T0124524

Heartstrings

RACHEL SPANGLER

HEARTSTRINGS
@ 2022 BY RACHEL SPANGLER

THIS TRADE PAPERBACK ORIGINAL IS PUBLISHED BY
BRISK PRESS, WAPPINGERS FALLS, NY, 12590

SUBSTANTIVE EDIT BY: LYNDA SANDOVAL
COPY EDIT BY: AVERY BROOKS
COVER DESIGN BY: KEVIN @ BOOKCOVERS ONLINE
AUTHOR PHOTO BY: ANNA BURKE
BOOK LAYOUT AND TYPESETTING BY: CAROLYN NORMAN

FIRST PRINTING: MAY 2022

THIS IS A WORK OF FICTION. NAMES, CHARACTERS, PLACES,
AND INCIDENTS ARE THE PRODUCT OF THE AUTHOR'S
IMAGINATION OR ARE USED FICTITIOUSLY. ANY
RESEMBLANCE TO ACTUAL PERSONS, LIVING
OR DEAD, BUSINESS ESTABLISHMENTS, EVENTS, OR LOCALES
IS ENTIRELY COINCIDENTAL.

THIS BOOK, OR PARTS THEREOF, MAY NOT BE REPRODUCED
IN ANY FORM WITHOUT PERMISSION FROM THE AUTHOR OR
THE PUBLISHER.

ISBN-13: 978-1-7343038-7-2

For Susie, who fills my life with music and always lets me over-schedule our adventures.

This is all your fault.

Chapter One

Mira's phone buzzed on the glass top kitchen table, startling her and pulling her attention from the spreadsheet on her laptop. Blinking a few times, she shifted her vision from the black and white tableau she'd been absorbed in. She squinted at the smaller screen in her hand to read the text message from Larry, a local real estate broker and one of her financial advisers she'd recently made the mistake of informing she might be interested in adding some property to her portfolios.

Larry: *Did you get a chance to see the building on Main?*

Mira: *No, but I read the prospectus and the property history.*

Larry: *And?*

She sighed. She'd done a rather thorough review of the large, three-story, multi-purpose structure, and while it did seem well-built and reasonably cared for, her assessment ended there. While the apartments on the upper levels appeared to have solid occupancy rates and several long-term tenants in good standing, the entire lower floor seemed a consistent financial loss. Cavernous and largely open if the pictures were to be believed, it had housed a steady stream of unsuccessful business ventures for the last five years, not one of them managing to celebrate a single one-year anniversary, which led to it being empty more often than not. She simply wasn't interested in an investment where the most optimistic projections suggested a loss on a full third of the property.

She shook her head as she typed back a quick, *Sorry, not interested in that one.*

It only took thirty seconds for Larry to shoot back.

Larry: *Come on, at least take a tour. I can meet you there or send you the security code.*

Mira: *No thank you.*

Larry: *It's got character you can't see on paper and personality you can't experience by crunching the numbers.*

She shook her head at how little he knew her if he had any hope in that line of reasoning.

She didn't make decisions based on anything other than paper and numbers. Character couldn't be quantified. Neither could personality. Those sorts of whims or gut-feeling judgements made for bad business, and she prided herself on being good at her job. She made decisions based on facts and trends and well-documented odds. If she were going to take a risk, the hard numbers would have to be stacked squarely in her favor and, in this case, they simply weren't.

She was still trying to find a way to politely say so when a knock at the door startled her for a second time in as many minutes.

She instinctively glanced at her watch to confirm what she already knew. At nearly 9:00 on a Thursday night, the acceptable time for visitors had passed. Of course, in her mind, the acceptable time for unannounced visitors started at never o'clock and continued from there into eternity.

The knock sounded again, and she froze, her mind the only thing moving quickly as she tried to process the possibilities. It could always be an axe murderer, though she knew enough about statistics to nearly negate that possibility. Solicitors, Girl Scouts, or Jehovah's Witnesses also seemed unlikely at this hour. It could be a harbinger of bad news. Her parents were in Florida for half the year, which gave her a dull headache every time she contemplated all the dire possibilities, but again, if something had happened to them in Tarpon Springs, surely the authorities would call rather than send someone all the way up to Western New York to break the news.

She sighed at the realization she'd run through every unreasonable option only to land at the most likely candidate: Vannah.

The knock came a third time, and Mira removed her reading glasses, folding them neatly and placing them on the keyboard of her computer before clicking "save" on the spreadsheet she had open. Then, pulling her cardigan a little more tightly around her, she walked to the door. Leaning close to the cool, wood surface, she pressed her eye to the peephole and took in the artificially bulbous view of her younger sister.

"I know you're in there," Vannah said as if the door didn't stand between them. And why shouldn't she? Doors had never meant much to her, not the door to Mira's bedroom when they were growing up, not the door to Mira's first apartment, and not the door to her office. The only reason she hadn't barged through this one was that Mira had never given her a key. "It's chilly. Ben's going to catch a cold."

Mira didn't bother explaining colds came from germs and not the weather. There was no use, and besides, as she flipped the deadbolt, she got the distinct feeling more important arguments lay ahead.

Throwing open the door, she stood back to let her sister in, followed by her sleepy, sheepish nephew.

"Hi, Aunt Mira," Ben mumbled as he shuffled past in a pair of navy-blue athletic pants and an oversized fleece. He had a black backpack slung over his shoulder, and his hard-plastic violin case in one hand, but he used his free arm to wrap her in a halfhearted hug. She gave him a more genuine squeeze, resting her chin atop his dark hair and breathing in the fresh scent of shampoo.

"Did your mom drag you all the way from Buffalo after your shower?" She hoped her tone came across as more playful than accusatory.

"He's all squeaky clean for you." Vannah set down a small suitcase with a spaceship on it.

She released her nephew and closed the door behind them as the sinking suspicion this wouldn't be a short visit spread through her chest.

"I thought I bought that bag for Ben last summer when he went to music camp," she said slowly. "Are you going to music camp, Vannah?"

Her sister laughed. "Actually, you're not far off."

"Do I win a prize for guessing correctly?"

"The best prize in the whole world." Vannah's easy smile never wavered as she looked past her toward her son. "Ben, why don't you head on into the guest room to play your games while I talk to Aunt Mira."

Ben stepped back, his dark eyes wide and soulful for a second before he lowered them and shuffled away with a mumbled, "Sorry."

"It's okay," Mira said quickly. Then for her own benefit she silently added, "Whatever it is will be okay."

Vannah wandered out of the entryway and perched on the arm of a dining room chair without being invited to do so. Mira supposed it wasn't unusual for siblings to make themselves at home in one another's houses, but everything else about this felt out of the ordinary. Despite Vannah's fly-by-the-seat-of-her-pants nature, she didn't just drop in. And as much as the family had feared otherwise over the years, she'd always managed to take care of Ben, at least as far as food, sleep, and some modicum of a school schedule went. For her to show up late on a weeknight with her child in tow and suitcase in hand, something had to be out of sorts, and when something was out of sorts in her world, Mira liked to put it right as quickly and efficiently as possible.

"Tell me what's wrong."

Vannah's smile faltered but didn't fade completely. "Hello. It's nice to see you, too."

"Please don't."

"Don't greet my sister, who I haven't seen in weeks even though she only lives thirty minutes from me?"

"Don't drag this out. You know I'm a nervous wreck about surprises."

"About everything," Vannah corrected, "but yeah, okay, I need your help. Which isn't exactly a surprise, is it?"

It wasn't, so she waited for more.

"I've been offered an awesome job opportunity. It's not exactly a music camp, but it's close. A friend from school—"

"Which school?"

Vannah rolled her eyes, but she'd attended any number of schools over the last decade trying to find herself, sometimes finishing programs in cosmetology, hospitality, massage, and music therapy, sometimes not. So Mira didn't think the question unreasonable.

"The music conservatory." Vannah seemed to anticipate Mira's argument that a part-time classroom, part-time garage band performance space qualified as a conservatory. "I got certified in several teaching methods on multiple instruments, and Kerry, he's the friend, remembered I also started an associate's degree in hotel management. That's why he found me online."

"Sure." She was willing to play along to get to the point of this story, though she suspected the guys who gravitated toward Vannah weren't interested in her lackluster professional credentials.

5

"Anyway, he bought some land down south in a beautiful area, and he's spent the last year building lodgings."

"What kind of lodgings?" She kicked herself for even asking, but she was a hopeless detail person.

"All kinds, tree houses, yurts, tiny houses, very diverse."

"Sure. Totally well-rounded."

"They are, and everything's built around a central long house to serve as a dining hall and arts space."

"Sounds right up your alley."

Vannah hopped off the arm of the chair excitedly. "It is, and the best part is he wants me to help him run the business as he gets ready for his first visitors. I mean not the financial parts because I'd be terrible at that."

Again, she didn't argue with the obvious.

"But I'd be in charge of scheduling classes and planning events and making sure the artists have everything they need."

"What artists?"

"Oh, did I forget that? The whole thing is a retreat center for all kinds of artists, from visual to musical to performance. Some of them won't be great, obviously. The first group Kerry lined up are like the super-rich kids doing gap years in exotic places, but once we bring in some money, we'll have scholarships and work study to make it more egalitarian."

"Can you back up to the part where you said exotic location, because when you said 'south,' I thought you meant, like, Alabama."

Vannah laughed and did a little twirl. "That's the best part. It's in Belize!"

Mira's brain exploded. Or maybe it only felt that way as her vision flashed white then red. "Are you out of your mind?"

"Kind of." Vannah showed no signs of chagrin. "Who wouldn't be a little loopy for a chance like this? It's everything I've always dreamed of."

"No. Nope. Not always." Mira began to pace. "You used to dream of being a dolphin trainer. Then you dreamed of being a trapeze artist. Then you dreamed of recording a sitar album in Bangladesh. Then you dreamed of teaching elephants to paint."

"People do that with elephants. It's a thing, but I didn't because I was being responsible and taking care of my kid, and that's what I'm doing here, too." Vannah sounded defensive for the first time. "Only this time I don't have to choose between doing right by Ben and following my dreams. If this works, it'll be an amazing opportunity for both of us. If we get this camp off the ground, it could offer a steady income and creative freedom. And if—"

"No," Mira snapped, heart hammering against her ribs. "Stop saying 'if.' You can't take Ben to the middle of a rainforest hoping this place might eventually turn into something legitimate. You can't expose him to God-knows-who while you try to figure things out. You can't uproot him from his entire support system based on wishful thinking. Who will watch him while you work? Where will he go to school? What about medical care? Too many ifs."

Vannah sighed and her shoulders slumped. "You're right."

"What?"

"I agree with you."

"You do?"

"Yes." Vannah snorted. "I know you think I'm some sort of imbecile as a parent—"

"I didn't say that."

"I get it. We've always been on opposite ends of the decision-making spectrum, but I'd never put Ben in danger, which is why I want to go to Belize and evaluate things first."

"Excuse me?"

"I need to see for myself how this place runs and what resources are readily available. I need to meet the staff and the first guests. I need to see how my days actually play out in order to know if it's a good fit for Ben, too. Then, once I get a sense of how stable the conditions are, I can make an informed decision."

All the words were reasonable. Too reasonable by Vannah's standards. Mira should've felt relieved at such a level-headed response, but the sweat pricking her palms spoke to the opposite emotion. "You're leaving him."

Vannah grimaced. "Please don't make it sound like I'm abandoning my child."

"But you are. You didn't bring the suitcase to travel with him. You brought it to leave him with me."

"Don't say it like I'm running off on some wild vacation. It's going to kill a part of my soul to be away from him. I hated him even going to camp last summer, but the stakes here are much higher."

She shook her head at the understatement of the year.

"I'm doing what's best for him, for us, and I get that you probably don't agree with me, but you love him almost as much as I do."

She stared at her sister, for the first time taking in her own dark eyes. There was a pleading to them she'd seen only a few times before. The first was on the night she'd found out she was pregnant, the second was when she'd brought Ben home from the hospital, the third was when he'd been two and had scarlet fever. Every time Vannah had been terrified, and every time she'd wanted Mira to help—not her, but Ben.

Mira had never said no.

They both knew she wouldn't do so now.

"How long?"

"I hope only a month or so."

Now it was Mira's turn to sink onto one of the chairs.

"It won't be a minute longer than I have to be away from him, but I need to be absolutely sure."

She nodded as if that were reasonable when nothing about this scenario felt reasonable to her. Reasonable people didn't fly off to Belize on a moment's notice to check out the child appropriateness of treehouses and yurts. Reasonable people didn't leave their children for months at a time unless they had no other choice. Reasonable people didn't ask family members to bail them out repeatedly.

Of course she could feed and house Ben, but what about work? She supposed he could come to her office after school, and she'd seen the school bus on her street in the morning. She could call the district and figure out what time school started and ...

Frustration swelled in her at the fact that either of them were even considering the practicalities of such a fool's errand, but she always considered the practicalities. She'd always had to be the one to do so whenever Vannah got one of her whims.

"I've never taken care of a child for more than a few days. I have a job. I don't know anything about being a primary caregiver. I don't know his schedule or his playmates or bedtime routine."

"You're overthinking. He'll tell you what he needs. You'll work out a schedule together. He's quiet. He always does his own homework. He can make his own grilled cheese, and he doesn't need you to bathe him or anything. He's eleven."

"I know how old he is." She bit off the words. "I was in the godforsaken birthing pool with you when he was born."

Vannah chuckled. "You didn't drown then and you won't drown now. He's a good boy. Honestly, he's more like you than I've ever been. You'll get along perfectly. I've got all the important paperwork in his backpack. I called the school here in town today, and he's registered. I had his school in Buffalo send his records over. You just have to show up with him on Monday morning."

She shivered at the thought of changing schools two-thirds of the way through the year even though she wasn't the one who'd have to do so.

As if reading her mind, Vannah said, "He's moved a lot. As long as he's got his violin, he'll be fine. Oh, which reminds me, I found him a violin teacher here who seems great. Young, peppy, cute. He'll love her. I made a lesson appointment for next Tuesday afternoon."

"How long have you been planning this?" she asked numbly.

"I just got the offer a couple of days ago. You know how I get once the right idea strikes. I jump right in and start moving pieces around."

"And I was the last piece."

Vannah blushed. "I know how you worry about details. I wanted to work them all out ahead of time so I could propose a cohesive plan. I knew if I did all the legwork, you wouldn't say no."

Mira didn't even know what to be more offended about, the fact that Vannah trusted her with Ben for an indefinite period of time but didn't trust her to handle his shot records. Or maybe the fact that she thought Mira's biggest concerns would center around scheduling rather than her nephew's emotional well-being. Or perhaps the worst part was the fact that her acquiescence was such a foregone conclusion.

Then again, why wouldn't it be? She'd always been the responsible one, the reasonable one, the levelheaded one. All through her childhood, she'd bailed Vannah out. She'd covered for her first with their parents, then teachers, then boyfriends. Now she'd do the same for Ben. While part of her wanted to break that mold of herself as dependable to a fault, another part of her clung to her own sense of stability, especially in the face of her sister's constant upheaval. Besides, even if she were to suddenly decide she wanted to break the patterns she'd spent her whole life developing, she'd never do so at Ben's expense.

Chapter Two

"Perfect," Shelby said as her dad and brother scooted the last piece of her new living room into place.

"That's the last thing I'm moving up those stairs," Darrin said as he flopped onto the newly positioned couch, sandy hair falling over his blue eyes. "Ever. Couldn't you find a place on the first floor?"

"Not one big enough to hold all my instruments."

"Did it ever occur to you that maybe you don't need enough instruments to stage your own orchestra?"

"Nope." She eyed the furniture she'd had her dad and brother arrange. The couch sat along the biggest wall, an end table next to it, and two cushy chairs that didn't quite match on opposite sides of a long, low coffee table. "You know, I actually think we might need to switch the couch and the TV stand."

Her dad hopped up immediately, his barrel chest puffed out and his biceps already straining the sleeves of his black T-shirt, but her brother groaned, "Are you freaking kidding?"

She bit her lip and made her most apologetic face, watching his consternation fade into submission before she finally burst out laughing. "Yes, I'm kidding! Everything's perfect. Thank you."

Darrin shook his head slowly. "I'd choke you, but I'm too exhausted."

"I still feel great," their father said.

"That's because you're a beast, Dad." Looking him over, she noticed how little he'd changed in the last ten years. Aside from a few more laugh lines, he still appeared every bit like the coach and gym teacher he'd been his entire adult life. "Too bad you didn't pass any of your athletic genes on to either of your children."

"Speak for yourself, Orch Dork." Darrin grumbled the nickname he'd given her when she'd joined her first orchestra in middle school.

"Nerd herder." She shot back her favorite childhood epithet good-naturedly. "Maybe if you spent less time playing with your chemistry set as a kid, you wouldn't be winded from carrying a few boxes up three flights of stairs."

"First of all, I'm an actual chemist, so you know, good return on my childhood investment, but that"—he waved his arm toward the fifty cardboard boxes in the next room—"is not *a few*. It's only been a year since you moved last time. How do you keep getting more stuff?"

"It's mostly music books."

"Yeah, my back noticed they weren't exactly pillows. What happens? Do they mate and multiply on their own?"

"It's called grad school. You'd think you'd remember how that worked, or was it too long ago for you, old man?"

"I got my master's at a place with a lab and offices and libraries, not some froufrou music conservatory."

"Oh, good Lord, are you two bickering about your master's degrees again?" Their mother pushed through the door with several paper sacks, which were likely loaded with more sandwiches than they could eat in four meals. She blew a long strand of fair hair out of her face and took on a classic mom tone. "When I birthed my children five years apart, I hoped for a little less sibling rivalry and a little more of a mentoring relationship."

"I tried, really I did, but he's beyond mentoring," Shelby said quickly. "The five years he was alive without me must've done irreparable damage."

Her father snorted.

"I'm the mentor here." Darrin sat up and motioned for the sandwiches. "Which is why I've now lugged a full-sized bass and two cellos from one apartment to another every summer for five years in a row. I'll accept my big-brother-of-the-decade award any time now."

She rolled her eyes. "Your certificate is probably in the mail, but I'll give you one thing, I do not want to move again any time soon."

"I'm not nearly as fragile as your brother, but I'm on board for the not moving thing, too." Dad eased into the chair on the other side of the coffee table. "I like this place, and I like having you close."

"I agree on both counts, and now that I have finished school and transitioned into being a stable adult—"

Darrin snorted.

"What?"

"Stable adult?"

"I am a stable adult."

He laughed while stuffing his face with a pastrami on rye.

"I have an apartment with no roommates. I have a new job at a great school. I've even got a lesson with an actual paying violin student next week." Her heart rate increased, and her voice went up an octave. "Mom, tell Darrin I'm a stable adult."

"Of course you are, honey." She turned to Darrin and gave him the stop-teasing-your-sister look. "She's a very stable adult."

"All I'm saying is that if you need your mom to tell people you're a stable adult, you're probably not."

"Says the health scientist who's eating a sandwich without having washed his hands."

"I have superior immunity. You should wash yours, though, because you're going to be around all those little vectors of disease starting Monday."

14

"Darrin," her father said in a warning tone. "I know that might be the scientific term, but we've talked about using better words for human children than 'vectors of disease.'"

"Yeah, maybe that's why women aren't lined up around the block to reproduce with you," Shelby shot off before she pushed up from her chair. "But I think I'll get cleaned up before I eat."

She walked through her new bedroom to her new bathroom. Neither one of them were big, but they were bright and open, and best of all, they were all hers. For the first time in her life, she didn't have to share her living spaces with anyone else.

She opened a box labeled "bathroom cabinet" and pulled out a bar of lavender soap. As she sudsed up, she took deep breaths of the calming scent. She'd never admit it in the living room, but all that talk of stable adulthood made her a little twitchy.

She was living by herself for the first time. She had a full-time job for the first time. She was making student loan payments for the first time. And for the first time in twenty years, she wasn't a student. She was a teacher. Her world was moving faster than ever, and she couldn't shake the sense that even bigger things were on the horizon. While part of that terrified her, it also thrilled her.

She rinsed her hands, then realized the box holding her towels hadn't made it in yet. Running her clean palms over the legs of her sweaty jeans, she had to laugh. Maybe she wasn't quite all the way to stable adult, but she was moving in a new direction, and she couldn't wait to see what lay ahead.

***

"You can do this," Mira mumbled to herself. "You're fine. You've got a schedule. Work the schedule."

She flipped open her leather-bound day planner and lay it atop her desk calendar. The calendar was for the bigger picture, but she'd devised a system of color-coded dots to remind her when she needed to check her more detailed daily list of chores and events. A red dot signified a work meeting or deadline. Green indicated some home-related errand to run, like the store or the post office. For Ben reminders, she'd chosen a cerulean blue.

The color reminded her of the boy, bright but deep. While his mere presence and the circumstances surrounding his sudden arrival threw her entire life and all her carefully constructed routines for a loop, she had to admit he was an easygoing kid. Always quiet by nature, he had little problem spending time on his own in his room. Even when he did join her in the living room, he chose mostly to read or play on his tablet. The only time he made any real noise was when he played his violin, but aside from the occasional squeak, the sound had been more soothing than bothersome. At times, it also sounded a little sad, and Mira didn't know if the sentiment came from the instrument or the boy.

She'd attempted to talk to him about his feelings over the last four days, and she'd tried to fill the house with some of his favorite foods. She'd even offered to watch a superhero movie with him, or shop for some new school supplies, but he'd been politely insistent that he was fine, and she'd seen little evidence to the contrary.

Apart from seeming tired after his first two days at a new school, Ben didn't appear shaken by the transition or his mother's abrupt departure. Maybe he was just an unflappable kid. Maybe he was emotionally stunted. Maybe he was used to being jerked around. Maybe she should take him to a therapist, but not right now because the little blue dot on her calendar reminded her she needed to take him to his violin lesson.

"Ben," she called as she closed her planner.

"Yes," he responded in a much less frantic tone.

She glanced up, startled to see him standing in the doorway to her office, jacket on with his violin case in one hand and a magenta folder tucked under his arm.

"It's time for your lesson," she said mostly for herself, since obviously he was more prepared than she.

He merely nodded and headed for the door. She followed him, glancing at her watch as she got into her trusty old Toyota Camry. They had plenty of time to drive the two miles across her small town so long as she didn't get lost or run into traffic, both of which were highly unlikely, but still, she hated being late. It made her feel out of control. As she backed out of the driveway quickly, Ben gave a little squeak. "Um, Aunt Mira ..."

She glanced in the rearview mirror to see his face had gone a little pale. "What's wrong?"

"I'm not buckled yet."

She hit the brakes hard, then kicked herself. Who slams to a stop with an unsecured child in the back seat? Thankfully she hadn't had enough speed to catapult him through the windshield, but even the thought made her nauseous.

"Sorry," he said sheepishly and fumbled with his shoulder strap. "I buckled my violin in first."

She turned to see that sure enough, the thick, black case sat upright next to him with a gray seat belt holding it securely in place. "It's okay. Just maybe next time, do yours first."

"Okay." He nodded, then hesitated before saying, "My mom usually asks, 'Ready spaghetti?' before she drives."

For some reason, tears stung her eyes as she quickly turned back to driving. "Probably a good policy."

She didn't know why her cheeks burned. There was no way she could've known there was a seat belt catchphrase, but it made her realize there were likely a million other things she didn't know, and she hated not knowing even more than she hated being late.

She drove down the quaint suburban streets, worrying each little inadequacy might be a ticking time bomb. She'd pored over his medical records—no food or drug allergies, and no medicine except for a seasonal nose spray when the pollen flared up. She'd read every line of his school transcripts, impressed by how well he managed to do academically even though she suspected Vannah had been more encouraging of his creative development. She'd met with his principal and his homeroom teacher and established solid lines of communication. She'd even downloaded a few books about adolescent development. None of them had told her to ask, "Ready spaghetti?" before pulling out into traffic, and wasn't basic auto safety more important than his third-grade spelling test scores?

She was still frazzled when she pulled into the parking lot of an old, brick industrial building that, judging by the fresh paint around the doors and budding landscaping, had been only recently refurbished. "I think this is the place."

She glanced again at the address, which seemed familiar even though she'd never been here.

"Yes, I checked the address." Ben waited until she came to a complete stop before unbuckling himself and his violin. "Her apartment is on the third floor if you need to find me."

"What? No. I'm walking you up. I need to meet this woman."

He shrugged and headed for the door.

Inside, they started up the stairs. By the second floor, her legs had begun to burn, and her mind began to whir. She had to get out of the office more. Ben didn't seem to have any trouble bounding on ahead, instrument and folder in hand. Mira didn't even have anything to carry, which now felt odd. When she went to meet with clients, she always had folders or pens or a briefcase. It felt strange to go into a meeting empty-handed. Maybe she should've brought something else. A teacher's gift? Ben's shot records? Did violin teachers need those? Regular teachers did. What if he couldn't attend violin school without them?

Her heart pounded from the mix of panic and exertion. She needed a minute to gather her thoughts, but Ben didn't hesitate to knock on the green metal door labeled 345. She fought the urge to pull his hand back. She needed to catch her breath. She needed to pull herself together. She needed to ask questions and find answers that made her feel like she wasn't destined to screw this situation, and by extension her nephew, up.

The door opened, halting all her swirling thoughts. Or rather, the door hadn't stopped them so much as the woman behind it.

She was beautiful. There was no other word, or maybe there were millions of them, but Mira couldn't recall them in the moment. And young. This woman couldn't have been out of her twenties. Her effervescent smile fell first on Ben, giving Mira a second to observe a few details like her tight jeans, and the oversized scoop-neck sweater hanging slightly off center to show a smooth expanse of shoulder, almost as creamy as the cotton itself. She didn't know what she'd expected in a violin teacher, but it wasn't smooth skin and sparkling blue eyes and cozy sweaters.

Then the woman turned to her, and the warmth of her expression faded to surprise. "Oh, you're not his mother."

Mira's breath left her lungs at the blunt summation she'd been struggling to hold at bay for the last few days. "Is it that obvious? In four seconds, you can tell I'm not mother material? What gave me away? Should I have brought something with me?"

The woman's brow furrowed. "No. I'm sorry, I didn't mean to imply ... I don't know, whatever I implied. I only meant I saw Vannah's and Ben's photos when she contacted me on social media. I expected her to be here."

"Yes, so did I, but circumstances have changed."

"I'm sorry." The woman shook her head as her grin returned. "I didn't handle this very well. I'm a little nervous. Would it be unprofessional of me to ask for a do-over?"

Mira blinked at the quick change. Could they do that? Admit they'd been nervous and start over? Apparently so, because Shelby made a show of ducking behind the door and swinging it open again.

"Hi," she said, extending her hand. "You must be Ben."

Ben smiled shyly but shook her hand.

"I'm Miss Tanner. I've been looking forward to meeting you." The genuineness of her tone made Mira marvel at how quickly and beautifully she'd recovered. She fought a wave of embarrassment for her earlier outburst and her inability to right herself with the same amount of grace and speed. Her hand still trembled slightly when the woman turned to her with a playful smile.

"And you can call me Shelby."

"Mira," she said with a nod, then feeling like she should say more added, "I'm Ben's aunt. I'll be bringing him to lessons for a while."

"Lucky you," Shelby said. "I hear Ben's quite the cool kid."

Mira smiled for the first time all afternoon as the truth of that statement hit her. Glancing down at her nephew, she took in his lightly feathered hair and deep, expressive eyes as he stared back earnestly. "He really is. And I've heard him practicing that violin. I think you're in for a treat."

"I can't wait." Shelby rubbed her palms together. "Come on in and show me what you've got."

Ben didn't hesitate to brush by her into the apartment, but as Shelby turned to Mira, she froze. Was she expected to go inside too? She didn't know the etiquette. She hadn't planned to stay. She desperately needed to answer some emails, and her parents had never come to her own practices when she was Ben's age, but the world had seemed much simpler then. Who even was this woman she was supposed to be leaving her nephew with? Had Vannah run a background check or called references? Oh Lord, she'd let Ben wander into a stranger's apartment, and she'd intended to leave him there. Wasn't that how child traffickers operated?

Admittedly, Shelby looked more like a super cute and chic yoga instructor than a hardened criminal, but wouldn't that make her all the more effective as a kidnapper? Why hadn't she thought of this before she got here? Then again, statistics said child abductions were at an all-time low. Had she become a helicopter parent in only four days?

"You're welcome to join us if you like." Shelby seemed to read her hesitancy. "Or there's also a little coffee kiosk in the main lobby of my building if you want to stay close by without having to sit through a full lesson."

All Mira's relief left her lungs in a rush. "That actually sounds like a good middle ground."

Mercifully, Shelby didn't ask what two horrible thoughts that middle ground lay between. Instead, she smiled sweetly. "We'll be fine here."

"Right. But Ben has my phone number if you need anything, or you can find me in the lobby, or—"

"Thanks, but really, you can relax." Shelby's smile widened. "Ben and I are going to get along famously."

She nodded. This woman exuded positive energy. Ben was already waiting eagerly for her. She was a teacher. Mira wasn't even leaving the building. "Okay."

"Bye," Ben called from inside, followed by the sound of him tuning his violin.

"He's starting without me." Shelby laughed lightly.

"Sorry," Mira said sheepishly. "It's my first violin lesson, and well, he's my only nephew."

If Shelby's expression had been warm before, it turned downright sweet, as her smile faded and her blue eyes glistened with emotion. "You're doing a great job. I promise I'll take good care of him."

And Mira believed her.

***

To say Shelby found Ben impressive was a sizeable understatement. The kid played with a technicality far beyond many of her new students at the high school, but more remarkable was his ability to play with emotion. As she'd asked him to run through some of his favorite pieces, he'd gone from slow and swaying on a ballad to the sparkling lilt of a jig. He moved his shoulders, his hips, his eyes as he played, his small chest rising and falling. Between songs, the kid was almost painfully shy. Despite Shelby's praise and attempts to draw him out with questions, he most often offered short, surface-level answers and averted his eyes before flipping quickly to a different song in his music binder. However, once he held his bow to the strings, his whole demeanor changed. All the tension left his body, and the music flowed out of him.

Most kids his age played stiffly, their eyes darting from their music to their fingers and back again, but Ben scanned his music in leisurely glances or sometimes not at all. The pieces he played seemed imprinted on his memory, and he closed those dark eyes as if surrendering to the melody. The serenity of his poise offered a stark contrast to the frazzled woman who'd dropped him off. With his eyes closed, only his deep brown hair offered any evidence he and Mira had sprung from a closely related gene pool.

Mira's complexion was lighter and slightly more creased either with age or stress, or both. Even Mira's smile had been tight, while Ben's lips curled sweetly as he played. She wished she could see Mira wearing a similar expression, one of relaxed pleasure and satisfaction. Her mind offered up some mental approximation of the image and her heart rate accelerated.

She shook her head slightly. Why had she let her thoughts wander back to Mira? Because she projected a walking contradiction between prim and proper mixed with a near frantic level of frazzled? In Shelby's experience, women who wore pencil skirts and sensible heels tended to be cold, but Mira's face had burned with the heat of frustration or embarrassment when Shelby made the stupid comment about not being Ben's mother. She kicked herself internally for the carelessness inherent in her assumption that only a mom would drop a kid off for lessons, or that a kid had to have only one mom. She'd let her own expectations get in the way of her introduction, and it wasn't just because Mira didn't look like the woman in the pictures.

She'd always assumed her students' parents would be considerably older than her, and certainly Mira didn't seem like any twenty-six-year-old she'd ever met, but she certainly wasn't some typical forty-five-year-old suburban soccer mom, either. Try as she might, she couldn't picture this woman in a sport utility crossover or passing out juice boxes at the park, not that either of those things were bad. Her own mother had been that kind of mom. She liked those kinds of moms. They made her feel comfortable.

Mira made her feel something else entirely with her angular face and deep eyes. The combination paired with her business attire and dark hair pulled up might have come across as severe on other people, but on Mira, it looked elegant, effortless, natural, and that was saying a lot because nothing else about their interaction had been natural.

Ben's song came to a close, pulling Shelby's mind back where it belonged as the child lowered his instrument and raised his chestnut eyes to her. A shot of affection surged through her, and she applauded exuberantly.

He blushed and started to turn away, but she reached out and placed a hand flat across his music stand, preventing him from choosing another piece that would undoubtedly confirm what she already knew.

"Ben, you're a gifted violinist. How long have you been playing?"

"Since I was four."

"Really? I didn't even start until I was nine. By the time I was your age, I could maybe play a handful of songs. You're way ahead of where I was then."

His shy smile quirked up again.

"But thankfully, I'm a few years past there, so I do think there are a few things I could show you. I'd like to try anyway, but only if you want. I promised myself I'd never give private lessons to kids who didn't want them, kids whose parents made them or who only played to pad their college applications. I get plenty of those kids at school, but you don't strike me as part of that group."

He shook his head quickly. "I love to play my violin. It's my favorite thing."

"Good. Then if it's okay with your mom—"

"She's in Belize," he blurted, then with a hint of pink to his cheeks added, "Aunt Mira has to watch me until my mom comes back."

Shelby raised her eyebrows, then got her curiosity under control. Mira and Ben's living arrangements weren't any of her business, and she didn't want to step into anything like she had earlier. "Then as long as it's okay with Aunt Mira, I'd love to work with you."

As if on cue, a knock sounded on the door.

"Oh, that's probably her. Let's ask." Shelby swung open the door to see Mira appearing a little calmer and wearing a polite smile.

"How did it go?"

"I had fun," Shelby said quickly and glanced at Ben. "What about you?"

"Yes, thank you," he said as he grabbed his case and began to pack up.

Shelby turned back to Mira and whispered, "Is it me, or is he not much of a talker?"

Mira frowned, tiny lines forming around her mouth that Shelby would've given anything to wipe away. "I think he's normally on the more reflective side of the eleven-year-old population, but we've had some upheaval lately, which reminds me—I want to apologize for my own behavior earlier."

"I don't know what you mean."

"You're very kind, but please don't think that totally inept introduction was normal for me. Generally, I manage not to look like the proverbial deer in the headlights when I meet someone new. Some might even go so far as to call me a pretty competent person."

"I never doubted that," Shelby said sincerely.

"I did for a moment, but I promise I'll do better from here on out. A lot has happened in the last four days, but I do think I'll get the hang of it."

The little hint of emotion under the statement plucked at Shelby's heart strings. She wanted to pull Mira inside and offer her a cup of tea or something stronger. She wanted to curl up on the couch opposite her and listen to all those things she wouldn't let herself say while standing in the hallway. Instead, she jumped at the sound of Ben's violin case snapping shut.

Mira too seemed hyperaware they weren't alone, as her shoulders straightened and her eyes darted to her nephew when the rustle of papers indicated he'd begun to pack up his music. "Anyway, I hope neither of us were too much trouble for you this afternoon."

"Not at all," Shelby effused, hoping her voice could make it clear how strongly she felt. "The opposite is true. Working with Ben, or rather simply listening to him play has been the highlight of my day actually, to the point that I'd selfishly intended to ask for more time with him."

Mira glanced at her watch, eyes going a little wide again.

"Not today," Shelby quickly corrected. "I don't want to wreck your schedule, but perhaps later in the week, if you have time?"

Mira opened her mouth then closed it, her brow furrowing as if she were trying to run through some tough mental calculations. Shelby held her breath. She didn't even try to put her finger on why. She just felt a strong pull to these two. Maybe she was merely lonely and trying to anchor herself in her new life, but Ben was clearly special, and she got the creeping suspicion Mira might be, too. Perhaps she merely connected with the shared sense of transition hovering around them all or maybe the tightening in her chest hinted at more, but she hadn't been lying about her motives being partially selfish.

"Honestly, I've never had the chance to work with such a gifted eleven-year-old. If the price of lessons is a hardship—"

"No." Mira smiled weakly. "It's not that. I don't know what's standard scheduling for a kid his age."

Shelby's smile erupted again. Of course, the schedule and Ben, she was starting to see a trend in those two priorities. Both turned to the boy as he tucked his binder neatly under his arm. He looked from her to his aunt. Then that little quirk of a grin lifted the corners of his lips once more and he nodded his assent.

"That settles it," Mira said with a certainty she'd lacked earlier, and endeared her even further to Shelby, for respecting him and accepting his verdict fully.

"So same time, same place, on Thursday?"

"That works for me, works really well, actually. Thank you."

"No, thank you for sharing him."

As they walked down the stairs, Shelby closed the door feeling lighter than she had in ages. Instead of packing up her own violin, she raised it to her chin and played a familiar little jig, her fingers flying over strings, as her bow seesawed like her heart had over the last hour. The music didn't lift her spirits so much as complement them, an outward expression of the feelings she couldn't put into words at the thought that their new trio, whatever it may become, would be meeting a little more frequently.

Chapter Three

Mira pushed through the door to her office, arms loaded down with folders and binders she couldn't fit into her work bag.

"Whoa there." Her assistant, Jane, hopped up from her desk. "Are you doing some sort of human Leaning Tower of Pisa performance art?"

She snorted and off-loaded half of her bundles into Jane's arms. "I wish. I've been taking more and more work home with me, to try to catch up after Ben goes to bed."

"And when do you go to bed?" Jane began to sort through the folders.

"When the work is finished."

"So, what? Midnight? One a.m.?"

"Sometimes." Mira yawned. "Coffee?"

"Already brewing."

"Do you need a raise?"

Jane laughed. "Always, but, in fairness, you gave me a nice bonus two weeks ago when we survived tax season."

"Was that only two weeks ago?" She glanced at Jane's desk calendar. "Is it really only May first?"

She nodded. "Time flies when you have kids at home, or so they tell me. I mean my mother tells me every time she mentions I'm not getting any younger."

"You're only thirty. You've got time."

"Of course you'd say that, you're thirty-six."

Mira frowned, not sure exactly what she was supposed to take away from that. Her mid-thirties might've snuck up on her, but she'd hardly wasted them. She owned a home. She ran her own business. She'd nearly paid off her student loans, and she had a little money in the bank in case of an emergency. She'd even started a healthy retirement fund. She'd done everything she suggested her own clients do, and she was in a better position financially than many of them were in their forties or fifties. What more could a woman her age reasonably expect to accomplish?

For some reason the thought made her think of Shelby with her sweet smile and small apartment and her eagerness to do more, and her casually stylish clothes and the easy way she rebounded from interactions that left Mira frazzled. Then again, a great many things left her frazzled these days.

"What?" Jane asked.

"I didn't say anything."

"You didn't have to. You frowned, then smiled real quick, and then frowned again."

"I did not."

"And now you're getting defensive. Come on, what is it?"

"It's no one."

Jane laughed a giddy little bubble of a noise. "I said 'what' and you responded like I'd said 'who.' That means it's not a thing, it's a person."

"There's no person, it's just ..."

"What?" Jane practically bounced with excitement.

"Really, nothing major, only I don't know. If I were to ask you what you think a violin teacher would look like, hypothetically, what would you picture?"

Jane pursed her lips as if this wasn't exactly the kind of exercise she'd hoped for, but she played along. "I guess I'd probably say female, though I'm not sure why."

29

Mira nodded and motioned for her to continue.

"Probably older, violin feels like an older, more classical instrument, kind of serious, so maybe I'd picture someone buttoned-up, blouses, long *Little House on the Prairie* kind of skirts. Oh, and black shoes with pantyhose. Hair in like a bun, not the messy kind. Like some old schoolmarm stereotype."

"Exactly," she agreed with a sort of triumph. "Violin teachers are supposed to look like teachers, old ones, not younger than me. They aren't supposed to be peppy or cute, or more comfortably dressed than me, either. They aren't supposed to—"

"Wait." Jane held up a hand. "I'm going to need you to back up a bit. Are we talking about Ben's new violin teacher?"

"Yes."

"And did you call her cute?"

She rolled her eyes.

"Point of clarification."

"No."

"Do you mean cute like a puppy, or like, check out that cute girl over there."

"No. Neither." She sighed. "Maybe both."

"OMG."

"Please don't text speak. We're not turning into teenage girls over this. The woman merely caught me off guard. I went in expecting some silly cliché and got something different."

"How different?"

"She's like those women from the Athleta catalogs. She's young and fit without being super skinny, so it seems natural. And she wears these clothes that would seem almost slovenly on me, but on her, they're effortlessly chic. And she smiles, not politely, but genuinely at every little thing."

"Wow, how much time did you spend with her?"

"Less than ten minutes."

"And you've been thinking about her all night?"

"No." She pointed to the stack of folders. "I did work all night."

"But you thought of her more than you wanted to."

Her cheeks flushed. "Maybe more than I had reason to."

"Ask her out," Jane said flatly, then picking up her desk phone thrust it toward Mira. "Call her right now and ask her to have coffee with you."

She pushed the phone away. "Are you insane?"

"I've worked with you for five years, and I've never seen a woman turn your head."

"Not true. I've gone on several dates over the last five years." She racked her brain to remember the specifics of any of them. None during tax season of course, because she didn't have time, and she'd spent New Year's Eve with Vannah and Ben, Christmas break she'd visited her parents, something before the holidays ... she snapped her fingers. "I went to an office party with Shawna from Price Waterhouse."

"Was that a date?"

She grimaced. "Not a great one."

Jane held out the phone again. "Call the violin teacher."

"Her name's Shelby, and you're blowing this way out of proportion. She merely surprised me."

"Because she's young and hot."

"I never said hot. I said cute, pretty, like maybe even beautiful in some ways."

"Yeah, doesn't sound like you're attracted to her at all."

"In that distantly appreciative way you can note someone's appearance without throwing yourself at them. I don't objectify women, and I barely even know this one. She might not even be gay." The thought sparked a little tightening sensation in her chest.

"There's only one way to find out."

"Wait patiently for her to self-disclose?"

31

"Ask her out."

"Not going to happen."

"Why?" Jane whined the word pitifully. "Romance is fun."

"That's never been my experience, and there's a million reasons why it would be a terrible idea to chase a personal relationship with Shelby."

"You're about to start making a list, aren't you?"

She smiled at the prospect of a good list. "One, I do not have time to date. Two, any extra time I may be able to carve out should be spent with my nephew, whose mother walked out on him. Three, Shelby is Ben's teacher."

"Yeah, what did he think of her by the way?"

"Honestly, they must've hit it off. She mentioned him being quiet, so I'm not sure what they talked about, but he was a little more communicative at dinner last night. He told me the names of all the songs he played for her, and what he wanted to work on. And when he went to his room to practice, the songs seemed to have a little more pep to them."

"That's good," Jane said excitedly. "Progress."

"Yeah, and he smiled a couple of times, like when she asked if he'd like some extra lessons. And later, when I mentioned putting her on our schedule for Thursday, he looked happy. Honestly, I think he might be a little smitten with her."

"He might not be the only one. You do know you've smiled more this morning, too, right?"

She rolled her eyes. "It's time to get to work."

Jane glanced at her calendar. "You've got fifteen minutes before your first appointment. Also, Larry called about the building on Main."

"Right. It took me a minute to figure it out, but that's actually the building where Ben has his violin lessons."

"Did you look at it?"

"I peeked in some windows at the vacant space, but I'd already seen the specs."

"Still, it might be fun to take a tour when you're there sometime."

She shrugged. "If I can't envision a likely business pairing from the financial prospectus, I don't see how standing in the middle of a big, empty room is going to help. I'll call Larry later. I don't think fifteen minutes is going to be enough time to put him off."

"But it is enough time to call Hot Violin Teacher and ask her out," Jane tried again hopefully. "She sounds perfect."

"You're overanalyzing." She headed to her own office before turning around to add, "She's like ten years younger than me. What could we possibly have in common?"

"You've got Ben. That seems like as good a start as any."

"Ben's leaving in a month."

"Then you better act fast." Jane gave her a little shooing motion, which Mira gratefully accepted as her indication she could leave. She wandered into her office and sat at her own desk. She didn't need to get the last word. She didn't need to convince anyone else. It would be foolish to entertain ideas about asking Shelby out, and thankfully for both of them, she'd never had any inclination toward foolishness.

***

"That's beautiful, Ben!" Shelby said, and not just for show. Apparently, the boy wasn't only well practiced, he was also infinitely coachable. They'd been working together for nearly forty-five minutes and while she'd made several suggestions, she'd never had to tell him the same thing more than once.

"Thank you," came his standard, polite response.

"Do you know how awesome you are, Ben?"

He blushed and shook his head.

"Let me tell you, because I was working on this same piece with some of my high school students today for a full hour, and some of them never took to it the way you have in fifteen minutes."

The hint of pink coloring his cheeks was the only sign her comment resonated with him.

"And the ones who did manage to play it were awfully smug about it, rubbing their accomplishments in other kids' faces like they were rock stars."

Ben shook his head. "Music isn't like that."

"How do you figure?"

"My mom says music isn't about what other people think or being better or worse. Music is about expressing yourself."

Her heart ached at the simple pureness of the statement. "Your mom's right, and I'm glad you understand."

He shrugged. "I love music. I like when it sounds right to my ears."

It was the most personal thing he'd ever said to her, and it only strengthened the kinship she felt toward him. "And when it sounds right to your ears, does it feel right through your whole body?"

He nodded.

"And that's why you practice so much to get it right." She explained her own process for him. "Because when it's right and easy and natural all at the same time, it feels like everything's right with the world, including you, at least for those few minutes."

He lifted his dark eyes to her, a depth of feeling there he hadn't let her see before. "My mom says it's deep peace."

"Your mom seems to say a lot of smart things."

He shrugged and turned back to his music. "Sometimes."

Her stomach dropped. Ben had mentioned his mother with such affection in his voice, but clearly there were other emotions there, too. However, before she even had the chance to process that information, much less decide what to do with it, someone knocked on the door.

She blew out a frustrated breath. Why did they keep getting interrupted? "Sorry, probably someone dropping off a package. I've had to buy some stuff for the new place lately."

She opened the door and Darrin bounced on through.

"Hey, Orch Dork, you wanna go get ... whoa." He caught sight of Ben and stopped.

"Um, I'm kind of in the middle of a lesson."

He grimaced. "I thought you had lessons on Tuesday, not Thursday."

"This is a new lesson since we last talked."

"Oops, yay, good for adding another student." He glanced past her. "Hey buddy, sorry to interrupt."

"S'okay," Ben said with a shrug.

"Darrin, this is Ben. Ben, meet my goofy older brother, Darrin."

"Hello Mr. Tanner," Ben said softly.

"Mr. Tanner. I like this kid. He's my favorite of your students."

"He's also my only private lesson student. We've decided to meet two days a week now because Ben is special."

Darrin arched an eyebrow.

"He's my best student, even including anyone I've seen at the high school. I was about to invite him to play a few pieces with my older students at our concert in a couple of weeks."

"Really?" Ben's excitement overrode his shyness for a moment.

"Really," she confirmed. "I already told you you're playing this piece better than most of my sophomores. I don't see any reason you can't learn the others in time if you're willing to practice."

"I am," he said seriously. "I love to practice."

Darrin shook his head. "How'd you find a mini you on the first try?"

"I'm pretty lucky," Shelby admitted, "or at least I was until my brother barged into my room like I'm still eight years old.

Ben laughed softly. It was the first time she'd heard the sound out of him, and it warmed her heart.

"What do you say, Ben, should we kick him out and get back to work or let him stay while we finish up?"

He shrugged again. "He can stay."

"Thanks, Ben." Darrin gave him a wink as he came into the entryway and kicked off his shoes. Shelby was about to close the door when she heard footsteps falling lightly on the stairs. She paused long enough to watch Mira come into view. She'd seen her when she'd dropped Ben off earlier, but Shelby's breath still hitched a little bit at the sight of her. Today she wore navy-blue slacks and a gray dress shirt open at the collar. Her dark hair swept away from her face and twisted up into an elegant clip, giving her an air of both class and command.

Mira lifted her chestnut eyes and caught Shelby watching. "Am I late? I set a timer so I wouldn't be, but maybe—"

"Not at all," Shelby said. "You're actually a few minutes early, but our lesson was interrupted by my older brother stopping by unannounced. I'm sorry."

Mira waved off the apology. "Don't ever feel the need to apologize for your siblings around me."

She got the sense she'd almost stepped into something again and chose to let the remark drop. "Thanks, and Ben just agreed to give a little performance of his last piece for Darrin. Want to come in and listen, too?"

"Of course," Mira said without hesitation.

"That's the offending brother." Shelby pointed to him.

"You can call me Darrin."

"I'm Ben's aunt, Mira."

"Good to meet you Aunt Mira," he said jovially, and Shelby was glad he managed not to be a total dweeb around her friends these days. Not that Mira was a friend, but she still didn't want her brother to make an awkward impression like he so often had in high school.

"I was learning what a rock star Ben is," Darrin continued.

"It's true. I was singing his praises," Shelby said, "but I really don't have to. Go on, Ben, whenever you're ready."

He nodded. Then, with a deep breath and slow exhale, he lifted bow to strings and began to play.

For a moment the room united in focus on him, three adults all looking through their own lenses and listening through an array of filters melded into one audience for one boy. Ben closed his eyes and swayed, his brow furrowing then smoothing as the emotions of the music spread through him, or maybe the feelings originated in him and then spread out through the music right into the hearts of each person in the loose circle around him. Shelby loved this communal experience aspect of performance. She barely knew Mira, Darrin didn't know Mira at all, and yet the three of them now shared a visceral memory of this moment and this music.

As Ben wound down the song with one full, long pull of his bow, the corners of his mouth curled up, and Shelby's eyes flicked across the room to find a mirror expression on Mira's beautiful features. The image of this woman, so close, and for the first time serene sent a jolt of something more powerful than the melody through her. She might have stared for an entirely inappropriate amount of time if Darrin hadn't broken the spell with his enthusiastic applause.

"Wow, I mean, I only played the trumpet for like two years in high school, so it's all impressive to me, but that seemed really good. Shel, was he really good?"

"Yes, really good is an apt description." She laughed lightly, then turned to Mira. "Ben's not only developing technical skills above his age level, he has a musicality, an ability to interpret that many adults never develop."

Mira blew out a little sigh of relief. "I suppose that's one area I don't have to worry about."

The comment struck Shelby as odd. She reminded herself she didn't know anything about their lives, but she had a hard time believing a sweet, quiet kid like Ben would inspire a great deal of worry on his own. She felt an overwhelming urge to smooth out the frazzled edges that always surrounded Mira in their brief encounters. "Yes, no need for any worries around me. Ben is a gem, and as far as I can tell, you've got an all-around good kid on your hands."

Mira nodded solemnly.

"Can I pack up now?" Ben asked.

"Absolutely." Shelby watched him collect his things for a few seconds before stepping closer to Mira and lowering her voice. "I don't want to overstep my bounds, but I work at the school, and if he's having trouble there ..."

"No," Mira said quickly, then frowned. "At least not that he's mentioned."

"Okay, I don't know, you seemed to have some concerns."

Mira smiled. "I'm a very concerned person, and I fell into this role unexpectedly a week ago."

Shelby waited for some elaboration that didn't come.

"He's a good boy," Mira finally said. "I know I should be thrilled, and honestly I'm grateful to you for taking extra time with him. I agreed in part so I'd have an extra hour to get work done, but seeing him smile means a lot more."

"It's okay to appreciate both," Shelby said.

"Thank you for that, too." Mira glanced across the room to where Ben was now chatting with Darrin, or rather Darrin was chatting with Ben. "But other than adjusting my schedule to fit his school hours, he hasn't been nearly as disruptive as a kid his age should be."

"Well, that's a good thing, right?"

"I suppose. Only I worry he should take up more time, more space, more energy. He doesn't ask for hardly anything, and I haven't been able to draw him out. What if something's wrong and I'm missing all the signs?"

A million questions filled Shelby's mind, but she didn't want to compound the hints of panic rising in Mira's voice again, so she reached out, placing a hand gently on Mira's arm in an attempt to anchor her and said, "I don't pretend to understand everything you two are going through, but I've been around a lot of kids this week, and I can assure you Ben is in better shape than many of them. He's centered, he has a productive hobby, and I'm sure he knows there's nothing you wouldn't do for him if he needed you to."

Mira's dark eyes watered, but before she had a chance to respond, Darrin and Ben approached, and she quickly blinked away the tears while forcing a smile. "Ready to go?"

Ben nodded. "But first, Mr. Tanner said I needed to ask you."

Shelby shot a questioning look at her brother. "Ask her what?"

"I told Ben about the open house at work this weekend for friends and family of the employees. There's going to be a picnic, but also tours of the facilities, and some science activities for kids to learn what it means to be a modern chemist."

"And you told him he could go?" Shelby asked.

"I told him he'd have to ask his aunt first."

"Did you ask if he's even interested in science?"

"I am," Ben said quickly.

"You are?" Mira sounded surprised.

Ben nodded.

"Of course he is." Darrin grinned. "As soon as I saw how smart he was, I knew this had to be a logical guy. Aren't you always the one telling me musical education helps with math and science?"

Shelby's cheeks flushed with embarrassment. "So, you invited him to work with you?"

"It's a family thing, and I don't have any kids."

"That's because you do weird things like this. Can't you invite Mom and Dad?"

"I did," Darrin said, not seeming to grasp how weird it was to barge in and co-opt one of her students since he didn't have kids of his own. "They're coming, and I thought you would, too, but the more the merrier."

She covered her face with her hands.

"What?" Darrin asked. "You're a teacher. Aren't you supposed to be concerned about STEM education? What kind of example are you setting, baby sister?"

Shelby sighed. She couldn't believe her brother was busting her chops in front of a student, and Mira. She didn't know which was worse, so she turned to them both. "You don't have to go."

"But I want to go," Ben said seriously.

"High five." Darrin raised his hand and Ben trotted over to slap his hand then and the two of them huddled together talking.

Mira smiled in a way that looked more like a grimace. "He wants to go."

"I'm so embarrassed," Shelby whispered.

Mira waved her off. "Don't be. I was just saying Ben doesn't ask for anything. I should thank you for drawing him out, first with the music and now with the science."

"Darrin did the science."

"Then I should thank him, too."

Shelby laughed sharply. "Oh, I'll tell him for you ... along with some other things."

Ben ran back over, and Shelby said goodbye. Then she started to close the door, intending to turn on Darrin, but this time, Mira caught her arm. The intimacy of the touch stopped her completely, and all the anger ran out of her as she turned to see a gentle pleading in Mira.

"I mean it. I'm sorry if I didn't seem thrilled immediately. I don't handle changing plans well." She managed a little chagrined smile. "It takes me a while to adjust to new ideas, but I'm not a total robot."

"That thought never occurred to me," Shelby said honestly. Nothing about Mira had felt hard or artificial to her so far.

"Thank you, and now that I've had a minute to rearrange things in my head, I'm warming to the idea of good educational fun with my favorite nephew."

Warming was a good word for the sensation Shelby experienced, not just at the rush of heat spreading from the place where Mira touched her, but at Mira's endearing self-assessment. She nodded, then bit her lip trying not to reveal the excitement building in her. "Then I look forward to seeing you both this weekend."

Mira broke the touch. Ben waved goodbye. Shelby held it together long enough to watch them disappear down the stairs before gently closing the door and whirling on her brother. "What the hell, Darrin?"

"What?" he called from the kitchen where he was already rummaging through her cupboards.

"You can't bust in on my lessons and chat up my students. It's not professional."

"First of all, I didn't know you had lessons on Thursday, or I wouldn't have popped in, but I'm glad I did, because wow."

Shelby walked over to her own violin and focused on putting it away so she wouldn't have to meet his eyes. "Wow what?"

He snorted. "Come on. That's a whole lot of woman."

She began to loosen her bow, wishing there were some sort of knob she could use to loosen her own internal strings. "I don't know what you're talking about."

He laughed outright. "You're a terrible liar. I assume from that little arm touching business that she bats for your team."

Her heart gave a thud. "Some women are more demonstrative."

"That woman is not demonstrative. She's super buttoned-up. That's a big change for you. I thought you liked the artsy-fartsy, free-spirit types."

She rolled her eyes, but he either didn't see or didn't care.

"This woman seems like she's got her shit together. Are you ready for that?"

She placed the violin in the case and got a little satisfaction at the sharp sound of the latches snapping into place. "I don't have to be ready for anything because nothing is happening. She's the guardian of one of my students. She's very focused on him. I don't know what's going on there, but I get the sense it's something big."

"Yeah, something big and romantic and directed at you," he teased.

"How would you even know such a thing?"

"I've seen movies."

"You've seen *Star Wars*."

"*Star Wars* is romantic!"

She finally laughed. "I love you."

"Because I got you a date for Saturday?" he asked hopefully.

"No, because you're dumb enough to think that an outing to your office with our parents could possibly count as a date."

Chapter Four

"So, I'll be in until about ten tomorrow morning with Ben in tow, but can you reschedule Mr. Markakis and block off the rest of the day?"

"Sure," Jane said eagerly. "I relish any reason to kick off early on a Saturday, but I still don't understand what's happening."

"I told you, it's a science thing Ben got invited to."

"At school?"

"No, at Altenech. You know, the drug plant up on Route 5."

"Who invited Ben to a drug plant?"

She ground her teeth. She'd been hoping to avoid these details. She hadn't wanted to overthink the event or the conflicting feelings it inspired in her, but somehow dodging direct questions only made the whole thing a bigger deal, so she finally admitted, "We met Shelby's brother after lessons last night, and when he learned of Ben's interest in science, he invited us to an open house for friends and family."

"I didn't know Ben was into science."

"I didn't either, but he said he wanted to go, which is more than he's said all week, so I'm clearing my schedule."

"Good for you!" Jane said. "I'm proud of you. Getting out of the office and taking him someplace where you won't know anyone else is out of your comfort zone."

She tried to keep her face neutral, but she must've failed because Jane's eyebrows shot up under her blond bangs. "Spill."

"What?"

"There's something else. You looked guilty when I said that about not knowing anyone. Oh wait, it's Hot Music Teacher, isn't it?"

"Damn," she mumbled. "How do you do that?"

Jane clapped her hands. "Tell me everything."

"There's nothing to tell. It's a science thing we'll both be at."

"It's a date!"

"It's not."

"What are you wearing?"

"I don't know, and it doesn't matter because it's not a date."

"Do you want me to come over tonight and help you pick something?"

"Stop," she commanded. She didn't need this giddiness. She didn't need anyone encouraging her less than logical impulses. She certainly didn't need anyone to help her remember the silly way she'd reached out for Shelby's slender wrist, or the fact that Shelby had actually touched her first. "This is about Ben. He smiled more in five minutes with Shelby and Darrin than he has in a week with me."

Jane's expression softened. "That's a good thing."

"Yes, and when I dropped him off at school today, he said he was looking forward to the fun weekend. Fun weekends and I don't normally go together. Forgive me if I want to focus on that for a few minutes."

"Okay," Jane said. "You're right. You're allowed to enjoy being the fun aunt for a while, but be honest, are you at least looking forward to a fun weekend a little bit, too?"

"Honestly? I am." Her surprise came through in her voice. "It's the first thing I've planned outside of work for months, plus Shelby emailed the event flyer last night for me and Ben to read together, and some of the stuff actually interests me."

"I hope it is. Fun, I mean."

"Thank you."

"And that's all?" Jane asked seriously. "You're not even a teeny bit looking forward to seeing Hot Music Teacher?"

"Her name is Shelby."

"But you do think she's hot, right?"

She rolled her eyes to prove how silly she found the question, but she couldn't quite deny the charge. "She's lovely in a myriad of ways."

"Like wanting to know her biblically sort of ways?"

She blew out a frustrated breath. "You're incorrigible."

"So, yes you're excited about the date?"

"Seriously, I'm going with Ben. Shelby's going with her brother and their parents."

"Right. That's a lot of baggage for a first date." Jane frowned for a second, then perked up again. "This brother who threw you all together, is he by chance single?"

"I have no idea." She smiled at the memory of Shelby ragging on him about not having kids of his own. "But judging by his rough social skills, I think he might be."

"Like how rough on the social skills, on a scale of living in his parents' basement to mildly nerdy?"

"He invited a kid he doesn't know to go to work with him."

Jane grimaced.

"Honestly, he also seemed pretty sweet and genuinely excited to teach Ben about chemistry."

"Hmm, middle of the road socially awkward, or perhaps, too soon to tell. I expect a full report Monday morning."

"I figured as much."

"And not just about Hot Music Teacher's brother. I want to hear all about your date, too."

She snatched a folder off the reception desk and headed for her office, not even stopping as she called back, "It's not a date."

***

"There they are in line." Darrin clutched Shelby's arm without any of the gentleness Mira had used when doing the same thing two days ago. "Play it cool."

She shook her head. "I'm not the one bouncing on my toes at the sight of them."

"Which ones are they?" Her mother craned her neck to see around him toward the front gates where volunteers checked bags and directed newcomers to various areas around the sprawling complex.

Shelby's family had staked out a location on the grass near a small pond where they could see both the main entrance to the lot and the front doors to the imposing building that housed Darrin's lab. She couldn't tell which one of them was more nervous about seeing them in this social setting, but there was no doubt Darrin was doing a much worse job of acting cool about it.

"Look for Mira first. She's taller than a lot of the women in line," he said. "She's the one with the dark hair pulled back and the sunglasses."

"Oh, she's lovely." Her mom reached back to pat Shelby's leg. "Very grown-up."

"I don't even know what to say to that." She wasn't sure if she should protest the unspoken assumption Mira was somehow there for her, or her mother's apparent surprise that someone interested in Shelby might be an actual adult.

Still, she couldn't deny that Mira more than warranted her mother's compliments and then some. Dressed down in blue jeans and a white V-neck with three-quarter length sleeves, she managed to appear both casual and effortlessly elegant. Her dark Ray-Bans added a hint of an edge to the ensemble, but more than that, she exuded poise Shelby found herself both attracted to and envious of.

"The boy's cute, too," her dad added. "Does he like sports?"

"I doubt it. He's pretty introspective."

"Do you think he'll like any of the sandwiches I brought?" her mom asked.

"Since you brought about twelve of them, I'm sure he'll be fine."

Her mom shrugged sheepishly. "Food is love."

"Here they come." Darrin hopped up to wave them over, and Shelby said a silent prayer her family wouldn't overdo the welcome.

Ben spotted them first and jogged in their direction, leaving Mira to weave among the picnic blankets on her own.

"Hey buddy." Darrin extended his hand for a high five.

Ben paused only a second before slapping it. "Hello, Mr. Tanner. Thank you for inviting us to your job."

"I'm glad you could come, and you should probably call me Darrin because that"—he pointed to their dad—"is Mr. Tanner."

"It's nice to meet you, Ben." They shook hands with great seriousness. "Wow, a nice firm handshake. I like that in a young man."

"And I'm Mrs. Tanner." Her mom wasn't one to miss out.

"It's nice to meet you, Mrs. Tanner," Ben said dutifully.

"Such nice manners," she cooed. "What's your favorite sandwich?"

"Mom." Shelby rose from the blanket. "Let him get settled first. Hi, Ben."

"Hi, Miss Tanner." He smiled shyly at her, then glanced over his shoulder as if finally realizing he'd left his aunt behind. Every eye turned to Mira as she approached. She stopped briefly as a couple of young kids ran past, and Shelby wondered if anyone else appreciated the few extra seconds to compose themselves. Maybe her mother had been right about Mira being more grown-up, because Shelby did feel a little bit out of her league as she stopped in front of her, wearing a polite smile.

"Hi." Not the most effusive greeting, but it's what came out of Shelby's mouth, followed by the even less graceful, "This is my mom, Mary, and my father, Ken, and you probably remember Darrin."

"Of course." Mira's smile widened at him, and Shelby felt a twinge of sibling envy. "Thank you all for letting us horn in on a family outing. Ben has been looking forward to this whole event."

"And we've been excited to meet him," her mom said. "He's made quite an impression on both of my children. Please join us."

Ben sat between Shelby and Darrin as they all took up a few squares on the checkered picnic blanket.

"Now, can I ask about sandwiches?" Her mom managed a little hint of humor.

Shelby sighed playfully. "My mother's greatest joy in life is feeding people."

"Never let it be said I'd deny someone their greatest joy in life." Mira patted her stomach lightly. "Also, I forgot to eat breakfast this morning."

"I've never in my entire life forgotten to eat a meal." Her dad helped his wife unpack their old-style wicker picnic basket.

"I get a little bit of tunnel vision when I'm working," Mira explained. "If not for my administrative assistant, I might go the whole day without eating."

"What do you do for a living?" Darrin asked.

"I'm a financial planner, mostly retirement, 401(k)s, IRAs, but a little bit of stock trading, too."

"Impressive," her dad said. "Maybe I should set up an appointment. I get statements from the teacher's union every month, but I haven't updated any of my contributions in years, and I'm probably past the age where I should be paying more attention."

"Probably," Mira said without a hint of judgement in her voice, "but then again, most people are."

"You hear that, you two?" He pointed to each of his children. "Start early."

Darrin agreed quickly. "Maybe I'll make an appointment in the coming weeks, if you have room."

"Absolutely," Mira agreed as they all glanced to Shelby.

Her cheeks warmed. "I should check to see how my first paycheck compares to my first student loan payments, but you might be waiting awhile on me."

Thankfully, Mira's eyes didn't go wide. She didn't purse her lips or grimace or do anything to express disapproval or trepidation. Instead, she adeptly steered around the minefield by asking, "Are you new to teaching?"

"I am. I've only had about two weeks on the job, and I'm lucky to even have that since I finished my master's work in December. I thought I'd have to wait until September, but the old orchestra teacher had some health issues and took early retirement mid-semester."

"Unlucky for her, but congratulations on landing a job so early."

"We're very proud," her mom interjected, "and we're happy to have her close. We worried she might have to go out of state to find an orchestra job."

"Did you grow up locally?" Mira asked.

"We lived up the road in Lakeshore. My parents still live there."

"And I'm in Westbrook," Darrin added. "Are you local?"

Mira nodded. "Born and raised. My parents still live in town six months out of the year, though they spend the other six in Florida."

"And what about Ben?" Her dad pulled the boy into the conversation. "I heard you're new around here."

He nodded slowly. "I lived in Buffalo, but we move around kind of a lot. This is my fourth school."

Shelby's heart clenched at the thought of attending four different schools by the end of sixth grade.

"Well, I hope you get to stick around awhile," her dad said jovially, but Ben's expression darkened.

"I might be moving to Belize."

All the adults turned automatically to Mira, whose complexion grew even paler under their inspection. "Ben's staying with me for a few weeks while his mom researches an employment possibility in Belize."

The answer was revealing and not, both in the words Mira seemed to have chosen carefully and the level, guarded tone with which she'd delivered them. Shelby got the sense Ben's mother may've dumped him with Mira while she went off on a wild goose chase, but Mira certainly didn't phrase it that way, whether to protect her sister or her nephew wasn't quite clear.

"There's a lot up in the air right now," Mira said, then forcing a smile added, "but I'm enjoying the extra time with my favorite nephew, and because of him I get to do fun things like science day."

And just like that she steered the conversation back onto neutral topics. Shelby felt a little in awe of her composure. She didn't know the extent of what Mira must be juggling in both time and energy, but she suspected it was considerably more than she let on. She also noticed Ben's shoulders had slumped and his smile had faded. She wanted to hug him. She wanted to hug them both.

Thankfully, her mother saved her from an embarrassing breach of personal space by holding up a plate piled high with wax paper-wrapped sandwiches, which of course was her version of hugging, but also worked as a distraction. "I have ham, turkey and swiss, egg salad, peanut butter and jelly, hummus and roasted pepper, beef on weck—"

"She's going to keep naming them off until you claim one, Ben." Darrin gave him a little nudge.

"I really like peanut butter and jelly," he said quickly.

"Beef on weck is one of my favorites," Mira added.

A little whoosh of relief went out of her parents and brother, causing Shelby to roll her eyes.

Mira froze. "Did I miss something?"

Darrin laughed. "We're all super relieved to hear you eat meat. Shelby's last girlfriend was a vegan."

"There's nothing wrong with being a vegan. Just for that I'm going to eat the hummus and roasted peppers." Shelby's defensive impulse kicked in first, but quickly on its heels burned the realization her brother had outed her. She met Mira's eyes with more hope than she should have, but the little sparkle she found there combined with the slight quirk of a half-smile sent a shot of something hotter than embarrassment spreading through her.

The flash of recognition, the hint of connection, the tiny spark of knowing each other in some small but quintessential way all swirled through her like a warm summer breeze. Shelby loved that feeling, and even more, she enjoyed the prospect of inspiring the same in Mira.

Chapter Five

"So. Much. Science," Shelby groaned.

Mira couldn't disagree as they wrapped up a tour of not only Darrin's lab but the production floor and an exhibit on clinical trials and FDA standards, too. Even after paying close attention for as long as she could, she'd been in over her head before they'd left Darrin's workstation.

"Did it hurt your brain a little bit, Orch Dork?" Darrin poked his sister.

"No, it was actually interesting. I don't know why they let a nerd herder work with such otherwise important people, though."

Ken placed a hand on each of his grown children's heads and made a move like he intended to knock them together. "Ben, do you know how many times I have had to threaten to separate these two in the last twenty-five years?"

He shook his head.

"Me either," Ken said with a laugh, "but trust me, it's a lot."

"Maybe we should make them run the three-legged race together to teach them a lesson," her mother interjected, then turning to Mira added, "Were you and Ben's mother like this growing up?"

She shook her head. She and Vannah had never had the easy ribbing relationship like Shelby and Darrin. While the two of them did spend more time sparring than most adult siblings, every joke was laced with endearment. Even the nicknames that may've carried a sting if delivered in a different tone managed to sound affectionate. "No, I'm afraid I'm very much the dour older sister to Vannah's free spirit."

"I find 'dour' hard to believe," Mary said kindly, "but I raised a scientist and a musician, so I know what you mean about two wildly different people springing from the same gene pool."

She smiled politely rather than try to explain how her relationship with her sister didn't feel at all akin to the playful personality differences she'd witnessed between various members of the Tanner family so far. Honestly, she felt a little envious at the lightness of it all. When she and Vannah bickered, the consequences always seemed too high.

The thought made her gaze wander to Ben. He strolled a few feet ahead of them between Ken and Darrin as they headed toward the field day-style games taking place on the wide lawn. His eyes hadn't glazed over once during the long tour and multiple talks. Several times he'd even asked questions about the science of various machines or equipment. She'd seen Ben play his violin so many times, and she'd always considered him a quiet, artistic soul, but he was still a little boy. Why hadn't it occurred to her he might have other interests and curiosities worth supporting?

As if sensing her eyes on him, he turned and offered his sheepish grin that almost made him seem his age. "Can I play?"

She cocked her head to the side, trying to make sense of the question. "You want to do the sports?"

"Do the sports?" Ken slapped his hand to his forehead and laughed. "Am I the only person here who speaks Field Day?"

She grimaced. "I mean, I could try to keep up."

Mary lay a hand on her shoulder. "Oh honey, we all stopped trying to keep up years ago. Let him run around with Ben for a while. It's what he loves. Plus, then maybe he'll sleep better tonight."

"Ben's actually always been a good sleeper."

"I was talking about my husband."

She laughed.

"I'm serious. I'll go keep an eye on them, but he's a middle school gym teacher. Ben couldn't be in better hands." She turned to include her daughter. "Why don't you two go relax. Field Day clearly isn't either of your fortes."

"I'm not a total klutz," Shelby protested, but she made no move to follow her mother as she rushed to catch up with the boys.

"I actually am," Mira admitted. "Try as I might to understand the appeal of sports, I'm not that kind of lesbian."

Shelby's smile widened, either at the joke or the confirmation of their shared sexual orientation. Mira wasn't sure which option she found more appealing. Of course, the former was safer. Humor made her feel like she wasn't in over her head or horning in on someone else's family outing. Humor helped her hold off the fear that she'd neglected Ben's interests as she'd striven to merely keep him fed and on schedule for the last week. Admitting she and Shelby could, at least hypothetically, fall into the same dating pool didn't make her feel safe, confident, or sure of herself at all.

In fact, she'd spent the last hour trying to ignore the little tingle she got every time she remembered Darrin's aside about Shelby's "last girlfriend." She hadn't known two simple words could be so loaded, and yet with them he'd told her not only did his sister identify as queer, she was single.

"Do you want to get off our feet?"

"Uh ..." The question felt both forward and abrupt given the thoughts swirling through her head. She blinked a few times to reorient herself and follow Shelby's line of sight to their picnic basket, then process that she hadn't been propositioned so much as invited to sit down in a public place while their respective family members played nearby. "Yes, actually, I think I'd better."

"Sorry my brother dragged you to work with him." Shelby sank onto the blanket and crossed her legs with a flexibility Mira wasn't sure she still possessed. Then again, she wasn't wearing leggings and a tan shawl-style sweater that managed to appear both stylish and comfortable at the same time.

"Oh, I'm not," Mira said as she sat next to her, choosing to angle her legs off to the side. "Ben's clearly having a great time."

"And what about you?"

She smiled. "I'm actually having more fun than I expected."

"Whatever do you mean? Touring the job site of a man you don't know while his parents cooed about how proud they are of him isn't your ideal version of a Saturday?"

She laughed. "Actually, I normally work on Saturdays. I sort of forgot other people don't."

Shelby shook her head. "I've had to work many Saturdays in my life, but let me tell you, I never once lost the sense that I shouldn't have had to."

"Then you're probably doing better at life than I am."

"I don't know." Shelby bumped Mira's leg with her own knee. "Remember what I said earlier about my salary-to-student-loan ratio? Maybe I should return to working Saturdays, but people keep telling me work-life balance is supposed to be a thing."

Mira glanced around at all the families playing, laughing, or lounging together in the springtime sunshine and wondered if this was normal behavior for them. Clearly the adults had jobs, or they wouldn't have been invited to the company picnic, but did they all manage to leave their work at work? The idea didn't shock her, but it did feel foreign to think of others relaxing at a time when she was normally in her office, and now it felt a little odd for *her* to be relaxing when she should've been at the office.

Still, as she allowed her line of sight to drift back across the lawn to Shelby, all cozy and smiling and only a few blanket squares away, she had the sudden certainty that she didn't regret missing work. She didn't worry about the files she'd have to bring home later, or the meetings she'd have to reschedule. The feeling was different, but that didn't mean bad.

"What?" Shelby asked, one eyebrow creeping up.

"Nothing. I mean something. I guess if this is what work-life balance feels like, it's not terrible."

Shelby laughed again. She did that a lot, and over even the littlest things. She almost made Mira feel funny, another new sensation. "That's a ringing endorsement."

"Sorry, I'm not used to ... I don't know, relaxing? I guess it's been a while."

"Since Ben arrived?"

She shook her head. It would be easy to blame the added tension his arrival brought, but she'd never been the type to lie around. Still, she liked this moment, and this woman, enough to not want to admit that, so she accepted the offered explanation at least in part. "There's been a lot going on."

"Long week?"

"That's perhaps an understatement."

"What's the full statement?" Shelby asked, her blue eyes kindly inquisitive.

Mira worried she might be dancing too close to a flame, and while she appreciated the brightness, she didn't want to get burned. "Oh, I'm fine. Everything's going to be fine."

Shelby smiled sweetly but waited.

"Can you tell everything's going fine?"

She nodded but still didn't speak. Mira shifted in the silence between them as the tight hand of tension started to squeeze around her chest.

"Does it sound like I'm trying to convince myself I'm fine when everything's clearly not?"

Shelby's smile widened. "Yes to the first part, no to the second."

"Fifty percent isn't terrible is it?" She shook her head. "Who am I kidding? You're a teacher. Fifty percent is a failing grade."

"I'm a very new teacher," Shelby said. "The whole grading thing is still fuzzy for me, but I'm pretty sure it only applies to my new students, not my new friends."

Some of the tension slipped at the fact that Shelby thought of her as a new friend, but she wasn't at all sure what she'd done to warrant such generosity, and without thinking, she basically said as much. "You and your family have been too kind to us. I'm sure it's because you can see I'm sinking here."

"No," Shelby said quickly. "I can't see that at all. In fact, I've spent most of the last hour wondering why a woman as put together as you are would deign to spend her Saturday hanging out with a bunch of nerds you don't know, doing something that clearly doesn't carry more than a surface-level interest for you, and all I keep thinking is you must be the best aunt in the whole world to jump in so fully."

Mira couldn't believe how far the summation differed from her own assessment of the situation. "I didn't even know Ben liked science. I'd never thought to ask him myself until Darrin did."

Shelby laughed. "Why would you? Darrin is a big, goofy, loveable nerd, but I don't know many eleven-year-olds who harbor a secret desire to spend their Saturday afternoon touring pharmaceutical plants. That's like getting down on yourself for not thinking to ask him if he really wanted chicken liver over rutabagas for dinner. Who does that?"

"When you put it that way ..." She sighed. "I feel like I'm missing things I should catch. I've managed to keep him alive, but—"

"Hey." Shelby gave her a cheesy thumbs-up. "That's not nothing."

"No, but neither does it feel like a very high bar. Getting him to and from school, feeding him, making sure he showers and sleeps, these things seem like the barest of minimums for childcare."

"You also got him to two violin lessons and a science day. Sadly, I see many kids in school who never get to do those kinds of things, much less in their first week in a new town, and that's with their actual parents. I don't want to overstep my bounds, but I sort of get the sense your new situation came about quickly."

She snorted. "Again, an understatement."

"I didn't mean to pry."

"It's okay," she said, and surprisingly she meant it. She wanted Shelby to know. She wanted to tell her herself. "Vannah, Ben's mom, well, my mom calls her a free spirit, and I guess it fits, but as flighty as she might be, she's always been a pretty okay mom."

"And now?" Shelby asked softly.

"She just left him with me. She showed up last Thursday with Ben and his suitcase and some story about a co-op in Central America, and honestly, she even sounded sort of reasonable about wanting to make sure it was the best situation for him, but the thing is, it's not reasonable to leave your son on a moment's notice with someone who's never had kids."

Shelby shook her head slowly. "I don't have kids either, but it does seem like a lot ... for both of you."

"It is and it isn't," she admitted, hearing the dismay in her own voice. "He's good, and I don't want him to feel like an imposition, but honestly, even when he's not an imposition, I feel

58

like maybe he should be. Maybe he's not a disruption because I'm not doing enough for him."

"Again, not a parent here, but I work with a lot of kids a little older than Ben, and sometimes that's how it goes. Some kids are naturally quiet and self-contained."

"But how would I even know if he's one of them, or if he's sitting in his room, playing those sad songs, wishing for something more, or missing his mom, or feeling lonely, or dreaming of science day and three-legged races?" She covered her face with her hands and stifled the urge to scream into them before composing herself. "I'm not that person. I have a small social circle. I work too much, and I forget to eat. I like numbers way more than emotions, and I never, ever think to do something spontaneous or whimsical."

"Hey," Shelby whispered. "You're okay."

"I'm not sure that's true," she admitted even as she kicked herself internally. Why was she sitting here on a picnic blanket on a beautiful spring day trying to convince a beautiful woman she was a total mess?

At least she didn't have to worry about the little spark she'd felt earlier creeping in to complicate things now. Surely no amount of shared sexual orientation could overcome the emotional load of instability she'd dumped at Shelby's feet, which was probably for the best given all the other things she needed to work on right now. Surely, the woman would extract herself from the situation quickly, mercifully ending the temptation.

Instead, Shelby scooted closer. "I understand you just confessed to being an emotionless animatronic workaholic, so this is probably super unprofessional for your nephew's violin teacher to ask, but could I give you a hug?"

She dropped her hands to her lap and stared at Shelby, who only smiled, mildly chagrinned, the corners of her blue eyes crinkling slightly as she added, "You can totally say no."

But she didn't want to say no. She wanted, shockingly, overpoweringly to say yes, only the lump in her throat wouldn't let her. Closing her eyes, she nodded.

In an instant, Shelby's arms wrapped around her, the warmth of her body enveloping Mira completely. Resting her chin on Shelby's shoulder, she breathed deeply, inhaling the scent of lavender and jasmine, and the tension that had knotted her shoulders from the moment she'd heard the late-night knock on her door melted away.

It would've been enough, it was already more than she could've expected, but Shelby didn't pull away. She squeezed gently and held on for several more steady breaths. Mira couldn't remember the last time someone had hugged her for more than two seconds. Perhaps in direct correlation, she couldn't remember the last time she felt so comforted, so connected, so close. A little part of her mind rebelled against that idea, saying she barely knew Shelby, but her body felt otherwise, and in another first, her body won out.

Chapter Six

"So, it was totally a date, right?" Darrin asked for the fourteenth time.

She rolled her eyes. "Here's the thing, and I get you haven't been on enough dates to fully grasp the concept, but when something isn't a date at the time, it's probably still not going to be a date four days later."

"Ugh. Are you sure you're a lesbian?" He stared up at the ceiling from his spot on her couch, the entirety of which he'd claimed as his own. She might have told him to get his feet off her furniture, or maybe even admitted she wasn't in the mood for their normal repartee and could he please go back to his own apartment, if only he hadn't brought Chinese takeout. Bad day at work or not, she was a real sucker for the total unhealthiness and inauthenticity of sesame chicken and crab rangoon.

"I thought you all had some syndrome about U-Hauls or something."

"That's only after a good second date. Mira and I have had zero dates."

"Okay, in straight-people world, cuddling on a picnic blanket would totally be a date."

She frowned and used her chopsticks to pull some of his lo mein onto her plate. "Actually, in lesbian world, that would probably constitute a date as well, but that's not what happened. I just hugged her because she was seeming overwhelmed. It was a totally platonic impulse."

"Totally?" He turned his head to give her his most skeptical glare.

She adjusted her position on the living room rug so her crossed legs were actually under the coffee table. Not because she was squirming under his inspection, though.

"Uh-huh," he said as if he'd scored some kind of point.

"Okay," she admitted. "I liked the hug. Doesn't mean I had ulterior motives. I honestly reached out because she seemed kind of overwhelmed and really hard on herself. I wanted to give her a little break from carrying all the weight of everything on her own."

"But then it turned sexy?"

"No," she said quickly. "I mean, she felt good, like absurdly good, the way she sort of melted into me."

"Melting is good," Darrin said hopefully. "I would've expected her to be a little prickly about people invading her personal space."

"I asked first," Shelby said.

"That's chivalrous of you. Some women like that old-fashioned stuff. Makes them feel respected."

"Like you'd know."

"Hey, I'm a feminist. Besides, I agree slow might be better with someone like Mira. She seems cautious, which makes it even more impressive you got as close as you did on your first date."

She dropped the chopsticks and stared at him.

"Okay, okay," he surrendered. "I'm just saying she seems like she'd appreciate slow and steady."

Steady. Given Mira's comments about work and routine on top of the massive transition she'd had forced on her, steadiness was exactly what Mira craved. Only Shelby wasn't sure she had any to offer. She flashed back to their conversation about retirement planning and shivered.

"You can turn the heat back on even in May," Darrin said. "We do live in Western New York."

"I'm fine." She hadn't shivered from the cold, though the weather had taken a downward dip about the time her first paycheck arrived. The latter cooled her more than the former. Initially, the numbers on her paystub appeared huge, certainly bigger than any she'd ever seen written under her name before, and yet after she compared them to her bills, they vanished. For the first time in her life, she had a respectable full-time job, but also student loan payments and an apartment she didn't share. She'd worked hard to get to the point where she was no longer a starving student, only to find out she'd still have to live like one for the foreseeable future. Which of course brought her back to the free Chinese food Darrin brought, and she took a few more bites before saying, "Can I keep the leftovers? Tomorrow is lesson day and I won't get to shop before then, much less cook."

"Sure." He sat up and began to fold the tops back down on the paper cartons. "Maybe you could invite Mira and Ben to stay after his lesson."

She rolled her eyes.

"Or maybe you should wait until you have a chance to buy matching plates."

She frowned at her brightly colored but mismatched yard sale finds. "My plates are eclectic."

"Keep on telling yourself that, but you know Mira has matching plates at her house, right?"

She hopped up. "You know what, I have to practice. I haven't played my own music in days, and I need to relearn a couple of pieces on the cello before the ninth graders come in second period, but all the school cellos are out of tune and—"

He held up both hands. "I'm sorry. I didn't mean to piss you off."

"I'm not pissed off." She sighed. "I had a rough day at work. Two of my students almost came to blows in the hallway before class, and then everyone was already tense when the principal came in to inform me I'd need to direct and/or maybe play in the pit band for the high school musical, which is in *four* weeks, because the band director is also the softball coach and maybe they'll be in a tournament or something that weekend, so 'tag-I'm-it' on this massive undertaking when I don't know these kids very well, and I don't know the music to *Guys and Dolls* at all. Plus, I can barely pay my bills, and now you're busting my chops about not having my shit together, and I'm just ..."

"Flustered, because Mira probably has matching plates at her house, and you don't?"

She shook her head. "I don't know why Mira's plates should have any bearing on anything in my life."

"They shouldn't," he said resolutely. "I didn't mean to make you feel bad about your place. I only thought maybe you were resisting this thing with her because she's more put together than you are, and then there's the age difference, and she's raising someone else's kid on top of already being a successful business owner and—"

"Stop! I don't even know what you're trying to do. First, you want to throw us together and then make something out of every little thing Mira and I say, and now you're burying me in all the reasons I'm not ready for a relationship with a woman like her."

"No, I didn't mean that. I'm totally on Team Shera."

She stared at him. "Team Shera?"

"Yeah, like Shelby and Mira put together. It's Shera."

"You've already given us a celebrity name?"

He grinned. "How could I not with such a good one right there for the taking."

She continued to stare at him in disbelief.

"Come on." He laughed. "She-Ra is a badass superheroine. Probably you're too young to remember her, but Mira totally would. You should mention it to her. It'll make the age difference between you two feel less awkward."

"Get out."

"What?"

"Shera?" She shook her head. "I have to practice, and if you mention our age difference or economic status one more time on your way out the door, I'll beat you over the head with a viola."

"Fine." He pretend-pouted. "Hug it out?"

She shook her head but managed to smile a little as he wrapped his arms around her and squeezed.

"Love you, orch dork."

"Love you, nerd herder."

She closed the door behind him and picked up her violin. She didn't even adjust the tuning pins before she began to play in the hopes that the sound of the strings would drown out the insecurities Darrin's comments had caused. She didn't need them. She didn't need all the answers. She was doing fine. She might not have everything she wanted yet, but she was moving in the right direction and that was enough.

She snorted as she played a long, low note. Matching plates. Would Mira really care about something like that?

***

"She's calling!" Ben sprang from the dinner table and sprinted toward a buzzing sound emanating from his room. It was the fastest Mira had seen him move since the field games four days ago.

It took her a few seconds to process the sound they'd heard was some sort of ringtone from his computer, and another second to piece together that the only person who would call

Ben's computer was Vannah, but from Ben's reaction he'd likely been waiting for this call, at least in the back of his mind, every minute since Vannah left.

Vannah managed a couple of emails and one letter over the last two weeks, letting them know she'd arrived and offering a bare-bones report, but now, as her voice filtered through laptop speakers in the other room, Mira battled a slew of emotions. Relief that her sister was not only safe, but also connected to some form of civilization. Happiness at Ben's excitement. Shame it hadn't occurred to her he'd likely hoped for this moment to come sooner and a little twinge of something she didn't recognize, that despite her best attempts to be more present, she was still a sad substitute for a real parent.

"Aunt Mira," Ben called, "come look! My mom's in a jungle!"

She sighed and pushed back from the table. "Of course she is."

She entered Ben's room to see him sitting on his bed, laptop perched on his outstretched legs as Vannah's voice extolled the virtues of fresh papaya.

"And what about bananas?" Ben asked excitedly.

"We've got bunches of them hanging right outside the window of our yoga studio. And guess where the yoga studio is."

He shook his head. "Where?"

"In a tree house!" Vannah practically squealed.

Ben grinned like the little boy he was. "Really?"

"There, look at it." There was a sound of rustling, and Ben's eyes went wide.

Mira couldn't resist peeking around the screen to see a slightly pixelated image of a low, long building suspended by trusses between two large trees.

Vannah's face spun back into view. "Oh, hi Mira."

"Hello." She sat lightly on the edge of the bed, so both she and Ben could see.

"It's good to see you both," Vannah beamed, her eyes sparkling, and her complexion significantly more tan. "I miss you."

"I miss you, too," Ben said quickly.

"I've been going crazy without being able to talk to you. I finally threw an all-out fit telling everyone who worked here that if they didn't have the Wi-Fi up and running by tomorrow, I was going to walk out and right back to Buffalo."

Mira thought she felt Ben's shoulders tighten next to her, but that may have been her own muscles constricting at the implications of the comment. Things weren't going quite to plan, and it had gotten bad enough Vannah threatened to quit. A part of her wished they hadn't gotten the Wi-Fi up by the deadline. Then she felt guilty for thinking such a thing. Who knows if Vannah would've actually made good on her threat. Follow-through had never been her strong suit, and even if it might have been better in the long run, Ben's smile at seeing his mom would've been a hard thing to trade away.

He seemed younger as Vannah told him a story about a monkey who kept stealing their construction supplies. He laughed easily as she described missing toolbelts and crowbars, then began to speculate on what he might be building with them. He hadn't been so carefree since Saturday when he'd run around with Ken and laughed with Darrin.

"Maybe that's why things are behind schedule here," Vannah said casually, setting off another warning bell in Mira's brain.

"How far behind schedule?" She tried to match her sister's nonchalant tone, without actually succeeding.

"Not too bad. We had to push back our first group of artists by a week, but they're still coming."

"What does that mean?" Ben asked softly.

Vannah waved. "Oh, just a little swaparoo. Nothing to worry about, but it does mean the paying group we hoped to have in after them had to reschedule for a couple more weeks, so we won't have a true handle on the finances for about a month."

"But you're still coming back in two more weeks, right?" Ben asked.

Mira didn't need to see the frown on Vannah's face to know the answer. She'd anticipated this from the beginning. Even under the best of circumstances with an ambitious team, it took more than four weeks to get a new venture off the ground, and nothing Vannah ever did had the best circumstances or an ambitious team.

"I'm sorry, bubby. It'll probably be closer to four more weeks."

His face went stony again. "Oh, okay."

"I hate that," she continued. "You know I hate it, right?"

He nodded.

"But we were apart for a whole summer when you were at music camp and we survived." She forced a grin. "Besides, this time you're at Aunt Mira's house, and isn't that nicer than Camp-wanna-hock-a-loogie?"

He snorted softly. "That's not what it's really called."

"But at least at Aunt Mira's you don't have to eat mystery meat and share a toilet with seven other stinky boys."

He grinned a little. "Yeah, it's way better here."

Mira wasn't sure she should feel great about managing to hurdle such a low bar, but for a second, she'd worried she hadn't even been doing that.

"Aunt Mira took me to science day," he added, "and I got to see where Darrin works and play games with Mr. Tanner."

"Wait?" Vannah asked, her own smile starting to return. "Who are these people?"

"Oh, Darrin is Miss Tanner's brother. You know, my new violin teacher?"

"Yes, I remember now. You hung out with her family?"

"They are super fun." Some of his earlier exuberance filtered back in.

Mira said another silent prayer of thanks for the Tanners and their influence over the last two weeks. She might have survived without them, but she doubted Ben would've thrived. He certainly wouldn't have had anything fun to report to his mother, and Mira wouldn't have memories of Shelby's hug to pull strength from.

She'd thought back to that moment so many times since Saturday, she'd even gone so far as to revel in the memory of Shelby's arms around her. She couldn't quite put her finger on why the gesture mattered. Nothing had changed about her actual circumstances, and her reaction defied logic, but she'd felt undeniably better since then. Calmer, more stable, less panicky. Even now, after the confirmation that Ben would be with her for another four weeks at least, she wasn't freaking out.

"And Miss Tanner is nice, she's letting me take lessons twice a week." Ben's voice filled with affection. "She's the best violin teacher I've ever had."

"Wow," Vannah said. "That's high praise."

"Yeah, we've already had three lessons, and I get another one tonight."

"So, you're not mad at me for needing more time?"

He shrugged. "No. I miss you, but I understand."

Mira bit her tongue, trying to hold back a comment about the fact that asking an eleven-year-old to not only understand such an absence but to also assuage his mother's guilt might be a little much. She didn't want to create a problem where Ben didn't see one or exacerbate an issue if he didn't want to. Then again, maybe he did want to. Maybe he wanted someone other than him to be the adult here and tell Vannah to come home and act like a responsible parent. How was she supposed to know?

"I appreciate that," Vannah said, her voice a little thick with emotion, "and I appreciate you, too, Aunt Mira."

She forced herself to smile as they both turned to her, then added, "He's a good boy. We'll be fine."

Those were the only truths she could bring herself to offer, not to let Vannah off the hook so much as an affirmation of Ben and herself. She didn't resent him or his presence. She loved him. She could do this for another month, and she'd find a way to do it as well as possible, which meant getting him off to his violin lesson with Shelby.

"We actually have to get going though, if Ben wants to make it to his lesson with his favorite violin teacher ever."

"We wouldn't want to miss that." Some of Vannah's natural enthusiasm rebounded. "And now that the Wi-Fi is working, we can chat every day if you want to."

"Really?" Ben asked, sounding guardedly optimistic.

"Of course. You're my number one, no matter what time of day or what continents we're on."

His cheeks turned a little pink. "Thanks, Mom. I gotta get my violin stuff packed. I love you."

"I love you, too, to the moon and back."

He shifted the laptop over to Mira and scrambled off the end of the bed, leaving her staring into the familiar eyes half a world away.

As soon as he was out of earshot Vannah began to apologize. "I really am sorry for the extra two weeks. If this wasn't so promising, I wouldn't still be here."

"I don't mind having him. I want to do what's best for him, always."

"I know," Vannah said softly. "I want that, too."

Mira believed her. She always believed that, but no matter how many times they ended up in a situation like this, she couldn't help but marvel how two women with the same genetic

70

makeup and the same goal in mind could come to such wildly different conclusions about what actions to take.

"I'll be in better touch now," Vannah offered.

"He'll like that," she said, then admitted, "so will I."

Vannah nodded. "I love you, too, you know."

"And I love you."

She had only a second to register her sister's smile before she disconnected the call and the screen went dark. It left her both warm and sad simultaneously. Vannah had always had that way about her. Mira preferred black and white, though she liked to think she was capable of seeing shades of gray, but Vannah had always insisted on living her life in full color. She'd never wanted to dim that light, but she had more than once wished it could be directed toward more productive, or at least more stable, areas. When they'd been younger, her desire had stemmed from her own need for stability. Now it focused more on Ben, because no matter how open-minded she tried to be, and how much her heart tugged in different directions, some things might still never feel right to her.

"Aunt Mira," he called from the hallway, "I think I'm ready to go see Miss Tanner."

The name caused a new sensation to spread through her, this one so much simpler, happier, less complicated—a direct contrast to everything she'd been trying to make sense of. She welcomed it like a person lost in the woods might welcome a compass as she called back, "Me too."

Chapter Seven

Shelby applauded before the echoes of Ben's last note had faded from the little alcove at the front of her apartment where she'd set two music stands side by side. It wasn't much in the way of studio space, but Ben had made it his own little concert hall over the last forty-five minutes.

"See," she exclaimed, "that was beautiful."

He shrugged. "I still cheated a little bit on the A-sharp."

She grinned at him. "It'll be our little secret because if I can't hear the difference, no one sitting in your audience around here will."

He frowned slightly.

"Uh-oh," she said. "That was a long face for a boy who's just been told he can get away with whatever he wants musically."

"My mom called today and her camp in Belize is kind of taking longer than she thought, but people are going to come soon, so when I move down there, artists will be around, and she said all kinds of them, which might mean some serious musicians."

"Hmm." Shelby took a seat on one of the bar stools she'd pulled over for conversations like these, as arts teachers often fell somewhere between academics and school counselors on the kid confidante scale. "Sounds like you've got a lot of things to think about in that equation, what with being away from your mom and a big move, and a new set of people to meet."

He didn't release his grip on either his bow or the slender neck of his violin, but he did ease himself onto the other stool.

"It might be helpful to break it all down into more manageable pieces, sort of like we do with the longer orchestra compositions."

He raised his dark eyes to her in both hope and question, and she remembered seeing a similar swirl of emotions in his aunt last weekend. The two of them could be so alike in that they appeared so competent, intimidatingly so at times, but beneath those steady surfaces Shelby suspected deep and possibly turbulent waters.

"Let's break some of those thoughts into stanzas. The first one seems to be that your mom's work isn't going as quickly as hoped. That must be kind of disappointing for both of you."

He nodded, his voice low as he mumbled, "I'm not going to see her for another month."

Her heart gave a low thump against her rib cage. "That's sad. I bet you really miss her."

He shrugged.

"It's okay to miss your mom, Ben."

"Aunt Mira's house is nice. She lets me pick out all my favorite foods, and I have a computer in my room, and she doesn't make me have an hour outside before I get screen time."

"Because she disagrees with that rule, or because she doesn't know it was a rule in the first place?"

The corner of Ben's mouth curled up.

"Ah," Shelby said, "well I won't tell if you don't, but it's okay to like Aunt Mira's house and still miss your mom at the same time. You know you're not letting either of them down by loving them both, right?"

This time he lifted only his eyes, regarding her from beneath thick, dark lashes.

"I mean it, but I'm sure you could even ask them, and they'd say the same. Your mom and your aunt are vastly different people who manage to love each other. I bet they actually know exactly how it feels to be a little torn between two very different things that matter to them a lot."

His chin lifted a little bit as he pondered this point.

"And one of the biggest things they have in common is how much they both love you," Shelby added.

He nodded a little. "I know."

"If two people who both love you have spent their whole lives learning to balance that love with the ways they are wildly different from each other, I don't think either of them would have a hard time understanding how you love both of them, too. So, I think you can stop worrying about that at least, and let yourself feel what you're feeling, the good and the bad."

"Okay," he said, his voice a little lighter.

"What about stanza two? A big move, right?"

"Just another move," he corrected gently.

"Oh right." She remembered he'd been through plenty of those. In fact, he was only two weeks out from the previous one and already thinking about the next. "You barely get time to settle in here before you're off again."

"Yes," he said with a little bit of force.

"And that's hard, because now you're in a bit of an in-between, right?"

"Because I'm going to be here another month, but like not forever."

"Probably feels like you don't know how much to invest," she guessed.

"I'm going to leave again soon," he confirmed, "but not as soon as I thought."

"Yeah, I know what you mean."

"You do?"

"Sure. I only finished college a few months ago, and college is a lot like that in some ways. It can feel like forever, but it can also feel really short and fast, too. Especially in the summer for my last few years when I did things called internships. Have you heard of those?"

"They're like short jobs you try out."

"Exactly, so I was lucky. I got to do one in California for eight weeks, and one in Scotland for six weeks."

"That's cool."

"It is, but it's also hard because you're there too long to live like you're on vacation but not long enough to settle in."

"What did you do?"

"Honestly, the first time I sort of floundered. I ate alone and worked a lot, and practiced all the time, right up until the last week when I realized I could've done the exact same thing from my apartment back home."

Ben nodded slowly. "I bet that made it easier to leave though."

"You would think so," Shelby admitted, her chest tightening at the memory, "but it didn't. I spent those last few days frantically running around trying to see as much as I could, and I met so many cool people, but we didn't have the time to become friends, and when I got on the plane to come home, I felt sad, like I'd missed out on all these possibilities. I swore I'd do things differently the next time around."

"Did you?"

She grinned. "I did. In Scotland, I took every opportunity to play. I said yes anytime anyone asked me to go to a pub. I climbed this huge hill outside Edinburgh called Arthur's Seat with a violin strapped to my back and played with a quartet. I learned traditional Scottish dances in an old castle. I can play a jig with the best of them now. And I still meet people from that trip at a Scottish festival in Ontario every summer even though we all live in different parts of the country now."

He raised his dark eyes, a new hint of hope glinting there. "But did it make you sadder to leave?"

She shook her head. "Strangely, it didn't. Mind you, I was exhausted, but I felt, I don't know, full. I had no regrets. I'd done what I needed to do there, and the memories and the friendships, they were going with me."

He considered this, but before he could offer up any more thoughts, a knock at the door pulled their attention away.

She glanced at her watch, surprised the time had gotten away from her. "That'll be your aunt."

"We didn't get to stanza three," Ben said quickly.

"Which one was that?"

"More practice." His voice took on a hint of panic. "I have to get good enough for real musicians."

Her heart swelled as she went to the door and opened it to Mira, before saying, "Your nephew is a dream child, and I might have to keep him here forever."

Mira blinked in surprise, her brown eyes clouding with confusion first before a sparkle cut through the haze. "I'm not sure I find your terms acceptable, as I also happen to be very fond of him."

"But he wants more practice." She laughed. "Do you know how hard it is to find middle school boys who beg for more violin practice?"

Mira smiled, a genuine smile that only managed to amplify the joy Shelby already felt. "He is pretty special, but I'm not sure how much more practice time he could get. He plays at home nightly, and he's already taking lessons two nights a week."

She sighed. "I'd offer to work with him every night of the week, but honestly I recently learned my schedule is about to get even more complicated."

"Oh?"

"Apparently, I have to help direct, and possibly play in the pit band for the ... wait, that's it!"

"The pit band for the wait that's it?" Mira's eyebrows went up. She wore a full pantsuit today, navy, with a cream-colored blouse that made her skin and eyes seem darker by comparison. "Is that the name of a musical because I'm not familiar with it."

"No." Shelby grabbed her hand and pulled her in excitedly. "The musical is *Guys and Dolls*."

"Then, I am familiar with it."

"You're way ahead of me because I've only had the music dropped in my lap two days ago. Apparently, it's not enough to start a new job halfway through the second semester. I'm also expected to jump into a musical mere weeks out, because the softball team is better than anyone expected, and also four of their starters were in the pit band, so we can't count on my top cello player or ..." Shelby and Ben exchanged a concerned and confused glance that made her realize she was rambling. "Sorry, too much information. The point is, I need more violinists who can catch up quickly."

Ben's eyebrows went up. "Are you asking me to play for the high school musical?"

"Yes," she said emphatically before remembering to add, "only if you want to, though. I might not have a choice, but you do. Despite how my tone may've sounded, I don't want you to feel any pressure."

"Statistics show that teenagers who get involved in extracurriculars do better in school and have higher rates of social satisfaction," Mira said as if weighing the pros and cons against some set of data she kept filed away in her brain for such occasions. "But it's a high school musical, and he's only in sixth grade."

77

"We're going to have to pull up top middle school students to cover for the softball players. I was mostly considering my eighth graders, but Ben outplays every one of them. Still, there will be at least a few other middle schoolers in the group. I promise I won't let him fall in with a bad crowd, not that there are a lot of unruly orchestra students in our theater program."

Mira cracked a smile. "No, I don't imagine that extracurricular activity draws gangs of juvenile delinquents."

She sighed. She was overselling things. She was overselling everything because she was frantic and scattered, and while she knew that, she hated the idea that Mira probably did, too. It had been one thing to lose her cool in front of Darrin, but she didn't want to melt down in front of this amazing picture of poise in a pantsuit. She wanted to come off as cool and confident, or at least as one of the actual adults in the room. Darrin's comment about matching plates came to mind unbidden, but she pushed it away.

"But I have to leave in four weeks," Ben said, "probably."

"The musical is in three and a half weeks. It may be your last weekend in town, but wouldn't it be a fun way to go out? On a big show with older musicians?"

He nodded slowly, then lifted his eyes, directing an unspoken question to his aunt, who mulled over the idea as if running through a mental checklist. "Won't he be behind the other kids?"

"Yes," Shelby admitted, trying to hold her own tension at bay, "but that's the beauty of this arrangement. We're all behind. The new middle schoolers, the production as a whole, me in particular. We're in the same boat, we can row together, which will give Ben a lot more practice time."

Mira turned back to him. "That's really what you want?"

He nodded seriously. "I want to play more, and if Miss Tanner needs help, that would make me feel better, even though I don't know what *Guys and Dolls* is about."

"Me either, Ben." Shelby sighed. "Me either."

Mira's expression brightened and with it, the whole room. "I can actually help there because I used to love *Guys and Dolls*. There's a movie version with Marlon Brando and Jean Simmons."

Ben and Shelby stared at her blankly.

"Seriously? Nothing? It also stars Frank Sinatra."

"Oh." They both said in unison then laughed.

"I should've led with Sinatra to the musicians, but the film's a classic. We can watch it to bring you up to speed. How about a movie night on Friday?"

Shelby froze. Had Mira just invited her over to watch a movie at her house, or had she only meant for her and Ben. She didn't want to ask. That would be stupidly awkward, and yet not knowing felt pretty awkward, too. She should be used to being awkward by now, what with all the practice she had.

"All of us?" Ben asked hopefully.

Mira caught her breath as if realizing she might've stepped off a cliff, then glancing between them, pursed her lips for a second before nodding. "Of course, only if you have time in your schedule, but I do own the movie, and I'd be happy to do a viewing. If you wanted, that is."

Shelby's heart pressed against her ribs as a myriad of emotions spun through her. "If you don't mind, I'd love that."

"Then it's settled," Mira said resolutely. "What time?"

"Practice starts right after school and runs until six. I could bring Ben home to you then."

"Perfect. I work until 5:30. How about I pick up some pizza on the way home?"

"Are you sure?" Shelby asked, mostly out of politeness rather than any actual desire for Mira to back out. She'd been thrown the most wonderful lifeline, and her heart beat rapidly at the prospect of having it withdrawn when she desperately wanted to cling to it.

"Of course. Watching one of my favorite movies and supporting local arts education from the comfort of my own couch while also giving my favorite nephew a chance to do something special? I see no downside."

When Mira smiled, Shelby's knees about buckled. She wanted to tell her how much it meant to be included in the offer. She wanted to admit how much she appreciated her not acting like this was a big deal or making her feel bad about being in over her head. She wanted to convey to her how much it calmed her to actually look forward to something, especially something she'd previously been dreading. She wanted to let this woman know what her steady assurance and easy grace meant to her at a time when she lacked in both. Instead, she only managed a slightly frantic sounding, "Thank you."

Chapter Eight

Mira straightened the plates and glasses she'd set out on the table, but seeing as how there were only three of each, the task didn't take long. So she glanced around the living room again to make sure nothing was out of place, which took another ten seconds. She strolled down the hallway and peeked in Ben's room. He'd already tidied up in there before leaving for school, which should've pleased her, but given her nervous energy, only produced a sigh.

She merely intended to watch a movie with her nephew and his music teacher, just a friendly get-together to help someone who'd been good to her and Ben. There was no logical reason to be obsessing over minutia around the house. She always liked to have a logical explanation for her actions, but her anticipation for tonight defied reason ... or at least any reasons she cared to consider.

She wandered back to the kitchen and checked the drink options in her fridge one more time, only to confirm she'd definitely gone overboard there, too. Still, she believed in overpreparing. So what if she'd purchased two kinds of juice, three types of soda, and two bottles of wine? It wasn't like any of those things would go bad, and in the meantime, she got to relax knowing she could meet whatever need might arise.

Only she couldn't actually relax. No amount of drinks or pizza topping combinations could quell the butterflies in her stomach, which left her pacing around the entryway and wrestling with the niggling suspicion her nerves had nothing to do with the details of entertaining and everything to do with the person she'd be entertaining.

She was still walking in aimless circles by the front window when a little Nissan hatchback pulled into her driveway and shuddered to a stop. She took a deep breath and threw open the door before Shelby had climbed out, but Ben didn't seem to mind her over-eagerness as he bounded up the front walk, his backpack bouncing and his violin case swinging from one arm.

"How was rehearsal?" she asked as he hopped to a stop and allowed her to drop a kiss atop his head in their usual routine, but this time he went a step further and wrapped his free arm around her waist and squeezed tightly.

"It was so much fun! They only practice one scene at a time, so we work on the same music over and over until we get it right, just like the actors keep practicing until they get it right. We play, and they sing and dance, and I've never made my music so that someone else can do their thing at the same time like that. It's the best."

She leaned back to see his beaming smile before curling over the top of him in a tighter hug and kissing his head once more, her own joy mingling with his. Only when he squirmed away and slipped past her into the house did she glance up to see Shelby waiting right behind him. Mira's heart skipped as she processed both her proximity and her role in making her nephew the happiest he'd been in weeks, and she had an overpowering urge to kiss her as well. Thankfully, her self-awareness and understanding of social norms hadn't vanished entirely, but now that she'd considered an inappropriate greeting, she no longer felt sure about what constituted an appropriate one. A wave seemed silly and reductive, a handshake too formal and stuffy for both the situation and the warmth this woman inspired in her, and the longer she stood there frozen in her indecision, the more awkward things became.

"Hi," Shelby finally said. The simple, single syllable and the shy smile accompanying it melted through the ice encapsulating Mira's brain, and she leaned forward on instinct. Wrapping one arm around Shelby, she hugged her gently, quickly, and much to her surprise, naturally. She soaked in the subtle press of her body, the silky strands of honey hair, and the light scent of vanilla. The half hug only lasted a few seconds, but the imprint it left on Mira's mind lingered much longer.

She stepped away, feeling some of the calm that had eluded her moments earlier, and said, "Come on in."

"Can I put on my pj's before we watch the movie?" Ben called from down the hallway.

"Sure."

Shelby followed her through the entryway and into the open living room and dining room area. "You have a lovely home."

"Thank you. It was a bit of a fixer-upper when I bought it. Nothing structural, just outdated, but I've enjoyed putting my own spin on it over time."

"How long have you lived here?"

"Almost ten years." She paused to do the math in her head again. "No, I bought it when Vannah was pregnant with Ben, so almost twelve years. Wow, I'm getting to the disconcerting age where I occasionally realize I've lost track of entire years."

"And how old is that?"

Mira paused again, not due to the math, but because of some internal screeching of wheels suggesting she didn't want to drive down that particular path, which was a first for her. She'd never been self-conscious of her age, but then again, she'd never examined her age in relationship to Shelby's. "I'm thirty-six."

"Ah, then I'm about ten years ahead of schedule when it comes to losing track of time," Shelby said with a bittersweet expression. "I feel like yesterday I was seventeen and ahead of the curve. Then I woke up this morning, behind on everything."

"I'm sure that's not true." Mira tried to focus on the emotions and not the confirmation Shelby was at least ten years her junior.

"I'll be twenty-six next month, but I'm only starting my first real job and moving into my first rental on my own, when it sounds like you owned a house when you were my age. Be honest, you'd opened your business by then, too."

She nodded. "I had, but it took almost two years to really thrive."

"And let's not even talk about babies. I feel like two years ago was the summer of weddings for my entire peer group. Now, I can't even count how many baby showers I've been to in the last eighteen months."

"I cannot concede that point, because if I were ahead of you in the career department, I'm even ten years further out from the wedding and baby seasons."

"Oh, I didn't mean to imply—"

"You didn't." Mira cut her off quickly, not wanting to wrestle their way any further down that road. "We're all doing the best we can to progress along our own paths. Besides, research shows families started later in life are more stable."

Shelby brightened. "Are they really?"

She nodded, unsure why she'd committed that particular statistic to memory. "Actually, according to the odds, your best chance of a lasting marriage starts in your early to mid-thirties."

Shelby's grin grew. "I'd never thought of marriage as something you calculated the odds on, at least not statistically, but is it wrong to find that really affirming right now?"

She shook her head, refusing to say the tail end of that particular statistic's window ended before age forty. Which meant, while Shelby wasn't running out of time, she might be. "I'm sure a lot of factors and intangibles come into play in a happy relationship—interests, worldviews, goals—and no one can predict every possible outcome, but I do like to account for the variables within my control, and the first step is understanding them."

"I think you picked exactly the right career field. You strike me as someone who's shockingly good at your job."

Mira's cheeks warmed at the compliment. "I like what I do, but you seem the same way."

"Most days, I'm not sure I'm very good at it yet, but," she added as Ben walked into the room wearing Star Wars pajamas, causing her smile to brighten once more, "I do love working with awesome kids like this one."

He blushed at the praise. "I like working with you, too."

"I like both of you," Mira said, "and I hope we all like pizza because I may've bought way too much of it!"

"I do!" Shelby said, her exuberance even outstripping Ben's, either from genuine hunger or gratitude for the shift to slightly more neutral topics.

Ben's eyes went wide as Mira unboxed two extra-large pizzas. "You did buy a lot."

"I wasn't sure what everyone liked, so I did half cheese, half pepperoni and sausage, half black olives and mushrooms, and half supreme."

"I like the way you think," Shelby said, and Mira didn't hate the warmth spreading through her core.

"Good, because I did something similarly comprehensive with drinks and basically bought one of everything at the store.

Shelby froze from where she'd been loading a slice of supreme pizza onto her plate along with one from the pepperoni side. "You're serious, aren't you?"

She nodded. "I may have gone a little overboard."

Shelby smiled. "It's nice you put that much thought into things. You're wonderful with details."

Mira's chest swelled, and she may have revealed a bit of a smile before turning to the fridge to begin pulling out the drink options. By the time she looked back, Shelby had returned her focus to the pizza, but Ben had cocked his head to the side with a curious expression.

Her chest tightened. Had she embarrassed him with her smothering? Was he pondering something they'd said, or had he sensed something more in their exchange? She reminded herself that tonight was about him. Everything she'd done for weeks had been about him. Well, maybe the bottle of white wine she'd purchased wasn't for him, but everything else. Just because she'd given a little thought to Shelby's preferences didn't change the fact that Shelby was Ben's teacher. The two of them wouldn't have even met if not for him, much less be sharing dinner and a movie together.

And still, as they all settled into the living room with drinks in hand and pizza balanced on plates on their laps—Ben chose to stretch his little legs out along the length of the loveseat, and Shelby sank into the other corner of the couch opposite her— Mira couldn't help but wonder when she'd last shared her personal space with someone so beautiful. Nephew aside, no one else had snuggled up on her couch in a long time. She stole another quick glance at Shelby, who sat with one leg curled under the other, one elbow on the armrest, and her hand tucked beneath her chin. Her long hair spilled over her shoulder, and her eyes sparkled as a sigh escaped her lips when the opening number of the show began. The sight of her, close and comfortable, kindled a wistful kind of yearning Mira didn't recognize in herself.

Shelby turned to catch her watching, and Mira's breath caught as their eyes met. She wasn't sure if she should look away or make some excuse. Instead, she simply smiled, suddenly sure she'd never shared this couch, or any other, with anyone as beautiful as the woman beside her now.

***

"This is terrible relationship advice," Shelby exclaimed, throwing her hands up in the air and letting them fall to her lap.

"What?" Mira asked.

"These women." Shelby gestured to the TV where two characters on the screen had launched into a routine about their gambler boyfriends' reluctance to settle down. "Marry the man today and change his ways tomorrow?"

"Well, that's a rather blunt way to put it."

"Blunt?" She laughed. "It's terrible. You shouldn't marry someone expecting to give them a personality transplant after the honeymoon."

Mira's eyes sparkled with mirth as she pressed her lips together like she was trying not to smile. "You don't think trapping your partner under false pretenses is the way to lay a solid foundation for a healthy relationship?"

She snorted and turned back to the screen. She was enjoying the movie, but she suspected her good mood had more to do with her current company, so she couldn't keep her eyes on the characters for long before turning back to see Mira still watching her.

She'd worried she might be in over her head when she'd arrived to find Mira still looking utterly elegant even when dressed down in jeans and a blue, cotton V-neck with the sleeves pushed up. Then her mouth had gone dry as Mira wrapped her in a hug that ended entirely too soon. Her head was still spinning as they moved inside and she watched her host take full command of her own space. Darrin's comments about matching plates had been a total understatement. This woman had it all, a beautiful home, a successful business, and such a multitude of drink choices, she put several local restaurants to shame. What's more, Shelby suspected the wine glasses might be real crystal, and she knew the wine she was currently sipping hadn't come off the bargain rack, but still, Mira didn't flaunt any of it.

Mira merely existed, moving through spaces and conversations with an easy kind of grace that made Shelby comfortable enough to forget how out of her element she was. Even their earlier conversations about how far behind she felt at this point in her life were met with genuine tact and an openness that left her feeling uplifted rather than insufficient. It was no wonder she couldn't stop glancing at the other end of the couch where Mira sat with one long leg draped over the other, and her long fingers draped over the armrest, the stem of her wine glass between her fingers, so her palm gently cradled the rounded crystal. Shelby could hardly believe someone like that would even give her a second glance, and yet she had several times tonight. Still, no matter how many times their eyes met, she couldn't get used to the way it made her stomach tighten, as if in anticipation of something more.

Finally, Mira asked, "Do you think the characters are right about love being a gamble though? You get no guarantees?"

She lifted one shoulder. "I guess not. I do think people can grow over the course of a lifetime, but they're talking about trying to use things like pot roast and Ovaltine to domesticate men who don't want to settle down."

"And yet, people do change," Mira said almost hopefully, "right?"

For some reason it seemed important, so Shelby nodded. "Some do. I guess. I suppose plenty of reckless youths have become good citizens as adults, and vice versa."

"I'm probably overanalyzing. I guess a part of me wants to suspend my disbelief when I watch things like this."

"What, you mean set aside your statistics for a bit?" Shelby teased.

"Something like that."

"I don't think there's any harm there. I'm a teacher and an artist. I'm one hundred percent on board with believing the best in people." Then, with a little laugh, she added, "So long as we don't give Ben the wrong idea about believing those women when they say that having nine babies is a good way to guilt someone into staying with you!"

"Agreed," Mira said enthusiastically.

"Did you hear that, Benny?" Shelby laughed. "No matter what you hear during the high school musical, using babies as human guilt machines isn't a good way to sustain a healthy relationship."

"Okay." He laughed, then rubbed his eyes before yawning.

Shelby turned back to see if Mira had noticed they were losing him to the exhaustion of a long day, but once again, when their eyes met, it became hard to focus on anything else.

"Glad we sorted that out," Mira said lightly.

"Yes, I suppose, we can be hopeless romantics in reasonable doses so long as we don't set a bad example for the kids."

"You may be on your own there," Mira said. "I think we already established earlier that I'm not exactly in a position to offer relationship advice beyond the idea that having nine babies is a bit excessive."

"If you're going to put it that way, I should probably count myself out, too." She lifted her wine glass to gesture at the TV once more. "Perhaps I should pay closer attention to that song about trapping potential spouses. Care to rewind it?"

"No, I think you were right the first time. Both of those women would be better off marrying someone they wouldn't have to domesticate."

"See, I think they'd be better off marrying each other."

Mira's eyes twinkled with new mirth as she shook her head. "You disagree?"

"Actually, I don't." She sounded genuinely amused by the idea. "I just can't believe I've been watching *Guys and Dolls* at least once a year for nearly thirty years and I've never realized Sergeant Sarah Brown and Miss Adelaide are absolutely perfect for each other."

"There you go. Maybe that means you were right all along."

"How so?"

"Perhaps someone can do the same things over and over for a long time and still leave room for someone else to help them see things in a new way."

As soon as the comment left her mouth, Shelby wanted to reel it back in. It was too much, too personal, too presumptuous, but instead of pulling away, Mira reached across the space between them and placed her hand over Shelby's, giving it the lightest little squeeze before saying, "Thank you."

Taken totally aback by both the touch and the sincerity of the simple words, she could only manage a soft, "You're welcome."

And then, just as quickly as the connection had been built, Mira sat back. The musical moved on, and the score struck up another raucous number, but Shelby didn't manage to follow along. She assumed things ended well enough for the characters in the movie, but she couldn't be sure about them when she still had so many uncertainties to sort through in her own mind.

She felt like something big had happened, but she didn't pretend to understand what, which wasn't unusual, but this time she desperately wanted to know what she'd missed with this woman. The ideas all swam together. Something about relationships and change and growth. Mira had almost seemed insecure, but why? She had everything Shelby lacked, and then some. What kind of affirmation could she possibly need from someone who she outstripped in every measure of success?

She was still pondering the question as the screen went dark and Mira rose to collect their plates. A quick check on Ben confirmed they'd lost him to sleep sometime during the closing sequence of the show.

"I don't think he found the movie quite as enthralling as I did at his age," Mira whispered as she slipped his empty cup from beside him on the couch.

"I wouldn't take it personally. He had a big day."

"He's had a big month."

"Maybe we all have."

"But we're all doing okay," Mira said in a way that made it sound a little bit like a question.

"You are," Shelby said sincerely. "I honestly don't know how you're handling everything with so much grace."

"I don't feel very graceful these days."

"Trust me. You are. I can't even imagine how I would've reacted if Darrin dropped his kid off at my house unexpectedly on his way out of the country. That scenario is so mind-boggling to me, but you've not only stepped into this role of taking care of him while maintaining all the stresses of your own life and business, you managed to offer me a lifeline tonight."

Mira shook her head. "No, you've been good to Ben. Dinner and a movie was the least I could do."

"It was so much more than that, and Ben is an easy kid to like, but tonight wasn't about him."

"Oh?" Mira's eyebrows went up.

"Tonight was about you offering me a break, a chance to relax and enjoy a quiet evening with a dinner I didn't have to cook or pay for, in a real home with two people I've grown very fond of very quickly. I won't overstay my welcome by burdening you with all the stress I'd been feeling when I walked through your door, but I want you to know that after a couple of hours here with you, everything feels a little more manageable."

Mira's smile spread. "You know what? I could actually say the same thing. I don't remember the last time I let myself relax and enjoy a quiet evening."

"Then, thank you for providing that for both of us." Shelby headed toward the door. "I hope if I can repay the favor in any way, you'll let me know."

"You already have." Mira followed her as far as the front steps. "I don't know what I would've done without you lately."

Shelby's whole body warmed at the words spoken with such genuine emotion, and so close. She turned to meet those dark eyes once more, but this time, her own gaze slipped lower to Mira's lips, and she fought an almost dizzying desire to kiss them. The urge came over her so fast, she barely had time to process it, much less step back before acting on it.

Mira reached out and caught her arm before Shelby slipped off the top step. "Careful."

Shelby's heart beat rapidly, and she closed her eyes as if that might somehow help her make sense of what was happening, but Mira's strong fingers around her bicep wasn't helping her ability to think clearly.

"Are you okay?"

She opened her eyes and nodded. "Yes, sorry. I guess I ... lost my balance a bit. I feel silly now."

Mira smiled. "No need. We've already agreed, it's been a long couple of weeks."

"Yeah," Shelby said quickly, once again glad for Mira's social grace. "I'm sure that's what it was."

She could blame the long days, not the fact that she'd spent the evening curled up on the couch with a beautiful woman who somehow managed to be simultaneously strong and vulnerable and graceful and approachable. Oh, and had she mentioned beautiful? Because standing there in the moonlight with her hand still on Shelby's arm, there was no denying that Mira was strikingly attractive, and still very close.

"I'd better go," she blurted as the unsettling urge to kiss her took hold again. She stepped backward down the stairs, afraid if she didn't, she might do something she'd regret way more than tripping over herself. "Thanks again for having me."

"Thanks for coming," Mira said lightly.

"It was my pleasure." She hung her head and trudged down the front walk, kicking herself for ending with such a cheesy comment.

As she got in the car, she hazarded one more glance to confirm Mira was still on the steps watching her go, then managed an awkward wave before backing out of the driveway with every intention of making a beeline for her own bed and hiding under the covers for the rest of the weekend.

Chapter Nine

"Okay, you're staying after school today for musical practice," Mira said as a sort of confirmation for both herself and Ben when she pulled into the middle school parking lot Monday morning.

"Yes." Ben nodded. "We're going to work on your favorite song today."

"Which one is my favorite?"

"'Marry the Man Today.'"

She pulled into a front-row parking spot before she turned to him. "Why do you say that?"

He shrugged and unclipped his seat belt. "You and Miss Tanner talked about it so much, and you've been humming it ever since then."

"Have I?"

He rolled his eyes. "All. The. Time."

"Must have an earworm." She tried to brush it off, but she couldn't keep from smiling a little at the memory. She'd done that a lot over the weekend. Both Ben and Jane had remarked on her good mood Saturday morning. She'd merely written it off as the product of a sound night's sleep, which wasn't entirely untrue. Still, if pressed, she'd have to credit their evening with Shelby as the catalyst for her more relaxed mindset, and even two days hadn't been enough time for the stress to creep back in.

She'd flown through her Saturday appointments, and on Sunday, she and Ben did some gardening together, then went out for ice cream after dinner, even though the weather was still a smidge too chilly to warrant it. The little hint of whimsy had felt like a luxury, and she hadn't even picked up her briefcase after he went to bed. She couldn't remember the last time she'd had such a well-balanced weekend. At no point did she worry about juggling her responsibilities or even feel a hint of guilt about not doing enough, and she strongly suspected she had the evening with Shelby to thank for starting her off on the right foot.

"So, you'll pick me up at 5:30?" Ben interrupted her reminiscence.

"Yes. I'll be right here, eager to hear how everything went. Maybe you can even play your new song for me when you get home."

He grinned so broadly it stretched his little cheeks all the way to his ears as he hopped out of the car. "See you later."

"Have a great day!" she called as he shut the door and marched toward the school, blending in with other kids as he went. Still, she stayed there, eyes tracking his mop of dark hair until he cleared the main doors. She didn't quite breathe a sigh of relief because having him out of her sight carried different concerns, but statistics around school safety generally offered a soothing picture despite horror stories on the news. There was also a sort of satisfaction in having developed a routine that worked for both of them, even more so now with the musical to work on.

She was putting her car into reverse when one more glance toward the school revealed a short woman in a denim jumper hustling as fast as her legs would carry her without bending her knees.

"Ms. Collins," the woman called, waving a hand in the air, as if she didn't already have the attention of everyone within a mile radius.

Mira took a deep breath and lowered her window. "Yes?"

"I'm glad I caught you. I'm Mrs. Graves, the middle school counselor. I was hoping I might speak to you."

Her stomach tightened, and she tried to tamp down her dread. "Sure, what can I help you with? I actually meant to call the school today to see if you needed any local businesses to sponsor the musical."

"How nice of you. Perhaps we can check on that on our way to my office."

"Your office?"

"Yes. Obviously, if you're in a hurry, we could schedule a time for you to come back, but I figured since you were here ..."

She sighed. An office summons was never a good thing. "Of course."

She detached her seat belt and turned off her car, straightened her blazer and checked her sleeve cuffs for good measure, then followed Mrs. Graves through the crowd and up the school steps.

She entered through the same doors Ben had used, then took a hard right, followed by a left, and down a crowded corridor lined with lockers and student artwork. They took another turn and passed a cafeteria filled with students eating breakfast, then ducked around what appeared to be an auditorium. All the turns and congestion only amplified Mira's mounting sense of worry as her head swam with the frantic momentum. Surely nothing had happened to Ben in the mere seconds he'd been out of her sight.

She'd just dropped him off.

He had plans.

He'd been smiling.

And yet, something had clearly prompted this woman, who strode through the labyrinth of a school with purpose, to stage a parking lot intervention.

They took two more turns, and Mira worried she should've been dropping bread crumbs. Instead, she began sneaking peeks into the classrooms they passed as if she might find the answers to a myriad of questions scrawled on the chalkboards. No, that would be silly. She wasn't seeking answers. She sought aid, comfort, a steady hand, or a calm voice to tell her she was doing okay. She almost stumbled to a stop as she realized she was looking for Shelby.

Shaking her head, she tried not to ponder when she'd started doing that. They'd only known each other a month. Was that really long enough to begin seeing her as some sort of a savior? She wouldn't have thought so, and yet she couldn't help hoping she'd emerge from one of the rooms with her easy smile and warm greeting to tell Mrs. Graves she must have made a mistake in calling her here because Mira was doing so well.

Only as Mrs. Graves threw open a door and motioned for her to enter the small office, Mira didn't feel like she was doing nearly as well as she had moments ago.

Mrs. Graves sat behind a desk slightly too big for a woman of her stature, and Mira fought the urge to check if the woman's feet touched the ground while she took the seat opposite her.

"Thank you for joining me." Mrs. Graves flashed what could only be called a sympathetic smile, and Mira's stomach turned. "I wanted to speak with you about how your nephew, Ben, is adjusting."

Her shoulders tensed. "I thought he was adjusting nicely given the circumstances, but I gather you wouldn't have called me in if you agreed."

"I wouldn't go that far. I like to check in with many of my students over the course of the year, especially ones I know are facing big transitions."

"Um-hmm." She wasn't buying it.

"Starting a new school with mere months left in the semester is quite a tall order, wouldn't you say?"

"I would indeed." She tried to keep the tension from her voice. "But I wasn't consulted in the matter."

"Yes, from what I learned from his last school, the move was rather unexpected." A pointed pause. "Have you ever had guardianship of a child before?"

The tension in her shoulders tightened exponentially. "I have not, but I assure you, I'm a responsible adult with a successful business and many excellent references, as well as a relationship with Ben that started only seconds after birth."

"Oh, of course, of course." The counselor used a placating tone. "I only meant this must be quite a big adjustment for you, too."

"It's taken some getting used to, but I've enjoyed having him with me." She chose her words carefully. "I am, however, always open to learning opportunities, and if you see room for improvement, I'd certainly be happy to hear your suggestions."

"I'd be more comfortable sharing observations, or perhaps you might call them concerns, and then we could formulate ideas together."

It took everything she had in her not to roll her eyes. She didn't need coddling. If there was a problem, and clearly this woman must think there was, she wanted to know how to fix it. Instead of screaming that at her, she laced her fingers together and nodded. "Please, go on."

"From my short interactions with him, and from every report from his teachers, Ben is a sweet, smart, conscientious student."

Mira waited for the "but."

"He's excelling academically, which is rather impressive given both his current situation and how often he's moved around in the past."

"He's a very bright and good-natured kid."

"I agree, which is why I find it concerning that he doesn't appear to interact with his peers."

She blew out a breath. "Oh, the problem is that he's introverted?"

Mrs. Graves shook her head. "No, we have lots of shy and/or introverted children in the school. Many of them enjoy quiet time or independent work, but they still manage to sit with friends at lunch or say hello to their peers in the hallways."

"He sits alone at lunch?"

She nodded. "At first, he was sitting at tables by himself, but after some nudging from our teacher's aide, he did eventually accept invitations from other children, but even when he sits with them, he doesn't speak unless spoken to. And during free time, he often turns down overtures for play. The gym coach made a special effort to include him, even offering him a spot as team captain last week, which most children find exciting, but Ben politely declined."

"Maybe he doesn't like sports," she said quickly, then remembered how eagerly he'd joined the field games with Shelby's family. "Are the other kids nice to him?"

"Several of the teachers say they've gone out of their way to put him in groups with the best, and most kind classmates, and I've personally made it a priority to keep an eye on him in the hallway, but I haven't noticed any evidence of mistreatment."

Whatever had been left of Mira's confidence crumbled. "I didn't know. I thought he was happy. He smiles, he plays his violin, he joined the musical."

The counselor's eyebrows went up. "What musical?"

"The school musical. The high school one."

"But he's only in middle school."

"Shelby said it was okay."

"Shelby?"

She shook her head. "Sorry. Miss Tanner. She said there were several younger kids helping out, and Ben seemed happy to be a part of it. Was that wrong, too?"

"No, that's rather wonderful. I knew several of our middle school students had been selected, but I didn't know Ben was among them, and you mentioned he likes to play his violin at home?"

"He loves it." She tried to tamp down the defensiveness and doubts.

"We can use that as an opening."

"An opening to what? He's already opened the door and walked through it. He started rehearsals at the end of last week, and he's been practicing for days."

"Right, I never doubted his dedication. Ben's clearly studious beyond his years, but I'd hate to see such a beautiful opportunity for social connection to simply become more work for him."

"I don't think he sees his music as work." But it *was* work. Lots of it. The buzz started softly in her ears but grew to a din as realization squeezed her throat. Too much work for a sixth grader? How would she know? As the whole world liked to point out to her on a regular basis, she'd never been great at understanding the difference between life and work. And though the two may have indistinct boundary lines for her, little boys needed *a life*, not a job. She tried to push away the panic that made her feel—about Ben, about herself—and focus. "But if you have suggestions, I'd love to hear them."

"If he loves music, perhaps you could use that as a catalyst to build relationships with other kids in the orchestra."

She nodded as if she understood, but her confusion must've shown through because Mrs. Graves offered more. "You could arrange some joint practice with one or two other kids or invite one of them to watch a local concert or just jam together."

She briefly thought about mentioning she'd had the teacher over to watch a movie, but she doubted Ms. Graves would think it fit the bill for play, or peers, or anything other than bringing his teachers home with him.

"Middle school is a critical time for a child's social development. If he doesn't learn to bond with peers now, it will be increasingly hard for him to do so going forward, which can lead to unhealthy relationships at work and home, even with intimacy as an adult. This is such an important opportunity to make sure we're fostering a well-rounded approach to living a full life."

Her face flamed at all the implicit judgement there. It no longer felt like they were talking about Ben, but rather her own life and choices. Was that why she'd hadn't seen the issues when this woman clearly did? Because she wasn't a well-rounded person with a full life? Was her own inability to balance things inadvertently turning the person she loved most in the world into a maladjusted workaholic built in her own image?

Breathing grew much more labor intensive, and her knuckles started to ache at the point where she squeezed her hands together. "Is there anything else I can do?"

Mrs. Graves offered that kindly patronizing expression. "Let's strive for a couple of social interactions with peers each week. Then, we'll see how it goes in a month and readjust from there."

She bit her tongue to keep from blurting out that Ben would be gone in a month. That was one horrible piece of news she wasn't ready to process, not on her own, and not in front of someone who would surely not be happy to hear he'd have even less interaction with kids his age while living at an artists' refuge in Belize. What if this were his last chance to build the skills necessary for fulfilling peer-to-peer relationships and she'd robbed him of that by failing to facilitate a good work-life balance?

"Well, this was a wonderfully productive meeting." Ms. Graves began to shuffle some papers on her desk. "Thank you for making the time. I'll let you get on with your day."

101

Mira stared at her, understanding she'd been dismissed but not quite able to process what to do about it. This woman had dragged her in here, dropped a bomb, leveled some veiled criticisms that made her question a great many of her own life choices, shaken her faith in her ability to adequately care for Ben, and then told her to have a nice day?

Was this one more thing she didn't understand about life?

She rose numbly.

"Oh, did you want me to direct you to the office so you can talk about sponsoring the musical?"

She shook her head. "No, I ... I think I can take care of that."

"Lovely. Do you need help finding your way back to the parking lot?"

She shook her head again, then stood there for what felt like too long. She didn't want to spend any more time with this woman, and yet she didn't seem to be able to leave.

Taking a deep breath, she managed to mumble a "No, thank you," before putting one foot behind the other as she shuffled backward out of the office.

It required all her remaining fortitude not to run through the hallways in an attempt to escape this place and the insecurities echoing through her core. She couldn't even see where she was going as she took turns at random, simply trying to walk with enough sense of purpose that no one would stop her or ask any more questions she didn't know the answers to.

She turned right, then left, then another right, with some vague idea that if she could simply find an outside door, she might be able to orient herself back toward the parking lot, or better yet she could abandon her car all together and simply jog all the way to her office. Which was probably a problem, since she'd willingly chuck her most expensive and useful possession if only she could reach the emotional safety she associated with her job.

"Oh my God, I'm a workaholic," she whispered frantically as she accelerated around one more corner and collided forcefully with another person.

***

Shelby gasped as someone smacked into her and sent the stack of sheet music she'd been carrying fluttering through the hallway. "Oh, I am so sorry."

"No, I'm—it was ... I'm—"

She stooped to pick up some of the papers. "Not at all, I charged right out of my room into your way. I do it all the time. I need to look before I leap, or in this case, walk."

"Shelby?"

She froze as the voice registered and her eyes fell on sensible navy heels before traveling all the way up deliciously long legs to a pencil skirt and brilliant white shirt under a business chic blazer. For one disorienting second, she thought she might've crashed into a walking J.Crew model until her eyes met their darker mirror, full of shimmering tears.

"Mira?" She stood quickly, abandoning the remaining papers where they'd fallen. Looping her arm through Mira's, she tugged her through the door to her classroom and pulled it closed behind them. "What's wrong?"

Mira shook her head. "Nothing."

"That's clearly not true," she blurted. But how could she not? Mira's complexion had gone completely pale, her voice sounded hollow, and the tears spilled over. "Is it Ben? Is he okay? Are you?"

Mira nodded, and swallowed so hard her throat visibly constricted.

"Come on." Shelby put an arm around her shoulder and steered her toward the nearest chair. Then, she pulled another

103

one at a 90-degree angle, for herself, so she could both hold Mira up and see her face at the same time. "Talk to me."

"You're working."

"I've got a prep period. I don't have any kids for another forty-five minutes."

"I bet you're really good with them." Mira hung her head.

"I do my best. What's going on? What happened?"

"I'm messing everything up. I thought I was doing okay. I thought we were happy, but apparently that's only because I don't have any idea what it means to be a well-rounded human, and now I've warped Ben, too."

"Whoa, that's a lot of burden to have picked up between Friday night and Monday morning."

Mira snorted softly. "I picked it up in the last fifteen minutes. I'm in my mid-thirties. How am I just finding these things out today?"

Shelby took one of Mira's hands in her own and placed the other on her back to rub in a small, soothing circle. "I'm not sure what you found out, but you are absolutely a well-rounded person."

"The guidance counselor disagrees with you."

"Mrs. Graves said you were maladjusted?" That didn't sound like a very counselor thing to say, if you asked Shelby, but she barely knew the woman. And whatever she'd said had certainly done quite a number on the strong, steady woman whom she'd spent Friday night admiring, so it must've been pretty rough.

"Not in those words exactly, but she did say Ben doesn't have any friends, and he's running out of time to make them."

Shelby's breath caught. "Mira, that's not true."

"Apparently she's watched, and he doesn't interact with his peers, and'" —Mira did a rather good impression of Mrs. Graves —"'if he doesn't develop the ability to bond with peers now, it will be increasingly hard for him going forward, which can lead to unhealthy relationships at work and home, or even with intimacy.'"

It took all the professionalism Shelby had developed in her short time teaching not to mutter, "What a load of shit." Instead, she took a deep breath before saying, "I can certainly see why that'd be upsetting for you to hear."

"You do?" Mira glanced up, her dark eyes full of questions.

"Of course."

"Because you see the same thing in me?"

"What?"

"Unhealthy relationships and trouble with ..." Mira bit her lip, and Shelby refused to finish that list for her, especially while trying not to fixate on the mouth she had fought not to kiss a few nights ago.

She closed her hand around Mira's shoulder, gently trying to squeeze away the tension there. "You're not maladjusted, and neither is Ben. You two have gone through a massive upheaval. I've already told you how impressed I am with your grace. And Ben is juggling so much emotionally and academically and musically, but he also mentioned being in a bit of limbo."

"What? When? How so?"

"A week ago, maybe. He knows he's not staying here long term. He misses his mom, but he's enjoying his time with you and thinking a lot about what's next in his life. I'm not surprised he isn't exerting tons of energy trying to make a new best friend. He won't be here long, and you're doing such a good job of meeting his needs in this moment, he doesn't need to seek support elsewhere."

Mira released a shuddering breath. "He told you all of that?"

"It came up when we were playing together."

"It hasn't come up with me."

"Because it doesn't have to. You get each other. It's adorable, really, how much you two think alike."

"And by adorable do you mean problematic?"

Shelby laughed and shook her by the shoulder. "No, I know the difference between adorable and problematic. Thanks for the vocab check though. I meant what I said. You two have the same eyes and the same frown when you're thinking about something, and the same earnest work ethic, but you're also intuitive and caring and reflective."

"But what about friends?"

"Ben's an amazing kid who will make friends easily when he's ready."

"What if he's not ready until it's too late? The counselor said he's running out of time."

"In the next three weeks?" She shook her head and pressed her fingers to the knot at Mira's shoulder, relieved to feel her lean into the touch. "That's absurd, and it's never too late to learn or grow or make friends."

Mira scoffed, "What about your mid-thirties?"

Her ribs constricted around her heart. "Clearly not, because you've managed to do so rather quickly."

Mira rolled her eyes.

"What? We're not friends?" She tried to sound playful, but her breath caught as she waited for her to answer.

"You've been wonderful. You're doing it again right now."

"And you did the same for me when I was frazzled about the musical, then again Friday night when I got down on myself. What's that if not modeling good social skills for Ben?"

"I hadn't thought of it that way."

"No?" She hadn't either, but as Mira relaxed forward until her forehead rested on Shelby's shoulder, she didn't have it in her to care.

"You've been rescuing me with all the extra violin lessons and the help and inviting us out with your family."

"Rescuing you? From what? You don't need rescuing."

"Mrs. Graves seems to think otherwise. She says I need to set up playdates and arrange outings to foster interactions with other kids."

"Okay, we can do that," Shelby said quickly. "Outings are fun, plus I happen to know lots of kids. It's one of the perks of the job."

Mira didn't even lift her head. "There you go saving me again."

"Not saving. Helping, supporting, making plans together. It's what friends do."

"This feels like more than friendship, Shelby," Mira whispered.

She tried to stifle a gasp at the soft seriousness of the statement, but she must've done a terrible job because Mira finally lifted her head off her shoulder. If the touch had felt close, the vulnerability in her eyes felt downright intimate.

"We don't have much time."

She nodded, no longer sure they were talking about time with Ben, or time together, or maybe the two were connected. When Ben left, the two of them would have little cause to ever be this close again unless they created it themselves. Mira's hand trembled in her own, or maybe it was the other way around.

"Shelby?" Mira whispered. "Do you honestly think I'm doing okay?"

"Yes. No. I mean." She ran her free hand up Mira's shoulder until she cupped her cheek in her palm. "I think you're so much more than okay."

Mira started to shake her head, but only ended up leaning into the touch. Shelby ran a thumb along her lower lip, then one of them sighed, and Mira closed her eyes.

There was something too sensual in the subtle surrender, and everything around them went white. There wasn't anything else in the room but Mira's mouth, and Shelby knew nothing but the need to kiss her.

She leaned in the inches necessary to connect them, but as soon as their lips touched, Shelby knew that inches might as well have been a cliff because she was falling for this woman.

Mira was soft and surprised as her lips parted, then pressed to hers. Eyelashes fluttered against her cheek in a butterfly touch, only to be replaced with a gradual, persistent pressure. They melted into each other, shifting, moving, seeking. She still held Mira's face in her palm and worked her fingers back into those dark, silky strands of hair as she cupped the back of her head.

Mira released a little whimper as she opened more, lips parting, the taste of her filling Shelby's senses as the urgency between them escalated. Mira slipped a hand around her waist, pulling her steadily closer, as if this were the natural culmination, or at least, an obvious next step.

They both rose together, bodies craving more, fingers still entwined as every other part of them eased toward each other in the same fashion. Shelby grew dizzy from the surge of sensuality this woman inspired. The pace of the kiss never grew frantic so much as deeper, but the same could not be said for the rapid beat of Shelby's heart. She hadn't let herself imagine this moment, but even if she had, she wouldn't have been able to do it justice. Mira's lips, Mira's scent, Mira's body reacting in time with her own stoked something at the center of her being, and she didn't know whether she might laugh or cry, but she didn't have time to find out because the kiss ended even more quickly and violently than it had begun.

Mira wrenched away with a force that left Shelby stumbling, awkwardly, emptily forward into the space she'd vacated.

Thankfully Mira caught her, stopped her from falling all the way to the floor, but instead of pulling her close once more, the way Shelby ached for, she locked her elbow, holding her at arm's length.

"I can't do this."

The words hit her harder than any fall would have, and she winced.

"Shelby, I—" Mira shook her head and glanced heavenward as if seeking divine intervention, "this is not my life."

"Okay," she said dumbly, but it was all she could muster with her brain on fire.

"I have custody of my nephew, and no matter how nice you've been about that, I'm floundering. An actual licensed counselor told me I'm not meeting his needs and made some real bank-shot judgements on my own life in the process. I'm reeling here."

She nodded. "I'm so sorry."

"No, I am. I barged in and melted down, and I'm doing it again right now, but I have to stop. For my own sanity, I cannot take one more thing making me feel unstable and out of control."

"I didn't mean to—"

"I know. God help me and my apparent complete insufficiency in all sorts of interpersonal everything. I feel completely out of control right now, and I'm not that person, despite all evidence to the contrary."

Mira's anguish ripped through the remainder of Shelby's haze, and she stepped forward, the instinct to offer comfort stronger than all the others. "You're not out of control."

"I am," Mira snapped as she stepped back. "I don't even know what's happening to me. This isn't my life. I like order and numbers and feeling competent. I don't even understand the things you make me feel, but I know I cannot face them right now. I don't know how you can, but I'm not that strong. I feel like I'm sinking, and it's too much."

"I'm sorry. Please, Mira, I never wanted to make things worse. I only wanted to be there for you in your moment of need."

"I don't know what I needed, but it's not this. Or maybe— god." She pushed her hands through her hair. "Maybe I did, but I can't. I just can't."

She didn't trust herself to speak around the emotions clogging her throat.

"I have to go." Mira sighed and her whole body sagged. "I have to go to work."

"Okay."

She shook her head. "None of this feels okay, but I don't know any better, and damn it if that doesn't prove some horrible points."

"Mira." She fought the urge to step forward again. She wasn't welcome in that space, perhaps she never had been, and that thought made it hard to breathe, but she'd deal with her own crushing sense of regret later. First, she needed to let Mira off the hook. It was the absolute least she owed her after misreading the situation so colossally. "It's okay. You're okay. Just go."

Mira stared at her for several excruciating seconds as if fighting her own silent war before grimacing her way into a curt nod. Then, she turned and edged out of the room. Slowly, she took one step, then again, pausing briefly at the door, but she didn't turn back, and Shelby didn't even know what to think about that, or anything else for that matter. She merely stood stock still, listening to the sound of heels clicking on linoleum, until the steady rhythm faded completely.

Then, she collapsed into a hard, plastic chair and hung her head in her hands, finding it in herself to utter a lone summation of her entire thoughts on the subject.

"Fuck."

Chapter Ten

Mira had no memory of finding her way out of the school, or locating her car, or even driving it for that matter, but she must have, because in the next moment of acute awareness, she found herself sitting in the parking lot of her office. She would've freaked out about how she'd gotten there if she hadn't been all full up on freak-outs at the moment, with no room left for another one.

She killed the engine and collected her work bag from the passenger seat, then made extra sure to straighten her clothes and lock the doors in the hopes that any semblance of mundane routine might begin to quiet her jangling nerves. However, no amount of squaring her shoulders or lifting her chin before pushing through the door could put off Jane.

"What happened?" Her assistant practically vaulted over the desk the second she laid eyes on her.

"What?" She jumped back like a skittish animal. "What do you mean?"

"You're late and you look like a ghost, and the back of your hair is a mess."

She sighed. She'd fixed her clothes but never even let herself remember the feel of Shelby's hands in her hair, as her mouth ... she shook her head and shuddered. "I'm fine, just a complicated morning."

Jane regarded her as if waiting for more.

"Do we have coffee?"

"Of course."

"Can I have some, please, easy on the sugar and cream."

"Is that a polite way of saying you want it black today?"

"Why don't you pour the cup and let me fix it."

"Sure." Jane kept eyeing her as she went about the task, but Mira did her best to shake off any outward signs of disquiet and anchor herself to work. "What time is our first appointment?"

"Not until 11:00. You set aside the first few hours to catch up on emails and run reports."

"Good." Her relief must've come through because Jane sent her another questioning glance.

"Are you sure you don't want to talk about it?"

"There's nothing to talk about."

"Okay, but like, I've known you for years, and something clearly has you shaken up."

Shaken. That was a good word for it. Physically, mentally, emotionally, it felt like someone had taken the entirety of her and shaken it violently. Everything seemed jumbled and tangled. Ben, the counselor, her sense of self, and Shelby. Most of all Shelby.

She closed her eyes and tried to take a sip from the mug Jane placed in her hands but only managed to scald the roof of her mouth.

"It's hot," Jane warned two seconds too late.

She barely managed to strangle a sob that threatened to shake her even further. She didn't even know who she was becoming, and yet she couldn't seem to go back to who she'd wanted to be. Or maybe not exactly who she wanted to be, but at least the kind of person she'd been comfortable projecting. She liked that clear-minded, confident version of herself so much more than the mess she'd devolved into, but even now that she'd run back to the place she felt safest, she couldn't summon any of the control she craved. If anything, being here with Jane in this haphazard state felt more discordant, and she fought the unfamiliar urge to confess as much. "I had a rough morning."

"I gathered as much," Jane said. "Would you like to tell me about it?"

She pondered the question. "I'm not sure 'like to' is an accurate description."

"Need to?" Jane offered.

She nodded slowly. "I fear I might."

Jane seemed to understand the gravity of what that meant for her and reacted with unusual tact. "Okay, let's go to your office. Whatever it is, we'll work it out."

She desperately wanted to believe whatever problems she'd faced or run from this morning could be handled with the proper amount of work, but even that desire brought up bad memories, and they'd no sooner sat down on opposite sides of her desk when she blurted out, "I got called to the school office today."

"Uh-oh."

"Yes, apparently Ben is excelling with his studies, but he's not interacting with the other kids in any meaningful, age-appropriate ways. Or at all really."

Jane worried her bottom lip with her teeth.

"What?"

"I didn't say anything."

"Exactly. You always say something."

"Just waiting to see where you take that news."

She shifted in her leather desk chair. "I took it a little personally if you must know."

"Sure, yeah, that's the least shocking part of any of this. Did you say something about apples and trees, or did you go with pots and kettles?"

"Neither. I sort of quietly panicked while the counselor gave me dire warnings about Ben's social development and his future prospects for relationships and intimacy."

Jane grimaced. "Ouch."

"Indeed. I agreed to set up playdates or kid-centric outings, but I'll admit, I wasn't in the best headspace when I left. What with all the reevaluating my own life choices and insufficiencies, as well as how they may have contributed to Ben's stunted social development, I'd gotten rather worked up by the time I ran into Shelby, quite literally."

"Shelby as in 'Hot Violin Teacher?'"

Mira didn't even fight against the description anymore. The last thing she needed was an argument over the semantics of descriptors like "hot" versus "beautiful" or perhaps "stunning," so she merely gave a nod of acknowledgement.

Jane practically squealed. "I've been waiting for this moment."

"What moment?"

"Come on, no other woman has turned your head in a long time. You didn't really think nothing would come of that."

"I did. Was I stupid to believe I could find a woman attractive, and enjoy her company, and share time with her and Ben without it turning into a crisis?"

"I have so many questions."

"Are they pertinent to the conversation?"

"How many times have you enjoyed her company?"

She rolled her eyes. "We went to the family thing, and we've spoken a few times after Ben's lessons, and then she came over Friday night for pizza and a movie with us."

"Oh my God." Jane's eyes went wide. "I can't believe you started dating someone and didn't tell me!"

"I didn't start dating someone!" Mira shouted, then caught herself.

Had she and Shelby been dating?

Surely not.

She would've known.

Then again, that would explain a great deal about what happened this morning. Her face burned hot all of a sudden as her brain spun.

"Are you sure you know what it means to date someone? Does Shelby?" Jane asked. "Oh Lord, is this the crisis part you mentioned? Please skip ahead to that part right now."

"Why do you figure this stuff out so fast? How's it possible for you to know what I don't even understand when I was there the whole time?"

"Sorry, you're kind of bad at being a lesbian. You never notice women noticing you."

"You say that like it happens all the time."

"It does, but one problem at a time here. If you don't tell me what happened with Shelby, I'm going to have a toddler-style temper tantrum in your office."

"I don't know what happened. We were in her classroom, and there were no kids in there, thank God, because I was a mess, and she was her usual wonderful self."

Jane held up a hand. "More details, please."

"I barely remember what I said." She stared up at the ceiling trying to replay what happened without letting the emotions grab hold of her again. "She was very close, and she was rubbing my back and telling me I was doing a good job. She said we could do more things together with Ben, and she thinks I've handled everything with grace, and she was holding my hand. Oh, also she said she thinks I'm so much more than okay."

She finally looked at Jane to see her jaw hanging open.

"When I say it that way, it sounds bad, right?"

"No. It sounds amazing!" Jane practically giggled with glee.

She sighed again. "It was, but I think I might've missed some big indicators, because when she kissed me, I was totally—"

"Hold the freaking phone." Jane about jumped out of her chair. "She kissed you?"

She pressed her lips together, still feeling the imprint of Shelby there.

"On the mouth?"

She shuddered as the memory overtook her. "She did this thing where she had her hand on my face and then she slid her thumb across my lower lip, and my brain short-circuited."

"No shit. I'm getting a little lightheaded over here thinking about it. Was the actual kiss as good as the buildup?"

Mira's heart rate moved into the anaerobic zone at the memory. "I think so."

"You think so? What does that even mean?"

"I mean yes, it was good, disorientingly good, but my emotions were ridiculously elevated. I wasn't prepared to judge a kiss. I wasn't prepared to be kissed at all." Her hands started to tremble again, and she clenched her fist to try to regain control over her own nervous system. "The whole thing caught me entirely off guard. I'm not sure that's the correct position to be in when making objective judgements on good or bad kissing."

Jane laughed. "I disagree. I think that's exactly the moment one needs to be kissed, but I've met you, so I get how much you don't like surprises."

"Hmm."

"Or did you like this one?"

"I don't know."

"There's a lot you don't know about this."

She lowered her head to her desk and rested her face on her large calendar as if it might somehow offer a sense of order via osmosis.

"Okay, and clearly that's taking a toll," Jane said, her voice kind, "but we can sort things out in a way that feels more natural to you."

She snorted softly at the absurdity of that statement.

"I'm serious. You're not sure about the kiss because it caught you off guard, and I can only imagine how well you reacted in that moment."

"Not good," she mumbled into the calendar. "I think I may've managed to say this wasn't my life and I needed to get to work, which reaffirms everything the counselor suggested."

"Okay, let's deal with one thing at a time. We don't need to completely psychoanalyze your perceived personality disorders. You need to kiss her again."

She rolled her head off the desk. "Are you serious?"

"Yes." Jane held up one finger to forestall argument. "And hear me out here, because you admitted yourself you weren't in the right headspace to make judgements, so let's hold on to them until you're in a better place."

"What if I never am? I feel like I'm drowning."

Jane's grin turned a little suggestive. "I've heard mouth-to-mouth can be rather helpful when one's drowning."

Mira pointed at the door. "Get out of my office."

"Okay, okay, I'm sorry. I know you're upset, but this is a little fun for me. I'm serious about the kissing, though. You owe it to yourself to try again."

"I don't follow your logic, if you even have it."

"I do, and that's the point. You're logical, you're analytical, you approach problems and new experiences head-on. You're like the queen of rolling up your sleeves and doing the research."

Mira shook her head, but she couldn't argue any of those points.

"This kiss knocked you off your axis, and maybe that's because you were already slipping, or maybe it's because this woman is worth falling for, but you don't have a big enough sample size to know for sure, and this isn't the type of thing you should guess at or make snap assumptions about. You need to approach the situation with the same dedication and attention to detail as you bring to every other major decision in your life."

She opened her mouth to offer a rebuttal, but instead said, "Do relationships work the same way as portfolio analysis?"

"Not at all." Jane laughed. "But *you* do, and anyone who wants to be with you needs to see that side of you eventually. You're coming apart at the seams, and I think you'll continue to do so until you make some sort of peace."

Tears stung her eyes at the truth of that statement, and she tried to blink them away.

"That's what I'm talking about," Jane said softly. "You say this isn't your life, but it kind of is right now, and you can either keep fighting it or have a real, honest conversation with Shelby about what it all means."

"What if she doesn't want that? Or what if it's too late? I ran out on her today. I'm not the only one who gets to decide if there's another kiss to examine and overthink. She might not have thought the first one was worth repeating, or she may've decided I'm a crazy woman with too much baggage to even know we're on a date, much less how to handle it."

"It's possible, but at least then you'd know you don't have anything else to worry about, and you can calm down. Then again, maybe you'll kiss each other again, and it'll all be fine, in which case you can also calm down and enjoy a nice, slow, easy time of getting to know each other."

Mira eyed her skeptically. Surely nothing could be so simple, at least not anything that made her head and heart feel the way Shelby's kiss had. "What if it's not either of those options? What if we pull this all up to the surface and it actually is as big and scary as it feels?"

Jane's grin spread once more. "Then you'll burn that bridge when you get there."

"That's not how that saying goes."

Jane laughed. "I know, but if what's happening between the two of you is good enough to rattle you like this, then something is certainly going to go down in flames."

***

"Fuck, fuck, fuck, fuck, fuck," Shelby said into the phone as soon as Darrin picked up.

"Um, is that an emergency fuck, an I'm-mad-at-you fuck, or a you-had-a-bad-day-and-need-to-vent-about-it fuck?"

"All of the above."

He laughed nervously. "Okay, but, like, since you called me and not 911, it's not a medical emergency, right?"

"I know the difference between my brother and an ambulance service," she snapped, "but apparently I don't know anything else worth knowing, or anyone else worth talking to about this, or at least no one else I wouldn't have to bring up to speed, which means I have to call you, even though I'm ridiculously mad at you for putting stupid, horrible ideas in my head." All the words came out in a rush and she had to suck in a huge breath to refill her lungs.

"Okay, I think you just admitted I'm your best friend, but we can circle back to that because calm down for a second and tell me what horrible idea I gave you?"

"You told me Mira was into me."

"She totally is."

Shelby fought the urge to rage scream into the phone. "No. She's not. And I now have empirical evidence to prove that point. Terrible, heart-kicking, self-respect-melting, and embarrassment-inducing proof."

"What did you do?"

"I kissed her!"

"How did it go?"

"Darrin, are you brain-dead? Would I be calling you from the school parking lot at eight o'clock at night in a total meltdown if it had been anything other than an utter disaster?"

"I didn't know you were in the school parking lot."

"Seriously?" This time she did scream. "That's your takeaway from this whole exchange? You know what? You're right. I shouldn't have called you. Goodbye."

She hung up and tossed her phone into the passenger-side seat and clenched both hands tightly around her steering wheel, double-checking that hers was the last car in the lot before pressing the horn with her forehead.

The long, loud sound offered only a few seconds of satisfaction, though, an artificial release for all the emotions she'd kept a tight lid on all day.

She'd sat in stunned silence for several minutes after Mira had left, her body still buzzing and the synapses of her brain refusing to fire properly right up until the next bell rang, and an exuberant band of eighth-graders flooded her room. She'd been on autopilot ever since, but not in a good way. She'd felt nothing but numb through all her classes and into play practice. The director even asked if she was okay when she'd continued to conduct the orchestra right through the end of the scene they were workshopping and into the next number despite all the action on stage concluding.

She'd managed a half-cocked lie about getting lost in the score and fixating on transitions, when really, she hadn't had a single cohesive thought all day. She wished she could fixate on something, anything other than the spinning whirr of memories. Maybe then she would've at least been able to summon some excuse when the director had asked all the faculty involved in the show to stay after for another meeting instead of nodding like a bobblehead.

Her phone buzzed on the seat beside her, and she glared at it. Darrin was no doubt calling her back to offer more wholly unhelpful and wildly off-base commentary, and she fully intended to let that go to voicemail. Except, she hadn't been lying about not knowing who else to call. She had friends, obviously. She'd been quite popular through college and grad school, and even though she'd moved away from most of them to take this job, she absolutely could call any number of them and they'd talk her through the entire ordeal. But it would be an ordeal. She'd have to start from the beginning and bring them up to speed on everything, and right now everything felt like an awful lot. She tried to think of several quick openings, but none of them sounded great when they contained phrases like, "one of my students' guardians was having a nervous breakdown in my room, so I kissed her on the mouth."

"Ugh." She snatched up the phone and accepted the call. "Are you ready to be even remotely helpful?"

"I don't know. Are you ready to calm down and act like an adult?"

"I'm hanging up again."

"I'm serious," Darrin said firmly in a man voice that sounded remarkably like their father, her fingers faltering before they reached the disconnect button.

She sat there, wordlessly trying to process both of their reactions amid all the other things swirling through her head.

"Are you still there?" he finally asked.

"Yes."

"Good, now take a deep breath and tell me the bare facts of what happened without any hyperbolic commentary or artistic license."

She rolled her eyes, but she didn't have any better plan for going forward, so she did as instructed, starting with the movie night on Friday. She told him how things had been more casual and comfortable, and how Mira had put her at ease about her own insecurities, and how she'd caught her watching her on the couch, followed by the urge to kiss her goodbye. Then she picked up again from the moment they'd collided this morning, obeying his order not to surrender to the panic as she talked about how upset Mira had been, and the way she'd looked at her with those big, dark eyes, and how she wanted nothing more than to pull her in and kiss her until the world around them blurred into oblivion. She managed to hold her emotions in check right up until the point where she replayed Mira's reaction to the kiss.

"She just started talking about how this isn't her life, and how she had work to do, and how she couldn't handle this, and then she bolted."

"Okay," Darrin said calmly.

"Okay?"

"Yeah, what did you do then?"

"What do mean, what did I do? I was at work. I'm still at work. I've been internally freaking out for twelve hours and trying not to die of embarrassment or the sheer horror of it, all while I had other people's children in my care."

"That's a bit extreme, and in typical you fashion, you're compounding the situation."

"What's that supposed to mean?"

"It means you're prone to dramatic fits. It's part of your artistic nature, and don't get me wrong, it works for you in music and in school, and maybe sometimes in romance, too, but here's a news flash: this situation isn't about you."

"It's kind of about me."

"Only because you're making it about you," he said quickly and firmly. "This situation shouldn't be about you at all, or at the very least only a little bit. Mira's in a free fall, and it might not look like it because she's exceedingly good at holding things in, but she told you she was melting down. She turned to you for help and stability and a break from feeling lost."

Shelby groaned. "And I gave her the opposite."

"Yeah. You acted on your desires, and I get you were trying to offer what you would want in that situation, but this isn't a golden-rule situation, it's a platinum-rule thing."

"Is that a scientist thing?"

"No, I read about it in a self-help book once."

She cocked her head to the side trying to imagine her big brother reading a self-help book but couldn't summon a clear image of such a thing, which gave him time to continue.

"The golden rule is 'do unto others as you would have done unto you,' which is a good impulse and one you're actually great at, but the platinum rule is 'do unto others as they want to have done to them.' It's a subtle shift, but an important one."

She opened her mouth, then shut it again, not sure she had anything to add. She'd done for Mira what she would want in trying to offer comfort via connection—a bold, beautiful, intimate sense of falling together. Only, Mira clearly didn't want to be falling at all.

"You see it now, don't you?" Darrin finally asked.

"Maybe." How stupid could she have been? Stupid and self-centered.

"And now you're beating yourself up, right?"

"Yes."

"Well, stop," he commanded, "because this is also not a good time to make it about you. You're embarrassed, and you've wallowed in that shit all day, but you didn't get rejected."

"I totally did." She remembered Mira backing away from her, eyes wide, expression stricken. "She definitely didn't want me to kiss her."

"She wasn't in a position to be kissed, not by you or anybody else. That doesn't mean she won't ever want you to kiss her, but

123

today she wanted you to step up and be there for her in other ways."

"And I wasn't. What if I can't? What if she's right? This isn't her life, and I'm too much for her. I clearly messed up pretty badly. She's dealing with stuff I cannot even imagine. She's got a kid and a business and a home, and I'm over here fixating on her mouth."

"And you don't have matching plates."

"Oh, damn the plates to hell, Darrin. This is bigger than fucking plates."

He laughed.

"It's not funny."

"It is, and I'm glad you realize that now. The job, the house— not Ben, he's a big deal—but the rest of it's all silly excuses, just like the plates. If you're interested in this woman, stop finding piddly differences and focus on the heart of it. If that's the age difference, then deal with it by acting like a grown-up."

"I am a grown-up."

"You're not, or you would've called her instead of me. You would've already started making things right instead of having a panicked pity party all day. If you want to be in a relationship with someone of Mira's caliber, you need to rise to the occasion. You can't sit around nit-picking every interaction or plucking daisy petals and repeating 'she loves me, she loves me not' like some moody teenager."

"Okay, I get it, and for what it's worth, I never did that daisy thing."

"Really?" He sounded genuinely surprised. "I totally did all through middle school, but that's the point. Adults are supposed to have actual conversations about their feelings. You owe that to both of you."

"What if she doesn't want to hear from me? What if I make things worse?"

"Then, you have to trust her to tell you so, and you have to respect her boundaries, but Shel, I don't think she was saying you were too much baggage for her. I think she was saying the emotions you inspired in her were too much to process in that moment."

She wanted to disagree. The burn of Mira pulling back, then running away still felt too raw against her skin and psyche, but even as her nerve endings still burned, some small part of her suspected he was right. Mira hadn't even been looking at her, not really. Her eyes had been frantic and unfocused long before the kiss.

The nervous churning that had plagued her stomach all day turned into a hard, hollow pit. "I made a mistake."

"Yeah," Darrin said softly, "everybody does, even adults. How are you going to deal with it?"

She sighed. "I think I better go."

"Sure, but I'm kind of invested here, considering the many times I've been right lately, so I think I'm also owed a phone call next time something goes well."

"We'll see."

"I mean, what with you admitting I'm your best friend and —"

"Goodbye, nerd herder."

"Good luck, orch dork."

Chapter Eleven

Mira paced around her living room, still wearing all her work clothes, right down to the heels. She wasn't sure if she'd failed to change in some vain attempt to cling to empty vestiges of a persona that used to help her feel more in control, or because she simply didn't have the ability to make any more decisions tonight. She'd used up the last of her remaining fortitude to make Ben a grilled cheese and apple slices for dinner. Thankfully, he'd kept up more than his side of the conversation by talking excitedly about play practice. She felt her only hint of pride in finding the wherewithal to ask him about the other middle schoolers and allowed herself some modicum of relief when he talked for a few minutes about a fellow violin player named Josh and a cellist named Izzy. Perhaps those little connections could lead somewhere productive, or maybe they should throw in the towel and start therapy tomorrow. She didn't know, and she didn't pretend she'd find the answer tonight.

Mercifully for both of them, the extra excitement and longer practice hours often left Ben not only excited but also borderline exhausted, and after a quick scan of his math homework, he requested to do his reading in bed. She found him conked out with the book on his chest shortly after eight. She'd been relieved in the moment, glad she didn't have to pretend to be okay anymore, but now she didn't know what to do with all the emotions that had threatened to overtake her multiple times throughout the course of the day. She'd held so much at bay, first because of work, then because she had Ben, but once she found herself alone, she didn't know how to let go.

A sense of insufficiency coursed through her veins, and she wandered from one open area to the next. She wasn't jittery or nervous. This was a deeper, seeping sort of discontent, more of an ache than a rattle.

Or at least that's what she thought until a soft knock at her door nearly made her jump out of her skin.

So much for not being nervous. Her heart rate skyrocketed as the memory of how this all began raked across her synapses. A thousand different possibilities assaulted her brain in a cognitive cacophony. A part of her desperately hoped it was Vannah returning to say she'd made a terrible mistake. But she was simultaneously seized with fear due to the knowledge that, even though today had been an exceedingly hard day, she still wouldn't have wished it away. A bad day with Ben in her life was infinitely better than one with him in Belize, and even the most mixed-up and mind-melting kiss with Shelby was better than not getting to see her anymore.

As if to drive home that point as sharply as possible, she opened the door to see Shelby standing on the front steps. She was so close and beautiful, Mira almost took a step back, unable to process the sight of her in her soft linen pants and the thin sweater that hung loosely enough to hint at her frame while also begging to be pulled closer. She'd pulled her hair back, and her eyes appeared more green than blue in the twilight.

For a few seconds, they stared at each other, gazes laden with emotions she didn't have the words or even the breath to speak.

Thankfully, Shelby seemed to have the opposite issue because once she started, she didn't stop.

"I'm sorry. I mean like heart-crushingly sorry. You came to me today in need of comfort or affirmation or a friend, and I want to be those things for you. I wanted it in that moment, and

127

I want it now, but instead of accepting you where you were and meeting you there, I reached for something more." She paused only long enough to suck in a deep breath and keep rolling. "You're going through so much, so amazingly. I think you don't even know how well you're doing, but I should've been focused on that instead of how amazing I think you are. When you said what was happening between us felt like more than friendship, a part of me ached to reach for that something more instead of realizing you didn't welcome that."

"I wouldn't go that far," she whispered when Shelby finally paused to breathe again.

"What?"

"I wouldn't say I didn't welcome it," she said a little more clearly as the idea took hold, carried forward by the ache Shelby mentioned. "I just didn't handle it very well. I think I owe you an apology."

Shelby shook her head, causing the low ponytail of long hair to sway against her shoulder. "No. You don't. You were overwhelmed, and I didn't mean to take advantage—"

"You didn't. And you're right. I've been overwhelmed a lot lately, but that's no excuse to run away."

"I didn't blame you."

She smiled sadly. "Of course not. You blamed you, which is even worse, because you don't deserve that. I should've stayed. I should've explained."

"You don't owe me an explanation."

"I think I do. I simply didn't have one, but I could've at least said as much because I hate to think you've been beating yourself up all day on my account."

Shelby tried to wave her off. "You don't need to worry about my emotions."

"But I do, because I contributed to them unfairly if I let you think you'd done something wrong or bad when the opposite is true. You've been so good to me, perhaps too good for me to handle." She gave a little shudder as the memory of the kiss and the power it still had over her summoned a wave of new emotions. "But there's no fault in being good, Shelby."

"I care about you, and Ben. I don't want to make things harder on either of you. I'd still like to be there for both of you in any way that makes you feel safe and comfortable." She bit her lip and shook her head. "If I can."

"I don't know if it's possible or not," she admitted.

"I understand," Shelby said quickly.

She laughed. "Really?"

"Yes, I want to do right by you and Ben. I can go before I interrupt your evening any more than I have."

"You didn't. He's asleep already. It seems all the extra excitement of the school musical is wearing him out."

Shelby smiled for the first time tonight. "I know how he feels."

Mira regarded her more closely now since the surprise of her arrival had worn off. This time, she didn't notice the fit of her clothes but the slump of her shoulders, and instead of the green of Shelby's eyes, she took in the faint, dark smudges underneath them. She suspected the musical wasn't to blame nearly as much as she was.

"Do you want to come inside?" she asked on total impulse.

"I'm not sure that's a good idea."

"No, neither am I." She shook her head. "We could, maybe, sit out here for a bit."

Shelby glanced down at the small porch steps, then the railing, then back at her. "Is that what you want?"

She shrugged. At least here, with Shelby in front of her and Ben tucked safely in the house, she didn't feel as though she was coming undone. What she wanted to do about that was another matter entirely, but she couldn't help hearing Jane's voice in her ears. *This isn't the type of thing you should guess at or make snap assumptions about. You need to approach this with the same dedication and attention to detail as you approach every other major decision in your life.*

"What is it?" Shelby stepped closer, then caught herself. "What do you want?"

"I think ..." She paused, then smiled nervously. "I think what I want most right now, for a myriad of reasons, is to kiss you again."

***

Shelby's breath caught, not in her chest but in her throat, which contributed to the squeak in her voice when she said, "I'm sorry, what?"

Mira hung her head. "That was bad, wasn't it?"

"No. I mean, I don't think so. I think I might've misheard."

"You didn't. I said I wanted to kiss you again, and I see that might not be welcome, given how badly I handled the first kiss."

"You didn't."

"I did, and you might not want to kiss me, given the sheer amount of baggage I keep dropping at your feet, but I felt a lot of overwhelming things this morning, and not all of those emotions were bad. Or at least I don't think they were, but I couldn't sort them out in that moment."

"Again," she sighed, "that's on me. I have a tendency to leap before I look."

"I don't," Mira said resolutely. "I do more than look. I do a full review of pertinent sources, then create a spreadsheet, and I've recently been informed those aren't appropriate steps in romantic situations, but I'm hoping it's not too much to ask for a little more warning or a second try before I make any rash decisions."

Shelby opened her mouth, her heart intending to agree before her brain could assert itself. She wanted desperately to feel Mira's lips against her own again, and the only thing stopping her from lunging forward was the aftermath of their previous attempt. Well, that and about a million other questions spinning through her brain like a manic carnival ride.

Mira wanted a second test-kiss? In lieu of a spreadsheet? Parts of her found that utterly endearing, but others worried that meant they were still in a precarious position.

"I know this probably isn't the most romantic offer ever," Mira said softly, "and I won't blame you if you want to back away, but you make me feel so many things, and they feel mostly amazing, but also scary. I can't make any promises, but I want to know if I'm capable of exploring the scary parts along with the amazing parts, because I think I want to."

She heard all the fear and uncertainty, and the bravery. A smarter person would heed the risk Mira had spelled out carefully and clearly, but Shelby couldn't seem to process much else when her eyes dropped to Mira's mouth. If this went awry, she'd have only herself to blame, and she simply didn't care. "I think kissing you was amazing and scary, too, and I'd love to try again as soon as you're ready."

Mira smiled nervously. "Thanks. How does right now work for you?"

She nodded and leaned forward. "Now would be good."

And it was.

So amazingly good, as Mira closed the sliver of distance without any hesitation this time. Their mouths met with a certainty that didn't extend past this moment, but the moment was all Shelby needed. In fact, she lived for it as the tension gave way to pressure and Mira took hold of her waist.

The tentativeness of the first kiss gave way to a subtle sort of searching, and Shelby opened herself to the press of Mira's lips, soft and yet also insistent. The grace and command she'd always admired in the woman came through in the way she moved, slowly yet steadily forward. Shelby circled her arms up around Mira's shoulders, wanting to let her set the pace but also cradling her close. Shelby ached to share some of her own certainty with her, because the longer the kiss went on, the more it grew within her. This woman was a force to be reckoned with, and whatever was happening between them could consume them both in the most wonderful ways.

Mira tightened her grip on Shelby's waist, strong fingers pulling their hips closer until every part of her body brushed tantalizingly against its mirror. Even behind her closed eyes, she registered a red tint of the heat spreading through her. She may've moaned a little bit or maybe the little purr of pleasure simply rumbled through her core, but either way, she felt it all the way down to her toes when Mira's lips parted. Up until that point they'd taken their explorations slowly, purposefully, with Mira in control even if Shelby wasn't, but as the pace picked up, all those ideas flowed away on a single, hot breath.

She cupped the back of her head in her hands and sank her fingers into her thick hair. Mira's tongue teased at her lips, and she swept her own up to meet it, inviting her in, ready to draw her as deep as she dared to go. And Mira did, but only for too short a second before pulling back steadily until their mouths parted only far enough to share a breath.

Every ounce of Shelby wanted to follow her, to walk her back until she had her pressed against the door, or better yet, stumble through it, but she didn't want to frighten Mira with the extent of her desire. She allowed her eyes to flutter open and search Mira's for any cue.

Her already dark eyes had become more pupil than iris at this point, but they held none of the fear she'd seen in them this morning. And tonight, the blush in her cheeks seemed more pink than red.

"That escalated quickly," Mira whispered, still clutching her tightly.

She nodded, waiting for more, not wanting to assume. The fact that Mira still clung to her, this close, chest rising and falling steadily but dramatically, sent all the right signs, but Shelby had read her body wrong before. She needed clear answers before she could relax enough to reach for more. "So, what's the verdict?"

Mira nodded, her expression serious, and Shelby's heart pounded through her ears so loudly she worried she might not hear the answer when Mira finally offered one.

"This still doesn't feel like my life," Mira started tentatively. "I'm not sure I really am this person, which scares me, but the kiss, your kiss ... when your mouth is on mine, I don't feel afraid of anything but falling."

As if to illustrate her point, Mira sagged against her, and Shelby held her tighter, relishing the weight of her, breathing in the scent of her shampoo and gently kissing the top of her head before whispering, "I'll do my best to catch you."

"I trust you. I'm not sure if I trust myself, though, and the logical part of me says I shouldn't be playing with something so much stronger than I am, especially with all the other things exacting such a heavy toll on my life." Mira released a slow, steady breath against her neck. "But, for the first time, I don't want to listen to the logical part of myself."

Shelby smiled and bit her own lip to keep from releasing some shout of exultation. "I know I'm probably supposed to say something calming and offer to go slow, or let you lead, and all of those things would be true, but can I also add I've never been so flattered to be someone's illogical choice before."

Mira lifted her head and gave her a lopsided little smile. "Maybe not illogical. Kissing you just feels beyond the reach of what I know how to process or put into words. Still, it doesn't really seem wrong. How about intuitive?"

Shelby cupped her cheek in her palm. "Intuitive works for me."

Mira kissed her again, this time more quickly, but also more comfortably, before leaning back. "I'm going to have to follow your lead then."

Her head swam again, both at the kisses and the idea of a woman like Mira deferring to her about anything. "I'll do my best, but I think part of intuition is trusting we'll know what we need to know when we need to know it."

"That's terrifying," Mira mumbled, but with more humor than trepidation in her voice. "What do you know now?"

Shelby glanced over her shoulder to the still cracked-open door, wanting very much to back her inside, lie her down on the couch, hold her and kiss her, and maybe go so much further, which was exactly why she shouldn't. This visit had already exceeded her most hopeful aspirations, and after the day they'd had, it would do both of them good to end on a win. "I know it's been a long, complex day."

Mira gave a hum of exhausted agreement.

"I know we should both get some rest." Hearing no objection, she pushed on, "but I also don't want to wait for happenstance to get another chance to kiss you."

"Something else we can agree on," Mira said with mock seriousness, "both the kissing and the happenstance. I need a plan."

"Okay. Tomorrow's Tuesday, so normally I'd have a lesson with Ben, but the musical practice covers our normal time."

"You're welcome to come over for dinner afterward, but I'll have to help Ben with homework and bedtime."

"I don't want to mess up your routines or intrude on your time with him."

"It might be good, given the apparent lack of social interactions I've provided for him."

Shelby leaned forward and kissed her temple. "One step at a time. Evenings are full for the rest of the week, but I have a double lunch period on Tuesday and Thursday."

"I've got an hour tomorrow at noon. I've no idea what the rest of my days look like, and not sure I could get too far from the office."

"And I'm not exactly suggesting we should make out there or anything ..." She paused long enough to cast doubt on her last statement. "What if I stopped by and we could go over calendars together and brainstorm a few outings that might offer Ben some kid interaction, and us a chance to hang out?"

"You had me at 'go over calendars together.'"

She laughed.

"But just a warning, I have an incredibly nosy assistant who may be inappropriately happy to finally meet you."

"Finally? Wow, I'm flattered."

"Maybe reserve judgement until after lunch tomorrow."

"Deal." She leaned forward once more, intending to steal another quick kiss, but when their mouths met again, the only thing quick about this one was the time in which it devolved. Without the initial trepidation that marked their earlier kisses, this one took on a life of its own. Searching, seeking, soulful, they tangled together before she had the wherewithal to understand how it happened. Hands, lips, even legs pressed fully against anything and everything they could reach. If things between them could go from where they had this morning to this kiss tonight, they'd be incinerated by Wednesday, but with Mira's fingers digging into the taut muscles at her shoulders, all she could manage to think was, *what a way to go.*

Chapter Twelve

"I don't know." Mira racked her brain as she did her best to explain to Jane what had happened. "One minute we were winding down nicely, gently. My heart rate had almost returned to normal. I at least felt like we had a viable plan for a next step."

"You felt back in control," Jane offered.

"I wouldn't go that far. I'm not sure I've felt completely in control in weeks, but things made sense for the moment, and then she kissed me again."

Jane did a happy little chair dance. "And then you swooned into her waiting arms."

She rolled her eyes. "Not quite, but all of a sudden we were basically making out on my front steps."

"Basically or actually?"

She grimaced and smiled at the same time. "Actually."

"Hurray!"

"Shhh, she's going to be here any minute, and I don't want her to hear you."

"Then you should've told me way sooner, so I had an appropriate amount of time to process." Jane waved her off. "That's on you."

"I needed time to process." She rolled her eyes. "Okay?"

"Okay."

"Nothing in my life so far has prepared me for my life in this moment."

Jane nodded thoughtfully. "That's fair. It's been a bit of a whirlwind lately. How does it feel?"

She cocked her head to one side and then the other. "Surreal, for sure. Also, I don't quite know how to explain one emotion. It's kind of creeping up through me, like anticipation, but without the dread."

Jane threw back her head and laughed. "I think the word you're looking for might be 'excitement.'"

"Really?"

Jane laughed again, apparently finding the entire idea of Mira being off-balance way too enjoyable, but she couldn't exactly argue. Certainly, she'd enjoyed herself last night. And she was looking forward to lunch, albeit guardedly.

"Oh," Jane craned her neck to see past her out the front window. "Is that her coming up the walk?"

Mira glanced over her shoulder and her heart about stopped. Shelby strode toward the building wearing gray slacks that managed to be both formfitting and business appropriate, topped off by a black, sleeveless top under a thin, maroon cardigan that offered a pop of color without much in the way of covering her shoulders. Her hair fell down over her shoulders and spilled down her back. "That's her."

"Holy hell, even I'm drooling." Jane feigned a swoon. "Also, let's go shopping this weekend and get you some new clothes."

"What's wrong with my clothes?"

"Nothing," Jane said quickly, while obviously eyeing the dark suit coat she wore over a gray shell. "I just think if you're going to date someone hip and trendy, we could maybe find a way to spice up—"

They both turned toward the reception area door as Shelby pushed it open, mercifully cutting short whatever anxiety-inducing ending Jane intended to add to that statement.

"Oh hi." Shelby smiled brightly. "I'm not interrupting a meeting, am I?"

"Not at all." Jane practically leapt over her desk, hand outstretched. "I'm Jane, and I'm so happy to meet you."

"Likewise," Shelby shook her hand.

"Come sit with me." Jane tried to pull her over. "Tell me all about you. What's your sign? How many instruments do you play? Where did you go to school? Mira mentioned a brother, right?"

"Okay, that's enough. Shelby, you can go into my office," Mira cut back in, "and Jane, you can go to lunch."

"What? No." Jane's expression resembled a child who'd been told they couldn't get a puppy for Christmas. "I don't get to ask her any questions?"

"None," Mira said, but Shelby laughed.

"It's fine. I'm a Pisces. I had to learn to play all the orchestral instruments in order to get my teacher certifications. I did my undergrad at NYU and my master's at the University at Buffalo, and what was the last one? Oh yes, Darrin, my older brother, is a good-hearted nerd, who I've recently learned might have more people skills than I ever gave him credit for."

Jane beamed at her, and Mira couldn't help but do the same. She was so unflappably good at social interactions.

"Well done, you," Jane finally said, then with a little nod to Mira added, "I release you to your lunch date."

"Actually, would you mind if I use your washroom first?" Shelby asked. "The tiny humans I teach are my heart, but they're also epic germ carriers."

"Of course," Mira said. "Toward the back exit, on the right."

Shelby headed down the hall, and no sooner had the door clicked shut behind her than Jane threw her arms around Mira in a tight hug.

"Oh, my word, I love her. Do you love her?"

She squirmed out of the vice grip. "What's the matter with you?"

"Too soon for the L-word? I understand. We'll play it cool. Don't want to seem needy, but you know she's a catch, right?"

She shrugged, not ready to admit she did know how special Shelby was.

"She's so freaking cute and trendy, and she's got way more personality than the people you usually date."

"Hey now."

"No offense. I mean I've only met like two of them in the last few years."

She didn't want to admit there had probably only been two of them in the last few years, so she merely folded her arms across her chest and tried to appear stern.

"You know what I mean though, right? You usually go for the kind of uptight, type A, good-looking, but in more of a severe way. This woman is soft and genuine, and her eyes dance when she looks at you. I'm not saying you have to marry her today, but I am saying I'm ready to meet her brother today."

She laughed. It wasn't funny that she'd pointed out all the contrasts between Mira's usual fare and Shelby, but she did like to think of being the one who made those eyes sparkle, and she couldn't deny any of her other assertions anyway.

"Thank you," Shelby said as she rejoined them. "I'm all washed up and ready for lunch. We didn't make concrete plans, so I packed sandwiches for both of us."

"Wow." Jane laughed, then picked up her purse and slung it over her shoulder. "Mira packed salads for both of you, and if you planned that, I don't even want to know. Let me get out of your way, and also out of the office entirely, so you can have the place to yourselves."

"You don't have to go on my account," Shelby said.

139

"No, really, she does." Mira gave Jane a gentle nudge toward the door.

"I do," Jane agreed. "It was nice to meet you, though, and also can I say, you are very pretty."

"Bye." Mira shoved a little harder this time as her cheeks started to burn.

Thankfully, Jane managed to make her exit without any more parting shots, and Mira exhaled her relief before turning to fully face Shelby for the first time all day. "Sorry about her."

"Why? She's like a walking self-esteem boost."

"Yeah, she can come on a little strong, but she's the best administrative assistant I've ever worked with, and she's not wrong."

"About what?"

"You are very pretty."

Shelby's smile softened. "Thank you, but the same could easily be said about you."

"No. When you arrived, she was critiquing my wardrobe. You interrupted something about adding color."

"Then, I'm super glad I did because I'm a real sucker for this power suit thing you're rocking here."

She raised her eyebrows.

"I'm serious." Shelby took hold of her lapels and gave them a little tug. "Since the first moment I saw you, I found your bearing alluring."

"My bearing? I was a mess when I met you."

"Only in your mind. I was totally taken in, and you've only upped my estimation ever since then." To emphasize her point, she pulled a little harder on the jacket until they met, lips first, in the middle.

The kiss was everything she remembered from the night before. Shelby's mouth was pure magic, and she hadn't even believed in magic until about twenty-four hours ago, but how could she not with so much evidence in her newly lived experiences? She would've gladly submitted to the spell this woman was casting over her right here and now, but no sooner had she gotten her hands settled along Shelby's sides than she pulled away.

"Sorry, I jumped the gun there."

She blinked a few times without making the apology compute. "I didn't complain."

"No." Shelby took her hand. "And I enjoy that about you, but we need to eat lunch before we start on dessert. Come on, show me your office."

"There's nothing in there as enticing as what you've already managed to show me out here, but if you insist."

"I do."

She somehow managed to make her legs work in tandem enough to take the four steps from Jane's desk to the door of her own workspace. "It's not much, but—"

"It's you!" Shelby exclaimed. "I love the cadet blue on the walls. It's very confident and yet calming. Oh, and your desk is a beauty. Is that cherry?"

"It is." She warmed at having one of her prized possessions not only noticed but also appreciated.

"And you sprung for the high-backed desk chair, very dignified."

She stood a little taller. "I'm glad you approve."

"I do, but I'm going to need a better visual. Go show me your work mode pose."

"I'm not sure I have a work mode pose."

"I don't buy it. You seem like a woman who slips into work mode both effortlessly and with great precision."

She lifted one shoulder. "I've never thought about it."

"That's because you're a natural," Shelby nodded toward the chair. "You've seen me at work. I think it's only fair I get the full treatment here. Go sit at the desk like I would find you if I happened to walk in some night when you're working late."

The request seemed more than a little silly, and not at all the type of thing she'd normally indulge, but in the grand scheme of out-of-character behavior, she supposed sitting at her actual desk wasn't nearly as big an ask as other things they'd done. Also, she didn't want to kill the mood Shelby had brought in with her, so she obliged and assumed a standard working position, scooting her chair into position, feet flat, slight forward tilt as she scanned a few FEC filing guidelines.

"Yes, that's very studious," Shelby said. "You were a straight A student, I'm sure of it, but wait, are those reading glasses by your right elbow?"

Her cheeks warmed immediately. "I have good eyesight, but a lot of forms I work with have deliberately faint fine print."

"Put them on," Shelby said, more commanding now than pleading.

She didn't argue this time, as her amusement mixed with a strong dose of attraction. Slipping the frames into place, she held up the paperwork again.

"Perfect," Shelby practically purred. "I'm going to picture that every time my students try to sword fight with their violin bows, or one of the band kids tries to take an unauthorized drum solo during play practice."

"Seriously?" Mira lifted her eyes to regard Shelby over the rim of her glasses.

"Oh yeah, and that right there. I mean I'm supposed to be the teacher here, but you've nailed the look that makes me feel all the inappropriate authority-based feels."

She finally laughed. "You're teasing now, right?"

Shelby shook her head slowly as she walked around the desk, then leaned down, placing a hand on each armrest of Mira's desk chair. "Not even a little bit."

142

Mira had no response, not to her proximity, not to the low intimate tenor of her voice, and not to the way either of those things set her nerve endings abuzz.

"Competence is sexy." Shelby leaned in to plant one hot, deep, fast kiss on her mouth before pulling away entirely too soon.

Mira kept her eyes closed for too long, attempting to steady her spinning brain and feeling grateful to already be sitting down. She wasn't sure she could've remained upright otherwise, but when she finally managed to open them again, Shelby stared down at her with a satisfied grin and a glint in her eyes that hadn't been there before.

"So, are you hungry?"

She nodded. "Absolutely famished."

***

"I can't believe we managed to pack such complementary lunches," Shelby said as she stabbed a bit of salad with her fork."

"You don't think it's redundant?" Mira took a bite of her sandwich.

"No, turkey and cranberry sandwiches with an apple and pecan salad? I can't even think of a more perfectly well-rounded midday meal. People in restaurants would pay good money for this combo."

Mira's eyes sparkled. "I hadn't thought of it that way, though I suppose that's no surprise. There are a great many things I haven't thought of lately."

"And yet, they all seem to be working out well anyway, right?" Shelby asked hopefully.

"Maybe not all of them as well as this meal," Mira said, "but that's a secondary reason for this not-so-businessy meeting, right? You're going to teach me about social outings for introverted tweenagers."

"First of all, can I say I'm glad you see that as a secondary reason, and you aren't just humoring this massive crush I'm developing for you as a way to co-opt my social directing skills."

Mira laughed. "No one could blame me if I did, but no. As much as I would've considered myself beyond the crush stage of my life, I have to admit the feeling is mutual."

"Wow." Shelby took a deep breath and held it for a few seconds before releasing.

"What?"

"Nothing. That's just me enjoying the moment when you admitted I'm not alone in this butterfly-fluttering-in-the-stomach sensation."

"I thought I made my feelings clear last night."

"You rarely make your feelings clear, but I'll say you gave me some rather strong indicators." Shelby tried to fight the light-headedness that accompanied memories of Mira's hands on her waist. "I could use a few more of those before I go back to work, but I worry we better stick to the topic at hand or I might not make it back at all. Did you have any ideas for kid-friendly activities?

Mira's eyes widened. "Wait, I thought you were bringing the ideas."

"I did, but you should go first."

"Sure, I can go first, as in I'd first like to say I have no ideas."

She laughed. "I find that hard to believe. You seem like a woman who knows how to solve problems."

"I used to think so, too," Mira admitted. "A few weeks ago, I would've called myself ... I might not have gone all the way to unflappable, but pretty close."

"I'd agree with the you of a few weeks ago and call you very close to unflappable."

"Even after the last few days?"

"Again, not completely, but very close. Yesterday morning being the exception."

"And last night?"

"Not an exception. You were magnificent, and not just at the end. You stayed calm and thoughtful and levelheaded, and approached a sensitive situation with openness and honesty. Your commitment to thorough research is something I admire."

Mira's cheeks turned that delightful shade of pink Shelby loved to inspire.

"I've no doubt that if left to your own devices, you could come up with some good leads," Shelby prodded, then waited.

"Well ..." Mira started, "Ben's mentioned two kids a couple of times over the last few days, though he commented on their playing more than their personalities."

"Any in is a good one when we're brainstorming. Lay the names on me."

"He said Josh plays well, and he seems to admire an Izzy, too."

Shelby beamed, both at Ben's choices and the attention Mira paid to the details. "He's right on both counts. Josh and Izzy are above average, which of course is why they're playing up with the high school group, but they're also sweet-natured kids from what I can tell."

Mira leaned forward. "Do you think they'd like Ben?"

"Of course. Anyone would like Ben once they get to know him, but more than that, I think their personalities are nicely matched to bring him out of his shell a bit. Josh is smart with a quirky sense of humor while Izzy is more gently outgoing with an easygoing streak that meshes with Ben's natural affability."

"Wow," Mira said, a hint of wonder in her voice. "You've only known these students a month, and already you can write detailed personality inventories for all of them?"

She shook her head. "Not all of them, only the ones who've stood out as special. I can't help it if Ben has great taste. Must be one more attribute he gets from his aunt."

Mira rolled her eyes playfully. "Well, his aunt is out of ideas from this point on. Even if I somehow knew how to rope two children I've never met into some sort of social plan, I wouldn't know what to do with them. The last social event I hosted was a holiday open house for my clients, and Jane did all of the preparations. Now that I think of it, she also did eighty percent of the small talk. I mostly stuck to conversations about Roth IRAs."

"I bet they were enthralling."

Mira snorted. "I've already mentioned many times, this situation you've found me in is not my natural state."

As if to prove her point, the phone on her desk rang.

"You can get that," Shelby said, but when Mira glanced at the caller ID, she shook her head.

"It's just Larry. He's a real estate guy who wants me to invest in a property. Your building actually."

"My building? Where I live?"

"Yes, and your place seems nice, but he's convinced that if I tour the commercial space, I'll have some sort of revelation to supersede all the financial calculations and projections I've already done, but that's not how business works. You have to crunch the ... oh my Lord, I'm boring you to death, aren't I?

"No," Shelby laughed. "You might have lost me, but not bored me."

"See, that's who I am at work—in my head, in the numbers, in control of my own little kingdom—not the shaky person who nearly falls apart after one kiss."

"And I know those moments bother you, but seriously, if this is you off your game, maybe you should go off more often."

Mira gave a little shiver.

"Maybe not all the way to temporary guardianship and meetings with the middle school guidance counselor, but like, on the 'this is not my real-life scale,' could you lean in to like, vacation territory?"

Mira seemed to think about that for a bit. "I can't remember the last time I took a vacation."

"Try."

She pressed her lips together, drawing Shelby's attention to one of her new favorite features. "When my parents retired three years ago, the whole family went to Disney World."

"That's a great vacation."

Mira gave a shrug. "It was hot and crowded, and for the happiest place on earth, there sure were a lot of children crying."

Shelby laughed.

"But there were some wonderful moments, too," Mira said almost grudgingly. "Ben loved meeting all the characters, and the rides were fun, most of them, anyway."

"Be honest, you screamed on Space Mountain."

"Of course I screamed. It's a rollercoaster in the dark. No one told me about the dark. I knew it was a rollercoaster, but I thought it was for children. Ben and I were both shaking profusely when it ended. He clung to me for the next half an hour, until I bought him astronaut ice cream and a Buzz Lightyear bubble gun while his mother rode it again."

"Aww." She could picture it all so clearly, and while she was definitely the type who loved rollercoasters, she enjoyed astronaut ice cream and bubbles, too.

"We did like the shows though, and the race cars don't actually go very fast. Oh, and the fireworks." Mira finally smiled. "Okay, and the Peter Pan ride was magical."

"There you have it," Shelby said. "Disney vacation is an apt metaphor. You're out of your element, and some aspects might be mildly traumatizing, but some parts are beautiful and entertaining, or even laced with magic. Can you think of this time as less of a derailing of your real life and more of a vacation?"

Mira pressed her lips together again, but this time the corners curled up a little bit before she nodded. "You're wonderful at offering perspective."

"Thank you."

"I think I can work with a vacation model. Ben is here only a few more weeks. The challenges of that time don't have to be permanent, and the memories we make can be. I've been focused on the rollercoaster aspects of it all, but I like the idea of letting go and enjoying the magic of these moments, too."

"There you go." Shelby's heart warmed at the hope rising in Mira's voice. "And lucky for you, you happen to be working with a vacation master here."

"I had no idea." Mira's eyes sparkled as she picked up the playful tone. "Please tell me more."

"I love vacations. Trying new foods, exploring new places, visiting all the cool landmarks, and checking out local events. In grad school, I even gave tours of Kleinhans Music Hall."

"You did?" Mira sounded impressed.

"Indeed, and I still know people who work there, so I thought maybe this weekend we could invite Josh and Izzy to go with us after we finish the Saturday morning rehearsal."

"All the way to Buffalo?"

"Don't make it sound like Siberia," she laughed. "It's only a forty-five-minute drive. I could give them a quick tour, let them see a real music hall, and then we could go to Delaware Park. There's an outdoor stage, and they've got a jazz band playing Saturday afternoon."

"How do you know all this?"

"You're not the only one who can research," she said, feeling more than a little proud she'd been able to impress Mira, who even in her weaker moments still managed to project an air of authority behind that big desk of hers. "Besides, in addition to being a fun and semi-educational trip for the kids, it sounds like kind of fun for you and me, too."

Mira paused to ponder the thought. "Actually, it does. We both get to work in the morning, Ben gets practice interacting with other kids, and we enjoy an afternoon in the park. It's all very well-balanced. More like a mini-vacation rather than full on running away from real life."

"There you go," Shelby said. "It'll let you ease into the new vacation mindset."

"I like it," she declared more emphatically. "Vacations are good. People take them all the time. They even look forward to them."

"They do."

"They go out. They get a break. They have a good time." Mira nodded resolutely. "And then they end, and people come back from them."

Shelby's heart kicked her ribs at that last line. She hadn't thought about that aspect of vacations when she'd been working this analogy. She rarely thought her metaphors all the way through. As with so many other things, she'd only considered what a vacation mindset might offer in the moment, but of course Mira had taken the time to consider the full trajectory.

Vacations ended.

Chapter Thirteen

"Here's to surviving the week." She raised a glass of wine, which Mira clinked with her can of Diet Coke. Then Shelby sipped, the cool sweetness settling across her lips, no match for the way the woman next to her made her feel.

"Not going to lie," Shelby said, "I had my doubts a time or two."

She chuckled. "When, like all of Monday?"

"Every minute of Monday, but also Wednesday night's head-splitting rehearsal. Plus, any time you were sitting behind your mammoth desk with all those calendars and your color-coded highlighters, I thought I might keel over from sheer admiration."

Mira rolled her eyes. "It's an efficient system."

"I know. It works for you, and it works for me too, just on a more visceral level."

The warm flush creeping up her cheeks was no longer a new sensation, nor was the easy sensuality of Shelby's compliments, but she hadn't grown inured to them. Part of her hoped she never did, though it was hard to believe she was the same woman who'd gone white as a ghost after their first kiss a mere five days earlier. They'd come a long way quickly, and she knew who she had to thank for that, among other things. "Thank you again for making today happen."

"You're welcome, and I'll accept full credit," Shelby said breezily, "but to be clear, it's not exactly a hardship for me to listen to great music while sipping wine and vaguely supervising three of the most well-behaved middle schoolers in the history of adolescents."

Mira glanced down the grassy knoll where Ben sat with Josh and Izzy. The classmates, and quite possibly new friends, all had their heads together talking intently as a jazz band played atop a small bandstand. "They do seem like nice kids."

"They are, and they like Ben because he's a nice kid, too. I didn't have to twist any arms. I merely issued the invite, and everyone involved jumped on board enthusiastically."

The way Shelby had retold it, she merely mentioned a trip to Buffalo for a chance to listen to some real musicians. Then, both the kids and their parents practically fell over themselves to accept. Mira couldn't have imagined it being so easy, though she suspected it wouldn't have been for her. Shelby had a knack for drawing people out. "Maybe, but I feel as though your own enthusiasm had something to do with inspiring theirs. It's had quite an effect on me."

She sipped her soda for fear of giving too much more away, but it wasn't easy with Shelby sitting close in a knee-length sundress, her shoulders dappled in shade, sun, and a few tantalizing freckles. It was perfectly appropriate for both the setting and the slowly warming weather, but Mira hadn't been able to keep her eyes off the little bits of exposed skin all afternoon.

"What are you thinking about?" Shelby lifted her wine glass and her eyebrows at the same time.

"Your shoulders," she said honestly, then realized that was an awkward thing to admit and grimaced, but it was too late to reel the words back in, so she tried to forge on. "I mean your dress, and well, yes, your shoulders, which are bare because of the dress, which is very cute on you, and—"

"Thank you." Shelby accepted the compliment gracefully and ignored the stammering. "It's still a little chilly, but I love summer dresses so much I sort of jumped the gun."

"Do you want to move more into the sun?"

"How about I scoot a little closer to you." Then, without waiting for a response, Shelby slid over to Mira's side of the table until their arms brushed against one another and their legs pressed together. "You're warm because, as always, you made much more appropriate choices."

Mira frowned down at her conservatively casual blue jeans and a lightweight navy-blue long-sleeve shirt.

"Don't do that," Shelby said.

"I didn't do anything."

"You did. You made a disapproving expression at your own clothes, the very ones exuding warmth and tempting suggestions of cuddles, especially since I was just sitting here trying to decide which version of you I found more alluring."

"Version of me?"

"You know, the sexy buttoned-up and together businesswoman, or the softer, casual version who makes every exchange feel intimate without even trying."

Her breath caught. How could Shelby see so much in her that she'd never even seen in herself? "And what's the verdict?"

Shelby's smile turned a little coy. "They're too good to choose between. I think I'm going to need a bigger sample size."

"Hmm, now you're speaking my language." Mira played along. "You should always have an adequate data pool before making any broad assertions. I might have to reference my calendars to see what we can do about that."

Shelby rested her head on Mira's shoulder. "You say the sweetest things to me."

She shook her head even as she smiled. She didn't even know who she was becoming on this little vacation of sorts but was no longer trying to fight it. Several times she'd even gone so far as to consider an actual vacation, at least from work, because their busy schedules hadn't afforded them nearly as much time together as she would've liked.

They'd shared two business-ish lunches spent in equal parts planning social outings for Ben and kissing passionately. And, while today's trip to Buffalo for a concert in the park felt more like a date on several levels, there'd been no kissing as they had three kids in tow. She couldn't find many similarities between their current trajectory and any other relationship she'd ever been in, and yet sitting near this woman on a late spring day with music in the air felt more real than all of the others combined.

"Aunt Mira?" Ben called, his voice jarring her back to the moment and the responsibilities inherent in it. "Can we go skip rocks on the pond?"

She froze, several terrible scenarios running through her head in an instant. Drowning, getting hit on the head with a rock, slipping and falling, perhaps also hitting his head on a rock. She started to consider the likelihood of each scenario though she didn't know the local drowning statistics, and before she could recall the probabilities of head injuries, Shelby placed a hand on her arm.

"The pond's only about three feet deep, and we'll still be able to see them."

Intellectually, she knew those weren't actual safety rails, and while a rebuttal about drowning in inches of water pushed up from the recesses of her brain, she didn't have any desire to give it voice with Shelby's gentle touch and soft assurance rising to the forefront, so she nodded, then turned back to Ben. "Sure, stay where we can see you."

The boy grinned and sprinted off with Josh and Izzy beside him.

She watched them jog through the sparse crowd, jostling each other as they went. She couldn't put her finger on any tangible difference. He seemed younger, smaller, lighter today. "That's how kids are supposed to behave, right?"

"I think kids can behave in lots of ways that are all valid," Shelby said evenly. "They really are smaller versions of adults. They each have their own personality and interests and learn at their own pace. If Ben wants to skip rocks, then that's appropriate for him. If he wants to lie on a blanket with a book, that's who he is. And if he wants to listen to music while staring at the clouds, that's Ben being Ben."

She took Shelby's hand and interlaced their fingers, wanting to intertwine herself with this woman in more ways than she could explain. "You make it sound simple."

"Maybe I'm naive, but I think it can be." Shelby ran her thumb along the back of Mira's hand. "I know teachers in core subjects like math or science have standards they have to cover, and so much pressure from standardized tests spills over onto the kids. Then the guidance counselor has to keep an eye out for red flags for good reason, but it can all create a hypervigilant state that puts people on edge or creates a pervasive culture of anxious expectation."

She tensed at the very visceral memory of her visit to the school, but Shelby kept talking in her soft, even tone.

"As a music teacher, I relish providing them with a space to explore and wander and express themselves. I love to watch them shed their notions of what's worthy, or other people's ideas of what's valid, and begin to pluck their own notes, or sway to their own tune."

"You make it sound like you hand them instruments and let them take it from there."

She laughed, a light, lyrical sound that hung in the air between them every bit as much as the strains of jazz wafting out from the stage. "No, that'd be a nightmare, utter chaos. I teach the classes of course. I cover form and positioning, posture and how to read music, and we have a wide array of basic benchmarks. Then, there's the big concerts at the end of the year, but I also know some kids will leave school and never pick up an instrument again while some of them will play for life. There's a freedom in that. What's more, I have one student who loves to play fiddle, and a couple who want to start a jazz band, and a few others who play in a traditional string quartet. I've only been on the job a few weeks, and already their personalities are coming forward and I get—" She stopped mid-sentence, free hand raised in an excited gesture cut short. "I'm sorry, that was way too much information, wasn't it?"

"Not at all. Please go on."

She shrugged self-consciously. "That's all. I get a little overexcited about all the doors music can open for a person. I imagine it sounds silly to someone with a real job."

"Music teacher is a real job."

"I know, deep down I do, and certainly it's been so much work to jump into a school year in the fourth quarter, but at the same time, I feel like it's still too good to be true." Her expression brightened once more. "I get to play instruments with kids all day, and people pay me an almost living wage."

Mira laughed. "I know what you mean about an almost living wage. My business actually lost money in my first year."

"No."

"Yes."

"The idea of you struggling at anything work-related doesn't make sense."

She liked how much faith Shelby had in her, but she couldn't mislead her. "Most businesses hemorrhage money for the first few years. I knew the statistics going in."

"Of course you did."

"I don't take gambles I can't afford, so I prepared to withstand a hit, at least hypothetically, but for someone who's used to succeeding, it stung to come up short no matter how hard I worked. And for what it's worth, I think that playing instruments with kids for six hours a day sounds like infinitely more work than what I do in my quiet, well-controlled office all day."

"I will grant that you do have infinitely more quiet and control if those are your metrics of choice." Shelby rested her head on Mira's shoulder as her voice returned to its almost dreamy quality. "But I've been making music my whole life for free. Even if I never got paid another dime, I'd still spend as much time playing as possible. I think I'd want to share that love with as many people as possible along the way, just maybe not with thirty-four fifth graders all at once."

She shuddered. "I can't even imagine being in a room with thirty-four fifth graders at once."

"It's ... a lot." Shelby sighed. "Too much to think about on a weekend in the park."

"Fair enough. I'd be remiss if I let you break my workaholic streak only to make you spend the day talking about your job. Why don't you tell me more about all the music you love enough to play for free?"

"You'll have to be more specific because that question is akin to me asking you to tell me about all the air you breathe."

"Wow. I don't even know where to start. I remember you told Jane you play basically all the instruments in the world."

"Maybe not quite that many. I at least understand the fundamentals of all traditional orchestral instruments. It's a requirement of the job. I can't teach a kid to play something if I don't know how, but I'm only concert grade in violin, viola, cello, and bass."

"Only those four? You slacker," she teased. "That's about four more than I play."

"You don't play any instruments?" Shelby held up her hand so their palms pressed together as she examined Mira's fingers. "I'd have put money on piano."

"My mother did her best, but I didn't even make it a whole year of lessons. All the musical talent in the family went right past me and into Vannah."

Shelby raised her eyebrows. "You don't mention her much."

"I don't think of her much right now," Mira admitted. "Is that terrible?"

"No. It could be out of sight, out of mind, or it could be a good sign that you and Ben have fallen into a routine akin to normalcy."

"I doubt it. Nothing about this feels normal to me." She glanced off in the direction of the kids, then down at their joined hands. "Maybe I've sort of locked that door, because while none of this feels like my real life, it does sometimes feel a lot more like hers."

"How so?"

"Vannah breaks routines. Vannah figures things out as she goes. Vannah gets swept away in the moment. Vannah spends afternoons at jazz festivals."

Shelby tensed slightly, and Mira pretended not to notice, but she certainly understood on some base level that she'd just described Vannah in ways that echoed much of what Shelby had encouraged in her. She hadn't thought of the two of them as being similar until this moment, as least not in many ways that mattered, but it'd be hard to imagine how she and Shelby would've ever met, much less found a way to where they were now, without the type of chaos Vannah always brought and Mira had spent her whole life trying to avoid. "She's a free spirit, and I don't judge her for that. I honestly judge her for very little."

157

"You judge her for leaving Ben," Shelby said matter-of-factly, "and you're allowed to. It doesn't mean you love either of them any less."

She tightened around Shelby's hand at the emotions the comment sent rattling through her. "I do still blame her, but even my anger feels more complicated now."

"Why?"

"There's so much back-and-forth. I do blame her for going places Ben shouldn't be, but I'm glad she didn't take him with her. I wish she'd given me more time to prepare, but I don't regret taking him. Sometimes I get mad at her for the impossible position she put me in, trying to do everything and be everything, but then I think that if she hadn't, I wouldn't have met you."

Shelby's breath caught audibly, but Mira forged on. "I don't generally believe in 'twists of fate,' or 'meant to be,' but I find myself wondering about the difference between who I've always been and who I feel like I am these days. Sometimes I think I should be more upset. I've never wanted to live like her in any way. Her life has always seemed disorienting to me, and now that I'm living such a small piece of it, I find I was absolutely right, but I don't feel vindicated."

"Why do you think that is?" Shelby asked cautiously, seemingly aware they'd tread onto some thin ice.

"I suspect it may be that even amid the chaos, there are also so many wonderful strands to reach for, which terrifies me." She shook a little, and Shelby must've felt it too, because she pressed against her a little more, offering something solid amid the shifting sand at her core. "I don't want the price of happiness to be chaos. I don't want to have to stay perpetually on edge, never knowing if the next emotional swing will be up or down. I don't want to have to trade my lifestyle for hers in order to have access to days like this."

Shelby smiled sadly. "I'm sorry you feel like you have to."

"And I'm sorry I've brought down the whole mood." Mira tried to sit back, but Shelby refused to release her hand.

"You haven't."

She shrugged and looked away, but Shelby pulled her in once more.

"I wish I could do more to convey how highly I think of you and how well you're wrestling with challenges that would've made any other mere mortal curl into a ball and cry."

She shook her head, unable to share the assessment, as she quite often wanted to fall apart, but she didn't have room in her schedule.

"You're dealing with some big changes, bigger questions about yourself, and rethinking your most fundamental relationships. You don't have to pretend that doesn't bother you." Shelby squeezed her hand to emphasize the point. "A lot of people would rage at having their lives upended, but here you are grappling with complexities and asking yourself hard questions, trying to make sense of discordant impulses."

"You make me sound much stronger than I feel most days."

"Good," she said resolutely, "because you've done the same for me. I'm in a time of transition, too. You inspire me every day, and I know living in the moment isn't your strong point, but you're doing it in a way that makes me feel better about my own lack of answers. When I watch you meet challenge after challenge in this crazy, endless loop, it gives me faith we can face the next one when it comes, whatever and whenever that may be."

"I'm glad one of us has faith because, despite what you see in me, I don't have a lot of experience working without a five-year plan."

She laughed. "I know. You're the only person I've ever met who buys calendars three years in advance."

"And that doesn't worry you?"

"Absolutely not. I find your type A tendencies endearing. And even more, I like having something to offer in return because I'm excellent at living moment to moment. It's all I've ever really been afforded, at least as an adult."

"You have so many things to offer," Mira said seriously. The corners of her mouth quirked up on that happy thought. "But please, don't withhold your wisdom on this particular front. If one were to choose to live in this moment, right here, right now, what would you suggest?"

Shelby bit the inside of her cheek as if trying to keep from smiling. "Anything?"

Mira fought the urge to add caveats, and instead just nodded.

She scrunched up her nose and forehead as if thinking hard before finally breaking into a huge grin. "I recommend ice cream for dinner."

"What?" Mira laughed. "Blasphemy! I was here for jazz and skipping rocks and not working Saturdays, and even with making out on our lunch hours, but replacing meals with sugar is insanity."

"I'm an artist. There's a fine line between genius and insanity." Shelby bumped her shoulder with her own. "But we're in this moment together, so make a counteroffer if you must."

Mira pursed her lips together more for effect than actual consternation. "How about a healthy dinner, then ice cream?"

"I hear your values coming forward, and I want to meet them," Shelby said, her eyes still dancing, "but also, I want whimsy. What if we kept all the pieces and rearranged them so we have ice cream right now and then a healthy-ish dinner when we get home?"

"Together?" Mira asked, feeling light and hopeful at the prospect of more time with this woman that she willingly skimmed over the "ish" addendum to dinner.

"Together."

"Then, you have yourself a deal."

Shelby lifted Mira's hand to her lips and placed a quick kiss on her palm.

Mira sat back contentedly. She'd made a lot of compromises lately, but none of them quite so sweetly satisfying.

***

"Aunt Mira, it's not that hard." Ben laughed, and Shelby found the sound contagious as it bubbled out of him and across the table to her.

"It's not that hard for you two," Mira shot back good-naturedly and pointed one chopstick at each of them. "You're naturally dexterous from all your violin playing. My hands don't work that way."

"They do," Shelby said as she demonstrated above her own plate of lo mein noodles. "Hold the bottom chopstick like a pencil. I've seen you use pencils on multiple occasions."

"Yes, but I generally only use one at a time, and at no point do I put them in my mouth."

"Maybe you should try some time," Ben suggested with another giggle.

"Ew." Mira tried to pick up another noodle and fling it into her mouth, only to have it drop inches short, eliciting another fit of laughter from Ben and Shelby.

They'd settled on Chinese food after dropping Josh and Izzy back at their respective homes on their way back into town. Mira had put up only a modest argument that crab rangoon and egg rolls hardly served as a healthy balance to their ice cream, but Shelby and Ben put her off by offering to eat a sizeable portion of vegetables in their lo mein. They had, however, also insisted on a chopsticks-only policy on the way home, inadvertently assuring only the two of them got plenty of vegetables, while Mira scrambled.

"I'm going to start stabbing carrots." Mira demonstrated by puncturing one and lifting it up triumphantly. "Look, carrot kabobs!"

Ben dropped his forehead to the table and laughed so hard his shoulders shook. "This is my favorite part of the whole day."

"Seriously?" Mira and Shelby asked in unison.

"Not the ice cream?"

"Not the jazz?"

"Not the friends?"

He shook his head. "Those were all good."

"But carrot kabobs are the best?" Shelby asked.

"Yes." He lifted his head to reveal happy tears. "It's just so silly."

She couldn't disagree. Mira's playful side injected something weird and wonderful into an already quite spectacular day.

"She's usually the best at everything," Ben continued, then turned to Mira. "I've never seen you not be able to do something."

Mira raised her eyebrows. "There are lots of things I can't do."

"I never heard of them," Ben said with a sincerity that melted Shelby's heart.

"I can't play the violin."

"That's because you never wanted to," Ben said quickly. "I bet if you did, you'd be good at it right away."

"What? Like I'm good at using chopsticks?"

Ben turned to her. "Don't you think Aunt Mira would be good at anything she wanted to be?"

"Yes." She didn't hesitate, and not just for Ben's benefit. She couldn't imagine Mira failing at anything she truly set her mind to. "I'm not sure she really wants to apply herself to the study of music, and that's okay."

"But shouldn't she at least try?" He jumped up, no longer hearing their counterpoints. "I'm going to go get my violin. Do you have yours?"

She shook her head. "I don't, but my cello is in my back seat."

"You keep a cello in your car?" Mira asked as if she found the idea absurd.

"Doesn't everyone?"

"Go get it," Ben yelled from down the hallway, then seemed to remember his manners and added, "please, Miss Tanner."

Shelby arched an eyebrow at Mira. "You don't have to do this."

"No, but he's happy today, which makes me happy." Mira took her hand under the table and gave it a little squeeze. "Besides, I've still never heard you play, and I'd like to. If I have to play along under the guise of my music lesson to get a private performance, then so be it."

She leaned forward and kissed her quickly on the mouth. "I'll play for you, or with you, any time."

She hopped up and hurried out to her car and back, lugging the cumbersome, hard case back through the narrow door with only fleeting gratitude she didn't have to commute with a stand-up bass. By the time she got the instrument safely into the living room, Ben had already uncased and tuned his violin.

"I've got some catching up to do." She unsnapped a few locks. "Why don't you teach Aunt Mira how to hold your bow."

She didn't even have to watch him to know he'd be gentle and detailed. The boy didn't have anything else in him, and she had little doubt Mira would respond well to the minutia of the task.

By the time she had all her own things situated, they'd moved on to positioning the violin under Mira's chin.

"It's awkward." She rolled her shoulder outward, but before Shelby could correct her, Ben placed a gentle hand on her upper arm and guided her into place. Mira's expression shifted into a mask of consternation.

"You don't have to summon Mozart," Shelby offered.

"Where do I put my hand?"

"Cradle the neck, soft but firm." Her lips curled of their own volition, and she couldn't stop herself from adding, "I know you possess that skill."

Mira lifted her eyes, something dark and sultry flashing through them before she settled her gaze back on the violin. "Do I need to do anything ... with my ... I mean, do I need to press anything with my fingers?"

Shelby's heart beat a little faster as she took a seat at one of the dining room chairs. "Not at the moment, but I'll let you know when the time comes."

Mira bit her lip and took a big breath, then held it.

"Relax, Aunt Mira," Ben instructed. "It's just making music."

"Is that all it is?" she asked, but instead of looking to him, her eyes found Shelby's.

Shelby's breath caught. Suddenly even the silly innuendo she'd stumbled into seemed insufficient. She couldn't say what she wanted to. Not with Ben there. Maybe not even on her own. She didn't know how to convey to Mira that they were making music, but there wasn't anything reductive in the act. There was nothing simple in the trust or the vulnerability inherent in learning to move together, to forge harmony or play notes in congress, not on any level. Instead, she made the best vow she could under the circumstances. "We'll go slow."

"You can play the open strings first," Ben offered, likely feeling the tension without understanding its depth.

"Yes, let your bow rest on the second string and pull it down, slow and steady."

Mira did as instructed, a little tentatively, but smooth enough to coax a single, sustained note.

"Good." Shelby and Ben both cooed.

Mira lifted the bow and tried again, this time applying more pressure without being told. The sound reverberated more fully, and Ben applauded.

"You're doing it. You're playing."

"I'm kind of a one-trick pony. I'm not sure this counts as playing."

"It does," Shelby said quickly, "but go ahead and play a different string. Then, you'll have two notes in your repertoire."

Mira shifted subtly and this time played one strong, clear, D note.

"Beautiful." Shelby took up her bow. "Play that again, then back to the other string, and then return to this one."

"Just those three notes?"

She nodded. "D-A-D"

"It's called the Dad Song," Ben said. "I started with that one, too."

Mira did as instructed, three long notes, clean if not complicated.

Shelby began to tap her foot. "Now keep it up. D then A then D, and then start the loop over again at the same, steady pace."

Mira's brow furrowed and her shoulders tensed visibly, but she didn't argue. She played through the notes again, and this time, as she started her second pass through the progression, Shelby began to play with her.

She started off in unison, keeping time with her toe and watching Mira for cues. As the first resonant sounds rang through the room, Mira stumbled, surprised no doubt by the strength of their combined volume, but Shelby gave her space, adjusting her pace to meet Mira's as they fell into a happy rhythm together.

Then, as the repetition grew stale, Shelby set about improvising a melody over the top. Mira's dark eyes lifted from the strings to meet hers, but caused her to falter, and she quickly refocused.

The brief eye contact was enough, though. Something shot through Shelby, something beyond surprise or fear of slipping—a connection, a recognition, a hope—and it soared with the music they were making together now. The feelings she'd been fighting to keep in check threatened to take flight with it.

They'd been careful with each other so far. Light touches, stolen kisses, easy, comfortable contact with hints of heat they never quite let catch fire, but the simple intimacy of this moment, the sensations of being safe and close carried something smoldering she'd never experienced with others. Even in the most domestic moments with Mira, there was a richness to their shared time that Shelby couldn't explain and didn't dare try to name, for fear doing so might dampen some of the magic in the mundane. But, for the first time, she didn't want to temper those feelings, either. She wanted to step nearer, trusting her own ability to build a melody over Mira's steady baseline, and merge the two into something more.

She might've kept playing all night if not for the blazing resonance coming from down the hall. At first, the sound seemed as though it might be trying to join the song, but that didn't make any sense, nor did the way Ben and Mira froze, leaving her to play several more awkward notes alone before trailing off.

"That's my mom!" Ben practically scrambled over them both and shot off down the hall.

Mira stayed much more measured in her movements, slowly lowering the violin from her chin, as if reluctant to let the moment pass. Shelby ached to hold on as well, to lift her bow once more to drown out the voices wafting from Ben's bedroom, but covering up their reality wouldn't change it. Instead, she smiled up at Mira. "You're a natural."

"I suspect anything I managed to do is more a credit to my teachers than any inborn talent." Mira gently set the violin back in its case before turning to face her. "But you are ..."

She held her breath as Mira searched for a word, her eyes pleading and hands reaching out for her as if understanding whatever one she found might be insufficient, but before either of them had a chance to find out, Ben called for her.

"Miss Tanner, come meet my mom."

She took Mira's hand and kissed it quickly, then raised her eyes, asking too many questions to find time or voice for.

Mira smiled weakly, then nodded. "Yes."

Chapter Fourteen

Mira held Shelby's hand until they reached the door to Ben's room, then stood back a half step to let her enter first.

"Mom," Ben said excitedly. "This is Miss Tanner, the one I've been telling you about."

Shelby gave a small wave.

"It's nice to finally see your face in real time," Vannah said. "When I found you online, I had a good feeling right away, but I didn't know you'd become my kid's new favorite person."

"The feeling is mutual." Shelby tousled Ben's hair. "He's a pretty special kid."

Mira couldn't see Vannah's face, but the pride in her voice came through the speakers clearly. "He really is. I love that you saw that in him, and you're dedicated enough to make house calls. Did I interrupt a lesson?"

"No, well, not for me," Ben said. "We were both giving a lesson to Aunt Mira."

"A lesson in what?"

Ben giggled. "First in chopsticks, but that didn't go great, so we moved onto violin, which went much better."

Now Vannah laughed, too. "You two gave Aunt Mira a violin lesson? Miss Tanner, you must be a miracle worker."

"Not at all. She's an easy student to work with." Shelby glanced back at her with a smile. "Not as easy as Ben, mind you, but still a joy to work with."

"Huh." Vannah's quizzical sound made the hair on Mira's arms stand on end.

"Mom, we had the best day," Ben cut back in. "I had rehearsal in the morning even though it's Saturday because the show is less than two weeks away now, and then Miss Tanner and Aunt Mira took me up to Buffalo with Josh and Izzy."

"I have a million questions." Vannah launched into all of them, asking Ben about Josh and Izzy, and then Shelby about the jazz festival, and both of them about the ice cream. Mira leaned against the doorframe and listened, trying to stay in the moment, but also knowing there'd be questions for her soon enough, and they likely wouldn't revolve around the virtues of mint chip versus chocolate peanut butter.

"Wow, you really did have the best day," Vannah finally said, then with a hint of teasing added, "I can't believe my big sister organized all that. She never took me to a jazz concert when I was your age."

"You wouldn't have wanted to go with me anyway," Mira said from her spot by the door. "Your friends were much cooler company."

Vannah laughed. "They really were, but I'm starting to suspect you've been cool in ways I never saw before. I never doubted you'd take great care of Benny-boyo here, but I had no idea you'd have him thriving there in a month."

"Thank you ... I think."

"No. Thank you." Vannah's voice took on a wistful quality. "Do you have time to chat for a couple of minutes?"

She and Shelby exchanged a quick glance, and another one of those silent understandings passed between them.

"Sure."

"Why don't Ben and I go practice a couple of our pieces for the musical and let you two catch up for a bit," Shelby offered.

"That sounds like a great idea," Vannah said. "Practice hard, Ben, and then when Aunt Mira and I get through all the boring, grown-up stuff, you can come back in and play for me."

He hopped off his bed and scrambled toward the door. "Okay, I'll pick a good one!"

"It was nice to see you," Shelby said, then gave Mira's hand a quick squeeze on her way out.

"Hi Van, how's life in the tropics?"

Vannah held up a finger in front of a mischievous smile, until the first strains of "Marry the Man Today" came in from the living room, before saying, "How long have you been dating Ben's violin teacher?"

All the air left her lungs, and Vannah laughed.

"Oh my God, Mir, she's so not your type."

"I don't, I mean, how did you ... did Ben say something?"

"No. He told me all the things you've been doing together. And I can read between the lines of extra lessons, movie nights, afternoons in the park. I honestly didn't know you had it in you. Where do you even find the time?"

She thought about saying she was on a sort of vacation, but it didn't feel quite right for reasons she didn't want to examine. "She's good with Ben."

"Sounds like she's good with you, too. I've never known you to be so open and outgoing. And she's young! Your girlfriends have always been older and established, even in college, remember you dated that woman who was like a professor or something?"

"She wasn't a professor. She ran the credit union, and she was only six years older than me."

"And how much younger is Miss Tanner than you?"

"Ten years," she said quickly.

"I didn't know you could up your game so much. No wonder you're breaking out of your comfort zone to keep up with this one."

"Did you have a pertinent point to make?"

Vannah laughed. "Yes. I'm happy for you. It's good to break the mold every now and then. She's cute and seems fun, and she's clearly been a huge help to you, not just logistically, but probably emotionally, too."

Mira couldn't argue, but she didn't want to divulge too much to Vannah either. She didn't need her speculating or making snap pronouncements about her personal life. Vannah might like to joke, or maybe she thought herself serious, but she wasn't exactly a relationship expert either, and her approval sent off warning bells rather than warm, fuzzy feelings of affirmation.

"Was there something you wanted to talk to me about?"

"Other than your new smoking-hot, young girlfriend and all the cool, out-of-character things she's getting you to do with my kid?"

She ground her teeth together. "Yes."

"I did, but playing around with you was more fun, so I wanted to do that before I got down to business."

"Of course you did." Play before work had always been Vannah's MO. "Let me guess, the jungle artist co-op is off to a slow start?"

Vannah blew out a heavy breath. "Actually, no."

"No?"

"We've had two big groups through now, and they've both been mostly successful. A few kinks here and there, obviously, but I'm learning, and I'm using so many skills I never really tested before. It's more work than I understood, like full-time days and some nights to keep up with the reservations and class schedules and dietary issues, but much to everyone's surprise, I'm genuinely good at the job."

171

She didn't know what to say. She hadn't expected the venture to be a success, and beyond the bigger picture, she'd never considered the possibility of Vannah enjoying a job that required actual work.

"I like facilitating and watching things come together. People are only in the space for a week, but I can see changes in them. We're creating connections here. The music, the art, I don't know how to explain it, but it feels like more than entertainment. There's a spiritual connection."

Normally, she would've rolled her eyes. A part of her still wanted to surrender to the knee-jerk reaction, but she couldn't, not after what just happened in her own living room.

She didn't pretend to understand the depth of the bond people like Vannah and Ben and Shelby shared with music, but she'd experienced a hint of it for the first time, and she couldn't deny its validity. When Shelby matched her own efforts, the cello deeper and more resonant, something powerful moved between and even inside of them. She couldn't read anyone's mind, and normally she wouldn't dare make assumptions about what anyone else felt in a given moment, but when Shelby lifted a melody from her muddling and carried them both upward, she knew on some deep, guttural level they were existing together in unison, or at least in a way she hadn't with anyone else before.

"Hey, are you still there?" Vannah interrupted her musing. "I think you froze."

"No. I didn't." At least not in the technological sense. "I'm glad you're happy. I take it you need some more time?"

Vannah shook her head. "Actually, the opposite is true. I think I'm ready to come get Ben."

"What? Now? Already?"

"Already?" Vannah scoffed. "It feels like I've been away from him forever, and I would've thought you'd be exhausted by now, too. Aren't you ready to get back to your routines?"

She shook her head, and then nodded, which only left her feeling even more shaken and jumbled.

"It's going to take some orchestrating, and I'll have to wait for a lull, but I think I can get an overnight flight two weeks from tonight, which should put me in Buffalo mid-morning that Sunday. So, if there aren't any delays, I'll be able to make it to the matinee of Ben's musical."

"He'd love that," she said genuinely, but the words came out a little strangled by all the other questions tightening her throat. "How long would you stay?"

"Only a couple of days. I can't miss too much work, but we can have a quick visit, and I want to take Ben to the pediatrician for his yearly checkup before he comes back with me, probably on Wednesday."

"Wednesday, hmm." Mira repeated the day as if she might have some scheduling conflict, when in reality, she felt as though she might actually be having a panic attack. Her heart hammered her ribs, and the room shrank and grew disconcertingly warm.

"I really appreciate everything you've done for him," Vannah said, her voice more distant through the cacophony ringing in Mira's ears. "You clearly went above and beyond to find him great experiences and the musical and friends. I'm sorry I didn't even know you had all that in you."

"I didn't," she said flatly.

"What?"

"I didn't have it in me. Shelby did. It never even occurred to me to get him involved in the musical."

Vannah shrugged. "Why would it? You always knew this was a temporary thing."

"Right." She had known. She'd even clung to the impermanence of it all to get her through her worst moments.

"Anyway, I'm glad you had help, and I'm glad he hasn't been unhappy, and I'm especially glad I'll have him down here with me before long. I'm ready to start our new life together, and I'm sure you're ready to get back to yours, so you can put me on your calendar for two weeks from now. There's a light at the end of the tunnel."

She managed a choked-off sort of laugh, but she couldn't speak yet for fear that light in the distance wasn't the sun, but rather a train barreling toward her in the dark confines.

***

Mira came out of the bedroom, and Ben hopped up, mid-progression, leaving Shelby's final notes hanging, the musical equivalent of going up for a high five only to be left stranded. She might've laughed or even teased him if not for the eager anticipation buzzing off him.

"Is my mom ready to hear my song now?"

"Yeah." Mira forced a smile Ben was too excited to register as clearly being fake. He trotted off, violin in hand, without a backward glance.

"Do you want to go listen?" Shelby asked, relatively sure she knew the answer.

Mira shook her head. "Let them have some time together."

"Of course," Shelby said, "we've had him all to ourselves all day."

Mira nodded, then turned away to start clearing the remains of their dinner, and for some reason, the room seemed bigger than before. Something had shifted, and while intellectually she knew the space between them hadn't grown, she couldn't quite make herself believe Mira was still where she'd been before Vannah called. "Is everything okay?"

"Yes, you know, Vannah stuff."

She didn't know, but she didn't want to ask either, and even that felt strange after all the other conversations they'd had. Even from their first meeting, they always jumped into the deep end together.

"I'm here if you want to talk about it."

"Thank you, but honestly, I think I'm crashing a little bit."

"Okay," she said slowly. "It's been a big day to wrap up a bigger week."

Mira sighed, her shoulders slumping as she paused over the half-cleared table. "I'm sorry."

"Hey," she stood up, setting her cello aside and coming over to place a hand on the small of her back. "You don't have anything to apologize for."

Mira turned to meet her eyes, her pupils expanding as if trying to search for something in the dark. "We had such a good day."

She smiled at the sincerity of the comment. "We did."

"I couldn't have done any of it without you."

"Nor I you. We make a good team."

"I don't feel like that's true."

Her chest tightened.

"You keep holding me up."

"I don't agree." She wrapped an arm tentatively around Mira's waist. "You're the one who realized Ben liked Josh and Izzy, you drove, you bought dinner, and most of all, you made me happy."

Mira raised her eyebrows. "Me?"

She kissed her temple. "Did you see anyone else holding my hand, chatting me up, and stealing little kisses when the kids weren't looking?"

"No," Mira admitted. "That would've been awkward."

She laughed. "No kidding."

"Vannah knows we're ... I mean, we haven't talked about what we are, but she noticed you and I, well we—"

Shelby kissed her to save them both from the tension building in that sentence. She'd only intended for it to be quick and kind, like the others they'd shared during the rest of the day, but the gravity of all the things she didn't know and several of the ones she did took hold. Within seconds, they were making out deeply, passionately, all-consumingly. Mira's mouth was sheer magic, and even if Shelby didn't know anything else about where they were headed, or even what they were doing in the moment, she felt all the way down to her curling toes how well they were doing it together.

Mira's hands closed around her waist, sure and strong and sensual as they held her up and held her close. This woman was such a delicious rush of complexities and contradictions. Shelby's head spun as she parted her lips, inviting her deeper, and Mira accepted the invitation. Their tongues swept along each other, sweet and hot as the tension melted away, or maybe the arousal simply singed hot enough to burn through the haze.

She wished they could always exist like this, the two of them ensconced in a scorching embrace, with no one else and no other responsibilities to push in and distract them from the important things, like how amazingly Mira's body melded with hers, or the scent of clean linen that clung to her clothes, or the singular focus she poured into exploring Shelby's mouth with her own.

She slipped her own hands up Mira's arms, pausing only briefly to work her fingers into the muscles there before moving on to sink them into the thick hair at the base of her neck. She had it held up with a clip, and Shelby was on her way to tugging the whole thing loose, wanting with a desperate kind of hunger to feel it cascade over her, when the door to Ben's room closed forcefully.

They jumped apart, gasping, and wide-eyed in anticipation of his arrival in the living room, but he didn't appear. Instead, another door opened and closed before the sound of running water filtered in.

"He's taking a shower," Mira said, nearly doubling over.

"Whew." She made an exaggerated show of relief, but her hands still trembled. She didn't think they were hiding their relationship from Ben, but neither had they had any explicit conversations about comfort levels or anything else, which now that she thought about it, didn't seem great. For all her experience and training with kids and teens, she'd never had any reason to consider her own dating life as part of those equations, but she knew enough about best practices to suspect that walking in on one's guardian and teacher mid-make-out session probably wasn't the best way to broach the subject. "Should we talk to him?"

"Not tonight," Mira said rather quickly and with enough conviction that Shelby didn't feel good about arguing.

"Okay." She nodded even while biting her tongue.

"It really was a great day," Mira offered in a conciliatory tone that also sounded slightly like a dismissal.

"Yeah. A good one, but a long one, and it's getting late. I guess I should let you two get some rest."

Mira's eyes suggested she wanted to argue or at least explain, but whatever other impulses she had won out, and she merely shrugged. "We're early to bed people around here. Sorry."

"There's no need to apologize. I'm thrilled we found enough time in our busy schedules to spend the better part of the day together."

"Me too."

She stood there a little longer, hoping for a bit more before conceding and going to pack up her cello.

She could feel Mira's eyes on her as she went about nestling the instrument securely and snapping clasps into place. She couldn't help but wish she had the ability to read minds.

Something felt off, and yet she had no evidence to support such paranoia, so she rose with a smile and kissed Mira on the cheek. "You have any time this week for a lunch date?"

"I'm not sure off the top of my head, but I'll check my calendars on Monday and see what we can figure out."

"You know how I love those organizational skills. I have faith you'll find something that works for both of us." She tried to inject a little playfulness into the comment, but it must've fallen flat, or maybe the excitement of the day had caught up with them, and they were bound to face diminishing returns from here on out.

Either way, Mira's smile didn't quite meet her eyes as she walked her toward the door.

"Tell Ben I said good night, and I'll see him at school, if not sooner."

"I will." Mira didn't bite on the idea of sooner. "You'll probably have more time with him this week than I do, since rehearsals are going even later."

"Then, we'll do our best to remember you fondly every time we play your song."

Mira did manage a little chuckle. "Please do. And thanks again for today."

"It's nothing."

"No." Mira caught her hand. "It was something ... a lot, really. The best vacation I've ever been on."

"Good." She leaned in and kissed her once more, wishing for more, but content to end the evening on a nice note.

As she walked to the car, she reminded herself of every good aspect of the day and the experiences she could hang her hopes on. From the in-depth conversations to the physical closeness to the joy of playing music together to all the laughter and little kisses, not to mention the one massive make-out session that spontaneously combusted between them when only given half a chance to catch fire. There were so many aspects to leave feeling upbeat about and absolutely no reason to worry.

And yet, as she started her car and backed away, she had to admit that in her experience, fear rarely yielded to reason.

Chapter Fifteen

"Morning, boss." Jane held up a steaming mug of coffee as soon as Mira walked through the door. "How was your weekend?"

Startled, she took a step back, a deep breath, and came back over the threshold again, accepting the coffee first before saying, "Fine."

Jane appeared nearly crestfallen at the one-word answer. "Seriously?"

"What?"

"I've been sitting all alone in my apartment for two whole days waiting for my chance to live vicariously through you and your hot, young, trendy girlfriend's experiences gallivanting around the city being impossibly cool with your jazz and liquor and loose morals."

She rolled her eyes. "How have you turned my educational field trip with three adolescents and their teacher into the plot of *Chicago*?"

Jane flopped into her desk chair. "I don't know. Perhaps if you gave me something to actually work with, I wouldn't have to fill in the gaps with fantasy."

"I give you plenty to work with, including all the actual work I pay you to do, but if you insist on hitting me up for a recap of the last sixty hours before both of my feet are inside the office, you're going to get lackluster answers like 'fine.'"

"Fair. Drink your coffee, and then come back and give me details."

"Or what?"

"Or I'll be forced to annoy you."

She snorted. "Have you been refraining from doing that so far?"

"I could've said, you know what people say 'fine' stands for."

"They don't say anything about it standing for something. It's a word, not an acronym." She walked toward her office, but something in her brain couldn't handle not knowing an acronym. "Right?"

"Wrong." Jane pounced on her weakness. "FINE means Feelings I'm Not Expressing."

She ground her teeth against any truth in such an absurd statement. "Where did you even hear that? Some internet meme or newspaper psychologist?"

"Probably," she admitted without any chagrin. "Doesn't mean it's not true."

"'Fine' is a totally normal word. It means 'okay,' it means 'even keel,' or 'acceptable.' It's not hidden code for some emotional inadequacy."

"Sure, and the fact that you're arguing about semantics instead of denying the charge isn't telling at all."

She sagged against the doorframe. When had the weight of her own shoulders become so hard to bear?

"What's wrong?" Jane asked softly.

"Ben is leaving," she blurted.

"When?"

"Less than two weeks, and I knew that, at least in theory. Maybe a part of me didn't believe Vannah would actually go through with this, or if she did, it would take much longer. Lord knows, sticking to a reasonable schedule hardly seems like the type of thing I can expect from her, but no. Apparently, she's

181

turning over a new leaf, which is ironic, as she's in an actual rain forest. Anyway, she called Saturday night and said she's making reservations to come get him in the blink of an eye."

"Ah." Jane frowned. "Saturday night. I guess that put a damper on the collective mood of your date day."

"It put a damper on my mood, and I think Ben's too, but he won't talk to me about it other than to say he's fine."

"Right, he's your Mini-Me. What did Shelby say?"

She shook her head. "She doesn't know yet."

"Had she already left?"

She shook her head.

"I'm confused."

"Join the club. I don't know what happened. We had the most wonderful day. I mean like idyllic. The perfect match of taking care of Ben and being present with her. Everything felt easy, the company, the food, the music. She was teaching me to play the violin. I was dreadfully dull as is my wont, but she did this amazing thing with the cello and layering notes, and it probably sounds ridiculous, but being with her in that way felt almost ... profound."

Jane's expression melted into some cross between awe and adorable. "Not ridiculous at all. You sound exactly how a person is supposed to sound at the start of a new relationship. You're falling for this woman, and that's a good thing."

"Is it?"

"You like her, right?"

"Yes."

"She makes you happy?"

"Yes."

"She gets you and appreciates you and makes you feel good about yourself?"

Mira nodded.

"She turns you on?"

She sighed. "So much, it's a little frightening."

"This all sounds perfect to me." Jane sounded all sentimental. "Except for the point where you hid something upsetting from her when she was right there with you. Honestly, I'm not even sure how you orchestrated such a thing in her presence."

"We all chatted with Vannah for a bit, but then she wanted to talk to me alone, so Shelby took Ben to practice his violin. After I finished up, he went back in to play for his mom, and I was thrown off. I think Shelby knew something was wrong. She seemed concerned, but somehow we ended up making out."

Jane nodded as if she totally approved. "Good option, get your kicks and comfort when the kid is occupied, and as a sidenote, I'm thrilled neither of you can keep your hands off each other because if anyone deserves to be ravished, it's you, but why not tell her after? Or yesterday?"

"I sort of shut down. I was worried about Ben, and then I worried about being worried because it occurred to me I shouldn't be as upset as I felt. I mean, I knew he'd leave eventually, and a part of me really looked forward to getting my real life back, but now, I just ... did I tell you Shelby calmed me down recently by telling me to think of this time not as a failure or crisis, but as a vacation?"

"She's good."

"So good. It helped me a lot in that moment and a lot of moments since then to relax and enjoy myself and my time with them, but the more I do, the more I want to stay on vacation a little longer."

"Oh honey." Jane frowned.

"But I can't. Vacations end. Last night, it hit me, and everything felt like my real life again, only not the life where I'm competent and in control as much as the aspects of my life where Vannah's going to show up again without any thought of me or what I want. I'm helpless to stop her from upending our world."

"Yeah, she's got a long career of wrecking your peace. I totally understand why her blowing back into the picture just when you're getting content would wreck your tenuous equilibrium, but what I'm unclear on is why you didn't invite Shelby into all of this."

She shrugged and tried to replay the moment. She'd been so lost and shaken, and then upset at herself for being upset, and Shelby had been there, beautiful and graceful and good. She'd had the cello between her knees and the bow in her hand as if they could simply go back to who they'd been and Mira'd known otherwise, but she couldn't be the one to shatter that sweet illusion. She didn't have it in her to play the heavy one more time. "I think because if I told her, it would make it real, and I didn't want any more real. For the first time in my life, I wanted to cling to the dream."

"Wow," Jane whispered.

"Do you think I'm wrong or weak?"

"I think you're human."

She might be human, but she didn't feel like a very good or mature one. "I think I did the relationship equivalent of burying my head in the sand because I didn't want to think of Ben leaving, and I didn't want to consider the prospect of what it would mean for me and Shelby if I went back to being the person I was before we met. That person would've never even met her in the first place, much less held her attention."

"Um." Jane grimaced. "Disagree."

"What?"

"You're a catch, and she's just as lucky to have found you as you are to have her."

"You don't have to lie to me. I know who I am, and the thing is, I actually like myself. I'm measured and thoughtful and successful. This isn't some bout of low self-esteem."

"Sounds like it might be."

"No, I'm a fan of honest self-assessment, which serves me well in evaluating strengths and weaknesses to adequately mitigate risk. It's not a slam on me to admit we actually have little in common without Ben here. I'm not musical or overly social. I don't generally have, or even look for, excuses to knock off work. I'm a strong investor, a solid community member, a responsible daughter, and an above-average sister."

"True," Jane affirmed, "and a great boss."

"Thank you. I'm proud of those attributes, but relationships have never been my strong suit. Ben's counselor all but called me maladjusted."

"She did not. Stop. She made general statements about a kid she barely knows, and she doesn't know you at all. You can't let a stranger feed your insecurities."

"Maybe not, but Vannah knows me, for better or worse—"

"Worse," Jane interjected. "She's the worst."

"Not when it comes to people. She knew Shelby and I were dating each other without even seeing us together, and do you know what she said?"

"I can only imagine what relationship wisdom she spouted from her Central American tree house with Wi-Fi while you hold guardianship of her son."

Mira ignored the truth of Jane's blunt summary. "She mentioned how far off Shelby is from my usual type and how much I'd have to up my game to hold her attention."

"Ugh, I have so many things to offer in rebuttal, from the fact that your 'type' has never led to romance success in the past, to the fact that you're actually holding Shelby's attention to the point where she sneaks over here in the middle of her school days with the hope of getting to ravish you atop your power-lesbian desk. Still, I think the strongest point I'd like to make is that there's literally no logical reason for a person of your caliber to take relationship advice from fucking Vannah."

She managed to laugh, even if she didn't feel completely humorous. "I do see your point."

"I should hope so." Jane shook her head. "And while I'm not exactly a relationship expert, I'd like to think my vote carries at least enough weight as your single, hippie little sister, and I vote for talking to Shelby sooner rather than later."

"What if I don't know what to tell her, or how? It's not like I have any practice at this sort of conversation, and I worry I'm constantly dragging her into my messes when I want to be the kind of person she can count on to be steady and make her smile and inspire trust, and also the kind of person she wants to keep kissing a lot."

Jane shrugged and smiled. "Again, no expert here, but I actually think that's a great way to start."

She took a deep, slow breath as she considered her options. None of them seemed fantastic, at least not in any clear-cut way. She craved black-and-white answers paired with hard numbers and well-researched statistics. She was aware enough to understand relationships didn't work like other kinds of investments, but that didn't mean she had to surrender to rash decisions. "I'll think about it."

Jane arched her eyebrows. "Think about what?"

Mira gestured vaguely around in an all-encompassing motion. "Everything."

"Okay, but like, the longer this goes, the harder it gets, so maybe don't overthink it."

She laughed humorlessly before heading for her own office, unwilling to make any such promise. "Overthinking is what I do best."

***

Shelby set down her bow and picked up her phone. Checking the screen again only confirmed what she already knew. Mira hadn't called or texted.

It wasn't unreasonable. They hadn't made plans. They both had incredibly busy weeks. It was only Wednesday. In short, there was no logical reason for her to worry or feel abandoned. The only problem was Shelby had never put excessive faith in logic. She followed her gut and trusted her instincts, both of which told her something wasn't right.

They'd had too good a day on Saturday to not communicate at all by Tuesday night. A few days without quality time was one thing, especially in a new relationship, but no quick chats? No playful messages? No sexy lunches? And it wasn't as if she hadn't tried. She'd asked Mira before she'd left when they could sneak in a quick visit, and she promised to check her calendar. Though the more she thought about it, the more she worried a woman like Mira should've already had a rough idea of her schedule stored somewhere in her impressive brain. Did it seriously take three days to schedule a forty-five-minute time slot?

She'd also tried to spark a few conversations by shooting a couple of texts to see how Mira's day had gone on Monday or if she wanted her to drive Ben home on Tuesday after practice, but got little more than perfunctory answers in response.

"Ugh." She grunted and drew her bow across the strings of the student cello she was trying to tune. The note sounded out of whack, but she played it again anyway, a sort of musical venting.

She understood being busy. Hell, she was living busy these days, with rehearsal every night until 8:00, plus her preparations for the end-of-the-year concert, and the daily challenges of first-year teaching. While patience had never been a great strength for her, she liked to think she would've handled this whole situation a lot better if not for the lingering sense of unease with how they'd left things.

She played a few more notes and tightened the requisite pegs accordingly, or at least the degree a school cello could be tuned in house after nine months of play by sixth graders who were not known for their gentleness of care. Over the summer she'd do major technical adjustments, but like most other things in her life right now, the bigger issues would have to wait in favor of smaller stopgaps. She shouldn't have been surprised Mira fell into a similar set of circumstances, where she'd settle for even a quick connection when she craved a serious conversation, but she'd be lying to herself if she said she hadn't hoped for more.

"Miss Tanner?"

She glanced up to find Ben standing, small and uncertain, in the doorway to her room, and her heart almost seized, both at the surprise of his presence and the sagging details of his appearance. "Hey buddy, what's up?"

He shrugged. "I thought maybe I could help you get ready for rehearsal."

"You know I'd love to have you with me, but aren't you supposed to be in class?"

"I have study hall, and I already finished all my homework. I got a pass if you want to see it."

"Of course you did. I trust you." She smiled and set aside the cello that was now as close to in-tune as it was likely to get today. "I'm tuning instruments for rehearsals tonight, but it might be silly of me since the humidity in here is different than the auditorium."

He nodded. "I usually wait until we get in there to tune my violin."

"That's because you're a gifted kid. Most of your classmates can't even tune by ear yet, much less think far enough ahead to plan the best places to do so."

He shrugged again without smiling, and she wondered if she should ask what was bothering him or let him come around in his own time.

"Do you want to check the violin cases and make sure the bows are stored correctly?"

"Sure."

"Thanks. I had a class of fifth-graders third period today, and they never remember to loosen them before running off to gym."

"Aunt Mira didn't loosen mine before she put it away over the weekend," he said, then kindly added, "but probably no one ever told her you're supposed to."

"I guess we left that out, or maybe she thought you'd come right back to it."

He nodded and popped open one of the cases along the wall. "Yeah, I thought we'd come back to it, too, but then I talked to my mom, and I didn't feel like playing anymore."

The hair on her neck stood on end as she sensed them circling closer, not just to what he wanted to say, but to answers about what happened out of her earshot on Saturday. "I was a little surprised you didn't come back after you gave her your mini-concert."

"I'm sorry I didn't say goodbye. I wanted to be alone."

"You don't ever have to apologize to me for taking time to process. We'd had a big day."

"We had a great day," Ben corrected more firmly. "I've had a lot of good days lately."

"I'm happy to hear you think so," she offered, trying to give him space to get to what he clearly wanted to say.

"Yeah. I really like it here, but I miss my mom a lot, too. I got excited when she told me she's coming for the last day of the musical, but then I got upset when she said we were moving back to Belize right after."

The news hit Shelby like a kick to the chest. She turned away under the guise of wiping some notes off the whiteboard. "Oh, that's a lot to process."

"She's happy there, but I'm happy here."

She bit her lip, letting him work through what he needed to.

"And I thought it would feel longer because six weeks sounds like a super-long time, but now it's only eleven days, and that doesn't feel like much." He paused and blew out a heavy breath before adding, "Or sometimes my mom says we're going to do things, but then we don't. So, when she said there were problems right away, I thought maybe this was one of those times, and she might come back to stay."

Shelby finally gained control of her facial expression enough to project a neutral sort of concern, so she turned to see him cross-legged on the floor in front of several open cases without actually working on any of them. Her heart broke, and she moved instinctually to sit beside him. "I'm sorry, Ben. It's a big change."

He nodded. "My mom says it's a new adventure."

"And that's true, but a lot of things can be true at the same time. That's one of the scary parts about getting older. The situations get more complicated, and people do too." Her chest ached at how deeply she felt that. "The same thing's happening with you. When you were little, you only had to process one emotion. Ice cream good, naptime bad, all the way happy, or all the way sad. Now there's a lot more stuff to think about, and you're smart enough to see all the moving pieces. You're also emotionally advanced enough to feel multiple things at once, which is a real credit to you as a young man."

He shrugged again. "What if I don't want to feel all of it at once?"

She put an arm around his shoulders. "I don't want you to stop feeling things, Ben. Closing yourself off might make you

190

feel a little better in the short term, but learning to process it all in its fullness will make you healthier in the long run. And I actually have two notes of good news on that front."

He finally looked at her with a hint of hope in his expressive eyes. "What?"

"One, you're off to a great start by articulating those feelings to someone else, and two, you don't have to process them by yourself. You have so many people who care about you. I'm here to listen and offer support. Your mom's love is strong enough to span half the globe for you, and your Aunt Mira absolutely adores you. You can talk to any and all of us."

He nodded. "My mom's really excited, and I don't want to make her feel sad or think I don't want to be with her."

"I understand, and I think you're a special kid for even considering your mom's happiness, but I'm sure she wouldn't want you to put your feelings behind hers."

"Maybe," he said without sounding convinced.

"And I know for a fact your Aunt Mira is super good at thinking things through and problem solving."

He brightened a bit. "Yeah. She's the smartest person I know, but I don't think she wants to talk about it."

Her shoulders tensed. "What makes you think so?"

"'Because my mom said she told her, too. That's what they talked about when we were practicing, but she hasn't said anything to me about it."

Shelby fought the urge to swear. So that's what had thrown Mira off. Vannah had told her she was coming to get Ben, and instead of sharing the information or her feelings on the subject, she'd clammed up. Even worse, she'd told Shelby everything was fine and let her spend the next few days feeling paranoid for believing something was off. It took all of her emotional restraint not to spin out of control wondering what that meant for their relationship or the level of trust between them and focus on Ben.

"I certainly understand where you might get the sense she didn't want to talk to you, but I was there. We were both waiting for you to come back in and let us know how things went." Shelby tried to keep her voice even and choose her words wisely. "And while she didn't talk to me about the conversation either, I wonder if she might've been giving you some space to process first. She tells me all the time what a great kid you are and how much she loves having you around. Maybe she wanted to let you decide how to bring it up."

He cocked his head to the side as if trying to consider the idea from a different angle. "I thought she might be upset, or maybe she's ready for me to go."

She squeezed his shoulder tightly as the pain of that comment lanced through her chest. "Ben, she might be upset, but not at you, and I swear she isn't eager for you to go."

"Are you sure?"

"Absolutely certain. There's a lot I don't know about your aunt, and a lot we haven't talked about." *Too much apparently.* "But I know without a doubt she doesn't just love you, she loves having you with her. There's nothing she wouldn't do for you if she knew you needed it or even wanted it."

He stared up at her for a few long seconds before nodding. "I think she likes you a lot, too."

She managed a tight smile because she got that sense too, sometimes, like when they couldn't keep their hands off each other, but even those memories felt tainted by the realization that Mira may have been up for deep kissing but not open to deep conversation. She didn't want to believe the two stood in opposition, but if Mira had used their physical connection as a substitute for an emotional one, that probably didn't bode well for them. Still, she wanted to give Ben as much truth as she responsibly could, so she said, "And I like her, too, but this conversation is about you. What do you need right now?"

He lifted one shoulder. "I don't know, but I think I feel a little better after telling someone."

"Good, you seem like a kid who likes to think things out."

"I do. My mom calls me an introvert."

"A lot of artists are, and I love that you know something so important about yourself. I think your Aunt Mira is an introvert, too, which probably makes it harder for you two to start important conversations when you aren't sure how you feel about them yet. Thankfully, you both happen to know an extrovert who's pretty good at talking."

He grinned. "Is it you?"

"Ding ding, we have a winner. It's totally me." She gave him a gentle nudge. "And I always want to respect your way of doing things, but at the same time, it's also a teacher's job to help provide opportunities for growth and support. So, if you want me to talk to Aunt Mira, maybe help you get the ball rolling a bit, so you don't have to figure it all out on your own, I'd love to help you."

He nodded slowly. "You don't think she might be mad?"

"At you? Never." What she had to say might make Mira mad at her, because at this point, those fears didn't even rank among her top five concerns. "But if talking about this makes you feel better, I think it's important for her to know."

He rested his head on her shoulder. "Okay."

"Okay?"

"Thank you," he whispered.

She hugged him tightly as her heart twisted, and silently vowed that whatever she had to do next, no matter how hard or personal, she would not let this kid down.

Chapter Sixteen

"You have a call," Jane said with an unusual stoicism, causing Mira to look up from the investment statement on her computer screen.

"Who is it?"

"Miss Tanner, from the school."

She smiled. "Pretty sure you can call her Shelby."

Jane's droll expression didn't change. "Normally I would, but she said to tell you 'you have a call from Miss Tanner at the school.'"

Her stomach tightened slightly. "I'm sure she's playing. She finds competence ... actually, can you put her through?"

"Sure, but for what it's worth, I don't think she's playing, and I also suspect you didn't tell her some things you should have."

Mira frowned at the truth of the second statement and her fading optimism about the first. "Can you close the door?"

Jane nodded. "Line one."

She waited until she heard the reception desk chair squeak, then lifted the receiver to her ear, trying not to read too much into the fact that Shelby had called her office line and not her personal cell phone. "Hey there. I've been thinking about you."

"That's nice to hear after four days, but I'm calling in a more official capacity."

"Oh?" She tried to keep her voice level. "How so?"

"I just had a troubling conversation with Ben about the fact that his mom apparently told you both on Saturday night she's made plans to come pick him up sooner rather than later."

She grimaced but didn't know what to say, so she did what she apparently did best, and stayed quiet.

"And while personally I have some serious questions about why I heard this from him well after the fact and not you in the moment, it's not the focus of this call."

"Shelby."

"Don't," she whispered. "I'm at work. That's what I'm doing here, working, and I may be a lot newer to my job than you are, but a student came to me while grappling with an emotional burden, and that's something I take seriously."

Her own emotions threatened to overtake her at the thought of both Ben and Shelby struggling. "I'm sorry."

"I believe you. And I also believe you probably have your reasons, but they aren't good enough anymore. I may have some doubts about how you feel about me, but I know you love him, so I'm telling you, you have to do better. He needs to talk to you. He needs to know it's okay. He needs support and help processing, and he needs you to take the lead."

"I didn't know he was upset."

"Because you didn't ask him," Shelby shot back. "You just shut down, and I get you're used to being an island, totally self-sufficient and self-contained. I don't pretend to know what you think that means for a relationship between you and me, but I'm a teacher, and I know very well what the rules are here. Consider this a first contact to make you aware of an issue."

"What's that supposed to mean?"

"It means I'm giving you a chance to deal with this before I move up the chain of command."

Red flashed through Mira's brain. "Are you threatening to report me to some authority? The counselor? The principal?"

"Seriously? I just told you Ben is struggling so badly he came to me during school hours. I'm worried about him. I'm telling you he's not getting the support he needs to process something absolutely bigger than he is, and you're worried about getting sent to the principal's office?"

She hung her head. "No. I'm sorry. I've never, I mean, I don't know how to do this, any of this."

"You have help. Or at least you did in the moment, and any number of moments since then."

"I didn't want to ruin the moment. God, Shelby, I don't like always breaking down in front of you. I don't like being helpless and in over my head. I don't want to spend every conversation pulling you into this void I'm facing."

"So, you decided to cut me out?" Shelby's voice shot up in both pitch and volume. Then she caught herself. "Fine, maybe you don't see me as an equal partner. Maybe it's too soon, or maybe you don't see me as being up to the challenge, but when you shut the door on me, you also put Ben on the outside, too. And that's not okay. He told me you're the smartest person he knows."

"Really?"

"Yes, and in most areas he's totally right, but he also said he thinks you don't want to talk to him, and he's worried it's because you're upset with him, or worse, ready for him to go."

"No," she said quickly, the word rasping out against the jagged edges of her own hurt. "I don't want him to go. Ever. God, but I'm not his mom, and I've never had any control over her. And I am upset, but at her, or maybe not even at her. Now I think I'm mad at me, and I can't tell him any of that."

"Well, you can't go on telling him nothing, either. This can't be about you, and it can't be about me, either. I'll continue to help in any way I can, but I can't do it for you. You're his person right now, even if you're not mine."

"I never asked to be a parent. I'm not equipped, and I didn't have any time to build skills or prepare myself—"

"Yeah, I know. This is not your life. Except it is now. Shit happens without warning all the time, even on vacations. You pride yourself on being someone who figures things out and pulls herself together and does research to make sound decisions. Be that person, Mira. Use your resources, put in the time and effort and emotion however you need to, but figure it out."

Her heart hammered in her chest at the magnitude of the challenge. She had no idea how she'd even begin to meet it, and yet in the moment, the only things more terrifying than trying to rise to the occasion were the stakes in failing to do so. "Okay."

"Okay?"

"Yes. You're right. I have to do better."

"That's it?"

She huffed softly. "You make a compelling argument."

"Oh," Shelby said, sounding as if such solid agreement may've taken some of the wind out of her sails. "Good."

She sighed. "Thank you for calling me, and for being there for him."

"Anytime," she said, with gravity back in her voice. "I mean it. Any time either of you need me, I'm here, but I hope you make the next call."

She pinched the bridge of her nose to try to staunch the pulse pounding there. "I promise I will, and I promise it will be sooner rather than later."

***

"Tyler," Shelby called in a singsong voice to a boy in the middle of the class who had his viola between his knees attempting to play it upright. "If you want to switch to cello, I could send a form home to your mom."

The class laughed, but most of them kept playing, and, more importantly, Tyler got the hint and lifted his instrument back to his shoulder.

She conducted them through the intro of the bass section, then tuned her ear to the violins, because someone was definitely off. Following the discordant sound, she honed in on a girl in the front row, Julia. The poor kid had clearly surged through a growth spurt recently, because not only did her hands seem too big, her jeans also seemed a full inch too short. Likely the parents didn't want to invest in new equipment or pants a month before summer vacation. She made a mental note to check the limited supply of full-sized violins in stock at the school. Then again, mixing things up this close to the concert might cause more harm than good, so she cued a quick uptick in the melody, even though half of the students never looked away from their sheet music long enough to notice her movements. Just one more thing she'd have to work on later, and by later, she meant next year.

She tried to remain upbeat, and generally succeeded, especially with students in the room. She loved their energy and good humor. Plus, nothing ever felt quite as dire when making music, but she still couldn't completely shake the sense she was running out of time. Class was nearly done for the day, and they hadn't made it through nearly as much as she'd hoped. The school musical would open one week from tomorrow, and the pit band wasn't at all as polished as she wanted. The end-of-the-year concert was two weeks later and only one of her four grade levels was ready. And of course, Ben wouldn't even be here by then. The first three issues caused stress. The last cut much deeper.

She lifted her baton higher as the song neared its close, and did her best to hold the last note as long as she dared before signaling a stop. The room fell silent on one suspended breath, each student taking the barest sliver of a second to collectively signal completion before descending into a chaotic cacophony of raised voices and frantic movement.

She glanced at the clock with the weakest intent to assert her right to the last three minutes of the class, but she didn't have the energy to waste on something so futile. Instead, she stepped back, leaned against her whiteboard, and waited for the merciful bliss of the day's last bell. When it finally rang, they stampeded out the door like the herd of wild beasts they were devolving into during the last month of middle school, though a few did manage to give her hope as they paused to say goodbye or wish her a nice evening, or better yet, shout that they'd see her at play practice.

She followed the last of them to the door, intending to make sure no one crossed the line between unruly and riotous, but when she stepped out into the hallway, she noticed someone nearly flattened against the wall.

It took a moment to process the person in such an out-of-context place and position, but when she did, her heart about jumped into her throat. "Mira?"

"Hi." Mira looked both ways before stepping forward. "I didn't want to interrupt you while you were working, so I waited out here, but I hadn't braced properly for the door."

She smiled in spite of the million questions screaming through her brain. "I think the coast is relatively clear if you want to come in now."

"I would. If you don't mind."

"My door is always open to you and to Ben, or anyone else in need for that matter." She nodded for Mira to follow her back into the orchestra room, and she did. "I do have to be in rehearsals in half an hour, though."

"I know, and I appreciate you giving me even a few minutes. I know this isn't the time or the place for a deep conversation."

"Then, why come?" It sounded blunt, but she didn't want to let her emotions drag her one way or another until she understood Mira's intentions. She'd clearly underestimated or misconstrued several things recently, and she wasn't sure her heart or her head could take more back-and-forth.

"I actually didn't come here to see you."

So much for keeping her heart out of it, because the statement twisted through her chest. And it must've shown, because Mira rushed forward.

"Which isn't to say I didn't want to see you. I did. I wanted to see you so much I almost drove over last night, but I had Ben, and I knew you wouldn't want me to leave him because you asked me to do better for him, and—" She shook her head. "I'm babbling. I'm sorry. I wanted to see you right after you called, but anything I said would feel hollow. I needed to prove I took what you told me seriously, so I talked to Ben first."

Shelby softened. "How did that go?"

"As well as anyone could expect when two introverts try to voice complex emotions we don't want to have, but I understand what he's feeling now, and he knows he can talk to me about anything going forward. I made it clear to him it won't be a one-time conversation. This is a learning process for both of us."

She nodded approvingly, but she didn't want to let Mira off the hook too quickly after several sleepless nights of trying to figure out what was going on, and several seething hours of trying to hold her hurt at bay after finding out what had really happened.

"What's more, after I spoke to you, I set up an appointment with the counselor, which is why I came to school today. She and I had a helpful, if uncomfortable, meeting about what Ben's going through, and ways I can offer support after failing to do so initially."

"Wow." Shelby didn't know what else to say. Mira willingly went back to the spot of her biggest meltdown and subjected herself to the same kind of vulnerability, this time of her free choice.

The corners of Mira's mouth quirked up. "A couple of days ago, I would've said I'd rather jam needles under my fingernails than chat with Ms. Graves again, but she gave me some pamphlets on anxiety and transitions, plus a few websites on adolescent development and communication. I'm going to go home and study while Ben's at practice."

The walls Shelby had tried to stack around her heart crumbled like the sand they were built on. She was terrible at staying mad at people, but she suspected such a genuine attempt at changing behaviors would have a similar effect on even a more hardened grudge holder. "When you decide to do something, you do it all the way."

Mira rolled her eyes. "I'm making up for lost time. I should've done more, sooner. I shouldn't have needed you to make some of the timely and salient points you leveled rather forcefully yesterday, but I'm glad you did. Ben and I will keep the lines of communication open, and then this weekend, after I have a better sense of what he needs, I'll start a conversation with Vannah, too."

Shelby heard trepidation creeping into her voice for the first time. "How do you think she'll receive it?"

"Honestly, I suspect she'll dismiss me as worrying needlessly, which is par for the course of our entire lives, but I'm used to having my concerns disregarded. Ben deserves to be heard, and I hold out some hope she'll agree there. She loves him."

"Loving Ben seems to be a strong common thread," Shelby mused, "and you're right. He deserves to be heard here."

"He does. He also deserves explanations and open, honest conversations," Mira said resolutely, then with the same certainty added, "and so do you."

"I didn't mean to make it about me."

"You didn't, but I am." Mira reached out as if she intended to take her hand, then pulled back. "I have a million reasons why I didn't talk to you. I was overwhelmed. I don't have a lot of practice letting people in. I didn't want to ruin the best day I've had in ages. I don't like looking weak and lost all the time. I preferred falling into your kiss to falling apart. I process internally and slowly. They're all true. Please know none of those things are empty excuses, and at the same time, I know none of them justify blocking you out."

Shelby covered her face with her hands for a second and then tried to take a deep breath, which was a little dumb since she had her hands over her face, but she clearly had no ability to think logically with Mira standing in front of her, utterly contrite and saying all the perfect things, and wearing a skirt. *Why hadn't she noticed the skirt until this moment?*

"I'm very sorry," Mira stressed again.

"I know. I get it." Shelby groaned and then dropped her hands to meet Mira's eyes. "Has anyone ever told you you're exceptionally good at apologies?"

"What?"

"Like professional grade. You should give a TED talk or something, because you hurt my feelings, and made me feel paranoid for feeling off, and clingy for wondering why you didn't call me, and immature for worrying. I wanted to stay mad at you, but you're making it hard."

Mira's smile turned shy. "Is that a good thing, or should I go away and let you rage, or, I don't know, maybe say something bad so—"

"No." Shelby cut her off. "Tell me what you want now, because I had one idea in my mind, and then over the last week you made me doubt whether or not we're looking for the same things. And I'm genuinely impressed with everything you've done to be present for Ben, but I'm still not clear what you want with me."

"I want to try," Mira said sincerely, "and honestly, that's all I'm doing with Ben, too. I cannot promise I'll be the perfect aunt or partner or girlfriend, or whatever you want to call the relationship, because clearly I'm bad at it, but this reaffirmed for me that I do want to get better."

Shelby closed the distance between them with the same unseen force as if Mira had tied an invisible string around her heart and given it a sharp tug. "You're not bad. You made a mistake because you're human and you're overwhelmed. I don't expect you to be perfect."

"What do you expect me to be?" she whispered.

Shelby reached up to cup Mira's cheek in her palm. "Present."

"That's all?" Mira leaned into her touch and closed her eyes.

"That's everything." She ran her thumb over her lower lip. "Or at least it opens the door to everything else I need."

Mira turned toward her hand and kissed it lightly before opening her eyes again. "I missed you."

"I missed you, too."

"I want to see you tonight, but I think I need a little more time on my own with Ben."

She stifled a groan. Never had she been so shattered by someone doing the right thing.

"What about Saturday? I'll take off work."

"We've got rehearsals all day," she whimpered. "Why is this godforsaken play so long?"

"How about dinner?"

"My parents and Darrin are supposed to come over because I haven't seen them in weeks, but I'd be happy to cancel."

"No," Mira said softly. "You have a great family. Don't take them for granted on my account. Maybe I'll use that time to talk to Vannah."

"I could come over after they leave. It might be later, but—"

"Please do. Ben will probably be in bed before 9:00, but I'd love to see you, no matter how late."

"That sounds really nice."

"Does it?" Mira sounded surprised. "Not boring? Not exhausting? Not beneath you?"

She shook her head. "Of course not. Why would you even think that?"

"I don't know. You're wonderful and bright and sweet and social, and sometimes when I look at you, I still can't believe you'd like to spend your Saturday night at home with me when surely you have any number of other options to be out."

Shelby laughed. "First of all, I'm currently more exhausted than I've ever been in my life. Second of all, I'm broke, flat broke. Third, have you seen the town we live in? There's nothing happening after 9:00. And yet, even if every single one of those things were untrue, I'd still choose to be with you. So, while I'm low-key thrilled you have such a high opinion of my social life and opportunities, I wish you had a higher opinion of yourself."

Mira sighed. "I don't know what I could possibly offer to hold your attention."

She eyed the open door to her room before catching hold of Mira's lapels and walking her backward until she bumped against it, pushing it closed and pinning her there. Then she kissed her, full and hard and deep.

Mira gasped, but her surprise barely lasted a second before shock gave way to surrender. She molded to the flat surface, then caught hold of Shelby's waist and pulled her in until their bodies met at every point available to them. Then, as if even that connection failed to satisfy the need building between them, she worked a hand upward from Shelby's hip and under her shirt until it splayed across the bare skin of her abdomen.

Mira opened her mouth in a moan, and Shelby slipped inside, running her tongue across her upper teeth and lip, wanting to explore each crook and corner from here to eternity. The only thing stopping her from devolving completely into a ball of utter arousal was the fear of permanently scarring whatever unsuspecting student drew the short straw and had to come looking for her when she didn't turn up for rehearsal. Though the longer Mira kissed her back with such fervor, the less important even that reason felt.

Shelby had to summon every last shred of her remaining wherewithal to pull back before she melted into oblivion with this woman, and even then, her whole body screamed in protest.

She opened her eyes slowly, blinking against the harsh onslaught of reality, and found Mira with the same sort of lustful sheen coating her unfocused eyes.

"There's your answer," she finally managed to say.

Mira let her head fall back to hit the wall with a soft thump. "I like that answer very much, but I have to admit, I forgot the question."

She laughed. "You asked what you can possibly offer to hold my attention. And that's your answer."

"Hmm." Mira made a happy little hum. "In other moments, I might argue that you're actually the one who did that, but I think you smothered my will to disagree, so I'll go with, 'See you Saturday night?'"

Shelby smiled. "I'm already counting down the minutes."

Chapter Seventeen

"Hey there, world traveler," Mira said as soon as Vannah's image pixelated on the screen of her computer.

"Hi," Vannah said, with a happy sort of weariness. "Everything okay?"

"Yes. Great actually. I was hoping Ben would still be awake to say hello when I called, but he fell asleep on the couch around 8:30, and when I woke him up to move him to bed, I promised I'd tell you he loves you and will call you tomorrow since he doesn't have rehearsals on Sunday."

"Aw, he's such a good boy."

"He really is, and the show takes a lot out of him, but he seems to love it. He comes home smiling every day and wants to play me the songs they worked on."

"He's a musician for sure." Vannah beamed proudly.

"You'd think he'd be so sick of playing after hours a day, but he still comes home and practices most nights, and even when his friends come over, they play together or talk about music ... well sometimes they complain about teachers and homework and sleep schedules that keep them from playing music."

Vannah laughed. "He might actually be my kid after all. I don't know where he got his studious nature, but wanting to blow off work to play music sounds exactly like me at his age."

"I hadn't thought of that." She paused to let the idea sink in now. She'd always focused on Ben's advanced work ethic in his approach to the violin. She hadn't considered it on par with

Vannah's teenage obsessions for electric guitar and drums and even a short stint with a saxophone.

"He's going to love it down here," Vannah continued. "Someone's always making music. We even had a sitar player last week. It's a constantly revolving door of talent."

The idea of a revolving door of anything brought Mira back to the moment, and the weight of what she needed to do now. "Actually, that's kind of what I wanted to talk to you about."

"Talent?"

"No, the idea of constant motion and change. I know it's not been a problem before now, and Ben's used to moving, but he's started to show some anxiety about this particular move lately."

"Oh, is that all?" Vannah waved her off. "He's a nervous kid sometimes, but he's going to love it once he gets here. There are monkeys and papayas, and lots of chances to play music, which is what he loves most of all, right?"

"I agree he's going to love all of those things. It sounds close to paradise by most standards."

"*Almost* Eden," Vannah emphasized.

"You might even get me on a plane to come visit."

Her sister laughed. "I'll believe it when I see it."

"I want to be able to help him get ready here on this end, and he shared some concern, and the school has shared some more of them, but I don't have answers to questions like, 'how's he going to go to school? Is there even a middle school close by?'"

"No, no, no. Middle school is terrible. He's going to be homeschooled, or better yet, world schooled. So many kids learn as they grow, and I think Ben is perfect. We already talked about how studious he is, and he loves to read, plus there's people here who can teach him real-life things. I'll order some math books or something to cover anything left over."

Mira clenched her fists under the table where they wouldn't show on the screen, understanding she needed to keep her own judgements under control in order to move forward and focus on Ben.

"Right, I can see where he'd like more academic freedom, but what about other kids his age?"

"We haven't had any yet," Vannah admitted with a light shrug, "but we plan to have some youth events at some point, or maybe even a whole summer program down the road. Plus, as we advertise more, I think we might get some families. Artists often travel with their kids. I'm sure some will turn up eventually."

"You're probably right. You know more about artists than me. I'm wondering if you have any plans to get him together with other kids until then? I've recently been told by people at the school that his social development is equally important as his coursework at this age."

"I think someone might be scaring you there." Vannah feigned sympathy. "You're an introvert. Ben is, too. You two love to be in your own heads, and neither of you ever had any trouble bonding with adults."

She couldn't argue the point at all. "Yeah the prospect of other people facilitating social outings for me has always been cringeworthy, but Ben's made a couple of fast friends here, and he keeps talking about how much he likes being part of the musical, which made me wonder, plus the school counselor gave me some pamphlets to read about peer groups' role in developing healthy —"

Vannah's laugh cut her off. "You're such a worrier. You're reading pamphlets? Mira, come on."

"What? I like pamphlets!"

"I know. You used to collect them at all the welcome centers when we went on road trips as kids, but what about actual lived experiences? You're a totally successful person, and you've never in your life been part of a big social circle."

She didn't know which part of that statement to take issue with first, and her head spun at the idea of arguing *against* her own way of life up until this point, but she'd promised to do better for Ben, and if that meant taking a few hits to her own pride, at least she'd had plenty of practice lately. "I like to think I've always had a couple of close friends. I still stay in touch with my college roommates even after all these years, and of course, there's Jane, who—"

"Jane is your secretary. She works for you."

"We're work friends."

"When was the last time you did something outside of work?" Vannah pushed.

"We went out to dinner together not too long ago?" She racked her brain to try to remember when. "Christmas, we went out to dinner together right before Christmas."

"That was five months ago!" Vannah kept laughing, which only made Mira's frustration rise. "And wasn't that your version of an office Christmas party, which would still make it kind of a work function?"

"Okay, fine. What's your point?"

"You don't have a ton of friends, and you turned out fine."

She blew out a heavy breath and hung her head.

"What?" Vannah sat forward. "You're fine, right?"

"Yes, I mean I'm the same as always ... mostly." She didn't have any idea how to explain all the little conflicts setting her sense of self on shaky ground lately. "But I've recently learned maybe I could do a little better at relating to people, both in general and on a more individual level."

"Did you learn those things from Shelby?"

"Yes."

Vannah laughed again. "Your young girlfriend is teaching you to be more open to human connections. That's sweet."

She bristled at the tone, something akin to the voice one might use with an adorable kitten. "My relationships are beside the point. We're talking about Ben and wanting better for him. This is a huge transition, and even if it's the right one, a major change in the middle of his formative years needs to be handled with the utmost care. Do you have a counselor or support staff there to help him if he needs it?"

"Yes." Vannah lit up like a little kid who'd gotten the answer right in class. "We do!"

"You do?" Mira sat back, not sure what to do with such unexpected information.

"Yes, we have the most wonderful yogi here full time, and she makes for a fantastic far-out spiritual guru. She opened my chakras like a champ."

"Wonderful," Mira managed, but only through gritted teeth. "A personal guru sounds like quite an ... experience. However, I wondered more about the availability of a licensed professional to make sure Ben gets the mental health support he needs after being pulled halfway across the globe into a foreign culture with no school or kids or any of the security a kid going through adolescence might need for a sense of normalcy."

Vannah tensed visibly even through the filter of a computer screen. "I'm Ben's support system, and I don't appreciate the implication he needs some social worker or something to step in. He and I have always been enough for each other, in case you've forgotten."

Goosebumps rose on her arm at the quiet warning in her sister's voice, but she'd come too far to back down now, and she didn't even want to anymore. "Of course, I haven't forgotten. Ben's a great kid."

"A kid I've raised, largely on my own, because I'm his mother."

"Vannah, I know you're his mom, and I've been here all along watching and helping and marveling at both of you. I'd never want to cross any lines, but I love him, too. I love both of you, but this move is much bigger than any of us have ever been through. Literally everything in his life will be turned upside down, and I'm not saying it can't go exceptionally well, but I'm asking if you've thought of the potential pitfalls and made plans to combat them."

"God, you're so condescending and judgmental. You assume everything's going to fall apart, and you're always making contingencies for when they do instead of putting your faith and energy into manifesting something better. I'm not even sure you'd know something wonderful if it hit you upside the head."

She thought of Shelby, beautiful and smiling, and pushing her up against the wall to kiss her senseless. "I disagree."

"Then prove me wrong. Look at what I'm doing right now, really look at it past the superficial details like locations and school schedules. Chances like this don't come up every day." Vannah shook her head. "They don't come along for me ever. You act like there's a million other options, but you're not exactly providing a better alternative. I've been working two dead-end jobs at a time in Buffalo for years."

She didn't have a rebuttal. Vannah's life had always been transient, though never on such a global scale.

"Maybe if I had a chance to make a real living doing something meaningful closer to home, I'd have to consider it, but this is my only chance to build a life for me and Ben. You keep talking about wanting to do better for him, but this is better than anything I've had access to back home, and yes there will be an adjustment period, but he's going to love it here."

She sighed. She couldn't prove her wrong, and she didn't even want to, but it felt like Vannah was pushing them all out onto a tightrope without a net. "I love you both and I want you both to be happy, you know that ... but—"

"But nothing. You don't get to put qualifiers on love. You can't want us to be happy, but only on your terms, ones you can control."

"I don't want to control you."

"You do. You want to control every aspect of your life, and ours by extension, but you can't control life. It's wild and unpredictable, and you have to hold on with both hands while it takes you where it will."

"That's absurd," she finally snapped.

"It's not. Happiness is a crazy, spinning mystery."

"No. There are a myriad of ways to find joy with nice, safe, measured steps."

"How's that working out for you?" Vannah laughed bitterly. "Is the safe path making you giddy?"

She ground her teeth so hard her jaw ached. "This isn't going anywhere productive."

"How do you know, Mira? You don't know. You can't know until you try. You have to take a chance sometime. There's a gamble in anything worth doing."

"But there are also ways to play the odds, to calculate risks and find ways to mitigate them. That's all I'm asking. Think things through, mitigate the potential for disaster, brace for various complications, have an exit strategy."

"You can't possibly plan for all things, and honestly, if you're carrying around all this negative energy or trying to micromanage disasters that haven't even happened yet, you're probably what's causing Ben's anxiety in the first place."

She opened her mouth to argue, then closed it. She wanted to deny the accusation, but how could she discredit a theory she hadn't considered fully? She'd been wrong too many times lately to do so with any certainty, and in her silence, Vannah continued to pile on.

"I appreciate you watching my son while I'm away, but even when I'm out of the country, I'm still his mom. I get to make the decisions. I get to decide what's best for our future."

"But the counselors said his interpersonal development—"

"Stop!" Vannah shouted. "This conversation is over, and if you want to keep meddling in someone's mental health or personal development, maybe you should look in the mirror instead of pinning all your insecurities on other people."

Mira winced, and her screen went black.

She sat back into her chair and curled her knees to her chest as her brain echoed with Vannah's parting shots and a million rebuttals she couldn't quite summon into coherency. All she knew for sure was that hadn't gone nearly as smoothly as she'd hoped.

***

Shelby dropped a take-out pan full of enchiladas on the table in front of her family and silently dared any of them to crack a joke about her culinary skills.

Perhaps she'd already conveyed her ample frustration, though, because they all smiled and dug in without so much as a hint of side-eye.

"I love Mexican food," her dad finally said as he heaped a serving of refried beans onto his plate, and she dropped a grateful kiss atop his head as she went to her own seat.

She'd initially intended to cook. Even when she'd woken up this morning, she fully expected to make a lasagna. She even purchased all the ingredients and figured out an assembly timeline that would allow her to get everything in the oven and take a shower before her parents and Darrin arrived, but she'd abandoned her best-laid plans even before rehearsals ended

213

because the one thing she hadn't planned on was a frightening level of sheer exhaustion seeping into her bones.

They'd spent the first three hours of play practice working on trouble spots, then taken a quick break for a lackluster cafeteria lunch before running through the entire show start to finish. She was dead on her feet by two o'clock, and she worried if she shook her head too quickly, her brain might crumble and fall out of her ears. The idea of adding two more hours of work and heat and mess had led to a bit of a manic mental meltdown, so she'd placed an early order for Mexican takeout and taken a nap. When she'd finally hauled herself out of bed to go collect her order, the restaurant declined her debit card due to insufficient funds. It had taken everything she had not to burst into tears as she pulled out the credit card she'd worked hard to pay down and tapped the machine.

By the time Darrin burst through the door without knocking, all the energy she'd stolen back during the nap had evaporated, but she simply hugged him and silently reminded herself she only had to get through a few hours with people who loved her, and then she'd get to see Mira.

The thought perked her up immensely, even now as she served the enchiladas on mismatched plates while her family chatted amiably about their respective weeks.

"I can't believe I'm only two more school years from retirement," her dad said between bites.

"From *possible* retirement," her mom corrected. "Just because you can doesn't mean you have to."

"You hear that kids?" He nudged her in the ribs. "Your mother doesn't want me home all day."

"I said no such thing. I only mean you need to think about what you intend to do with yourself all day. It's one thing to have a retirement plan financially. It's another to have one socially."

He winked at his wife. "Point taken."

"Hey, speaking of retirement plans," Darrin cut in, "I called Mira to make an appointment next week. Well, I didn't talk to her. I talked to her secretary, but on Wednesday, I'm talking to Mira."

Shelby stiffened. "Why?"

"My company changed some of their specifics on the match program for my 401(k), and they're offering me stock options for five years of service. Plus, one of my other stocks split recently, and I wanted her advice on whether I should keep everything or maybe sell some to contribute to my Roth IRA.

She stared at him, trying to make sense of those words coming out of his mouth. She hadn't even known he owned stocks, much less knew anything about how to manage them.

"I think that's a wonderful idea," their mom said. "She strikes me as a smart woman, and every man needs a smart woman managing his money."

He scoffed. "Reverse sexism."

"There's no such thing as reverse sexism. It's just sexism, or it's not," Shelby said, still trying to imagine her brother having a meeting in Mira's office with her behind the desk where the two of them had sexy lunches.

"Have you seen Mira and Ben lately?" her dad asked. "I've wondered a couple of times how they're adjusting."

"They are doing as well as can be expected," she said evenly. "Ben is playing in the pit for the musical."

"That's good," Darrin said. "I was worried there, after the whole debacle. I almost didn't make the appointment, but I figured since I hadn't heard anything else that the two of you must've patched things up."

Her parents exchanged a confused glance, and she fought the urge to kick Darrin in the shins under the table.

"What did you need to patch up?" their mom finally asked.

"Nothing. A little miscommunication. It's fine."

Darrin snorted. "Little? You said she was basically having a nervous breakdown and you—"

There was no more fighting the urge. This time she actually did kick him.

"Ouch," he yelped. "What?"

She gave him a death stare, then shifted her eyes pointedly to their parents.

"Oh shit, sorry. They don't know you two are seeing each other?"

"Now we do." Her dad chuckled.

Darrin grimaced. "I didn't know it was a secret."

"It's not a secret. We're just, I don't know, taking things as they come."

"I think that's wise," her mother said diplomatically. "I imagine both of you have a lot on your plates, what with a new job for you, and that poor woman has Ben to look after, and a business, and a home to take care of. I can't imagine having a little boy dropped into your already full life with no warning."

Shelby nodded. "It's a lot, but I like to think I've been helpful to her along the way."

"Except for the one time you kissed her at school when she was crying," Darrin pointed out.

"Seriously?"

"What?" He popped a chip into his mouth. "You said it wasn't a secret. I thought we were catching them up."

"I'm never telling you anything again," she said before turning back to their parents. "He's making things sound way worse than they were. We got some wires crossed. We worked them out along with a few other things, and that was weeks ago. We're spending time together casually when we're able."

"I think that's a wonderful idea," her mom said placatingly. "You don't want to rush into anything too serious. Give you and her both some time to get your feet under you. It might be best to set the bar low and then raise it in time."

She cocked her head to the side, trying to decipher all her undertones, but before she had a chance, her dad cut back in.

"I don't know. Mira didn't strike me as the kind of woman you mess around with. I think if you want to make a go at this one, you might have to up your game."

"That's what I said!" Darrin jumped back in enthusiastically.

"There's nothing wrong with my game. I'm not playing a game."

"Good." Her dad nodded resolutely. "Women with kids take a special kind of care."

"Mira can take care of herself. And she doesn't have a kid. She has a nephew staying with her until his mother comes back to collect him a week from tomorrow, which is actually making everyone a little emotional." Her voice cracked, betraying her own status on the edge. "Actually, can we talk about something else now?"

"Absolutely." Her mom shot the men a warning glance, and they both straightened up immediately. "We trust you'll take care of your own issues with Mira in your own time. Why don't we finish up dinner and then play Trivial Pursuit?"

She wanted to declare that she didn't actually have an issue to take care of with Mira, but instead she only managed, "Darrin's the only person who ever wins at Trivial Pursuit. It's a terrible game." The comment sounded pouty and immature, but that's how she felt with her whole family weighing in on her budding relationship with silly warnings and half-baked comments to ping her insecurities.

"How about cards?" her dad suggested amiably.

She nodded, agreeing to move their collective focus onto something else, but even a couple of hours later and many hands behind, she'd yet to win a single one. She might as well have played Trivial Pursuit because her brain refused to key in on any details outside of their previous conversation or her upcoming meeting with Mira. The immediate past and the immediate future tugged her back and forth but never allowed her to center in the moment. By the time she finally got rid of her family around nine, she practically bolted down the stairs.

As she hopped into her car, the energy slowly leaching out of her all day returned in a rush of anticipation. Her whole body buzzed, eager to be taken into Mira's arms and kissed. She'd ached for her on so many levels and almost every minute since breaking apart yesterday, and while she was socially aware enough to understand she couldn't jump Mira the moment she opened the door, she did hope they ended up in a position similar to the one she abandoned back at school.

Pushing the key into the ignition, she turned it, and the whole car jerked forward, shuddered, and then fell silent.

"No, no, no."

She tried again, and this time she didn't even get a rumble, just a sad, empty click. It was as if the car registered the key turning, but didn't know what to do about it.

"Please be a dead battery," she prayed aloud as she grabbed the portable charger her father insisted she keep in her trunk. Popping the hood, she connected all the cables in a rush of muscle memory and resentment. Her car had failed her before, but never when she had anything quite so appealing to get to. She waited the requisite time, then, without even shutting the door, reached in and tried the key again, only to nearly double over when it produced the same, hollow response.

A part of her, the eternally optimistic part, suggested she might wait a little longer, maybe check the cables and try again, but that part of her had been kicked around too much over the last week to make a very strong argument. She'd had enough car problems over the years to suspect either the starter or the spark plugs needed replacing, which wouldn't likely break her financially, but also wouldn't happen tonight, which was an absolutely unacceptable outcome. She had to get to Mira. She was almost frantic to do so, as her mind swam from one uncomfortable option to the next.

She could call a cab if cabs even existed around here, but her memory of having to use the credit card to buy dinner still stung. She could also call Darrin, who probably wasn't even home yet, and would turn around to give her a ride, but the echoes of him broadcasting her secrets at the family dinner table grated across her nerves. Mira would've been the obvious option, only she'd have to wake up Ben, which would also mean answering questions, plus Shelby would have to admit she drove a broken-down beater of a car she couldn't afford to fix.

Still, she needed to feel Mira against her so badly it hurt. The anticipation of her all-consuming mouth was her last, thin thread holding her sanity together.

In a rash moment, she slammed the car door, spun on her heel, and strode right out of the parking lot onto the sidewalk that would lead her through town. It might not be her proudest moment, but it wouldn't be a helpless one, either. She simply had to get to Mira, even if she stumbled every single step along the way.

Chapter Eighteen

Mira checked the large grandfather clock in her dining room for the twelfth time in two minutes, only to reconfirm it was nearly quarter to ten.

She'd spent almost an hour sitting alone with her own thoughts, replaying the conversation with Vannah, reliving the anguish and wishing she could redo a great many things, even though she didn't quite know how she could've done better. She'd rehashed the entire disaster so many times, every pulse point in her head and neck throbbed from the strain, but she still couldn't put her finger on exactly the moment everything had gone off the rails, and now she'd added another set of concerns to the pile by wondering why Shelby hadn't shown up.

Shouldn't she be here by now? Surely her parents didn't stay so late. Did people's families really come for dinner and stay until 10:00? Even the thought exhausted her, but then again, not everyone's families inspired as much stress as her own. Perhaps the Tanners were currently enjoying a lovely evening. Then again, maybe some emergency had occurred. Maybe Shelby had been in a car crash. Or perhaps she'd confided in them all the ways Mira had fallen short over the last week and they'd convinced her to walk away.

She shook her head and stood, trying to stretch her legs and roll the tension from her shoulders. She couldn't let her brain run away with itself. What-ifs weren't productive, and she rarely did anything without a sharp focus and a clear objective. If she had any real reason to worry, she could text Shelby, but she didn't want to come across as needy or put more pressure on anyone tonight. Still, she walked to the entryway and pulled back the curtain, hoping she wouldn't have to wait much longer.

She peered into the darkness, down her quiet street dappled in silver moonlight and dotted in the amber glow of the occasional streetlamp. The stillness soothed her somewhat, and she lingered there, trying to slow her pulse, but as a lone figure strode into view, her heart rate jumped once more.

Shelby walked purposefully toward her, her gait graceful even in a hurried state, and Mira threw open the door as soon as she came close enough to see her form fully. Not even thinking, she stepped onto the porch barefoot, then as if pulled to her, continued right down the driveway to meet Shelby at the street's edge.

"What happened?" she asked only after she secured her in a crushing hug.

"Rough night," Shelby whispered, burrowing into her neck.

"Are you okay?"

"I am now."

Mira held her back and searched her eyes, waiting for more.

"It's nothing major, just a million little frustrations all merging together, and I feel silly."

"No." Mira kissed her quickly and pulled her toward the door. "Are you kidding me? I could never think you silly, especially after all the crazy things you've seen me through."

Shelby shook her head. "You're dealing with real problems. I'm getting run over by my own everyday existence."

"What happened?" She shut the door behind them and handed Shelby a glass of wine she'd set out to breathe forty minutes ago.

Shelby took a sip and closed her eyes in the most stunningly beautiful expression of surrender, and when she opened them, their clear focus nearly stole Mira's breath from her lungs. "It really is nothing worth recounting, I promise, and believe me, I fully understand the hypocrisy of this request given the mountain I made you climb to get back to me this week, but could we please not talk about it right away?"

"Of course," Mira agreed and nodded for Shelby to join her on the couch. "I'm more than happy to accept a reprieve on recounting tonight, as long as it goes both ways."

Shelby curled into a cozy little ball beside her and regarded Mira over the rim of her glass. "I'm going to take it things didn't go great with Vannah?"

Mira grimaced.

"That bad, huh?" Shelby shook her head. "Sure, then. Let's be done with it all for tonight. I feel certain everything we set aside right now will keep until tomorrow anyway."

"Unfortunately, I agree," Mira said. "The question is, what shall we do with ourselves in the interim?"

The corners of Shelby's mouth curled up, and Mira's heart did a little stutter step that reverberated all the way through her stomach. She hadn't intended to imply anything with her question, but now that she apparently had, she could think of little else. Shelby wanted her, she'd apparently walked miles to get to her, and now here they were in a dimly lit room, wine in hand, curled up on the same couch. Everything seemed to be leading in one specific direction, and yet she hadn't prepared herself to go there, which was particularly disorienting as she generally overprepared. But her lack of planning did nothing to forestall the desire building in her now. Could she simply jump into something of such magnitude without forethought? She searched her rapidly clouding brain for some reason not to, and must've frowned when she didn't find any.

"It's okay," Shelby whispered.

"What is?"

"Whatever worry is causing your brow to furrow right now." Shelby took a long, slow sip of her wine. "I'm not in any sort of hurry, and I'd love to be with you in whatever way feels right. We don't have to do anything you're uncomfortable with or not ready for."

"Hmm." She hardly recognized the low hum as coming from her own body, which was now decidedly moving in the same direction as her brain. "That's what I was worrying about, actually. It seems as though I should have several things I'm not comfortable with or ready for, but when I look at you, I can't think of any of them."

Shelby's smile spread even as her eyes darkened. "That may be the sexiest thing anyone's ever said to me."

She drained her wine glass, less for the liquid courage and more because her mouth had gone dry. It had been a long time since she'd seen that look in a woman's eyes, but clearly her body hadn't forgotten what it meant. Setting her glass on the table, she motioned for Shelby to come a little closer.

Shelby accepted the invitation without hesitation, setting her own glass down and then leaning forward to practically crawl down the couch with a mischievous glint in her eyes. "Has anyone ever told you you're distractingly beautiful?" she asked as she got nearly close enough to kiss.

Mira shook her head as she bit her lip.

"What a travesty. I wanted to tell you the first day I met you."

"I find that hard to believe."

Shelby cupped her cheek in her hand. "Then I'll have to convince you."

Then she kissed her, or maybe it was the other way around, but either way they met mouth first, and everything followed easily from there.

She sank her fingers into Shelby's hair and practically pulled her onto her lap, the weight of her settling something in her she hadn't even known she'd ached to have held together.

She tasted like red wine, smelled like chocolate, and felt like heaven. A million silly clichés filled her senses, but she could only groan in confirmation of their inherent truth.

Shelby's tongue slipped into her mouth and stroked her own, taking time to explore in languid sweeps. She wanted to pull her in deeper, more completely, easily, as if they'd been kissing each other for ages. She'd depended on that mouth to build her up and unravel her several times over the last week, and yet never had she experienced it with the luxury of time. Every other kiss had been stolen or frantic, some even on the edges of sanity. Tonight felt different, with the only urgency born purely of desire. She wanted to know this woman, wholly, intentionally, completely.

Shelby's hands settled on her hips, thumbs drawing little lines up and down the curve of her waist with tantalizing pressure and urging her forward. Pulling herself away from the lips she'd fixated on with exclusionary focus to this point, she kissed a line along Shelby's jaw and down to her neck. Relishing in the soft surround of her long hair, Mira breathed deeply, imprinting the scent of her shampoo and the smoothness of her skin on the sensory center of her memory.

She worked her way slowly down to the hint of collarbone peeking out from Shelby's shirt and gave a little moan as she traced it with her lips and a great deal of reverence. "This drives me crazy."

"What?" Shelby asked distractedly as she wiggled her fingers under the hem of Mira's top.

"You wear these sweaters and sweatshirts with oversized scoop collars showing this spot right here." She kissed it again to demonstrate her point. "And this one, here at the base of your throat."

She laughed lightly. "You like that? I just wear what I'm comfortable in."

"What you're comfortable in made me decidedly uncomfortable several times early on."

"Oh." Shelby turned her head so she could kiss Mira's temple. "We don't want that. I only want to make you feel good tonight. Maybe you should take it off."

She sucked in a little gasp at the escalation, but once the seed had been planted, she could think of nothing other than removing the barrier she'd, only seconds earlier, found delightfully revealing.

She dropped her hands lower and worked them between their pressed bodies, pulling the soft cotton up unevenly as she went.

Shelby nibbled on her earlobe in encouragement until she had both palms on the newly exposed skin of her midriff before biting down a little harder and whispering, "I want to feel your skin against mine."

Another stellar idea she fully intended to bring to fruition, but even in her drive to make that dream come true, the logistics of the tasks also came with an awareness that the couch might not be their best venue for a myriad of reasons, ranging from vertical space to the remote possibility of interruption. Thankfully, this time her mind didn't even hesitate to process questions that started with "why" or "what if" and instead moved quickly to "how."

"Bedroom," she murmured in answer to herself.

"Where?" Shelby asked, easing back enough to stand and pull Mira up with her.

"Opposite side of the house from Ben's."

"That's handy." Shelby kissed her again, then wrenched herself away. "Show me."

She took her hand and wound her way through the dining room and past the front door, pausing only briefly because she couldn't take more than ten steps without kissing this woman. She intended to pull back and resume her course, but once their mouths met again, she no longer had the strength to separate and instead settled for walking backward the rest of the way into her own room. Thankfully Shelby had the wherewithal to push the door shut behind them before articles of clothing began to hit the floor.

Shelby's sweater, Mira's shirt, a pair of sweatpants followed by a set of slacks. Hands splayed across new expanses of skin followed by the heat of their mouths on shoulders, backs, chests, and when even that wasn't enough, she encircled Shelby in her arms, pulling them flush. They luxuriated in the increased contact, and Mira marveled at how amazing it felt to hold her so tightly, drawing a lazy line down the length of her spine.

Shelby nipped at the strap of Mira's bra with her teeth and then lowered her head to trace the top of the cups with her tongue, before meeting her eyes and asking, "Can I touch all of you?"

All the air left her lungs at the subtle hint of pleading, but she managed to nod while cupping the back of her head and urging her forward, hoping to signal not only her consent but also her enthusiasm.

Shelby's skilled fingertips skimmed across her back and unclasped the straps, but as soon as the bra fell away, she replaced the cover with both her palms.

This time, they groaned in unison.

"God, you feel amazing," Shelby said before capturing her mouth once more. Mira didn't even have a chance to respond before they took off again, which was just as well because she knew no words adequate enough to convey what she felt in this moment. Something primal and unspoken surged through her, and she managed to remove the final barriers between them with less finesse and more efficiency than Shelby, then pulled her the final step to the bed.

Spinning them in a half circle without breaking the kiss, she pulled back the comforter and lowered Shelby onto the sheets with great care and into a position where she could worship the body beneath her the way it deserved. Mira hovered over her for a minute taking in the sight of her, every perfect curve from her lips to her hips, the ridges of her ribs, and the dip of her navel. She didn't know which part she wanted to touch first, but indecision didn't equate to insufficiency so much as an embarrassment of riches. There were no wrong answers. She decided to start right where they were and dipped her head lower until her lips grazed against Shelby's collarbone again. She kissed down the length of one and up the other before running back to circle her tongue through the hollow in between.

Shelby cupped the back of her head, kneading lightly into her scalp without pushing in one direction or the other, but the way her chest rose and fell on each heavy breath drew Mira's attention along the incline of her breasts. Shelby arched up slightly to meet her, and Mira had a fleeting awareness this might be the moment when others would tease or make her wait, but she only wanted to satisfy her need, deeply and completely. Taking a nipple in her mouth, she received her reward in the sigh coming from the lips she loved to kiss. The high of that confirmation kept her mouth in place even as her body settled between Shelby's legs.

Soft and strong thighs tightened around her waist, and she flicked her gaze up to see Shelby watching her intently. "You're beautiful."

She would've echoed the sentiment if her mouth weren't focused on expressing something similar. Instead, she simply grazed her teeth lightly against sensitive skin and Shelby's fist tightened in her hair. The thrill at being the one to cause such a reaction pushed her onward to the other breast, and no sooner had she closed her lips around it than Shelby's hips began to rock against her. The feeling of her moving to some unheard rhythm beneath the weight of Mira's body offered the most erotic sensation she'd ever experienced, and she responded on an almost primal level.

Running her hand down along impossibly soft skin, she paused only briefly to massage the indent of her waist before sliding lower than she ever had, to the muscles of her thighs, caressing her way down the outside and then back up, urging the hold they had on her to relax. Shelby clearly understood, and slowly eased open in the most awe-inspiring way. The vulnerability and trust in the movement made Mira's brain spin with a sense of privilege and responsibility flooding in to meet her already heady arousal.

She pulled her fingers through the wetness pooling between them, and this time they both sucked in a sharp breath in unison as she circled the point of Shelby's need. Suddenly, she wasn't working for her so much as they were moving in tandem. The two of them surged and fell in equal parts and always together. She shifted her mouth back to the other breast, but held steady with her hands as they rocked.

The friction of their bodies grew exquisite as Shelby's muscles contracted below her. The pressure built, slow and steady, and still she refused to rush, or surrender to her basest impulses, choosing instead to give singular focus to the cues this amazing woman provided. A hitched breath, the tilt of her hips, the rise of her back off the bed to match a certain stroke. She wanted to learn her nuances and play them the way she'd seen Shelby play the cello, intuitively layering melody atop the foundation of her desires.

As they began to crescendo, Shelby swayed with more urgency, lifting almost off the sheets. Mira slipped her free hand underneath her shoulder, both offering support and holding steady as the first shudders shook through her. She continued with the same pressure and pace as Shelby surged, then turned into her body, burying her head against her shoulder, and biting at the muscle there to muffle her cries of release. Still, Mira didn't relent until the beautiful body in her embrace went limp. Cradling Shelby in her arms, she slowly trailed off and kissed a lazy path up her chest over her shoulder, along her neck, until their lips met once more.

Shelby kissed her, clinging tightly to her shoulders, until she fell back onto the pillow and shook her head. "Oh Mira, when you do something, you damn well do it."

She laughed. "You're not hard to focus on."

"Thank you, but your attention to detail so far outstrips anyone else I've ever met. You've got like superhuman focus." Shelby stared up at her in awe. "I didn't have to tell you anything or offer guidance. You read me like one of your spreadsheets."

"You're much more appealing to study than a spreadsheet."

"Aww, honey, that might be the sweetest thing you've ever said to me."

Mira laughed again. How could she not? This woman exuded so much joy, it seeped into her own pores and worked its way into her bloodstream. "Do you have any idea the effect you have on me?"

Shelby bit her lip and shook her head.

"I've never fallen into bed with anyone like that before. There's always been dancing back and forth and wondering 'what if,' and weighing pros and cons, and making plans. Then you walked through the door tonight and looked at me like I was the thing you wanted most in the world, and I became a foregone conclusion."

Shelby propped herself up on her elbow. "Nothing about you has ever been a foregone conclusion to me, but I do love to think my desires have so much power over you."

Mira rolled forward until their heads touched. "Why?"

"Because right now, the thing I want most in the world is to make love to you." She pushed slowly but firmly with her whole body until Mira rolled onto her back.

Not that she needed any convincing, but the soft expanse of Shelby's skin sliding along her own would've done the job. She couldn't remember a time she'd been so immersed in the luxuriousness of someone moving against her. Shelby kissed her mouth long enough for Mira to sink fully into the pillow, then nibbled at her bottom lip before moving lower. As Shelby ran her mouth down her jaw and along her neck, she paused long enough to nestle in the sensitive curve, causing Mira to sigh.

"You like that spot?" Shelby whispered.

"I've never given it any thought before," she admitted.

Shelby sucked a little harder. "How about now?"

"Yes." She gasped, tilting her chin up to provide easier access.

Shelby slid over to the other side, lavishing it with attention before shifting once more. She worked lower, never breaking any contact between their bodies or even lifting her lips as she drew light circles around her breasts, spiraling closer with each pass, then pulling back again.

Mira didn't generally enjoy being teased, and yet with Shelby, it felt less like a game and more of a dance. She took her time covering as much ground as she could, setting her own steps to the rhythm of their breathing while the rise and fall of Mira's chest kept a kind of beat. She ached for this woman deep in her bones and yet with the same feather lightness she felt each time strands of Shelby's hair brushed against her skin.

Then, after one more tantalizing pass, Shelby ran her tongue right across the center of the circle, and Mira gasped. The contact was so satisfyingly sharp, it changed the tenor of their entire trajectory. Her hands shot up on pure instinct, one clutching tightly to Shelby's back and the other cradling her head, not quite holding her in place so much as simply holding on. She needed this woman close to her. She wanted to keep her there always with a ferocity that frightened her, though to be fair, Shelby showed no signs of wanting to go anywhere.

She kissed and sucked, both toying and soothing every place Mira could've wanted without ever finding the voice to convey. Though perhaps she should have, because how could Shelby know? How could she possibly sense what was happening inside of her, the way her core trembled and her mind began to blur. Could she feel the beat of her heart accelerate or hear the way her own pulse pounded through her ears, so fast, too fast.

Everything escalated quickly, and yet no part of her wanted to slow down. On the contrary, the way she massaged the muscles flexing along the arch of Shelby's back and sides only to urge her on. The heat of her mouth moved southward once more, and she bit her lip not to cry out at the absence of attention on the sensitive nerve endings, but the sense of loss didn't last.

Mira's legs parted, seemingly of their own accord, and she thrilled at the sensation of Shelby sinking between them. Still not lifting her mouth, she painted a hot, wet path across Mira's stomach while she raked her fingernails across the sensitive skin of her inner thighs, sending the most erotic set of chills back up her spine. Mira fought the urge to throw her head back and surrender to the moan building in her chest because she simply couldn't succumb to anything requiring her to tear her eyes away from the amazing woman currently driving her past the edge of reason.

Then, dipping her head, Shelby ran one of her own hands through her hair, sweeping it out of the way so Mira could see her face as she ran her tongue along the length of her need.

That did it. Her vision tinged red as every part of her trembled. She wouldn't survive much longer. She had nothing in her frame of reference to make sense of the consuming way her body took hold of her brain. She barely had enough functioning synapses left to realize Shelby could do anything to her in this moment and she'd be powerless to stop her. Yet, even in that distant sort of awareness, she understood on a deep level that she didn't want her to stop. Not now. Not ever.

The orgasm ripped through her, unexpected in both its speed and strength, as the ferocity of their shared physicality collided with the gravity of her own awareness. The two swirled and blended to shake her thoroughly. Her climax came in wave after relentless wave as Shelby pulled everything out of her as surely and skillfully as she could pull a bow across a taut string, until only a blissful silence remained.

Chapter Nineteen

"Good morning," Shelby said groggily before even managing to open her eyes. She didn't have to actually see anything to sense the sun was up, and Mira was watching her sleep. Normally, either one of those things might've been disconcerting after so few hours of actual sleep, and yet today they seemed only like two more perfect details in a sea of others like them.

"It does indeed feel like a rather good morning," Mira said, a new dreamlike quality in her voice. "A bright new day of sorts."

She snuggled a little closer in the nook of her arm. "Just a new day? I feel like it must at least be a whole new week."

"Hmm," Mira hummed lightly near her ear. "After mentally referencing my beloved calendars or color-coded schedule, I think you're right."

"I'm right a lot."

"You'll get no argument from me." Mira kissed her neck. "Why don't you tell me about this new week of yours."

"Well." She stifled a yawn. "I can already tell you it's a lot better than last week."

"Lord, I hope so. Can we set the bar a little higher?"

"Fair. How about if we make it the best week ever?"

"Wow, big jump." Mira nipped at her earlobe, and she finally allowed her eyes to flutter open.

"Not as big as the jump we took last night."

Mira stared down at her from her position propped up on one elbow. "It was a big deal, right?"

"So big, and so good." She tilted her head up to kiss along her chin. "Some might even say a game changer."

"I'm not someone who generally takes to change very well, but this one seems to have considerable upside."

"I'm glad you think so. I don't know what I would've done if you'd performed some sort of cost-benefit analysis while I slept and decided I didn't stack up."

Mira shook her head until dark locks spilled over her shoulder. "You more than stack up. You're amazing and stunning and life-alteringly good at everything you do."

"I like the sound of that, though are you sure you're not talking about yourself?"

"Nope." Mira kissed her forehead this time. "Besides, now that I've had a teaser for the best week ever, I'm excited to learn what else it entails for us."

Shelby gave a little purr of contentment. "A part of it feels like, if we did nothing else but this all week, it might still fit the bill, but seeing as we both have jobs—"

"Do we?" Mira asked, a playfulness in her voice Shelby had never heard before. "I don't recall."

"High praise from someone of your stature in the local business community, but I must remind you, you've got clients and an assistant and an impressive desk, which I'd very much like to do what we did last night on top of."

Mira's hips gave a subtle little thrust, and the involuntary response sent Shelby's heart thudding again.

"And sadly, I have a school full of middle schoolers to prep for a musical performance."

Mira sighed. "One of those middle schoolers is likely to be awake in the next hour and ready for breakfast."

"Do I need to go?"

"No," Mira said so quickly there left little room for argument. "I don't want to go back to stealing kisses and settling for half-hour lunch dates. I want more, Shelby. Best week ever might come with some life constraints, but I want every free moment to be spent with you."

She nearly melted into a puddle at those perfect words and the sincerity with which they were delivered.

"I just can't neglect Ben," Mira added. "I've only got one more week with him."

The thought caused her chest to constrict and her mind to rebel. There had never been a them without Ben there. "We have to pull him in."

Mira arched an eyebrow.

"It wouldn't be the best week ever without Ben. We have to tell him about it and let him contribute. He's the one who brought us together. He should have a say in the fun, or at least large parts of it, in age-appropriate ways, of course."

"Okay, what did you have in mind?"

"Nothing." Shelby laughed. "You're the planner. I'm the idea woman."

"Well, don't you at least have some ideas for me then?"

Shelby pretended to think hard, but she couldn't quite pull off consternation with Mira staring down at her all beautiful and bare-chested save for the nearly translucent sheet covering them both. "How about a general sort of understanding that while none of us can cut out of work completely, we do everything we can to make the most of the hours we have together. No worries about responsibility or respectability or what happens down the road. We'll keep our heads and our hearts right where our feet are and live each moment the way we want."

Mira's smile turned a little lopsided. "Under normal circumstances that idea might give me heart palpitations, but given our current reality, I'm willing to try if you'll help me."

Shelby pulled her down and kissed her with renewed purpose before releasing her to say, "Let's start now."

Mira ran a hand across her stomach until it settled along the curve of Shelby's hip, and tugged her even closer until their bodies molded together. "And by start right now, you mean ... what?"

This time, Shelby kissed her nose, not trusting either of them to stop if she started again. "I mean breakfast. A big one, covered in lots of syrup, so it's ready and so are we before Ben wakes up."

"Right," Mira said with a hint of a frown. "When did you become the responsible one?"

She laughed and gave her a little shove. "You must've rubbed off on me, but I don't know how long it will last, so don't test your luck."

"Fair enough." Mira rolled over and stood up, causing Shelby's mouth to go dry. She had never in her life seen anything so beautiful in the first light of day. A part of her wanted to call Mira back and say she'd made a terrible mistake in letting her leave the bed, but another part of her finally dared to hope they might find their way back here sooner rather than later.

***

"So, your car wouldn't start?" Mira asked as she ladled pancake batter onto her cast-iron skillet.

"I suspect the spark plugs might be to blame." Shelby leaned up against the counter and took a sip from her coffee as if trying to fortify herself. "This car is not my first lemon. I've learned all the different sounds of a breakdown, and this one didn't have that extra expensive grind to it."

"Well, that's promising," Mira managed, which seemed like quite an accomplishment while still trying to process the sight of Shelby barefoot in black sweatpants and one of her plain, white T-shirts. Somehow, despite being one or two sizes too big, the clothes fit her better than they ever had Mira.

"Do you have chocolate chips?" Shelby changed the subject and pulled her attention back to breakfast.

"I think I may have some left over from the holidays. Check up in the corner cabinet with the baking supplies."

She turned toward the spot Mira indicated with her spatula. "This is the most organized cupboard I've ever seen, and yes, sure enough, there's half a bag of chocolate morsels right next to the red and green decorating sugar. You're an absolute wonder."

"Because I have chocolate?"

"No, because you have *leftover* chocolate, and you knew it was there all along." Shelby unclipped the bag and dropped a few chips atop the batter in the pan. "The only way chocolate survives in my house is if it falls behind the flour and I forget it's there."

"But surely when you reorganized your pantry during spring cleaning, you'd be happily surprised."

Shelby tilted her head to the side and crossed her eyes playfully. "I know all those words, but when you put them together in such a nonsensical order, they hardly compute. Organize pantry? Spring cleaning? What do those things even mean?"

Mira flipped the pancake, but before she could summon any sort of comeback, Ben shuffled into the kitchen in his Star Wars pajamas.

He stared at the two of them for a moment, and Mira's heart missed a beat for fear he'd know something profound had shifted for all of them and they were merely fiddling while Rome went up in flames, but instead he merely yawned before asking, "What are you making?"

"Pancakes," Shelby declared cheerfully, "with chocolate chips."

His eyes lit up. "And whipped cream?"

They both turned to Mira expectantly, and she didn't have the heart to suggest chocolate and syrup should be more than enough to feed their sugar cravings, so she merely smiled. "I have some heavy cream in the fridge if one of you wants to whip it up."

"I'll do it!" Ben jumped forward eagerly, and soon the three of them were moving around the kitchen and each other with ease.

She poured and flipped pancakes while Shelby made them sweeter, and Ben prepped the cream to serve as literal icing on the cake, or hotcakes as the case may be. As Mira stacked their offerings onto plates, she couldn't help but think about how their shared meal mimicked their own roles in their trio.

As they all gathered around the table and passed the maple syrup, Ben finally asked, "When you did you come over, Miss Tanner?"

They both froze and stared at each other like deer in the headlights. Mira might have stayed like that for all eternity if Shelby hadn't slid a hand onto her knee under the table and given her leg a little squeeze before saying, "I actually walked over last night."

Ben took a bite of his pancake as he seemed to ponder the news. "Why did you walk?"

She laughed. "A very good question with a sad answer. My car is dead, or at least in a coma, and since it's the weekend, I think I'm stranded."

"I'm sorry," he said sincerely.

"Thanks. I was pretty unhappy about it, too, but your aunt Mira made me feel better and offered pancakes."

"Pancakes do make everything seem a little better." His tone suggested he wasn't just talking about Shelby anymore.

"Yeah?" Shelby asked. "Mira and I were discussing how last week was kind of rough on all of us, and we wanted to start this one off better."

He turned to her. "Did you talk to my mom last night?"

She sighed, and her stomach gave an unpleasant drop, but she tried to force a smile. "I did, and I do think she heard what I had to say."

"Did you come up with any new plans?"

She shook her head slowly, and his shoulders sagged. "No, not yet, but your mom knows about our concerns now, and I think she'll take them as seriously as she can. She did say there were some good support systems in place and more on the way soon. Plus, I was thinking maybe you and I could work out a few more of our own."

He lifted his dark eyes to hers and asked a hundred questions without giving voice to any of them.

"For instance, you've been talking to your mom on your computer, so we know there's good internet connections there and here, which means you could just as easily chat with Josh and Izzy, right?"

He pondered the prospect for a few seconds before nodding. "I suppose so."

"I do online game nights with some friends from college. It can be really fun," Shelby added.

"Do you know any music games we can play that way?" he asked.

"So many of them, and listening parties, oh and virtual recitals, plus, if you all didn't mind a teacher horning in every now and again, I could even do some group lessons over video chat."

His expression brightened, and Mira's mood lifted along with it. She hadn't even considered the possibility of Ben continuing to work with Shelby from a different hemisphere. "Can you really offer lessons online?"

"Sure? Why not? I mean I'm clearly going to need a summer job to keep afloat financially and keep my car running."

"I'd be happy to pay for lessons, or even pay ahead of time if you need to fix the car now," she offered.

Shelby straightened, pulling her hand from Mira's leg as she sat back. "I don't need you to pay for my car. I'll figure it out. I always have before, and I actually have a real job now."

"Of course. I didn't mean to imply you couldn't." Though that was clearly how Shelby had taken the offer, and Mira got the sense she'd added one more sensitive topic to a conversation already overflowing with them. "I only meant the lessons have been a godsend for Ben and for me. I want to make sure I continue to pay for those, starting with a down payment, so we all know we won't let them slip in the transition of the big move."

Shelby nodded, but once again deferred to Ben. "Would that make you feel a little better if you knew you already had some lessons paid for and waiting as soon as you get settled, or even if you need them to help you feel settled?"

He nodded again, this time with a little more enthusiasm. "I think it would make me feel less homesick, but when will I see you, Aunt Mira?"

This time, when another little piece of her heart broke, it didn't feel all bad. A part of her thrilled he even wanted to keep in touch with her at the same level he did with his friends and his music. The love welling up in her seemed almost too strong to bear. Nothing in her life experience had ever prepared her to handle the magnitude of emotion she'd felt over the last few days, and even those felt small compared to the prospect of letting him down. She didn't know how to fight everything clawing up from her chest, so instead of trying to hold it all in, she surrendered.

Without thinking, she shifted out of her chair and crouched down next to him. "Ben, I swear I'll always be here for you. I was there the moment you took your first breath, and I'll be there for the rest of my life anytime you call, whether it's in person or on the phone or via a computer."

He worried his lower lip and swallowed. "Okay."

"I promise. We can set up regular chats, and you can play for me, whatever music you're working on, and maybe we can even find a way for the two of us to watch movies online together."

They both turned to Shelby as though asking if such a thing could be possible, but when their eyes met, she was clearly fighting to blink back tears.

"I think that's a great idea," Shelby said finally, her voice thick. "I hope you'll invite me anytime you watch an old musical."

"What do you say?" she asked Ben. "Can she come to a couple of movie nights?"

His smile spread to something less guarded. "I think so, 'cause she's kind of like your girlfriend, right?"

Her breath caught again, and she whirled one more time from him back to the other half of that equation. They hadn't put any terms on what they were doing, and even if they had, what they were doing had shifted drastically last night. She knew what she wanted the answer to be, but she didn't want to put words into anyone else's mouth.

Still, Shelby didn't seem to want to be the first to blink either because, despite a hint of pink rising in her cheeks and the crook of a smile playing at the corners of her lips, she didn't give much away.

"Well ..." She drew out the word and tried to think of a way to address both of her audiences simultaneously. "We haven't actually discussed the topic in detail yet, but I do like Miss Tanner, or rather Shelby, a lot, even more than as a friend. I think she's special, and she makes me feel good about things I might otherwise find frightening, and those are qualities I'd like in a girlfriend if she felt comfortable with such a label."

Ben giggled. "That was a lot of words. I thought girlfriends just liked to kiss each other and stuff."

She and Shelby both burst out laughing, and it took a few breaths before she could pull herself back together enough to say, "Now that you mention it, I do enjoy kissing and stuff too."

She turned to Shelby, who now beamed at her before agreeing. "Same here, on all counts, but if the kissing stuff makes us girlfriends, I guess I kind of became yours without us ever using the word."

Mira rose and reached for her hands, taking them in her own and intertwining their fingers, before asking Ben, "So, there you have it. Can we both have lots of video chats and concerts and movie nights with the coolest kid we know?"

He didn't answer, at least not verbally, but he did stand slowly and wrap his arms around them both, pulling them close until they met in a giant group hug.

Chapter Twenty

"Okay, okay." Shelby held up her hand as they all recovered from their third giggle fit in the last hour. "So far, we have ice cream, pizza, Putt-Putt golf, movie theater popcorn, the Buffalo Museum of Science, sleepovers, bubble baths, bike rides, and healthy, well-balanced breakfasts."

"Don't put that on the list!" Ben called, still laughing.

"Why not?" Mira teased. "I don't get a say in the best week ever list?"

"You do, but you can have a healthy breakfast anytime. These are things I'm going to miss when I move."

"You aren't going to miss my healthy breakfasts?"

He grimaced. "I feel like I'm supposed to say yes, but I think I can still get healthy breakfasts in other countries."

"How about this?" Shelby jumped back in. "Pizza has all four food groups, and it's already on the list. I can verify it is also an acceptable breakfast food."

"Is it?" Mira questioned, but her tone didn't convey much seriousness.

"Totally legit breakfast," she confirmed. "How about if we all eat leftover pizza before school tomorrow? Protein, carbs, and tomatoes make you happy, right?"

Mira smiled. "You two make me happy, so I'll allow the pizza plan."

"Way to compromise there. What else do we need to add to the list?"

"Can we invite Josh and Izzy to have pizza, too?"

"Of course," Mira said quickly. "We can get you as much time with them as possible this week."

"You're going to be with them a lot at play practice anyway," Shelby added. "The only night we have a full run-through is Tuesday, then again with tech on Wednesday, and Thursday is full dress rehearsal."

Mira frowned. "I think you're going to see more of Josh and Izzy than me this week."

"That means we have to make the most of today," Shelby said quickly, "and our evenings."

"You should stay here with us, Miss Tanner," Ben added.

She bit her lip, not sure how to navigate the complexities he couldn't possibly comprehend in such a suggestion. "I'm not sure that would be appropriate."

"Why not?"

She shot a glance at Mira, hoping for some assistance, but she merely folded her arms across her chest and fought a smile. Shelby suspected this may be payback for not jumping in to help her with the girlfriend conversation, but she wasn't sure she could've handled it as well as Mira managed. Still, the memory did give her a little shot of confidence because she wasn't an interloper, or even Ben's teacher anymore. She was Mira's girlfriend. She was allowed to have opinions and a say, at least a small one, in how they spent their time together. "I don't want to distract either of you from your quality time together."

"You won't," Ben said. "Aunt Mira could pick us both up after school, which is good 'cause your car doesn't work."

"I hadn't considered that particular hurdle yet."

"And now you don't have to," Mira said, "at least not on one of the busiest weeks of the year. I'll be on carpool duty until after the musical. It's the least I can do to support the arts and my two favorite artists."

She met her eyes and held her gaze a little longer, trying to do that thing other couples did where they could ask each other questions without saying them aloud. Did Mira know what she was offering? Did she really want her to stay there for a week? Was this part of their vacation philosophy until Ben left, or was it another huge step? It felt like the chips could fall in either direction, and she certainly didn't want to make assumptions.

Mira nodded and gave her another soothing smile, seemingly to say everything would be okay. Shelby believed her even if she wasn't at all certain her own concerns had been adequately conveyed.

"Oh, what about Doritos?" Ben bounced up and down excitedly.

"What about them?" Shelby asked, not quite able to follow the non sequitur to her own internal thoughts.

"Do they have them in Belize? Or should it go on the list?"

"The list? I mean, right, the list!" She kicked herself for making this conversation about her when they only had a week left with Ben. She'd never had to navigate the start of a relationship with so many other important things at play. "I have no idea about Doritos' international availability."

He turned to Mira, who shrugged. "Don't ask me. I don't even see their American appeal."

Shelby laughed. "We better add them to the list just in case. Which flavor?"

"Cool ranch," he said, as though he found her need to ask such a question a little silly.

"Right, the obvious choice," she agreed. "Big blue bag of deliciousness. What else?"

"I don't know." He scrunched up his face as if trying to think real hard. "Do you think we can do everything on the list?"

"We can certainly try." Mira took the sheet of paper from Shelby and scanned the items with the intensity of a professional planner. "We'd better start today, though. I think I see a trip to Buffalo in the cards to cross off the science museum and Putt-Putt, with a side order of ice cream."

Ben hopped off the couch. "Yes! And I could take a bubble bath when I get home."

"That sounds like a pretty perfect day," Shelby said sincerely, then turned to Mira, who smiled and nodded.

"I guess we better get moving."

"I'm going to get dressed." Ben sprinted down the hall before bolting back to hug them both quickly, then sped off again.

Shelby rose more slowly, but she couldn't deny his excitement had rubbed off on her, and those feelings went up another few notches when she turned to see Mira watching her, her dark eyes intently focused. "What are you thinking about?"

"You." Mira took her hand and pulled her closer.

"What about me?"

"You being amazing, and being my girlfriend, my amazing girlfriend."

"Me? What about you? You've been such a champ this morning, and last night, honestly, but never in my life have I seen someone go from turning me to Jell-O physically to melting my heart like you did this morning. When you got down on his level, so steady and strong, I could see how much it was killing you to admit his mom didn't bend, but he didn't see it. He saw you modeling hope and faith and honest assurance." She swooned a little thinking about it now. "Seriously, I would've agreed to be your girlfriend days ago, but you sealed the deal today by proving yourself to be the total package."

Mira chuckled lightly. "I don't think anyone has ever seen me quite the way you do."

"Good." She kissed her. "I don't want to share you with anyone but Ben."

"You don't have to. And, I mean, I'm not sorry he's here, because I love having him here, but I want you to know that I see how amazing you're handling all this as well. Most women wouldn't see a family breakfast and a trip to the science museum as an appropriate way to spend the morning after what we did last night."

"Then I'm not most women, because I love the science museum, and consider this your fair warning, I'm a closeted Putt-Putt pro, too."

Mira managed to look both duly impressed and genuinely happy. "Noted."

"Besides, since you're apparently driving me to work tomorrow, you should know I also plan to partake in the bubble bath portion of the evening after he goes to bed tonight." Then she leaned close enough to whisper, "How big is your tub?"

Mira snuggled into her neck and kissed the curve with enough skill to make her knees a little wobbly before standing back with a new glint in her eye. "Definitely big enough to fit two and still have plenty of room for suds."

***

"Good morning, Jane." Mira breezed through the door to work on Monday morning. "How was your weekend?"

"Same old, same old." Jane poured steaming coffee into a mug. "A whole lot of only half-watching movies while looking at houses I can't afford online. What about you? More spreadsheets than a normal human could even imagine?"

"Actually, no." Mira accepted the mug. "I worked Saturday during the day, then had a terribly futile and frustrating conversation with Vannah."

"So, pretty standard."

"Certainly not unexpected." She grimaced at the memory, then moved past it. "But otherwise, I had a lovely time with Shelby and Ben. We went to Buffalo and behaved like silly kids all day on Sunday."

Jane finally turned to her fully. "You spent a whole day behaving in a childlike fashion? Are you ill?"

She laughed. "I know, perhaps a bit out of character, but I actually feel wonderful. We did science experiments and played games and ordered entirely too much pizza followed by ice cream."

"Are you sure you don't have a fever? Your cheeks are a little pink, and your lips have a bit more color than ... wait a second, are you wearing lip gloss?"

"No."

"You are!" Jane hopped up and inspected her face at entirely too close a distance to be comfortable, then pointed to additional evidence on the rim of her mug. "When did you start using lip gloss?"

"I haven't." Her face warmed, and suddenly the coffee felt too hot to even take another sip. "I think, perhaps, Shelby wears lip gloss."

"Then how did it get on your ... never mind, I got it." Jane laughed. "Took me a minute. I don't know if I'm slipping or if you just blew my mind, but you've been kissing your hot, young girlfriend before work, which means either you snuck into the school at drop-off or she spent the night. Which one of those equally exciting options was it?"

"I drove her to work this morning because she's having car trouble."

"Seems reasonable." Jane nodded. "A little too reasonable for how red your face is, so I have to ask—"

"You don't, actually."

"Did you drive her from her house or yours?"

Mira sighed. She didn't have to answer the question, but a part of her inexplicably wanted to. "From mine."

"Oh. My. God."

Jane collapsed into her chair. "I can't believe this is happening. You're knocking boots with the hottest teacher in town. I'm proud of you."

"Thank you?"

"You're welcome. I assume your new sleepover status contributed to your wonderful weekend and your stellar mood this early on Monday morning."

"Perhaps," she admitted, then didn't know why she felt the need to keep pretending she wasn't as close to giddy as she ever got. "Actually, yes, yes it did. A part of me will never forget all of this could come crashing down on Sunday. Honestly, a smaller part of me expects it to, but for now I'm enjoying myself immensely, and I'd like you to reschedule any appointments I have between noon and one this week."

"I'd be thrilled to serve as an accomplice to your sexy lunch routines."

"Good, go ahead and take a full hour for yourself."

"I intend to." Jane laughed. "I mean, I like working for you all the time, but having you hopped up on whatever pheromones are surging through your brain right now really does make this the best job ever."

She laughed in spite of it being unprofessional. She couldn't argue. This was the best week ever after all, and Jane deserved to benefit as much as anyone else in their periphery. "Excellent, and while you're at it, go ahead and cancel anything we have slated for Saturday morning."

"Wow, already planning ahead for a wild Friday night?"

"Actually, the musical opens then and runs all weekend. I want to be able to be present and available for Shelby and Ben during the whirlwind."

"Aww, that's actually sweet and thoughtful. You're going all in, aren't you?"

She ground her teeth against the urge to downplay things, to make them feel smaller, and by extension, safer. She didn't want to get ahead of herself, but she didn't have to undercut the joy she'd been steeped in for the last thirty-six hours. Maybe Shelby was having a greater influence on her than she thought, but she felt calm and almost confident as she said, "We're keeping our heads and our hearts in the moment, but I'm committed to making the most of those moments while they last."

Jane beamed. "I'm so in awe. This is like the greatest thing that's happened to me in ages, and it's not even happening to me, but I feel like we should throw a parade or something to celebrate."

She laughed. "Let's not go quite that far. Taking lunches and Saturday off is as close as I get to a parade, but Shelby's putting in long hours this week, I can at least manage to keep up with a few of my responsibilities along the way."

"You got it, boss, and actually when it comes to Shelby and responsibilities, I wonder if they might be about to collide in the form of your first appointment."

"How so?"

"Your 8:30 is a new client named Darrin Tanner. I didn't put it together until he was off the phone, but two new Tanners coming to visit during office hours can't be a coincidence, can it?"

"No, they're related."

"Please say he's the single brother and not the dad who's about to retire."

She rolled her eyes. "Yes, he's the single brother."

Jane did a happy little chair dance. "Do you have a picture of him?"

"No."

"Why not?

"Why would I? I've only met the man twice. You think I keep photos of my girlfriend's family members on my phone? Is that a thing people do?" She had a brief moment of worry that perhaps she knew less about relationships than she'd previously thought, but Jane merely shrugged.

"Probably not, but I'm excited."

"Don't make a big deal of things. Darrin's coming in as a client. I don't even know what Shelby's told him about us."

"Good point." Jane winked. "Totally professional. No hanky-panky happening in this office. Secret sexy lunches, never heard of 'em. No one here is sleeping with the hot music teaching sister of people whose money they manage."

She wasn't sure that was quite the tone she'd hoped for, but before she had a chance to say so, the front door opened, and Darrin strode in with a smile.

"Good morning, good morning, how's my favorite future sister-in-law?"

Mira froze, her brain flashing white at its complete inability to process such a greeting and its vast disconnect from everything she'd just said.

Then Jane and Darrin burst out laughing simultaneously.

"Wow, I wish you could see your face," Darrin finally said. "You went all white."

"Like a ghost," Jane piled on.

"Be honest." He leaned in. "What caused the deer-in-the-headlights look? The implication you needed to propose to my sister, or the fact that I even know the two of you are dating?"

She tried to force a smile but feared it came across more than a little cringey. "You merely caught me off guard. I only learned about your appointment moments ago, and I expected us to discuss your financial planning."

"But we were totally talking about your sister before that," Jane offered in what was probably supposed to be a helpful tone.

251

"She's amazing, like a living doll, and you two have the same exact eyes."

Darrin grinned sheepishly. "I mean, she's all right, but yeah, good genes in the Tanner pool. I'm Darrin by the way."

"Jane." She extended her hand. "It's a pleasure to meet you."

Mira watched the exchange with detached interest, like one might watch an instructional video on casual greetings.

"So, you met my sister, huh?" he asked. "I take it she's been in to visit during office hours, which is weird because she keeps putting me off and saying she's so busy at work."

"She's incredibly busy," Mira cut back in, "and I'm sure you have a full schedule, too. Why don't we head into my office and get started."

"I'm actually off work today," he said nonchalantly, then glanced back at Jane to explain. "I'm a chemist at Altenech.

"Wow. I've never met a chemist before."

"Really? I know tons of them."

Jane laughed. "Not surprised given your frame of reference."

"Right." He seemed to see some humor in the comment. "Anyway, it's a good place to work, and I had a few personal days left to burn before the end of the fiscal year. I actually have a good insurance plan, too. Lots of benefits."

Jane smiled up at him, recognizing the comments as an attempt to flirt but his ineptitude at subtlety.

Mira tried not to picture how Shelby would've slapped him upside the head or called him a dweeb if she'd been there. Then she smiled at that image in her mind.

"How long have you worked here?" Darrin asked.

"Five years," Jane said.

"You like it?"

Jane glanced at Mira and gave an awkward little grin, like "Who is this guy?" before telling him, "I've got a pretty cool boss who recently upped my lunchtime from thirty minutes to a full hour."

"Nice," Darrin nodded. "I can take an hour for lunch sometimes, too. Maybe, I don't know, if you wanted to, we could take an hour lunch together."

Jane's smile turned sweet and if Mira wasn't mistaken, her cheeks tinged a little pink, too. "I do think I might like that."

Darrin gave a triumphant little bounce, then caught himself and tried, too late, to play cool. "Great, I think you have my number probably from when I made the appointment. I won't pressure you or anything, because professionalism and feminism, but you could let me know if you really do want to meet up."

"How about today at noon?" Jane offered, then shot a covert wink toward Mira. "I think my boss has plans."

"I think I do," she cut in, not sure she could stomach the ease of their mating ritual any longer. "And now the two of you do, too. Shall we move to my office now?"

He startled slightly as if he'd forgotten she was still in the room, then grinned sheepishly. "Right, we have an appointment, to talk about retirement, which is why I came in."

She stared at him, not sure why he'd needed to summarize any of those things, and not at all sure how she should respond.

"Good." He nodded before turning back to Jane. "Also good."

She had to save him, if not for his own sake, for hers. She had a low threshold for other people's awkwardness, so she motioned to her office. "Right this way."

He followed directions well enough, scooting past and waiting for her to close the door before sagging. "Oh my God, did she just agree to go out with me?"

"I believe she did."

"And it's a date, right?"

"Seems so."

"Do you think she knows it's a date?"

She finally laughed. "I'm pretty sure she does. Do you?"

He paused as if replaying the conversation in his head before his face split into another huge grin. "I think so."

"Have you ever been on a date?"

He sighed. "Yes, I have, but in my experience, they usually take a lot more work on my part."

She softened at the sentiment. "I know what you mean."

"Right." He seemed to really notice her for the first time. "Things are complicated, huh?"

"You have a gift for understatement."

"Not usually." He took the seat she indicated and waited for her to settle in behind her desk. "You might not believe this given what you just witnessed out there and the stellar advice I tend to give Shelby, but I often have a hard time talking to women I like."

She actively worked to keep her face neutral. "I would've never known."

"Right? I think probably we have to remember to stay open to it being easy sometimes. Like maybe it's supposed to be easier, right?"

"Right," she said as a pang of something akin to jealousy pricked her chest. Easy wasn't something she'd even dared to strive for. Even the little moments with Shelby, where they'd fallen into each other without overthinking, had only been facilitated after weeks of worry and emotional work.

She fought down the rising echo of the school counselor suggesting that lack of easy relationship building might be a sign of maladjustment. She'd moved past that mentality. She was doing okay, well even, or at least better than she ever had. There was no reason to let the exchange shake the confidence she'd strode in with today. Still, she could feel okay about her own efforts and simultaneously be a bit bemused by the contrast.

Right.

***

"Do you have any more meetings with any members of my family?" Shelby asked as she scooped up a handful of bubbles and dripped them along Mira's arm.

"God, I hope not." Mira kissed her bare shoulder and shifted slightly so Shelby reclined more fully along the length of her, both of their bodies submerged in the warmth of their new nightly bubble bath. "I mean, they're truly lovely people, but I'm running out of staff members in my office who aren't completely smitten with Tanners. No one is going to get any work done if you people keep distracting us with your seductive wiles."

"Ew, Darrin doesn't have seductive wiles, and please don't mention him while we're naked, ever."

She laughed so hard the water rippled around them, causing the lush layer of bubbles to shiver. "Fair enough, but Jane appears to disagree with you. They've had two dates in three days, and she thinks he's sweet and funny with better-than-average personal hygiene."

"Ugh, have you considered running her through concussion protocol, because he's not funny, and he's not nearly as smart as he thinks, but I guess he's kind of sweet. Also, I think straight women may have a lower bar for their partners' personal hygiene."

"Shame. Just think of all the great bubble baths they're missing out on."

She made a happy little hum, and shifted for no other reason than she enjoyed the slide of their slick skin against one another. The fact that Mira had a tub big enough for two only added to the long list of reasons Shelby had come to think of her as the perfect partner to spend the best week ever with. She also made love with a consuming intensity, and her attention to detail made almost every part of their lives better. Despite being one of the busiest school weeks of her entire life, she hadn't dropped a single ball or missed a meeting, or even felt frazzled enough to fear she might.

"What are you thinking about, if not your brother?"

"Your superior scheduling skills."

Mira laughed. "Sure you are."

"Seriously, I am. It's sexy how you keep all the plates spinning and have this aura of command like you hold all the logistical keys to the kingdom in your superhot brain."

"I can never tell if you're teasing me or not."

"I'd never tease about the schedule. If I wanted to tease you, I'd do this." She rolled her hips in a small circle to apply pressure to the apex of Mira's splayed thighs.

She groaned. "I think I'm done with the bath. Let's go to bed."

"Not so fast. You need to remind me what's on tap for the rest of the week."

"We can go over everything in the morning."

"No. After what you keep doing to me at night, I'm always a total waste in the morning. I can barely keep the kids from becoming wild banshees until I have a second cup of coffee. Give me your super competent rundown like it's foreplay."

"Fine. Tomorrow's a long day. School and work followed by dress rehearsal right after class until about 8:00. I already packed you and Ben both an extra snack to eat in between."

"What is it?"

"An apple, some sliced turkey, cheddar cheese, a few almonds."

"Did you put a charcuterie board in a box?"

"Basically."

She sat up and turned around quickly, causing some water to slosh over the edge. "I'm going to eat that tomorrow with my door closed and the lights off so no one can interrupt me while I daydream about kissing you so freaking hard."

Mira smiled at her. "You're quite easy to please. Are you sure you aren't also setting the bar a little low?"

"She asks while soaking with me in a luxurious bath after picking me up from work, feeding me a home-cooked dinner, packing my lunch, and turning down the sheets on the bed, which heavily implies a thorough ravishing exists in my immediate future."

Mira's cheeks colored beautifully, but clearly not from embarrassment as she placed both hands on Shelby's hips and pulled her forward until their legs tangled. "We could move on to the ravishing right now."

This time she wavered, but she didn't want to rush. "Tell me what else is on the schedule first?"

"Friday, you and Ben are having dinner at school, sorry, but I'll be there in the sixth row center when the curtain rises."

"And you will be held spellbound by the score if not by the acting."

"Absolutely. The music really is the draw, which is why it's called a musical."

"Good point. Go on."

"Then after you all take your well-deserved bows, Ben is spending the night at Josh's house to fulfill his list item of sleepovers, and you and I will have a sleepover of our own. This one isn't going to end with a six a.m. alarm."

"Heaven." She kissed her, letting both her mind and her body relax. "The idea of waking up with you and not having anywhere to go, or having anyone to tend to is literally giving me the life I need to make it through the next thirty-six hours."

"Good." Mira kissed her back, this time lingering a little longer before adding, "then I'm going to start a mental countdown to Friday night at 9:00. You can ask me anytime how much longer we have to go."

"Perfect, and that's enough schedule for me."

Mira eyed her for a second, her dark irises swirling with desire and something else. Shelby's throat constricted as she tried to ignore the unspoken, about where they always cut off these conversations: Vannah would arrive over the weekend.

No matter how many times they reviewed the agenda, they always stopped before they got to the place where everything would change. There had been zero discussion about who would pick her up, Shelby's role while she was here, or how their lives would change after she left. They'd chosen to steadfastly stay in the best week ever while pretending there was no such thing as a weekend.

She kissed her again, and this time, there was nothing quick about it. Their mouths, tongues, and bodies all slid together, blurring both physical and mental boundaries.

If denial was their collective coping method of choice, she wouldn't be the one to shatter any illusions. While she understood enough about choosing ignorance to be worried about the consequences down the road, she'd had plenty of practice putting off problems and pretending they didn't exist. She had some pause about how easily Mira managed to do the same, as it seemed much more out of character for her, but Mira had much more at stake. If she wanted to continue living in the bliss of playing house a few days more, Shelby wouldn't force her to face facts.

Besides, even if they were only playing house with their shared commutes, stolen lunches, family dinners, and erotic evening routines, she didn't see why she shouldn't let herself enjoy the game. Or more importantly, the woman in the tub with her.

Chapter Twenty-One

Mira double-checked the seat number on her ticket before settling into her spot in the sixth row of the high-school auditorium. Excitement buzzed around her as teenagers ran about and families with small children scooted past. Surprisingly, she found she wasn't immune to the energy. Six weeks ago, she wouldn't have even given a second thought to a youth production of a musical from the 1950s, and yet tonight she opened her program proudly and scanned the orchestra listing until she found both Ben's and Shelby's names.

She smiled at the idea of them somewhere backstage, probably tuning instruments, both wearing the all-black outfits they'd picked out together the night before without letting her see. They'd worked so hard over the last month, and she'd been aglow all day thinking about how happy they'd both seemed when she'd dropped them off that morning.

The lights dimmed, then came back up twice, and the murmurs around the cavernous room took on new urgency as conversations gave way to sounds of people dropping into seats and programs rustling. She craned her neck to see the students file in toward the rows of folding chairs in front of the stage. It took a few seconds, but she finally spotted Ben with his violin amid the jumble. He noticed her at the same time and flashed a smile but didn't return her wave before scooting into the middle of the pack and opening his music with great seriousness. By the time all the other kids filled in around him, she could only see his feet and the neck of his violin, but at least she'd know where he was at all times. She also knew he'd be his happiest self for the next two hours, which gave her immense comfort.

The emotion that hit her when Shelby emerged and took her place in front of the assembled students was decidedly less comfortable. She wore the quintessential little black dress. Sleeveless with an hourglass cut and playful flair just above her knees, it accentuated each stellar quality in the body she'd worshiped every night all week, and Mira's brain felt as though it had caught actual fire. She pressed her hand to her own forehead as her eyes ran down the length of those toned legs to the perfect pair of black, sling-back heels, and yes, she actually felt a little feverish, or perhaps that was the friction caused by all her synapses firing at once in some vain attempt to process the sight of Shelby in her absolute element.

She smiled over her shoulder, and Mira's chest seized at the radiance of the expression, but as Shelby took up her baton and with one flick of her wrist commanded the attention of every eye in the room, a new emotion settled someplace lower in Mira's core. Then, with another subtle sweep of her skilled hands, music broke forth, strong and sweet and steady. She marked time almost effortlessly, and yet the score she controlled with the most minute movements held hundreds of people utterly spellbound. The sight of her working with such grace and control caused Mira to shiver as Shelby's words echoed through her brain, low and sensual. *Competence is sexy.*

At some point, some young thespians burst onto the stage wearing zoot suits and fedoras. Songs were sung about horses named Paul Revere, and bets were placed while teenagers dressed like grandmothers tried to save wayward souls. Mira did make genuine attempts to watch them. To their credit, on those occasions when she was able to lift her gaze all the way to stage level, everyone did seem to be in step, and no one's voice had fallen flat enough to catch her untrained ear. If anyone had asked, she would've given the cast a respectable review, at least vocally, but she wasn't sure she could've picked any of the youthful leads out of a lineup since she couldn't manage to tear her eyes off Shelby long enough for anyone else to make a lasting imprint.

The woman exuded something so alluring, Mira had to grip the armrests on her seat to keep from moving toward her as she conducted. She seemingly had the ability to keep an eye on every student and the sheet music simultaneously, and if that weren't commanding enough, she occasionally took up an instrument of her own to fill in gaps only someone of her own ability could ascertain. During one song, she sat down long enough to play a complex section on a cello before setting it aside in the next number to grab a violin, and Mira lost all track of the play. She sat transfixed, watching Shelby sway in the dim light. She simply embodied the music and imbued all aspects of the performance with grace and a natural sensuality.

By the time the number ended and the audience signaled their approval with an extra-boisterous round of applause, Mira practically trembled with desire. She shook her head and forced her eyes off the flex of Shelby's shoulders. She'd never be able to look at herself in the mirror afterward if she didn't pull herself together. She was at a school function for crying out loud. Arousal was not an appropriate response to any part of this event. She'd never had any reaction like this to anyone in her life, at least not in an auditorium full of families. Still, she couldn't help but feel as though she was becoming someone else. She didn't want to become the type of person who got carried away by emotions any more than she'd wanted to be the person who fell apart or spun out of control weeks ago, but this time, the sense of falling didn't carry the fear it had then. Tonight, she couldn't summon any serious reminder of why she needed to stop, or even a strong desire to slow down. Tonight, she was so completely taken with Shelby, the sight of her overrode every moderating influence of her psyche.

By the time the production progressed to "Marry the Man Today," she was an utter internal mess, but she did manage a quick shot of laugher when Shelby turned and gave her a little eyebrow waggle and wink. It was the only real indication she had any awareness of Mira's eyes on her, but it injected enough lightness into the connection for Mira to survive the final numbers of the musical and the interminable wait afterward while parents were herded like cattle into the cafeteria to collect their kids.

Thankfully, Ben, Josh, and Izzy exited the orchestra room quickly enough, and Ben made a beeline for her, his cheeks rosy with a happy sort of exertion. He threw his arms around her and squeezed tightly, the perfect balm to her frayed nerves.

"You did so good." She placed a kiss atop his head.

"I had so much *fun*." He practically shivered on the last word. "I don't think I've ever had so much fun at school in my whole life."

She laughed. "I'm glad to hear it."

He leaned back enough to look up at her. "Thank you."

"For what?"

"For letting me do the play, and stay with you, and coming to watch and everything."

She pulled him back to her fiercely. "Thank you! I wouldn't have missed any of it for the world."

"Come on, Ben!" Josh ran by and tapped him on the shoulder. "My parents said Izzy can come get pizza with us before the sleepover."

The kid skidded to an almost stop and said, "Oh, hi, Miss Aunt Mira."

"Hello, Josh. Good job tonight."

He grinned. "Live theater is a blast."

She laughed. "I'm glad you think so."

Ben released her slowly. "My bag is back in the orchestra room. You can come with me, so you don't have to wait in this sweaty crowd."

"Thank God." She did her best to follow him as he threaded his way upstream against the throngs of people heading for the exits. Still, he beat her by a considerable margin, and by the time she made it to the room she'd come to think of simply as Shelby's, he'd already collected his overnight duffle and was hugging her goodbye.

"You did great tonight, kiddo." Shelby tousled his hair. "Don't party too hard."

"I won't," he vowed seriously. "We have two more shows to go. I want to be sharp."

"Attaboy." She patted him on the back. "Have fun."

"Come on, Benny!" Izzy yelled from down the hall.

He paused only long enough to give Mira a one-armed hug. "Love you."

"Love you, too," she called as he took off once more, then watched him all the way until he turned the corner before recognizing the distinct sensation of Shelby's eyes on her.

She closed her eyes to simply let the awareness settle across her skin like a warm breeze before opening them to find those blue irises swirling. Shelby bit her lip as if trying to hold in the extent or maybe the tenor of her smile, but when she finally released it to speak, her voice sounded as low and resonant as the cello she'd played earlier. "Take me home."

***

"I just need to pick up some more contact solution and a change of comfortable clothes, because the thought of putting on a school outfit tomorrow or having to do laundry in the morning

263

makes me want to weep," Shelby explained as Mira pulled into the parking lot of her building.

"I understand." Mira killed the engine. "I'll come up with you."

"Are you sure? You don't have to. I'll only be five minutes."

"Five minutes feels like a cruel eternity after watching you without being able to touch you all night."

"Then, by all means," she said, opening the door of the car. "I'll race you up the stairs."

She heard Mira laughing behind her, and the pure joy surging through her overcame the ache in her feet as her heels clicked their way upward. She didn't falter until she reached her door and had to pause to pull her keys from her clutch. Mira used the full stop to catch up and wrap an arm around her waist. Pulling her close so their bodies spooned together even while standing, she brushed Shelby's hair aside and kissed the back of her neck.

She almost dropped the keys at the press of that mouth against her skin, and didn't quite manage to keep a moan contained as she fumbled with a lock. Finally, the obstacle gave way, and as they tumbled inside, so did any illusions that they'd make it to Mira's tonight.

Kicking the door closed behind them, she barely had time to toss her things on the table in her entryway before they crashed into each other. Mira's hands were everywhere at once, hot and insistent like her mouth. Shelby practically swooned in her arms.

"Steady," Mira whispered. "I've got you."

Shelby tried to say she felt okay, but instead, it only came out as "okay," which also worked, because she had no intention of arguing. She clung to Mira with one arm around her waist and one around her shoulders, as if they intended to ballroom dance their way to the bedroom. They kissed passionately as Mira provided the momentum, and Shelby steered them through another doorway, then toward the mattress and box springs still on the floor.

"Sorry about the mess," she mumbled as she kissed her way along Mira's jaw.

"What mess?" Mira asked, pulling back only enough to meet her eyes. "I only see you."

"Oh, that was smooth."

"I'm serious." Mira lowered her all the way to the bed, kissing her mouth, before standing to shed her blazer. "I've seen only you all night."

She quickly and nimbly unbuttoned her lavender dress shirt and tugged it from her slacks, revealing a black bra, and Shelby shivered in anticipation, knowing everything else would match. Mira was nothing if not perfectly coordinated, but instead of slipping out of any more clothing, she bent to catch one of Shelby's sore feet in her hands. Flipping open the strap of her cute but toe-crushing shoes, she tipped up her heel and slipped it free. Then, without so much as a pause, she began to massage the tender arch.

Shelby tipped her head back and moaned in relief. "You're a goddess."

Mira's laugh rumbled low and smooth. "What celestial being does that make you?"

"What?"

"If I, a goddess, stand completely in awe of you and almost desperate to show my devotion, what does that make you?"

She squirmed as Mira reached her toes and pressed each one. "I think that makes me one very lucky woman."

Mira gently lowered her foot, leaving her bereft for only a second before taking the other one and giving it the same treatment. Never one to miss a detail, she massaged thoroughly from the heel to the tips of her toes, only this time when she finished, she didn't let go. Instead, she replaced her hands with her lips, kissing from the arch up to Shelby's ankle and along her calf muscle.

She eased her legs apart, both creating space and offering invitation as Mira edged onto the bed and upward, pausing to kiss the bend of her knee before dragging her tongue over the increasingly sensitive skin of her inner thigh.

She tried to sit up, eager for the best view of this amazing creature as she did even more amazing things, but her body trembled when skilled hands pushed her dress up out of the way.

"Relax," Mira whispered, and slipped her fingers into the waistband of the French-cut bikini bottoms she'd chosen in anticipation of this exact moment. No sooner had they been stripped away than Mira replaced them with her mouth.

Shelby fell back and released any last intention of doing anything other than melting for this woman. She couldn't even find the wherewithal to tangle her hands in the silky hair still pinned up in a clip, so she settled for clutching the sheets as Mira used her trademark diligence and attention to detail to pull her right to the edge of reason before easing back enough to hold her there. Never in her life had Shelby ever been touched by someone so meticulously attuned to her body. She surrendered to the rhythm of her strokes as the orgasm built from the tips of her toes and flowed up through her veins to curl at her core.

She groaned as Mira eased back once more, leaving her in a flood of her own arousal before the tide began to rise once more. Waiting wasn't a burden, not with the mind-melting things Mira could do with her tongue, and yet the next time she got close, Shelby nearly lifted her hips completely off the bed in an attempt to maintain contact with the source of her pleasure. She didn't want this to end, but something about tonight, Mira's urgency, her persistence, her desire to make this last, gave Shelby just enough reason to think they might not end at all.

The gravity of the thought combined with the physical sensations coursing through her sent her spilling into ecstasy.

Chapter Twenty-Two

Mira yawned and rolled over, eager to snuggle closer to Shelby for both warmth and comfort, but as she worked her arm under the pillow, she became aware that no one's head was weighing it down. She cracked open one eye to confirm she was alone, and not in her own bed. The memories of last night rushed back, and she smiled. Not only had they failed to make it back to her place, they'd barely managed to make it through the door here before she'd simply had to have Shelby. She shook her groggy head, trying to make sense of the person she'd become under the spell of this woman, but she suspected no amount of wakefulness would dull the sharp edge of attraction that cut through her last night.

However, as her other senses roused from sleep, she became aware of a melody wafting faintly in from another room. Straining her ears to hear music, she realized it wasn't a radio. Shelby must be in her practice room. Mira lay back and tried to picture her, relaxed and lithe as the notes poured out of her. The rich, lush sound of the cello soothed, and the emotion Shelby poured into each note spoke volumes even when muted by distance.

Then, a new level of recognition caused her heart to seize as memory made sense of the tune. She sat up, snuggling her knees to her chest as she began to pick out the classical composition of "Can't Help Falling in Love."

A million thoughts raced through her all at once as she processed the meaning of why Shelby would be driven from bed so early to pour that song out into the ether. She suffered conflicting urges to go to her, and also to stay still and listen forever. The warmth flowing through her on every level served as inspiration enough to stay put. Despite her own surging emotion, she had no need to rush through the perfection of this moment.

She swayed slightly as Shelby arced through the bridge of the song and took up the chorus with more vibrato, and as the notes faded out, a steady, pulsing buzz remained. It took her a second to understand that the sound wasn't some underlying hum of music, but rather a series of messages coming through on her phone.

She sighed and reached for it, intending to power it off completely, but at the last second, she realized it might be Ben. A quick glance at the screen filled her with instant regret.

Not Ben, but Vannah had sent her six texts in rapid succession. She closed her eyes as if she could rewind, but her brain simply didn't know how to unlearn some things. Opening them again, she scanned the messages to quickly ascertain that her little sister's disregard for schedules and good order knew no boundaries, and she'd not only caught an earlier flight, she'd now arrive in Buffalo a few minutes after midnight, because of course she would.

She fought the urge to throw the phone across the room and settled on the more restrained avoidance of tucking it under the pillow as she tried to process her own grief. She and Shelby wouldn't even have one last night together before Vannah came crashing in with all the chaos she always carried. She hugged her knees, wishing desperately she'd known last night had been a last of sorts, but as she replayed the evening in her mind, she took solace in knowing she wouldn't have changed a thing.

Rising from the bed with new urgency for the day ahead, she found her underwear but decided to forgo her wrinkled blouse, and instead chose a sweatshirt that smelled like Shelby.

She needed to go to her. They'd already had precious hours stolen from them. She needed her to know, she needed them to face this together, and still, she didn't want to face it at all until absolutely necessary.

Moving through the apartment with an almost desperate desire to find some better way, she pushed open the door to the practice room to find Shelby in all her glory, her profile cast in golden rays from an overhead window. She sat in pajama shorts, completely bare chested with a cello resting between her splayed knees. Her eyes were closed as she played from memory, so serenely beautiful it almost hurt to look at her, but neither could Mira look away. Every other thought that had addled her brain seconds earlier fled, completely overwhelmed by the full sensory overload of this woman. Sight, sound, smell, all surrounded her now. She ached to touch ... and taste.

Stepping forward, she whispered, "Keep playing."

Shelby's eyes flashed open, startling clear and blue, but she didn't miss a beat as she continued to pull her bow languidly across the strings.

Mira shifted to the side then bent to kiss her neck, her shoulder, her spine. She ran her lips up over flexing muscles and down to her collarbone, before turning upward. Placing a hand on the curve of Shelby's waist, she kissed the arc of her throat and along her jaw before reaching her ear. She nibbled at the lobe, and Shelby's concentration finally faltered. Smiling against her temple, Mira slid her hand over the ridges of her ribs to cup the breast not covered by the cello. A discordant note rang out, and when she ran one fingertip around a hard nipple, Shelby's bow failed her completely.

Throwing her head back, she growled, a low rumbling sound. "I cannot play this thing while you play me with the same sort of intensity."

Mira didn't argue as Shelby slipped the cello into its stand. Instead, she merely inserted herself into the spot it had occupied.

"Good morning." Shelby reached up to cup her face in her hands. "I didn't mean to wake you."

"I'm glad you did." Mira kissed her on the mouth. "I love to listen to you."

"It's not like I haven't had enough practice time this week. I just woke up feeling moved by the musical spirit."

"Moved. That's a good word for the power it has over me when I hear you." She glanced down with a smile playing across her lips. "Or see you, for that matter."

"The feeling's mutual." Shelby wrapped her arm around Mira's waist and pulled her close. This time when their mouths met, she deepened the kiss.

She parted her lips, surrendering to Shelby's playful exploration as skilled fingers skimmed over the back of her legs and under the hem of her purloined sweatshirt.

"You look good in my clothes," Shelby murmured as she teased the corner of her mouth with her tongue. "But you look better out of them."

"That could be arranged."

Shelby's only response was to push her hands farther up under the hoodie, causing it to rise as she cupped her breasts in each hand. She got the hint to shed the barrier quickly, but as it fell to the floor, she had to fight not to fall with it. Shelby's fingers burned hot on flush skin, and she rolled her head back to luxuriate in the touch.

"You're stunning." Shelby replaced one of her hands with her mouth, as hot and wet as Mira felt at her center.

She also wanted to touch her everywhere. She wanted it with a ferocity that may've terrified her if she were capable of processing anything other than need. She ran her hands through silken strands of hair, then clutched strong shoulders as Shelby lavished as much attention on her breasts as a person could withstand. Then her knees buckled, and she found herself sinking between toned legs once more, her mouth watering with an almost instinctual intent, but before she was able to kneel fully before her, Shelby caught hold of Mira's ass and pulled her up.

"Oh, no you don't." Closing her legs, she blocked off the access Mira had taken for granted and then used her confusion against her to flip the script by easing her forward until she straddled her lap.

"What?" It wasn't her most eloquent utterance, but she could hardly form a complete thought, much less a coherent question, while her brain remained overwrought from processing so many baser impulses.

Shelby laughed and tugged her down onto her legs, then raked her nails across her inner thighs. "You don't get to take the lead all the time."

"I didn't mean to lead. I only wanted to—"

Shelby cut her off with a kiss. "And I wanted to do this."

She pushed the thin strip of silk and lace between them to the side and skimmed her fingers over Mira's sex.

She gasped and arched back, but Shelby's hand at the base of her spine held her steady as she pushed inside. She inched forward and curled into her. Mira's forehead rested atop Shelby's hair, and she steadied herself with a hand on each shoulder. And then they moved together. Rocking against the friction of their bodies, they rose and fell with each slide of Shelby's fingers in and out. She'd never been this free or filled with anyone, ever, and any shred of restraint she'd clung to evaporated as she surrendered to the sheer eroticism of their coupling.

Her breath came hot and ragged as they clung to each other, working in tandem and at an increasingly insistent pace. She called out as the fervor rose between them and within herself. "Shelby, yes, please."

"Yes." Shelby urged. Curling her fingers upward with exacting pressure at the same time, she ground the heel of her palm in an excruciating circle. Mira's already incoherent babbling devolved into a cry she barely recognized as her body pitched forward and doubled over once more. Shelby held her close, her strong hands both steadying her and driving her higher simultaneously. Shelby was everything, did everything, inspired everything, and in this feverish, transcendent moment, that made more sense than anything Mira had ever known.

***

Shelby lay propped up on one elbow in her own bed feeling languid and sated as Mira stood in front of Shelby's closet in her slacks and a bra. She pushed through several hangers in rapid succession, searching for something, anything in Shelby's wardrobe that would both fit and not look insane with the rest of her attire.

"You can put your blouse from last night back on until we get back to your place."

"No," Mira said with a hint of force in her voice. "I mean, we don't need to go to my place."

"Why not? Your place is comfy, and you could get some more relaxing clothes. Not that I wouldn't actually like to see you in that blazer with nothing underneath. On second thought, let's go with that plan. Put on the blazer, and then we'll go back to your place."

Mira cast a knowing grin over her shoulder and started to turn back toward the bed, then caught herself. "No, we can't. I can't. I can hardly walk after last night."

"I didn't notice anything inhibiting your performance in the practice room this morning ... or the shower afterward."

Mira did finally turn to face her fully and placed her hands on her hips, but when she opened her mouth, no words came out. She only closed it again and shook her head.

"What's wrong? No argument means agreement, doesn't it?"

"You." Mira sighed as if the word constituted a full response.

Shelby had never seen her quite like this before. She'd clearly been thrown off-kilter multiple times over the last twenty-four hours, but what Mira had lost in verbal coherency, she'd more than picked up in sexual acuity. Their lovemaking had been earth shaking. The way Mira took command of the situation, pouring the quiet sort of confidence she displayed in so many other areas into an all-out assault on Shelby's senses, still made her a little light-headed when she remembered it. Then this morning, the sex had taken on a more desperate edge, but they'd managed to convey quite a lot with few words. She shivered at the memory of Mira's mouth sliding up her legs, and thought, not for the first time, that talking might be a bit overrated.

Still, she couldn't quite shake the idea that something in the unspoken undercurrent flowing around them might need articulation.

Mira spun around once more and said, "You know what? Toss me that hoodie again, and we'll figure out breakfast before we head out."

Shelby snagged the sweatshirt and passed it to her. "You're welcome to anything I have, but I'm afraid my cupboards are close to bare, and the milk in the fridge is almost certainly out of date."

Mira grimaced.

"Sorry. I haven't been here all week, and I don't get paid again until Wednesday. Unless you want dry Cheerios, there's no sense scouring my kitchen."

Mira paused long enough to confirm the news threw her off a bit before forcing another smile that didn't quite crinkle her eyes. "Then we'll go out. Do you have a favorite breakfast spot? My treat."

Her jaw tightened, and she rolled back onto the bed. "You've been treating a lot lately."

"I don't mind."

She squinted up at the ceiling. "I think I might be starting to mind."

Mira finally came over to sit on the bed next to her. "Why?"

"Because I don't want to be a freeloader."

"I've never once thought of you that way."

"Thank you, but I'm not exactly your equal in this area. You've been carting me to school all week because my car won't start."

"Yes, but you said you can afford to get it fixed as soon as things slow down at work after the musical."

"And you've paid every time we've gone out to dinner."

"You're helping with Ben. You've completely immersed yourself in the chaos of my life right now. The least I can do is cover some of the expenses associated with you being so present with us."

She bit her lip, wanting to believe that was the only thing behind Mira's generosity.

"But what if I weren't helping with Ben or consumed by the musical? Would you expect me to carry more financial weight?"

Mira hesitated, then opened her mouth and closed it again, affirming Shelby's worst fears.

"I knew it. I mean you're not wrong. I know I'm deficient in this area."

"You aren't deficient in any area."

"It's okay. You don't have to coddle me."

"It's not coddling to acknowledge we're at different stages in our careers."

She laughed. "Thanks for saying careers instead of lives, but yes we are, and I'm trying not to be embarrassed. I know I'm going to need a second job, but I haven't had the chance to search with school taking all my time."

"Ben and I are taking up a lot of your time, too." Mira took her hand. "And I'm not offering to pay you for those hours or anything, but can't I show my appreciation by picking up the tab at Denny's?"

"Why do you have to make everything sound so reasonable?"

Mira finally smiled for real. "I'm an exceedingly reasonable person. I'm told it's one of my most maddening traits."

"It really is, and I suppose I can overlook it a little longer, but I'm serious about getting another job. I could work full time somewhere during the summer."

"Okay." Mira nodded. "Did you have something in mind?"

"I haven't thought about it much." She rolled onto her side. "I hate to fall back on something I thought I'd moved past, but there's a summer camp in the Adirondacks I worked at for several summers through undergrad."

"Summer camp?" Mira sounded almost confused by the concept.

"Yeah, it's a sleepaway thing for music kids. There's cabins and rowboats, but mostly it's music lessons and campfire sing-alongs. It's a bit rustic for my tastes, but the money is good, and they attract great kids. The director all but begged me to come back."

"That's quite a vote of confidence." Mira hopped off the bed. "I'm sure you're very good at the work."

"Yeah." Her chest tightened as Mira began to pace.

"Ben went to a camp like that a few years ago and had a great time."

"Good. Are you okay?"

"Uh-huh. I'm glad you've got an idea to start from, and now we can start planning today. One day at a time, right?"

She arched an eyebrow. One day at a time didn't sound like Mira at all. She planned people's retirements for a living. Something was certainly off, and she wanted to know what before they spun further down that road again. "Hey, what's on your mind right now?"

"Breakfast," she answered too quickly, and then kept talking too fast not to be considered a little frantic. "I think you're right. We could run back to my place, and I'll change before we have to go out again. Let's go to a diner because I'm famished."

Shelby was actually also famished, but more pressingly confused about what sparked this almost manic response. "I actually think we should pause and—"

"Oops," Mira said as her phone began to vibrate in her pocket. "That's probably Ben."

She nodded for her to answer it and ground her back teeth at the timing.

"Good morning, kiddo," Mira said into the phone. "Sure. Did you have fun? That's great. We were just talking about getting breakfast ... no, we haven't eaten yet ...we slept late."

Shelby finally smirked at the explanation, and Mira shot her a conspiratorial grin.

"We'd love to have you join us," Mira continued to Ben. "We're at Shelby's place to pick up a few things. Let me check with her, but I think we can be there to get you in like half an hour if that works for Josh's mom."

Mira turned to her, a subtle pleading in her eyes, and Shelby caved. She didn't want to put this off, whatever *this* was, but she also didn't want to impede any of their fleeting time with Ben, either, so she nodded.

"Yes, that'll work," Mira said. "We'll see you soon, and then we can all go to breakfast together."

Mira hung up the phone. "Thanks for that. He sounds happy."

"I'm glad," she said honestly.

"Me too. And we'd better head out if I'm going to get home and change, but I'm sorry we got interrupted. Was there something else you needed to say before we run?"

Her heart kicked her in the ribs, trying to nudge her forward, but whatever questions were trying to push up from her chest never made it to her voice as she bit her tongue and waved off her concern one more time. "Nothing that can't wait."

Chapter Twenty-Three

"So, you have to leave, like when?"

Mira tensed at the edge in Shelby's voice, and she hated knowing she'd put it there. She hadn't meant to. She'd started to tell her about Vannah's impending arrival hundreds of times over the course of the day, but something else always got in the way. First, Ben wanted to invite Josh and Izzy to breakfast, which ended up being more of a brunch, and then they'd had to run by the school because there was a problem with the sound system, and then by the time they got home, they'd barely had enough time to unpack Ben's overnight bag and begin collecting everything he needed for the next performance. She'd made an honest attempt to connect with Shelby while she showered and got changed, but then her parents had called with an offer to take everyone out for a late meal after the show ended at 7:30, and from then on, they hadn't had a single second alone until right now.

She shook her head. Replaying all the excuses didn't change anything. "I should probably get on the road soon if I want to make it to Buffalo with enough time to park and meet her outside security. I'm sorry."

Shelby seemed almost mystified. "Sorry about what? Telling me this on your way out the door? Not telling Ben at all? Driving through the wee hours of the morning while I worry about you?"

"All of it, and that we haven't had any time to process the fact that my sister will be here in a couple of hours, bringing with her

279

the trauma and grief and chaos she always brings." Her voice cracked. She hadn't meant for it to. She didn't want to get emotional about what was about to happen. She didn't want to think about any of it at all, much less feel the fear and sadness and panic of the changes barreling toward them. "I'm also sorry I'm asking you to stay with Ben while he sleeps, because he needs a full night's rest, but neither his mother nor I can provide that for him tonight, or God knows when again. None of this is fair to you, or to anyone. I understand if it's too much to ask."

"Shh." Shelby lifted a finger to Mira's lips. "Stop. Is this what's been bothering you all day?"

She nodded.

"God, Mira, for someone who's so good at almost everything, you could use some serious work in the communication department."

She nodded and let her chin fall all the way to her chest. "I wanted to tell you. I started to at least five times, but I didn't want to talk about it in front of Ben because he'd want to come with me, and I didn't have the heart to tell him no, but I need time to talk to Vannah, and he needs rest."

Shelby shook her head. "You could've pulled me aside. You could've told me this morning before we picked him up."

"I should have," she admitted. "I have several legitimate excuses, but honestly, if I'd made it a priority, I would've found a way."

"Then why didn't you?"

"Because if I told you, that would make it real, and I don't want it to be real. I wanted to make love to you without anything else between us. I wanted the three of us to have a couple more happy meals. I wanted to watch you and Ben play one more time completely unburdened by sadness or anxiety. I wanted to steal a few more hours of what's been the happiest week of my entire life."

All the defensiveness slid from the set of Shelby's shoulders as she stepped forward and wrapped her in a hug.

Mira leaned into her embrace and rested her chin on her shoulder, filling her lungs with the soothing scent of her. "I'm sorry I'm not better at this."

Shelby squeezed her tighter. "On the bright side, you're fantastic at avoidance. Professional grade really."

"Do you think I should put that on my resumé?"

Shelby's laugh rumbled through her chest. "Probably, but you'll have to wait awhile to make those changes, because right now you need to go pick up your sister."

"What about Ben?"

"I'll stay with him." Shelby straightened and held her at arm's length. "Damn it, Mira, you don't even have to ask. I'd do anything for that kid, but you and I, we need to ... never mind."

"No, go on."

Shelby shook her head. "We both have to brace ourselves for what comes next, and I hoped we'd do the hard parts together."

"I didn't want to do the hard parts at all."

Shelby bit her lip like she wanted to say more, but instead merely hugged her one more time and whispered, "I'll be here when you get home."

The promise echoed through her ears all the way to Buffalo, and yet it didn't quite dispel the sadness settling through her stomach. Shelby would still be there, but nothing else would be the same. Maybe it wasn't even the same right now. It hadn't felt the same since the morning. She hadn't been open and honest, and more than once, she'd noticed Shelby biting back comments as well. Things were unsettled between them, and while a part of her ached for Shelby to blow open all the closing doors, another part of her feared what lay on the other side. They'd lived in blissful oblivion all week, but they hadn't done anything to address what their lives would be like from here on out. Vannah was coming. Ben was leaving. Shelby might be taking a job on the other side of the state for months.

Her teeth chattered as ice spread through her chest at the idea of losing them all at once. By the time she pulled into a parking space, she could hardly make her feet move toward the terminal with the tight grip of dread encasing her.

She shuffled mindlessly, restlessly through the nearly deserted corridors, not bothering to check the arrival board. She couldn't process any more details until a lone figure striding toward her caught her attention.

Suddenly her eyes focused on the most familiar face she'd ever seen, and the two of them ran toward each other. She didn't even mean to run. There was no thought, only instinct, and when she and Vannah collided, they wrapped around each other with the fervor of the small children they'd once been together.

Tears burned Mira's eyes and spilled warmth down her cheeks as Vannah trembled against her chest. In that moment, she knew so fully it was possible to want to love someone deeply and want to shake them senseless at the same time. It wasn't as though Vannah's arrival solved anything. In reality, it potentially made things much worse, and yet she never, ever stopped wanting to have her baby sister safe and close. For all their fights and faults and resentment, she loved her dearly, and when all else failed, at least there was a comfort in the consistency of their dynamic. Mira welcomed consistency wherever she could find it these days.

She pulled back to look Vannah up and down, eager to anchor herself to the familiarity of her, but on closer inspection, she noticed more changes than she'd expected. Without the distance and filter of a computer screen, she could clearly see dark smudges under Vannah's eyes, and her cheekbones seemed more prominent too.

She hugged her again, this time feeling the ridges of her ribs through the thin T-shirt. She'd definitely lost weight she'd never had in abundance. Worry sparked through her, serving as a gateway to the other fears she'd carried since she heard the knock on her door all those weeks ago.

"Come on," she whispered, nudging her toward the exit. "Let's get home."

Vannah nodded. "Sounds good."

She took her single suitcase and wheeled it to the car for her, then waited until they'd pulled onto the thruway before testing the waters. "How was your flight?"

"The one from Belize City to Miami was a bit rough, but this last one went smoothly enough, and they had snacks."

"Do you need to stop for something? I don't know what's open this time of night, but maybe some fast food, or a gas station?"

"No, I'm ready to hit a nice, soft bed."

"I'm not sure how great my foldout couch will be. Maybe I should've had Ben sleep out there so you could take his bed."

"No, the couch will be heaven, and I want to surprise him in the morning."

"He'll be surprised all right."

"Happy surprised, though, right?"

"Of course," Mira said. "He's missed you so much."

"He hasn't answered a couple of my calls this week."

Mira hadn't known that, but she tried not to let it show. "This week has been super busy. We've been trying to fit in all the things he wanted to do before he left, and the musical has consumed our lives. Any spare minute he's had has been spent running around with his new best friends. He actually spent the night with Josh last night, and then they made us pick up Izzy for brunch this morning. He's hardly been home."

Vannah didn't respond. She merely rested her head on the window and stared out at the passing cars.

Finally, Mira couldn't take it anymore. "What's wrong?"

"Nothing."

"Come on Van, you can talk to me."

"Why do you assume something has to be wrong?"

"Because you've lost weight, you've got circles under your eyes, and you're barely talking, which is totally not like you."

"Can you not start right now?" Vannah snapped.

Mira gripped the steering wheel a little tighter and waited.

"Look, I'm tired from traveling. I worked right up until the moment I had to leave. I work all the time, but so do you, so no lectures about spreading myself too thin, please."

"Okay."

"I've got a lot to do in the next few days, but I'm handling it, and I don't need you questioning my methods or reading too much into things that are totally normal for people executing an international move."

"Okay," she said again. Of course, Vannah was right. Everything could be explained. Nothing had to be wrong for someone to be tired during a major transition. The logic all checked out, only this time, logic felt as hollow as the darkness starting to creep in around her. Something was off. Vannah wasn't telling her the whole story. Ben was leaving in a matter of days. Shelby might be leaving for months, too. Everywhere she turned, she found something else she didn't want to face, something she couldn't control, or something she didn't know how to manage.

The world spun around her. Vacation had ended. So had the best week ever.

What was next?

No. She couldn't think that way. She couldn't play what-ifs or go poking around trying to find the next disaster. She had to focus on what she could control and shut the doors on all extraneous threats. She didn't know any way to make it through other than to choose the most direct path straight forward.

Only as she began to shut down parts of herself, slamming doors one by one on everything she didn't have the skill or energy to deal with, she couldn't help but realize she didn't have much of anything good left, either.

***

Shelby hadn't been able to sleep. She couldn't make herself lie down in Mira's bed without her, so she'd sat in the living room for the last two hours trying to replay the conversation she'd had with Mira ... and the ones she hadn't.

She couldn't argue with any of the base facts. Their day had gotten absurdly busy, and of course they didn't want to talk about Vannah in front of Ben or her parents, and she even shared Mira's desire to hang onto the good they'd created before Vannah came crashing in. She understood avoidance. She still had a broken-down car in her parking spot. She could avoid problems with the best of them. So, if she understood all the things leading to this moment, why did it still feel horrible?

She was still pondering the question when Mira pulled into the driveway. Shelby went to the door and opened it, only to be surprised when someone smaller and more frantic pulled her into a hug. The hair was the same, but the body was different, as was the smell, but the voice was almost the same as it said, "Thank you for taking care of Ben!"

Shelby's brain struggled to process being hugged rather fiercely by Vannah.

"You're welcome." She finally let herself relax into the embrace this woman clearly needed to give. This was Vannah, the person whose shadow had hung over their lives for weeks. Mira's sister, so alike and so not. And this was Ben's mom, the woman who brought him into the world and into her life, and also the one who'd take him away.

Vannah stepped back and looked her up and down. "You're even cuter in person."

"Um, thanks."

Vannah glanced over her shoulder and gave Mira an appreciative nod. "I'm impressed."

Mira rolled her eyes and held out the suitcase she'd pulled up the walk. "You're sleeping on the couch."

"Fine, fine. I can take a hint."

Shelby stood back and let them enter. Mira stopped to give her a little kiss on the cheek before saying, "She's not wrong. You are very impressive."

She smiled despite her misgivings moments earlier. "I'm glad you think so."

"I do," Mira said solemnly. "I appreciate everything you've done for me and Ben lately."

"I love Ben." She cupped her cheek in one palm. "And I'm pretty fond of you, too. Are you okay?"

Mira cast a pointed glance over at Vannah, who'd lifted her suitcase onto the coffee table and begun to rummage through it. "I'm fine."

She heard the words, but she also heard the tone in which they were delivered, and the two didn't go together.

"I'm going to go peek in on Ben," Vannah declared.

"If you wake him up now, he won't get back to sleep for hours."

"Seriously?" Vannah said quickly. "I haven't seen my kid in weeks."

"I know. That's why I'm worried that if you peek in on him, you won't be able to stop yourself from hugging him."

"Then, I'll hug him. I'm his mom."

"That's never been in dispute, but if you're going to wake him up, I don't know why we went through this whole midnight surprise airport run in the first place."

Vannah shook her head and turned to Shelby as if she might help. "Has she been like this the whole time?"

Shelby didn't know what to say, and she definitely didn't want to step into the tension between those two, but she rose to Mira's defense anyway. "She's been amazing with Ben."

Vannah's expression softened slightly. "I know ... but I'm still going to watch him sleep."

She tiptoed down the hallway and pushed open Ben's door softly before Mira turned to Shelby looking utterly exasperated. "I say this a lot, but I'm sorry things are such a mess."

"Me too. Was it weird picking her up?"

Mira shrugged. "Yes and no."

She waited for more, but Mira kept stealing glances down the hallway.

"What do you need?" Shelby finally asked.

"What?" Mira blinked at her as if she'd forgotten she was still in the room. "I don't know. I mean nothing. What do you need?"

"I guess some guidance. I want to help you through this, but there's clearly family dynamics at play, and I don't want to step on any toes or get in the way."

"Yeah." Mira rubbed her face with her hands. "I suppose Ben and Vannah are going to need some time together in the morning. We've probably got a lot to process, and I don't even know what my role will be."

"I get it." Shelby bit back her own unease. "I should probably sleep at my place tonight."

"Probably." Mira accepted the offer a little too quickly for Shelby's liking. "I can drive you home. Do you need to get any of your stuff from my room?"

"Let me go check." She didn't need anything she couldn't do without until tomorrow, and honestly, it was already tomorrow, but she welcomed the opportunity to step away and collect herself. She walked into the bathroom and tried to anchor herself. She stared at the massive tub, wanting to believe she'd be back there with Mira soon. Then she noticed her toothbrush on the vanity. Should she take it home? She had another one at her apartment, and an extra bottle of contact solution, too. She wasn't leaving for good, and yet this did feel like an ending.

No, she was being melodramatic. It was nearly 2:00 a.m. after long, busy days. She needed sleep. They all needed sleep.

She plastered a smile on her face and returned to the entryway where Mira and Vannah both waited wordlessly.

"I think I've got everything I need at home," she said. "It was nice to finally meet you in person, Vannah."

She beamed and pulled her into another hug. "You, too. I'm thrilled you've been here for Mira and Ben. I can't wait to talk more tomorrow. We're hanging out, right?"

Mira cleared her throat. "She and Ben both have a matinee tomorrow, and school on Monday. Let's play it by ear."

Vannah waved her off. "Ben doesn't have to go to school on Monday. You should play hookie, too!"

Mira pinched the bridge of her nose. "Tomorrow. Can we please press pause until tomorrow?"

"I should get to bed," Shelby said to Vannah, and caught Mira's arm and steered her out the door.

They walked to the car in silence and wound through the dark streets of town in the same fashion while Shelby began to rack her brain for something, anything to break through the chill radiating off Mira. In the end, words failed her, and she reached for her hand. The touch soothed her, and she intertwined their fingers.

Mira turned into the parking lot of her building and put the car in park but didn't turn it off. "It's late. Do you want me to walk you up?"

"I'll be okay, but what about you?"

"I'm sure I can find my way back to my place."

"That's not what I meant."

"I know." Mira rolled her head to either side. "I don't know what else to say."

She squeezed her hand. "What else do you want to say?"

"Nothing. I just want to go to sleep."

"Okay." She didn't love that. She didn't love much about this whole scenario. She didn't love not knowing what was running through Mira's mind. She didn't love not knowing where they'd go from here. She didn't love feeling helpless or lonely. She didn't love the prospect of pushing her for more than she had to give, but she absolutely hated Mira feeling closed off.

"We'll talk tomorrow?"

"Sure," Mira agreed. "We'll pick you up before the show and take you to school."

That hadn't been what she meant at all, but the longer this went on, the worse she felt, so she leaned in and kissed Mira on the cheek. "Call me if you need anything before then."

"I will," Mira said, then waited until she was about to close the door before adding, "and thank you ... for everything."

Her heart twisted at the gravity of her tone and the subtle hint of finality in the words.

She wanted to climb back in the car, grab her face, kiss her senseless, and then demand she tell her what the hell she was thinking. She wanted to throw a fit, to shout, to shake her, anything to bring Mira's attention back and force her not to pull away. She wanted to drive back to her house or pull her up the stairs and refuse to let her go until they found something, anything to hold onto the closeness they'd shared less than twenty-four hours ago.

However, when she ducked down to try to meet Mira's eyes, she realized it was too late. She was already gone.

Chapter Twenty-Four

"What did you think?" Ben bounded up to them exuberantly after the matinee performance.

"I think you're a superstar," Vannah said with dramatic flair before Mira had a chance to speak.

"I meant about the show."

"Ah, yes, that was wonderful, too, but you outshone everyone else on stage or off it."

"Mom." He laughed. "You couldn't even see me."

"No, but I could *hear* you." Vannah closed her eyes and swayed to music in her memory. "I know the sounds of my son's songs. I could always pick them out even when you were a baby in the nursery, and now you're sharing them with the world, and my heart is so full of pride and joy."

He smiled at her so broadly it stretched his whole face.

Mira's own heart felt full as well, but in a way that caused a little stress and strain. He'd smiled at her plenty of times over the last few weeks, and there were moments when he absolutely exuded joy, but at no point had his eyes carried the complete adoration they did in this moment.

Mira's gaze wandered over to Shelby automatically at the mere thought of adoration. She was chatting with a couple of parents only a few feet away and wearing another black dress, though she'd traded the heels for ballet flats. Mira had to stifle the urge to go to her, to slip an arm around her waist, to snuggle into her neck and breathe in the soothing scent of her shampoo.

She didn't deserve to seek comfort from her, not after the awkwardness between them over the last twenty-four hours, which she took full responsibility for, and yet had little idea how to offer amends. She wondered again why it couldn't be easier for them. Darrin and Jane had met, decided they were interested in one another, and gone on three dates in seven days. There'd been little waffling or wavering, no family drama, no communication complications, and little overthinking as far as she could tell. Was that how these things were supposed to work? And if so, where did that leave her?

"Hi, Ben's Aunt Mira." Izzy rushed up to her. "Josh said Ben can't come to the cast party. Is that for real?"

Mira shook her head, trying to pull herself back together. "No, I don't mind if he ... I mean, he needs to ask his mom."

"Oh yeah, duh," Izzy said sadly. "I forgot his mom came to take him away."

"I'm the mom." Vannah stepped forward. "You must be Izzy, and what's this about a cast party?"

"Hello, Ben's mom. All of us, everybody who helped with the play, gets to go to a party in the gym and have dinner and dancing and celebrate."

Vannah glanced at Ben. "Did you not want to go?"

He shrugged. "You just got here. I didn't think I should leave you again so soon."

"I did plan to take you out for dinner to celebrate your success, but a cast party is a pretty big experience to miss out on." Vannah hugged him. "You're the best boy in the whole world, which is why I think you should do whatever you want to do."

He looked from her to Izzy and back again. "It won't hurt your feelings if I stay?"

"Not a bit. We'll be together all the time for the next few months."

He grinned. "I do want to play with my friends some more."

Vannah pulled him close once more, and Mira noticed her smile faltered slightly as she said, "Then, go. Party on!"

"Yes!" Izzy cheered and caught him by the arm before giving it a sharp tug and shouting, "Joshie, he can stay!"

Shelby glanced up at the commotion, and Mira caught her eye. She nodded toward the door, wanting to talk to her, to touch her, to take her home, but instead of smiling, Shelby shook her head, and once again, she was at a loss as to what to do. They hadn't had any chance to talk, not seriously, for two days. After the total mess she'd created the day before, her whole morning had been consumed with Ben and Vannah. They'd given Shelby a ride to the school, of course, but a car full of people didn't offer an optimal opportunity to have meaningful conversations. Mira had pinned her hopes on tonight to regroup.

"I have to chaperone the cast party," Shelby said casually over her shoulder as she picked up her cello by the neck.

"You do?"

She nodded.

"I didn't know." She kicked herself for not having something better to say.

Shelby finally turned to face her fully. "We didn't get this far in the schedule planning."

"No, I guess not." She hadn't gotten this far in planning anything. She'd steadfastly avoided imagining this weekend, and now she felt almost bereft at the realization that, in refusing to acknowledge she might need Shelby with her, she hadn't considered the possibility of her not being there.

"I'll need to stay until all the kids are accounted for, and then help clean up. I'll have one of the other teachers drop me off at home."

She tried to take deep, steady breaths as this kept getting worse.

293

"I want to let you all have some family time tonight," Shelby continued evenly, "but maybe you can call me later if you're up for it?"

She nodded. "Okay. And we'll still give you a ride to school tomorrow."

"I'd appreciate that."

"Me too," Mira admitted.

Shelby smiled as if she found the response endearing, but before she had a chance to say anything else, a child called her from the doorway to the auditorium. "Sorry, I have to go."

"Yeah. Sure. Go." The words sounded staccato leaving her lips, but she didn't think Shelby noticed as she turned and wound her way between chatting families. Mira watched her go, and her disappointment must've shown because Vannah threw an arm around her shoulder and said, "We both got dumped for the appeal of an after-party."

"She's a teacher. She has to stay."

"And mine's a kid. He's supposed to want to be around his friends more than his mom, but that doesn't make it sting any less."

"I guess not. Is this the first time he's chosen his peers over you?"

Vannah nodded as they walked toward the exit. "Yup. What about you?"

"Shelby's worked insane hours for weeks, but last night was the first we've spent apart in a while, and it looks like tonight will be another."

"You know you don't have to on my account, right?"

She did, only she couldn't remember why she hadn't the night before. Had she been too overloaded to process how much she'd wanted Shelby to stay, or afraid to admit it? "I think I'm not great at relationships."

Vannah snorted.

"What?"

"I've never heard you admit to needing improvement on anything."

"I've never thought myself flawless."

Vannah pushed open the door to the school, and they stepped into the cool air of early evening. "No, but you've never been one for introspection, either. You've always gone about things so efficiently, and anything you didn't know, you simply learned. Remember when I got pregnant and you read those books on sleep patterns and placentas and swaddling?"

"I found them very helpful."

"No doubt, but you were still terrified the first time I handed Ben to you."

"He was still slippery!"

Vannah laughed. "You learned by doing, by holding, except for swaddling. You were already a pro there, but the rest you figured out by guess and check, just like I did."

"It's an awfully big risk to play guessing games with people's lives and emotions."

"All of life is a pretty big risk."

They reached her car, and Vannah climbed right in, but Mira paused as her stomach tightened. She didn't appreciate the sentiment, or the way it made her feel, so when she finally settled in behind the steering wheel she said so.

"I don't agree. I'm sorry. I know you accept risk as a given, but it has to be balanced with rewards. It has to be calculated and mitigated, not something you shrug your shoulders about and plunge in anyway. You have to constantly assess possible outcomes."

"Oy vey." Vannah threw her head back and stared at the roof. "Are you going to do this right now?"

"Do what?"

"The bit where you try to talk me out of going back because it's not the choice you'd make?"

"No." At least that's not what she'd intended to do.

"I know this seems wild to you. And maybe it didn't to me enough at first, I can admit that. I didn't understand the full scope of what it takes to get a business off the ground at first. I work all the time." She sighed wearily. "All the time."

"Is everything okay?"

"No, not all the time, but the upside is that it has the potential. For the first time, I can envision a real life for Ben and me."

"And you can't do that a little closer to home?" Mira's voice cracked.

"It's not like I haven't tried, but we haven't exactly thrived here. I'm not like you. I can't sit in an office all day, and working in bars and salons and picking up odd gigs barely keeps us scraping by. I want to do something more with my life and create something better for Ben at the same time."

"But he's got something good here now."

"I know," Vannah snapped, "and I hate that I'm pulling him away from it. I see it now. I see how happy he is with his lessons and his friends and the school, and I both love and hate that you were able to give him those things when I never could."

The anguish in Vannah's voice caught her off guard.

"Maybe if I'd been able to do more for him here, we would be having a different conversation. Maybe I would've kept working the dead-end jobs, but it wasn't an either-or choice. We had *neither*."

"But if there were a safer option where you'd both thrive, you'd take it?"

"Why do you keep asking me that? I know I'm a free spirit, but do you really think I'm some hopeless thrill junkie? Because so far, I feel like I've played it too safe." Vannah shook her head sadly. "I haven't taken any major chances. I've merely traded one unfulfilling prospect for another, and I'm tired of being run down and lonely. I want Ben and me to be part of a community. I want us to feel connected. I want him to see me chasing my dreams to show him how to chase his. I want to show him balance and beauty and passion and meaningful relationships with work and joy, both with other people, and to his own sense of self-worth."

Mira sat back. She didn't have any easy answers or rebuttals. She couldn't claim to offer solutions for Vannah that she hadn't found in her own life. She had a job and home and retirement plan, but she didn't have any of the things her sister was actively working toward, and for the first time, she understood her pursuit.

"I know this could end badly," Vannah finally said, "but the same could be said for me staying here and continuing to do all the things that haven't worked for years. Life is a gamble either way."

Mira shook her head, still not ready to grant her that point.

"Don't shake your head at me," Vannah said. "Maybe you'd have gotten away with being sanctimonious six weeks ago, but not after I saw the way you look at Shelby."

She tensed. "What's that supposed to mean?"

"You're rolling the dice with that one."

"I don't know what you're talking about?"

"She's like ten years younger than you. She's an artist. She seems fun."

"So?"

"Does she want kids? Does she want to travel? Does she have a solid investment portfolio?"

"I don't know," she snapped, sounding defensive, but she didn't know why.

"You've known her six weeks and you don't have a five-year plan?" Vannah laughed. "You must be slipping. When was the last time you had something this big in your life without making a myriad of contingency plans?"

Her palms pricked with sweat. "I don't know."

"I'm not busting your chops here. I'm impressed. I approve of you doing something wildly out of character."

"I wouldn't go that far."

"Then you're not being honest with yourself. Shelby's a huge change in your life. She's already forcing you out of your tiny box of control. She's a wild card, and yet you look at her like she's the most perfect thing you've ever seen. I saw you watching her tonight. I see how much you're already leaning on her."

Mira couldn't deny the charge. She'd leaned on Shelby constantly over the last few weeks. She'd come to depend on her as both a companion and a source of comfort, not to mention the way she'd connected with her romantically or sexually. Shelby had seen every part of her stripped bare.

"It takes a lot of guts to open yourself up to that kind of vulnerability, a much bigger risk than trying a new job. People switch jobs all the time. A relationship, that could be forever ... or not."

The tension in Mira's chest tightened nearly to the point of pain. She hadn't seen anything she'd done with Shelby as inherently risky, and yet now that Vannah had spelled things out so clearly, she couldn't think of anything else. Was that why she'd had trouble articulating her feelings? Why she hadn't let herself plan too far ahead? Why she'd all but shut down when Shelby'd mentioned taking a summer job far away? Had a part of her always, if subconsciously, braced for her to leave? She'd said so herself several times that she wasn't good at relationships. She'd never managed one successfully before, and with Shelby, there seemed to be more at stake than with anyone else.

"Have you stopped speaking to me?" Vannah finally asked.

She shook her head, then realized that might still constitute not speaking. "I think you may be right."

Vannah clutched her chest. "What? Me? Right? Did people in hell just get some ice water? Please tell me more."

She didn't. She couldn't. She merely started the car and pulled out of the parking lot, driving numbly toward home. She hadn't considered a future with Shelby a risky proposition. She hadn't considered a future with her at all.

She'd learned to trust her. She'd leaned on her. She'd wanted to protect and be close to her and feel her wrapped around her. She'd made love to her. She'd admitted, at least to herself, that she didn't want Shelby to leave, but she hadn't told her the same. She hadn't told her hardly anything.

"Hey," Vannah finally whispered. "I'm sorry. I didn't mean to joke. What's wrong?"

"Shelby accused me of not being open enough with her, and I believed I was doing the best I could. I thought I wasn't good at it yet. I even worried I might be incapable of that kind of intimacy, but now ... now I'm worried it's worse. After hearing you talk about the risk, and actually thinking about her leaving, I'm worried I might not *want* to be capable of assuming that level of risk and I'm not sure what that means for the future of our relationship"

***

Shelby stood outside her apartment building on Monday morning feeling like a silly, overgrown kid waiting for the school bus. She shot a disdainful glance at her car, feeling its betrayal more acutely after a restless night when even her sheer exhaustion after a weekend of middle school musicals couldn't overcome the disappointment when Mira didn't call.

She was quickly approaching the point where she didn't have a right to be surprised at the lack of communication, but it still hurt. She wanted to be understanding, and she certainly had plenty of empathy for the upheaval Mira faced this weekend, but she'd risen to every challenge she'd faced so far. Why couldn't she do the same with Shelby? One phone call wasn't too much to ask after everything they'd been through.

Mira pulled into the parking lot right on schedule, and Shelby's traitorous heart beat a little faster at the mere sight of her, but the rhythm faltered when she pulled close enough to reveal she was alone in the car.

"Where's Ben?" she asked the moment she yanked open the door.

"He's not coming to school today. He's sleeping in, and then he's got a physical and a dentist appointment in Buffalo."

"But he's coming back tomorrow?" Shelby tried to sound confident as she climbed in, but it came out more like a question.

"No." The word sounded strangled, and Mira put the car back in gear and pulled out of the parking lot, her eyes refusing to meet hers. "He's leaving Wednesday. They fly out at 5:00 p.m."

Shelby almost doubled over from that kick to the gut. "He's not going to get to say goodbye to his teachers, his classmates, me?"

Mira finally turned to look at her. "I wouldn't let him go without saying goodbye to you."

"Really?"

"Of course not. Do you think I would—"

"I don't know." She cut her off forcefully. "I don't know what I think you would or wouldn't do in the way of communication right now. I don't know what you're thinking at all. I don't know when you planned to tell me any of this."

"I didn't know any of this until last night."

"But you didn't call me when you found out. I'm not the first person you thought to reach out to when you got that news?"

"I'm sorry."

"I don't want any more apologies. I want explanations. Mira, you owe me that. Did you not want to talk to me? Did you go hide and pretend none of this was happening? Did you talk to someone else?"

"I," Mira started, then her face twisted as if she didn't want to say what was about to come next. "I called Jane and had to amend my schedule for tomorrow and move up a meeting to today."

"The schedule." Shelby laughed bitterly. "Of course. The schedule needs care and tending, but I don't."

"It's not that simple."

"It never is, Mira. There's always some complexity, and I've been here for all of it. I haven't once shied away from the fact that your life is a mess. My life is a mess, too."

"It's more than that today. I don't have time to explain everything on the way to school, and even if I did, I don't even know how to start."

"I need you to try."

"And I will, but this morning, I have an important meeting I need to face with a clear head. I might be able to call you tonight, and maybe I'll have more, but I don't know what I can say at this point."

"Might? Maybe? Do you hear yourself? You can't even commit to speaking to me openly and honestly sometime in the next twenty-four hours?" Shelby's voice rose with her righteousness.

"I know you want answers—"

"I want more than I'm getting. I'm not asking you to go lasso the moon, or pull out a crystal ball, but it's not unreasonable to want my girlfriend to tell me what's happening in her head or her heart. I've been with you for the good and the bad and the fear and the confusion and the joy. I've felt every emotion, grappled with every decision, worried about every possible outcome, dreamed of a better way. I don't deserve to be cut out now."

"I'm not cutting you out of anything good or solid or worth hanging onto," Mira snapped back as she turned into the school parking lot. "Is it such a crime to not want to drag you into my darkness and confusion?"

"That's what you *are* doing by shutting the door on me." Shelby refused to relent. "I'm still scared, confused, and angry. Can't you understand that whatever you're facing, I'm facing it too, and I'd rather have you by my side in the dark than be here alone."

Mira parked the car and turned to face her, looking genuinely mystified. "No."

"No what?"

"No, I didn't think you'd rather be caught up in my chaos than on your own. I don't know a lot of things right now. I've never been in this position before."

"Neither have I. I've never fallen head over heels for a woman so fast or become so completely enamored of a kid. I'm not sure what you think my life is like, but I've never forged something so meaningful or strong in such a short period of time and then had someone else blow in and shake everything back to its foundation." Shelby shook her head, waiting for some spark of recognition or connection from Mira, but her eyes had grown hazy and unfocused, so she pushed on. "There's no playbook for what we've been through in the last month and a half. I know I'm younger and less experienced and flat broke, and I don't have my shit together nearly as much as you do, but did I miss a memo somewhere?"

"What do you mean?"

"Does someone ever sit you down and give you directions on the proper procedures for when your girlfriend's sister arrives to take her nephew, who you adore, to a foreign country?"

Mira shook her head. "I don't think so, but to clarify, when I said I'd never been in this position before, I didn't just mean with my family. I mean the position I'm in with you."

"And what position is that?"

"A relationship. I mean I have been in relationships, but not like this." Mira gestured between them as if that explained anything.

"A relationship like what?"

"Like the way you make me feel. The others have always been calm and measured and logical, and you ..."

"Aren't," Shelby finished, her voice hollow. "Okay. There it is. I'm not calm or measured or logical. Right, because I'm sitting here yelling at you while you drive me because my car is broken, and I'm too scattered and broke to get it fixed. Oh my God, you're not pulling away because your life is chaotic. You're pulling away because I am."

"No, of course not."

"Why not? You've said all along, this isn't your real life, the steady existence you crave. Here's your opportunity to get back to that, right?" Her heart seized with the pain of the realization. "Vacation is over."

"Shelby, please give me some time to sort out my feelings."

"What about my feelings? Have you thought about those?"

Mira blinked a few times and cocked her head to the side as if trying to process the questions.

"Clearly no. I've spent all our time together biting my tongue and giving you space and making accommodations for every single complication, and I never once resented that because I always thought it went both ways. I believed you'd do the same

303

for me. I thought that when it was my turn to freak out or fall apart, you would be my person."

"I want to be."

"But you aren't actually doing it," she sighed, "and I refuse to believe you can't do better. Each time you set your mind and your heart and your focus to do something, you rise to the occasion. I deserve the same, Mira. I didn't let myself believe so until right this moment, because I'm less established and more insecure and my problems seemed so trivial compared to what you're dealing with, but I've been a good partner to you."

"You have been," Mira said solemnly.

"I may not be your equal in every way, but I've listened and pondered and shared everything, and damn it, that has value. It has to have value because let me tell you, being on the other side of the equation where you need those things and you don't get them feels awful."

"You're right, one hundred percent." Mira's voice trembled. "And I'm so sorry I haven't been able to give you the parity you deserve."

"Haven't been able to?" Shelby pushed. "Or won't?"

Mira's face went white. Her mouth opened but no words came out, and the absence of them actually spoke rather clearly.

"Great." She opened the door. "That's exactly what I needed to hear, or not hear as the case may be."

"Shelby." Mira finally reached for her hand, too late.

She pulled back and got out of the car. "No, it's fine. I mean, it's not fine, but I will be. You go ahead and get to your meeting. Wouldn't want my chaos to wreck your carefully laid plans."

"Please," Mira pleaded.

She shook her head. "You don't have a right to ask me for anything else until you figure some things out. Call me when you do ... or don't, because if you're not ready to let me in all the way,

I'd honestly rather you not open the door a little only to close me out again next time things get messy."

Then, she slammed the car door, turned on her heel, and walked away without letting Mira see the pain spiking through her with each step.

Chapter Twenty-Five

Mira watched her disappear into the school, but she couldn't bring herself to drive away. She couldn't do anything. She couldn't think or even breathe fully, the same way she couldn't bring herself to spit out an answer when Shelby gave voice to the one question she hadn't been able to fully face.

Why hadn't she just told her she didn't want her to go? Or said she needed her and wanted to be with her? For so long, she'd worried saying those things out loud would leave herself vulnerable to getting hurt, but here she was, vulnerable and hurting anyway. And pretending like she wasn't about to lose everything hadn't stopped her fears from coming to fruition. Then again, she hadn't built a great track record for getting what she asked for either. She'd all but begged Vannah not to take Ben, and look where that got her.

Ben. Her heartache doubled. What would she do if she lost every person she loved in the space of two days? How could she return to her empty house or her quiet office and not crumble under the grief and isolation, or the meaninglessness of it all?

She froze, or maybe she'd been frozen because she hadn't moved since Shelby slammed the door, but something about that last thought caused her brain to stop whirring. Had she really just thought of her old life as empty and isolated, or worst of all, meaningless?

No. She pursed her lips and shook her head. That couldn't be right. Her fears centered around losing Ben and Shelby, and even

Vannah, but not because she didn't want to go back to being who she used to be. She liked who she'd been before everything got turned upside down. She spent weeks wanting nothing more than to return to her real life. She loved her quiet little house and her steady job and time to think.

She backed out of her parking space and drove slowly as she ruminated on the last item of her list. When was the last time she'd been able to think clearly? She mentally traced a path back through recent events until she hit the moment before Vannah knocked on her door. She'd been talking to Larry about business. She'd pored over facts and figures in black and white. She'd made objective decisions based on fact and reason. Most importantly, she'd felt secure in her steadfast refusal not to take silly gambles. More than secure, she'd felt superior.

She drove through town, not paying much attention anymore to where she was headed or who she might be headed toward. Her body moved on autopilot, almost detached from the path her mind had wandered down as she compared the old to the new. Previous versions of herself had accomplished everything she'd striven toward, never failing to achieve any serious goal, in sharp contrast to her inability to master the level of self-revelation Shelby expected of her. She'd been confident in her competence as opposed to worrying she might be incapable of learning the skills she needed to be successful in a relationship. She'd kept her schedule orderly as opposed to the chaos consuming her now. She'd been reasonable and levelheaded as opposed to emotional and out of control, like she felt when begging Shelby to stay and accept her apologies, yet again.

Literally everything about the person she'd been before seemed preferable to everything she'd become, and yet the thought of going back left her near panic.

She pulled into her own driveway without intending to return home instead of going to work, and her hands trembled as she fumbled with her seat belt, but she didn't fight her own instincts as she strode shakily toward the house. She moved like a ghost past Vannah sleeping on the couch and down the hallway, pausing only when she placed a hand on the door to a room that would be Ben's for only two more nights.

The emotions rushing up nearly clogged her throat completely, and she struggled to get enough air to her lungs. Tears stung her eyes, and her chest burned, giving way to a distant sort of awareness that she might be having an anxiety attack, but understanding something and knowing how to change it were two different skills.

Leaning on the door, she eased it open slowly and waited for her eyes to adjust to the dim light until she could make out Ben's sleeping form under the covers. The sight of his serene features felt like another sharp jab to the heart. Nothing in her former life, superior as it may have been, had prepared her for this kind of pain. She would've thought safety preferable even an hour ago, but now, faced with the very real prospect of saying goodbye, she started to wonder.

Did safer actually mean better?

She gritted her teeth against the reality she'd never wanted to face, the one where she might be forced to admit the existence she'd cherished might pale in comparison to the one she'd always avoided.

Her brain burned in rebellion. She couldn't think of the life she'd always striven to lead as hollow or broken, but then she looked at Ben again. He'd been there only six weeks, and she carried a profound certainty that he'd take a part of her heart when he left. How much worse would it be when Shelby did the same?

She sank lightly onto his bed, no longer trusting her body to hold her upright under the weight of her own realizations. If she let Shelby in deeper, if she opened up fully only to lose her when she came up short or was inflexible or incapable, it would shatter her in ways that saying goodbye to Ben never could. At least when he left, she'd have Vannah to blame. She'd spent a good deal of her life blaming Vannah, but with Shelby, she'd finally have to contend with the fear of her own inadequacies. Without logic and statistics, fear would be all she had left.

Half of all marriages end in divorce. She'd heard the quips enough times to understand the odds of long-term success, and she and Shelby weren't even married. They'd practically just met. How many relationships failed somewhere between the one-month mark and marriage? She didn't have hard numbers, but probably more than half. To bet her whole heart on someone she'd known only a short time felt almost idiotic. She wouldn't take those odds in any other area of her life. She couldn't gamble something as valuable as her sense of self or her emotional future on some wild hope or whim. She didn't have that level of risk in her, and she found it horrifying so many others did.

Her heart tried to make a rebound, pushing against her chest, but she didn't make decisions with her heart. She made them with her brain. She wasn't a wishy-washy person. She couldn't make life-altering decisions like falling in love ...

This time she gasped, and Ben stirred slightly but didn't rouse.

Had she fallen in love with Shelby?

Without considering the cost or the consequences?

She couldn't. She simply couldn't surrender to that line of reason, or lack of reason. Being in love with someone didn't change the odds. If she surrendered to her emotions simply because she felt good, or because her gut or her heart had decided to insert itself into a process in which it didn't belong, she'd be no better than ... Vannah.

And there it was.

The door she'd fought to keep locked flung wide open. The worst of all her fears. The one that kept her from processing Ben's departure, the one that held her tongue instead of being honest with Shelby, the one that pushed her silently every day in every situation. If she let her emotions overrule her sensibilities, she'd be just like Vannah.

She built her entire world in opposition to the terrifying possibility of being like the person who frightened her most, and falling head over heels in love with someone in a matter of weeks would be exactly like Vannah. She'd watched her do it time and time again. Each new job, each new rock band, each new hobby, they were all supposed to be "the one" like every boy she'd met along the way.

She glanced down at her sleeping nephew. That's where he'd come from. Vannah had been absurdly in love with his father from the first night she saw him, until well after he'd left her alone with a baby on the way. Mira had been livid at him, but not nearly as mad as at Vannah for making such a silly, stupid mistake of trusting him enough to let him take so much from her.

Ben rolled over onto his back, his small, smooth face angling toward the light from the hallway, and tears filled her eyes, making the scene shimmer before they spilled down her cheeks.

How had she ever been so painfully wrong? This perfect, beautiful, sensitive, artistic, joy of a little boy had brought nothing but love and light into her life. How could she have seen any part of making him as a mistake?

Vannah had known the truth since the moment she found out she was expecting. She'd understood immediately what a gift he was. She'd given him all the pieces of herself, refusing to clutter them with worry or regret or trepidation. She'd seen only the blessing he'd be.

Mira leaned forward and brushed a strand of dark hair from his forehead. What if Vannah had been more responsible? What if she'd tempered her responses or measured her approach to love differently? What if she'd listened to Mira with her statistics and her forecasts about love and relationships? What if she'd protected her heart and played it safe?

There would be no Ben.

And without Ben, she'd have no Shelby in her life.

The thought was the final break in a series of them that shattered the last of the walls around her heart.

Chapter Twenty-Six

"Miss Tanner." Her name coming over the loudspeaker in her classroom startled her out of a stupor.

She hopped up and pressed the intercom button on the wall. "Yes."

"You have a call in the office."

Her breath caught.

"Someone will be down to cover your class in a minute."

"Thank you." She glanced around the room. Several students had looked away from the movie she'd turned on as a reward for finishing the school musical. Or at least that's what she'd told them since she didn't want to admit she may've gone through the most crushing breakup of her life because the woman she'd given everything to for weeks didn't know if she wanted to offer her the same in return.

Mrs. Graves cracked open the door and waved her into the hallway.

"They're watching *Fantasia* today." Shelby tried not to sound embarrassed. Maybe counselors didn't know every music educator kept that particular movie in their back pocket for days when they didn't have it in them to teach.

"I've got this. You go ahead and take the call."

She nodded and hurried toward the office where one of the secretaries directed her to a side room. "Line one."

She picked up the receiver and took a deep breath, refusing to let fear or hope rush in. "This is Miss Tanner."

"Shelby, I'm sorry to bother you at work."

She didn't recognize the voice at first, "Who's this?"

"Jane. I didn't know who else to call."

Her brain struggled to make sense of Mira's assistant interrupting her workday. "What's wrong?"

"Darrin said you don't have your cell on during school hours."

"Is Darrin okay?"

"Yes. God, I'm so frazzled. It's Mira. She didn't come to work. She's not answering her phone. She missed a meeting with a client. Vannah said she was supposed to pick you up this morning, and that's the last any of us heard from her."

"Oh God." She groaned, causing both of the school secretaries to look up.

"Did you see her?"

"Yes, but it didn't, I mean, she and I ..." Her voice trailed off. She simply didn't know how to describe what happened. They'd argued, certainly. She'd snapped at Mira. She hadn't thought she'd said anything she'd regret, but she had laid down an ultimatum. Had Shelby pushed her over the edge?

"Do you know where she might have gone?"

She racked her brain. "No. She said she had an appointment. We didn't ... we didn't leave things well."

"Oh." Silence filled the line for too long before she finally asked, "Was she upset when you left her?"

"I didn't leave her. I asked her to be there for me, and she ... you know what? It doesn't matter right now." She tried to focus on the question at hand. "Yes, she was upset. We were both upset."

"Okay." Jane drew out the word. "I'm sorry I bothered you. I'm worried."

"Me too," she admitted.

"I'll let you know if we find her."

"I'm going to help."

"Seriously? You're at work, and it sounds like maybe you're mad at her."

"So mad," she admitted, "and hurt and frustrated, and also in love with her."

"Wow." Jane said, a little awe mingling with her worry. "Does she know that?"

"Only the first part. I wasn't sure about the love part until it came out of my mouth, but now it has, so I'm going to have to deal with it when I find her."

"Thank you." Jane breathed a sigh of relief. "I'll let you know if I hear anything. You do the same."

She hung up and turned to the secretary. "I don't know how this works, but I've had a bit of a family emergency, and I need someone to call me a substitute."

The woman nodded. "We can do that."

"Thank you." She started for the door and grimaced. "Could you also call me a cab?"

She jogged back to her room and collected her things in a hurried rush, then exited the school as a cab pulled up. She hadn't even been certain the town was big enough for a taxi service, or rather for a guy with a taxi sticker on the passenger-side door. The setup seemed shady enough that she might've questioned her safety, but with Mira missing, she didn't even hesitate to hop in.

"Where to, miss?"

She didn't know what to say. Jane had already checked the obvious places, and she couldn't have a stranger drive her all over the place all day. She cursed her broken-down car once more. She should've dealt with it sooner. She should've called a tow truck or a mechanic, credit card be damned. She shouldn't have let herself come to feel like such a burden, and then maybe she wouldn't have snapped at Mira about her desperate need to be seen as her equal.

"Miss?"

She shook her head. "Actually, take me home first, please."

"Sure ... but where's home?"

She rolled her eyes and gave him her address. Refusing to fall apart, she started to google roadside repair companies nearby and had selected one with decent reviews by the time the cab driver pulled into the parking lot to her building.

She paid him with the stupid card she hadn't wanted to use all week and hit the call button for the mechanic. Holding the phone to her ear, she glanced over to her broken-down hatchback, but something else caught her eye. Mira's car sat right next to hers.

"Dunn Tire and Auto," a voice on the phone said.

"Can you hold please?"

"Um, you called us," the voice said, but she didn't care. She sprinted into the building and up the stairs.

"Mira," she called as she reached her door and fumbled for her keys. A part of her brain told her Mira couldn't be inside if it were locked, but she checked anyway, power-walking through each room, scanning for anything out of place. "Mira? Are you here?"

She got no answer and slowed, trying to process too many things that didn't make sense. Why would she have come here if she knew Shelby was at school? And why leave the car if she couldn't get into the apartment? It wasn't like Mira to be illogical. None of this was like Mira at all.

She wandered back into the hall, leaving the door unlocked in case Mira returned. Backtracking down the stairs, she tuned her ear to any unusual sounds, but found each floor still and quiet until she reached the bottom and heard footsteps approaching. Heels clicked on concrete, and she turned instinctively toward the rhythm of a purposeful stride. Then, when she turned the corner, she nearly collided with someone.

No, not just someone. Mira. She sensed her even before she fully saw her, and catching hold, pulled her into a hug.

Mira gasped. "Shelby?"

"Are you okay?"

"Yes," Mira said quickly, then sagged against her. "No. I mean, what are you doing here?"

She stood back. "What are *you* doing here?"

She glanced over her shoulder to an older man in blue jeans and work boots. "I was getting a tour."

"Of my apartment building?"

"Yes. Not because it's your apartment building, but because I ... it's complicated, but this morning I think you may've suggested everything is complicated, and perhaps I needed to learn to deal with complexities better."

Her cheeks burned. "I'm sorry."

"Why? You were right. You've always been right, Shelby ... well, maybe not when you worried you weren't my equal, because you are. I still don't know why you're here instead of at work, but I'm glad because I just told Larry I couldn't make any decisions without talking to you."

Shelby turned to him and he shrugged. "Honest. She told me so not five minutes before you appeared."

"Talk to me about what?"

He held out a set of keys to Mira. "Why don't I make myself scarce? You two take all the time you need."

"Thank you." Mira accepted the keys and waited for him to walk away before turning back to her. "Will you walk with me?"

"Of course, but I still don't know what I butted in on. Jane called and said you never came to work, and Vannah didn't know where you were. She's worried, and I panicked, too. I don't know what's happening, but you're safe and you're here, and I don't know what I'm feeling, but it's a lot."

Mira took her face in her hands. "I know exactly what you mean, and I want to do a better job of conveying those big emotions. I know I've apologized a lot, and I'll probably have to keep doing it until I learn to do better, but you stumbled into the process of me trying to figure out if I actually *can* do better."

Shelby hesitated. As much as she wanted to pour all her relief at finding her safe and close into a crushing kiss, she also heard the uncertainty behind those words. Yes, Mira said she was trying, but she hadn't quite answered the question of whether or not she was capable.

"Look." Mira took her hands. "I see the concern in your eyes, and I know I put it there. You needed more from me this morning, and I failed you. I'm not even asking your forgiveness yet, but if nothing else, I need you to know I heard you. I did a terrible job of conveying my feelings, but I did listen when you shared yours. When you asked me if my shortcomings were a matter of 'can't' or 'won't,' I froze, and that must've felt terrible to you, but I swear it didn't take me long to realize, I want to be your person, and I dropped everything on my plate today in an attempt to start testing my capabilities."

She bit her lip. It was a great speech, but she'd also heard phenomenal apologies before. "If you're still uncertain, maybe I shouldn't have interrupted."

"You're not an interruption." Mira's eyes watered, and she blinked away the tears. "You're the reason I'm here, or at the very least, the reason I have the courage to be here. Please stay, because without you, none of what I'm debating internally will even matter. I need you beside me. You were right when you said I didn't treat you as my equal, but that's only because I know you're my better."

She wavered, pulled in by the emotion behind Mira's plea. The woman before her now bore little resemblance to the cool and closed off person she'd walked away from earlier. Ultimately, passion overrode reason, and she smiled slightly at the realization they'd shifted roles. "Okay. I'm here. Show me what you've got."

***

Mira turned the key Larry had given her and slid open the heavy industrial door, then flipped on a power box protruding from a rough brick wall. Overhead lights flickered and buzzed as they came to life. Her body hummed with electricity, too. She wasn't someone who believed in coincidence or fate. She understood Shelby had shown up here this morning only because Mira's absence from work had apparently kicked off a chain reaction she'd have to address almost immediately. Still, even understanding those facts from a logical standpoint, she couldn't shake the sense that if Shelby's concern for her was enough to bring her to this very spot, they might be on the right track somehow.

"What do you think?"

"Of what?" Shelby glanced around.

"This space."

"It's um, cavernous. And sort of rustic industrial?" She shook her head. "I'm not sure how I'm supposed to be evaluating it."

"Me either," she admitted. "Larry wants me to buy it. He wants me to buy the whole building, actually. He thinks it'd be a good property investment, but it didn't look like one on paper."

Shelby shook her head, still clearly confused about where this was going.

"The apartments are nice, as I can verify from personal experience." She paused to offer a wistful kind of smile at the memories she'd made upstairs only a few days earlier, but returned to the task at hand. "But this space here has always given me pause. I couldn't envision any business that I'd ever worked with that might be suited to the space. I let my own

318

experiences and the lack of vision outside my tiny box of possibilities close me off from bigger pictures."

Shelby worried her lower lip between her teeth as she began to wander around the space while Mira kept talking.

"Then over these last few weeks, my life got turned upside down, and suddenly I had to see the world from a whole different angle, and I honestly found that horribly disorienting. I spent so much time trying to right myself, to get back to where I was and who I had been. I kept thinking the circumstances were forcing me to look at things the wrong way, and maybe I should've caught on quicker, but it took you slamming that door this morning to make me realize all my attempts to get back to living the way I used to kept me from an opportunity to examine the new viewpoint."

"And now?" Shelby asked.

"And now, I'm trying. Everyone told me to stand in the space and dream or seek a connection to it, but when I stand here alone, it's just a huge, empty space. And maybe I'm incapable, but I thought maybe the pure desire for a new outlook might mean suddenly seeing new potential, but I can't. Not without you beside me."

"Potential for what?"

"An art space?"

Shelby turned her head to the side.

"Yeah, I know it's vague, because I don't know what goes into such art spaces, but Vannah said she's really taken to the work she's doing, though she sort of admitted the setup in Belize isn't perfect for her or for Ben."

"Of course it's not." Shelby rolled her eyes.

"I know. I felt the same way, but she also made some beautiful statements about wanting to model healthier relationships to work and joy and balance for Ben, and I realized

I couldn't offer those things to him, either, because I didn't have them in my own life."

"Mira." Shelby reached for her hand, but she wasn't ready to be comforted yet.

"It's true, and it sent me into a tailspin you got swept up in this morning. I might be more stable than Vannah, but I'm not more well-balanced. So how could I ask anyone to take a risk on a workaholic schedule-addict who couldn't even envision a life full of art and love and growth beyond all odds? But you were also right when you said every time I set my mind and heart and focus on something, I rise to the occasion. I want to do that right now, right here, for myself and Vannah and Ben, and most of all, you."

"So, you're scouting prospective art spaces without even knowing how to use one?"

She sighed. "I know it's thrown together and half-cooked, but Vannah said if she had a better option to thrive closer to home, she'd consider it, and this isn't how I do business, or anything, but maybe I need to learn to do things differently. Maybe I need to learn to have faith or look past the numbers."

"Why start now when you've been successful using the methods you know?"

"Because I haven't been successful," she blurted, "or maybe I've been successful in some ways, but after having you in my life, I'm not sure those ways matter, because you and I don't look good on paper. The age difference, the personality difference, the way we see the world, we don't look like a great long-term investment, but for the first time in my life, I don't care. I want to be with you. For the first time ever, I assessed the odds, the risks, and I fully understand you could shatter me, but I'm still desperate to take a leap with you."

This time when Shelby reached for her, Mira took her hand. "Do you really think we're a risky investment?"

"Yes." She didn't see any reason not to be fully honest. "I've never had a successful relationship. I've behaved erratically for weeks. I have no solid plan for growth, only goodwill and an earnest work ethic. If I were a stock, I'd totally tell you not to add me to your portfolio."

"But you're not a stock," Shelby said.

"No. And I remember when we watched *Guys and Dolls*, you were adamant you shouldn't marry someone with the hopes of changing them, so I know I'm a gamble here. You don't have to make a decision about till death do us part, but I'm wondering if maybe you might be willing to enter a relationship with the hope, if not for change, maybe for growth? I promise I'll do everything in my power to become a more well-rounded asset."

"And this building?" Shelby glanced around one more time. "You're buying it to prove you're diversifying your prospects?"

She shook her head at her own absurdity. "I guess it probably sounds pretty stupid."

"No, not stupid, but I'm not sure how I fit in. You want me to create an artist co-op or something here?"

"Actually, I want Vannah to run it. I'm mostly planning to dangle it in front of her in the wild hope she and Ben will stay. And she may tell me to shove it, but I didn't intend to even bring it up with her until I talked to you first."

"Why?"

"Because, while I love Vannah and Ben, I am *in* love with you and I *need* you to be with me if I go forward with this venture. You bring so much to the table that I don't have. You see possibilities where I only see problems."

"Wait, did you say you love me?"

"Yes." Mira's voice and hands both trembled. "I know it's soon, and I've had a funny way of showing it, but only because I haven't had any frame of reference for the things you've made me feel. It's totally out of character for me to rush into anything, but you inspire me to be better."

Shelby kissed her, the soft press of her lips soothing the burn of everything else that had happened this morning. She leaned into Mira, soaking up the comfort and the confirmation that she hadn't merely imagined the power of their connection. Numbers and metrics and odds be damned, she surrendered to the pull of her own heartstrings, the answer that had been there all along.

She leaned back to meet Shelby's blue eyes, so clear and sparkling. "So, what do you say?"

"I'm in favor of you making all the bad investments you want to make so long as you keep kissing me."

She laughed. "Good, but to be clear, I don't think either one of us is making a bad investment, and between the two, you're making the riskier choice."

She kissed her quickly as if to prove her willingness to assume such a risk. "But?"

"But, you've shown me some of the things that matter most in life can't be quantified."

Shelby hooked a finger through the belt loop of her slacks and tugged her closer. "Like what?"

"Like the way my heart feels stronger when you smile at me, or how it moves me when you play your cello, or the hope that flows through me when you open my eyes to wonders I'd never considered before, or how happy you make me simply by being by my side ..."

"Or," Shelby cut in, "the fact that I'm also utterly and absolutely in love with you, too?"

"Yes," Mira agreed, because she would've granted Shelby any point she wanted to make, but as the words sank in, she shook her head, afraid wishful thinking had affected her processing skills. "Wait. What?"

Shelby smiled. "I never thought you'd beat me to the punch on some big, emotional reveal. I think you must be a quicker learner than we thought, but I need you to know I came to the same realization this morning. I love you, and I did even before you made this amazing grand gesture."

Mira's heart pressed against her ribs almost painfully, as if trying to burst out of its confines. "Really? Even before now?"

"Yes, I'm serious. That's why I came looking for you in the middle of a school day. Ask Jane."

"Jane? Why would I ask Jane?"

"Because I told her when she called."

"You told my secretary you loved me before you told me?"

Shelby laughed the most melodic sound in all the world. "Yes, I was worried about you, and it sort of came out. It caught me off guard. Honestly, I think it shook Jane up a little, too."

"I'm glad the news got its proper due even if I wasn't the first to know."

"Good, but also we probably need to call her, and Vannah, too. You scared everyone today. I don't think anyone saw you running off on impulse to buy my entire apartment building as something within the realm of possibilities."

"Me either," she said with a smile. "But so far, I have to say the experience has been much more fulfilling than I could imagine. I promise to tell the whole world about this bold new aspect of my personality you have uncovered, only they're going to have to wait a few more minutes while I kiss you, because I've also learned one more lesson on impulses this morning."

"What's that?"

"Once I set aside all the silly excuses and empty logic and realized that I want to be with you all the time, in all the ways, I also realized I couldn't stand to waste another minute more than I already have."

Epilogue

"See you at school tomorrow," Shelby called after Ben, Josh, and Izzy as they bolted from her lesson room out into the larger, communal hub where Vannah had wrapped up a basket-weaving class.

"Whoa," a familiar voice said from the other side of the open door.

She smiled. "Mira, are you flattened against the wall again?"

"Maybe a little."

Vannah laughed from across the room. "Totally, a lot."

She peeked around the corner to see Mira straightening her suit jacket and shaking out her dark hair. Shelby's mouth went dry at merely the sight of her standing within arm's reach. They hadn't seen each other since seven that morning, and ten hours apart still felt like entirely too long.

"Someday I'll try to learn that middle schoolers do everything in herds and with great urgency, but today is apparently not that day."

Shelby caught her by the lapels and pulled her in for a quick kiss before releasing her reluctantly. "You've learned a lot quickly. The travel habits of preteens aren't on the top of your need-to-know list."

Mira smiled. "I love it when you itemize and prioritize my lists."

"Yeah, well, I've learned a lot, too."

"Me three," Vannah said as her eyes swept over the space that had held them together more than a time or two over the last year.

Every step along the way had brought a new set of challenges, but none of them quite as daunting as taking the first leap together. And while they'd had more long days, short nights, and deep discussions than she could've possibly anticipated the first time she'd met Mira outside, she wouldn't trade a minute of the experience.

Vannah nodded for them to join her. "Come look. I think the summer schedule is finally done."

They followed her to a large desk she'd built almost entirely from driftwood she and Ben had found along the lake shore. Together, they'd staged it as a sort of reception-area-meets-open-concept office for herself. Pulling out a large, trifold board, Vannah laid it out for their inspection.

"Oh, it's beautiful," Shelby gushed, and she wasn't merely saying it because she knew how hard Vannah had worked to make all her dreams fit together. The calendar was an actual work of art in both its visual appeal and its clarity of function.

She'd been more than a little terrified that first day as she'd accompanied Mira to spring the idea of a local arts haven to Vannah, but after a brief flash of defensiveness, she not only agreed to listen to their proposal, she took to her new role better and faster than anyone else involved in the process.

Mira had shared her suspicion that Vannah most enjoyed the prospect of having full control over something from the ground up, but over time, Shelby had come to appreciate that some of the qualities she'd initially prescribed to flightiness might better be described as adaptability. She had a knack for rolling with the punches, and often served as a calming influence when the infinite possibilities overwhelmed Mira. Though, examining the gorgeous, intricate, and fully color-coded three-month calendar before them now, Mira's personality had clearly had a stabilizing effect on her sister as well.

"I love how vibrant it is." Mira's voice exuded admiration.

"Right?" Vannah seemed pleased. "I wanted people's eyes to be drawn to it as soon as they walk through the door. I chose colors that were bright but also coincided with the type of activity they represent."

"You kept Ben's cerulean blue for the music classes," Mira noted with a hitch of emotion.

"When you're right, you're right." Vannah bumped her shoulder. "He's going to have the best summer ever."

"He said last summer was the best summer ever."

"Last summer was all planning and construction, which was kind of exciting," Shelby said. "He did enjoy getting his own hard hat."

"But this summer, we'll see full payoff of all our hard work."

They'd held numerous classes and workshops in the space since winter, but as she scanned the stunning document before them, she certainly understood Vannah's sentiment. The entire building would be filled with life, morning, noon, and night. Shelby was slated to offer six different group lessons a week plus two week-long youth day camps in July. Vannah had connected with local potters, painters, and weavers to teach recurring courses, and starting in two weeks, they'd be offering yoga classes and a workshop on herbal medicine. Vannah was also piloting a whole foods nutrition series, and she was personally leading guided meditations by candlelight most evenings. Still, the calendar entry that probably amused her the most came about when Darrin and some of his colleagues convinced their company to sponsor kid-friendly chemistry workshops each Wednesday afternoon. Shelby fully intended to sit in the back and mock his nerdiness whenever it was his turn to teach.

"Mom!" Ben called, pulling their attention away. "Can I show Josh and Izzy our new apartment?"

"Sorry buddy, I can't go up right now. I've got to be here to meet the drum circle group in five minutes."

"We could take him up," Shelby offered. "I have a few more boxes to grab."

"Boxes of books?" Mira feigned trepidation.

"Yes, so you'd better come help, and maybe we could put the kids to work, too."

"You hear her, Ben?" Vannah called. "Aunt Shelby says you can go up as long as you promise not to report her for child labor violations."

"Hey now." She laughed. "You're the one who's always telling me kids learn best by doing."

Vannah shot Mira a look. "I'm still impressed you manage to keep up with this one."

"Me too," Mira said, then added, "I'm learning by doing, too."

"Yeah you are." Shelby nudged her toward the door before dropping her voice into a lower register. "And I can think of a few things I want to do to you when we get all my stuff into your house."

"Into *our* house," Mira corrected as she picked up the pace of her heels clicking against the stairs.

Our house. The idea had taken some getting used to. She'd initially worried that since Mira had owned her home before she even came along, she might have a hard time seeing it as equally hers to shape or inhabit the way she had with the business, but Mira had made a conscious and concentrated effort to merge their lives. She'd cleared out half of the garage for Shelby's newest used car, and traded her glass top table for Shelby's bigger, if slightly more worn, wooden one, saying it made more sense for the big family dinners they'd taken to hosting with Ben, Vannah, and the whole Tanner clan.

She'd also converted her home office into a music room, which felt like a rather big and somewhat metaphorical statement, but Mira pointed out that she usually worked at the table most of the time anyway, and even that had slowed as she brought the office home with her less and less these days.

As they reached the door, the kids ran ahead, eager to follow Ben to his new room, but Shelby caught hold of Mira's hand and pulled her into the practice area. "We can get to the books in a moment. I've missed you."

Mira slid her hands along the curve of Shelby's waist and tightened them possessively. "I missed you, too."

They stole a kiss that wasn't nearly as quick as it probably should have been with the kids still roaming the apartment, but in all the things they'd learned together, restraint wasn't one of them. Mira's steady confidence and competence still drove her wild with want, and it took everything in her not to shoo Ben and his friends back downstairs so she could run her hands up over her strong shoulders and push that blazer to the floor.

Instead, she sighed and eased back enough to say, "This isn't my apartment anymore."

"Are you going to miss it?"

She shook her head. "No, only it's convenient proximity when you stop by to see me in between lessons."

Mira sighed. "Agreed. I would've never believed the five minutes it takes to get to the house a long commute, but all things are relative."

Shelby kissed her cheek and pulled her lips up to Mira's ear. "Not all things. I still want you the same no matter whose space we're in, and I'm sure Vannah wouldn't mind if we occasionally —"

Mira laughed. "I'm not sure I'm up for quickies in my sister's bed ... but we did pay for her very nice couch."

Shelby laughed loudly and pulled away. "I can't believe you've turned into such a bad influence. One of us has to be the responsible one."

Mira's smile turned coy, but before she could respond, the kids came racing back around the corner.

"It's cool Ben gets your apartment now, Miss Tanner," Josh said.

"Yeah," Izzy glanced around. "Does he get your practice room in here, too?"

She shrugged. "I don't know. It's his and his mom's to make into whatever they want, but he's got plenty of practice rooms downstairs, too."

Izzy made a little swooning motion, then turned to Ben and said, "You don't even have to go outside to get to music heaven. I'm jealous of how cool your family is."

He blushed slightly, but even his budding teenage stoicism couldn't manage to hide his grin. "Yeah, I'm pretty lucky."

Shelby slipped an arm around Mira's waist and tugged her close the same way the sentiment tugged at her heartstrings. "I'm pretty lucky, too."

Mira leaned into her, resting her chin on her shoulder before whispering, "I'm the luckiest."

Acknowledgements

First and foremost, I want to thank my readers. My last few books have run the gamut from erotic linked stories, to an Olympic sports romance, to a fluid, English aristocratic romp, and you just keep coming along with me no matter what the adventure. I hope you enjoyed this return to a good-old-fashioned-girl-meets-girl love story as much as I enjoyed writing it. Your continued support allows me to keep doing my dream job, and I'm forever grateful to you.

Next, I'd like to thank my awesome team, who takes the work I do and makes it fit for human consumption before delivering that most polished version to you. Every time I go through this process, I feel the urge to shout, "Avengers assemble!" and yet I still manage to be pleasantly surprised when they do, starting with my beta reader Barb who always handles that first feedback with care and enthusiasm. Lynda Sandoval, my substantive editor, has been with me for seventeen books now and still finds new ways to make me a better writer (and to make me laugh). Avery Brooks brings a keen eye with an author's sensibility to my copy edits, and I'm thrilled she's joined my core group of regulars. This book is graced with a cover from the newest member of the cadre, and I couldn't be happier with what Kevin brought to the table, not just to capture a slice of the book, but also the tone I worked hard to create. My proofreaders are the last line of defense between typos and the printed page, and this time Diane, Ann, Monna and Anna all stepped up to save me from those stubborn mistakes that evaded eight professional writers and editors. If you're reading this as an eBook, we both have Toni to thank again for the meticulous formatting. And everyone who's read this far in any format owes the greatest debt of gratitude to Carolyn and Susan of Brisk Press. Every time I have a new book for them, I hold my breath, afraid they will have realized that I'm a lot of work for them and tell me it's time to figure out my own stuff, and every time they amaze me with their generous welcome, support, and a home away from home.

On the more personal side, this book took nearly 3 years to write. It was started in a moment when I was pretty well shattered by grief, and I eventually set it aside because I believed this story and these characters deserved better than I was capable of giving them then. What followed was years of hard work and healing. Thank you to everyone who stood by me in the interim of grappling and growing. Anna Burke understood the heartache of loss and what it can do to a creative process, and graciously shared her own vulnerability to help us both slog through. Nikki, Melissa, and Georgia never gave up on me, even when I tried to disappear. My therapist, Leah, has been a lifesaver all along, and in recent months has really risen to every challenge, now in the form of "Can we talk about my books again?" I wouldn't have been able to return to this project without the work we've done on the other ones. I'm so thankful for everyone who kept faith in me, and to these characters who stayed patient and persistent, then rewarded me by being absolutely worth the wait.

While this book didn't take the same level of research as some of my previous ones, it did take a lot of inspiration from some amazing music educators over the last ten years. As someone whose musical inclination ends at the appreciation stage, I'm so enormously indebted to the people who've stepped up to foster a deeper love and understanding in my son. Thank you to Kay Barlow, Kathy Petersen, April Hartung, Laurie Tramuta, Kevin Way, Andrew Bennett, Ben Wendell, Alexandra

Goff, with a special additional note of gratitude to Emily Greetham and Kristin Terreri, whose patience and compassion with my own young violinist informed Shelby and Ben's early interactions.

And, as always, none of this would matter without my family, who makes my life worth living and my job worth doing. In this book, more than most others, I pulled so much inspiration from your loves and strengths. To Will, who always fills our house with music, thank you for sharing that gift with me and supporting those beautiful impulses in Jackson. And to Jackie, my boy on the strings, when you were born I could've never imagined anyone from my gene pool becoming the musician you are today. From the violin, to the ukulele, to the guitar to chamber orchestras and school musicals, you blow my mind every day. I pray that no matter where you go or what you do, there will always be music in your life. Now, to Susie, who fills the best of these characters with her steadiness, her compassion, her creativity, and commitment. You represent every best quality I aspire to write, from the dedicated educator to the steadfast provider. I wish you could see yourself through my eyes, but I promise I will keep trying to show you how much I love you every day, come what may.

As always, the final and deepest gratitude goes to an all-loving creator, redeemer, and sanctifier, from whom all these blessings and more has been given without being earned. *Soli Deo Gloria.*

ALSO BY RACHEL SPANGLER

Learning Curve
Trails Merge
LoveLife
Spanish Heart
Does She Love You
Heart of the Game
Perfect Pairing
Edge of Glory
In Development
Love All
Full English
Spanish Surrender
Fire & Ice
Straight Up
Modern English
Thrust
Plain English

THE DARLINGTON ROMANCES

The Long Way Home
Timeless
Close to Home

ABOUT THE AUTHOR

Rachel Spangler never set out to be a *New York Times* reviewed author. They were just so poor during seven years of college that they had to come up with creative forms of cheap entertainment. Their debut novel, *Learning Curve*, was born out of one such attempt. Since writing is more fun than a real job and so much cheaper than therapy, they continued to type away, leading to the publication of *Timeless, The Long Way Home, LoveLife, Spanish Heart, Does She Love You, Timeless, Heart of The Game, Perfect Pairing, Close to Home, Edge of Glory, In Development, Love All, Full English, Spanish Surrender, Fire and Ice, Straight Up, Modern English* and *Thrust*. Now a four-time Lambda Literary Award finalist, an IPPY, Goldie, and Rainbow Award winner, and the 2018 Alice B. Reader recipient, Rachel plans to continue writing as long as anyone, anywhere, will keep reading.

In 2018 Spangler joined the ranks of the Bywater Books substantive editing team. They now hold the title of senior romance editor for the company and love having the opportunity to mentor young authors. Rachel lives in Western New York with wife, Susan and son, Jackson. Their family spends the long winters curling and skiing. In the summer, they love to travel and watch their beloved St. Louis Cardinals. Regardless of the season, Rachel always makes time for a good romance, whether reading it, writing it, or living it.

For more information, visit Rachel on Instagram,
Facebook, Twitter, or Patreon.

You can visit Rachel Spangler on the web at
www.rachelspangler.com